PRAISE FOR HANNAH ROTHSCHILD's

The Improbability of Love

"Riveting. . . . With its colorful cast of characters and richly layered plot, *The Improbability of Love* is entertaining and suspenseful." —*USA Today*

"A scintillating new novel." —*Harper's Bazaar*

"A propulsive yarn. . . . Makes an impassioned case for art—as a companion to the lonely, as a restorative to those in pain. . . . Beauty inspires both passion and violence; in *The Improbability of Love*, you get a generous helping of both." —*The New York Times Book Review*

"Rothschild whets our appetite for art world intrigue." —*W*

"[A] romp through the art world. . . . [Rothschild] understands how great art humanizes. . . . Her writing shows brain as well as a heart." —*The Economist*

"Enormously readable. . . . Energetic, clever, sometimes funny, sometimes sad and serious . . . with a romance, at least one mystery, even some thriller elements." —*The Washington Times*

"Deftly pings between comedic romance and biting satire of London's art world." —*Sotheby's*

"Totally delicious; conspicuous consumption on this scale hasn't been seen since the Eighties." —*The Times* (London)

HANNAH ROTHSCHILD

The Improbability of Love

Hannah Rothschild is the author of *The Baroness: The Search for Nica, the Rebellious Rothschild*. She is also a film director whose documentaries have appeared at such festivals as Telluride and Tribeca. She has written for British *Vanity Fair, Vogue, The Independent,* and *The Spectator,* and is vice president of the Hay Literary Festival, a trustee of the Tate Gallery, and the first woman chair of the National Gallery in London.

www.hannahrothschild.com

ALSO BY HANNAH ROTHSCHILD

The Baroness

The Improbability of Love

HANNAH ROTHSCHILD

Vintage Books
A Division of Penguin Random House LLC
New York

FIRST VINTAGE BOOKS EDITION, SEPTEMBER 2016

The Library of Congress has cataloged the Knopf edition as follows:
Rothschild, Hannah.
The improbability of love / Hannah Rothschild.
pages cm
1. Single women—Fiction.   2. Painting—Collectors and collecting—
Fiction.   3. Art dealers—Fiction.   I. Title.
PR6118.O8755147 2015   823'.92—dc23   2014047753

Vintage Books Trade Paperback ISBN: 978-1-101-87257-4
eBook ISBN: 978-1-101-87415-8

Book design by Iris Weinstein

www.vintagebooks.com

Printed in the United States of America
10 9 8

For Nell, Clemency and Rose

The Improbability of Love

Prologue

THE AUCTION (3 JULY)

It was going to be the sale of the century.

From first light a crowd had started gathering and by the late afternoon it stretched from the monumental grey portico of the auction house, Monachorum & Sons (est. 1756), across the wide pavement and out into Houghton Street. At noon, metal barriers were erected to keep a central walkway clear and at 4 p.m. two uniformed Monachorum doormen rolled out a thick red carpet from the fluted Doric columns all the way to the edge of the pavement. The sun beat down on the crowd, and the auction house, as a gesture of good will, handed out free bottles of water and ice-lollies. As Big Ben struck six mournful chimes, the police diverted normal traffic and sent two mounted officers and eight on foot to patrol the street. The paparazzi, carrying step ladders, laptops and assorted lenses, were corralled into a small pen to one side, where they peered longingly through the door at three television crews and various accredited journalists who had managed to secure passes to cover the event from inside.

"What's going on?" a passer-by asked a member of the crowd.

"They're selling that picture, you know, the one on the news," explained Felicia Speers, who had been there since breakfast. *"The Impossibility of Love."*

"The Improbability of Love," corrected her friend Dawn Morelos. "Improbability," she repeated, rolling the syllables slowly over her tongue.

"Whatever. Everyone knows what I'm talking about," said Felicia, laughing.

"Are they expecting trouble?" asked the passer-by, looking from the police horses to the auction house's burly security guards.

"Not trouble—just everyone who's anyone," said Dawn, holding up her smartphone and an autograph book that had the words "Rock and Royalty" embossed in gold lettering across its front.

"All this hullaballoo for a picture?" asked the passer-by.

"It's not just any old artwork, is it?" said Felicia. "You must have read about it?"

At the top of the broad steps of Monachorum four young women in black dresses and high-heeled shoes stood holding iPads waiting to check off names. This was an invitation-only event. From certain vantage points, the crowd outside could just glimpse the magnificent interiors. Formerly the London seat of the Dukes of Dartmouth, Monachorum's building was one of Europe's grandest surviving Palladian palaces. Its hallway was large enough to park two double-decker buses side by side. The plaster ceiling, a riot of putti and pulchritudinous mermaids, was painted in pinks and golds. An enormous staircase, wide enough for eight horsemen to ride abreast, took the visitor upstairs to the grand salesroom, an atrium, its walls lined with white and green marble and top lit by three rotunda. It was, in many ways, quite unsuitable for hanging and displaying works of art; it did, nevertheless, create a perfect storm of awe and desire.

In a side room, two dozen impeccably turned-out young men and women were being given their final instructions. Luckily, on this hottest of nights, the air-conditioning kept the room a steady eighteen degrees. The chief auctioneer and mastermind of the sale, Earl Beachendon, dressed for the evening in black tie, stood before them. He spoke firmly and quietly in a voice honed by eight generations of aristocratic fine living and assumed superiority. Beachendon had been educated at Eton and Oxford but, owing to his father's penchant for the roulette table, the eighth Earl was the first member of his illustrious family to have sought regular employment.

Earl Beachendon appraised his team. For the past four weeks they had rehearsed, anticipating all eventualities from a broken heel to an attempted assassination. With the world's media in attendance and many of the auction house's most important clients gathered in one place, it was essential that events were managed with the precision of a finely tuned Swiss clock. This evening was a game changer in the history of the art market: everyone expected the world record for a single painting to be smashed.

"The attention of the world's media is on us," Beachendon told his rapt audience. "Hundreds of thousands of pairs of eyes will be watching. One small mistake will turn triumph into disaster. This is not just about Monachorum, our bonuses or the sale of one painting. This event will reflect on an industry worth over $100 billion annually and our handling of this evening will reverberate across time and continents. I don't need to remind you that this is an international arena. It's time that our contribution to the wealth and health of nations is recognised."

"No pressure, my Lord," someone quipped.

Earl Beachendon ignored his minion. "According to our extensive research, your respective charges will be the highest bidders—it is up to each of you to nurture, cajole and encourage them to go that little bit further. Convince them that greatness lies in acquisition; excite their curiosity and competitive urges. Use every weapon in your arsenal. Bathe them in a sea of perfectly judged unctuousness. Remind each of them how unique, how indispensable, how talented, how rich they are and, most importantly, that it is only here at this house that their brilliant eye and exquisite taste are appreciated and understood. For one night, forget friendship and morals: concentrate only on winning."

Beachendon looked along the line of faces, all flushed with excitement.

"You are each to make your assigned guests feel special. Special with a capital 'S.' Even if they don't succeed in buying what they are after, I want these Ultra-High-Net-Worthers to leave this evening longing to come back, desperate to win the next round. No one must feel like a loser or an also-ran; everyone must feel that some tiny thing conspired against them but next time they will triumph."

Beachendon walked up the line of employees looking from one to another. For them the evening was an exciting experience with a potential bonus; for him it boiled down to penury and pride.

"Now remember, particularly the ladies, you are expected to serve and delight. I leave the interpretation of 'serve and delight' entirely up to each of you, but discretion is the name of the game." Nervous laughter rippled through the ranks.

"As I read out the names of the guests I would like their minders to step forward. You should all be familiar with your charge's appearance, likes, dislikes and peccadillos." Beachendon paused before offering his well-practised, deliberately politically incorrect joke: "No offering alcohol to Muslims or ham sandwiches to Jews."

His audience laughed obediently.

"Who is looking after Vlad Antipovsky and Dmitri Voldakov?"

Two young women, one in tight-fitting black taffeta, the other in a backless green silk dress, raised their hands.

"Venetia and Flora, remember, given the chance, these two men will rip each other's throats out. We have managed to keep their personal security to a minimum and have asked them to leave their firearms at home: prevention is our best policy. Keep them apart. Understood?"

Venetia and Flora nodded.

Consulting his list, Beachendon read out the next name. "Their Royal Highnesses, the Emir and Sheikha of Alwabbi."

Tabitha Rowley-Hutchinson, the most senior member of guest relations, was encased in royal-blue satin; only her long neck and slender wrists were visible.

"Tabitha—what subjects will you avoid at all costs?"

"I will not mention Alwabbi's supposed support for al-Qaeda, the Emir's other wives or the country's human rights record."

"Li Han Ta. Are you fully briefed on Mr. Lee Lan Fok?"

Li Han Ta nodded gravely.

"Remember: the Chinese may not triumph today, but they are the future." Looking around the room he saw that every single person was in agreement.

"Who is in charge of His Excellency the President of France?"

Marie de Nancy was wearing a blue silk tuxedo and matching trousers.

"I will ask him about cheese, his First Lady and French

painting, but I won't mention another British victory in the Tour de France, his mistress or his popularity ratings," she said.

Beachendon nodded. "Who is managing the Right Honourable Barnaby Damson, Minister of Culture?"

A young man hopped forward. He was wearing a pink velvet suit and his hair was coiffed in a style once known as a duck's arse.

Beachendon groaned. "More subtlety, please—the minister might be of that 'persuasion,' but he doesn't like to be reminded in public."

"I thought I might talk about the ballet—he loves the ballet."

"Stick to football and cinema," Beachendon instructed.

"Who is looking after Mr. M. Power Dub-Box?"

In recent months, the world's most successful rapper had surprised the art world by buying several iconic works of art. Standing at nearly seven foot tall, weighing 250 lbs. and flanked by an entourage of black-suited minders and nearly naked women, Mr. M. Power Dub-Box was unmissable and, apparently, unbiddable. His behaviour, fuelled by various substances and pumped up by infamy, frequently led to arrests but, as yet, no convictions. Two large men in black tie stepped forward. Vassily was a former Russian middleweight boxing champion and Elmore was an ex-Harvard sports scholar.

Looking at the towering men, Beachendon offered a silent thank you to Human Resources for hiring these colossi in a world populated by fine-boned aesthetes.

"Moving on. Who is minding Stevie Brent?" Beachendon asked.

Dotty Fairclough-Hawes was dressed as an American cheerleader in a tiny striped skirt and bra-let.

"This is not the baseball finals," Beachendon snapped.

"It might make him feel at home," said Dotty.

"He's a hedge-fund manager trying to create a smokescreen

around significant recent losses. The last thing he needs is a demented Boston Red Sox fan drawing attention to the fact that he can't afford this picture. Dotty, you are the only person here whose mission it is *not* to let Stevie Brent buy. According to our sources he has negative equity of $4 billion. I don't care if he sticks his arm up at the beginning, but sit on his paddle when the bidding gets above two hundred million pounds."

Dotty left to locate her blue taffeta ball gown.

"Oh and Dotty," Beachendon called after her. "Don't offer him Coca-Cola—he shorted the stock far too soon—it's up eighteen per cent."

Earl Beachendon continued through his list of VIPs, making sure that each was linked to an appropriate minder.

"Mrs. Appledore? Thank you, Celine."

"The Earl and Countess of Ragstone? Thank you, John."

"Mr. and Mrs. Hercules Christantopolis? Thank you, Sally."

"Mr. and Mrs. Mahmud? Lucy, very good."

"Mr. and Mrs. Elliot Slicer the Fourth? Well done, Rod."

"Mr. Lee Hong Quiuo—Xo? Thank you, Bai."

"Mr. and Mrs. Bastri? Thank you, Tam."

Venetia Trumpington-Turner raised her hand. "Who will be looking after the vendors?"

"That important and delicate job falls to our chairman," replied Earl Beachendon.

Everyone nodded sagely.

"The rest of you are to make sure that the lesser mortals are in the correct place," Earl Beachendon continued. "The directors of the world's museums are in row H. The editors of the newspapers are in I. The rest of the press are not allowed out of their pen, apart from a few named journalists—Camilla has their details. The other High-Net-Worthers are to go in J, K, L and M. Top dealers in rows P and Q. I want the odd model and actress scattered in between the others just to add a bit of sparkle, but no one over the age of forty or a dress size eight is worthy of an upgrade. Any celebrity who is not an 'A lister' can stand."

Beachendon stood tall and looked around. "Girls, go and reapply your lip gloss; boys, straighten your ties and line up by the entrance. Do your best."

Mrs. Appledore's limousine was making slow progress. The drive from Claridge's to Houghton Street normally took ten minutes, but there were roadworks and diversions in place and traffic had slowed to a crawl around Berkeley Square. On this unusually warm July evening. Londoners, convinced that this was the first and last glimpse of sun, spilled out of pubs and on to pavements. Men took off their jackets, revealing dark damp patches under their arms, while women wore sundresses showing off pink prawn-like arms and legs. At least they look reasonably cheerful for once, Mrs. Appledore thought. The British are so dreary and taciturn during winter. As her car crept up Berkeley Street, she wondered if this would be her last great sale. She was eighty next year and her annual trip to the London auctions was losing its sheen. Once she knew everyone in the saleroom; more importantly, everyone knew her.

Mrs. Appledore kept her eyes fixed on the future but aspired to the manners and modus operandi of the past. She was born Inna Pawlokowski in Poland in 1935, and her youth had been spent on a Polish farm and then in a nunnery near Krakow. Cared for by nuns for the rest of the war, the young Inna was then sent, with three thousand fellow orphans, to America in 1948. She met her future husband Yannic on the refugee boat, the *Cargo of Hope*, and although they were only thirteen years old, he proposed as they passed the Statue of Liberty. She promised to bear him six children (she carried nine) and he vowed to make them both millionaires (his estate, when he died in 1990, was valued at $6 billion). On the day of their marriage in 1951, Inna and Yannic changed their names to Melanie and Horace Appledore and never again uttered a word of Polish. Their first business, started the day after their wedding, was a hire company that rented suits and shoes to impoverished immigrants needing to look smart for job interviews. Soon Appledore Inc. expanded into properties, sweatshops and then private equity. Knowing from personal experience that immigrants worked far harder than natives, the Appledores provided seed funding for start-ups in return for a slice of the equity plus interest on capital. Thanks to the Displaced Persons Act, wave after wave of immigrants arrived on American shores and the Appledores helped and fleeced Europeans, Mexicans, Koreans, West Indians and Vietnamese. By the turn of the new century, Melanie and Horace owned small but significant and highly profitable stakes in family businesses across all fifty states.

Melanie understood that money alone did not guarantee a seat at the top table. Determined to make her mark on the upper echelons of Park Avenue society, she knew she needed to learn about standards and expectations in order to be part of a seamless flow of gentility and accepted behaviour. To this end, she employed Nobel Prize winners, museum directors and society ladies fallen on hard times to teach her every subject that would help her progress. She learned how to arrange silver at a table; about grape varieties; artistic movements; the difference between allegro and staccato; the amount to tip a duke's butler; which way to turn at dinner; and the direction of travel for a bottle of port. This new generation, Mrs. Appledore thought wistfully, parade their vulgarity like a badge of honour.

Horace and Melanie gave to many cultural institutes; they supported the rebuilding of La Fenice in Venice and the restoration of a tiny church in Aix-en-Provence. However, their principal love was a mansion built by the industrialist Lawrence D. Smith in 1924 as a token of love for his French wife, Pipette. Located on the banks of the Hudson River, forty-five

miles north of Manhattan, it had a three-hundred-foot-long
façade and a floor space of nearly three acres. Unfortunately,
Pipette died just after the house was finished and the broken-
hearted billionaire never moved in. It remained empty and
unloved until Horace and Melanie bought it in 1978 for the
princely sum of $100.

The Smith house was renamed the Appledore Museum of
French Decorative Arts. Horace and Melanie spent the next
decades and the lion's share of their fabulous fortune restoring
the building and creating one of the greatest collections of
French furniture and works of art outside Europe. For them,
having matter made them feel they did matter. Now in her
eightieth year, with a weak heart and a bad case of osteopo-
rosis, Mrs. Appledore had decided to blow every last cent in
her charitable foundation on *The Improbability of Love*. She
didn't care if that cleaned it out: she was almost dead anyway
and her children were already provided for.

Mrs. Appledore's Chanel dress, made in a lime-green silk,
a shade almost identical to the foliage in *The Improbability of
Love*, was chosen by her and Karl Lagerfeld to complement
the painting. The outfit was completed with a simple diamond
necklace and ear clips—nothing should distract from her last
great purchase. That morning she had asked for a new permanent wave, with a slightly looser curl and a blush of pink.
She wanted to look perfect at the moment of her last hurrah.
This time tomorrow, every paper would carry a picture of the
painting and its new owner. At a press conference she would
announce the immediate donation of her personal collection, complete with *The Improbability of Love*, to her beloved
Appledore Museum. If only her dear late husband had been
around to see this final masterstroke.

Sitting at his computer in his new house in Chester Square,
Vladimir Antipovsky punched in seventeen different codes,
placed his eye against the iris reader, ran his fingerprints

through the ultraviolet scanner and transferred $500 million into his current account. He was prepared to risk more than money to acquire the work.

The Emir of Alwabbi sat in his bulletproof car outside London's Dorchester Hotel waiting for his wife, the Sheikha Midora, to join him. The auction was the Emir's idea of torture. A private man, he had spent a lifetime avoiding the flash of a camera, the peer and sneer of a journalist, indeed any kind of life on a public stage. The only exception was when his horse, Fighting Spirit, won the Derby and on that glorious day, the summation of a lifetime's dream, the Emir could not resist stepping up before Her Majesty the Queen to accept the magnificent trophy on behalf of his tiny principality. It pained the Emir that so few understood that all thoroughbreds were descended from four Arabian horses. The English, in particular, liked to think that through some strange alchemy of good breeding and natural selection, these magnificent animals had somehow morphed out of their squat, bow-legged, shaggy-haired moorland ponies.

The Emir wanted to build a museum dedicated to the horse in his landlocked country. His family's livelihood had for many centuries relied on the camel and the Arab horse; oil had only been discovered in the last thirty years. But his wife said no one would visit that kind of place; only art had the power to persuade people to travel. She pointed to the success of neighbouring projects in Qatar and Dubai, to the transformation of nowhere towns such as Bilbao and Hobart. When those arguments failed to impress her husband, the Sheikha raged that it would take less than one week's output of crude oil to build the biggest museum in the world. The Emir gave in; her museum was built. It was universally agreed to be the masterpiece of the world's leading architect, a temple to civilisation and a monument to art. However, there was one fundamental problem that neither the Sheikha nor her legions of advisors, designers and even her celebrated architect had anticipated: the museum had nothing in it. Visitors would wander around the cavernous white spaces marvelling at the shadow lines, the perfect temperature controls, the cool marble floors, the ingenious lighting, but there was little to break the monotony of the endless white walls: it was artless.

Four floors above her husband, in the royal suite, the Sheikha sat at her dressing table. Betrothed at nine, married at thirteen, mother of four by the time she was twenty, the Sheikha was now forty-two years old. As the mother of the Crown Prince, her future was assured. There was little that her husband or courtiers could do to rein in her spending; they could only watch as she scooped up the best from the world's auction rooms and drove prices to new heights. The Sheikha needed a star turn, but unfortunately most of the great works were already in national museums or private collections. The moment she saw *The Improbability of Love*, she knew that it was the jewel for her museum's crown. Here was a picture capable of drawing tourists from the world over. Unlike those who wanted to buy the painting for a reasonable price, the Sheikha wanted the bidding to go wildly out of control. She wanted her picture (she had made that assumption a long time before) to be the most expensive ever bought at auction; the more publicity the better. While her husband won horse races, she would triumph in the great gladiatorial arena of the auction room— the image of the Sheikha fighting for her picture would flash on to every screen all over the world. After a long and bitter battle, the rulers of Alwabbi would snatch victory from the claws of the world's wealthiest and most avaricious collectors. It would be the final endorsement of her dream and the ultimate advertisment. Sitting in her hotel suite, the Sheikha drew a last line of kohl around her beautiful dark eyes.

She clapped her hands together and seven ladies in waiting appeared, each carrying an haute couture dress. The Sheikha wore only a tiny percentage of the clothes made for her, but she liked to have options. Tonight she looked at the dresses—the Elie Saab, McQueen, Balenciaga, Chanel and de la Renta—but after some deliberation she decided to wear a new gown by Versace, made from black silk and real gold thread edged in solid gold coins that chimed gently as she walked. The dress would be hidden by a long black abaya, but at least her Manolo Blahnik booties would be visible: mink-lined, white-kid leather with 24-carat-diamond-studded heels that would flash in the photographers' bulbs as she stepped up to the podium to inspect her latest and greatest acquisition.

In another corner of London, east Clapham, in her one-bedroom flat, the art historian Delores Ryan sat mired in despair. The only way she could imagine salvaging her reputation was to destroy the picture or herself, or both. It was universally known that she, one of the greatest experts in French eighteenth-century art, had held the work in her hands and dismissed it as a poor copy. With that one poor misattribution, one wrong-headed call, she had eviscerated a lifetime's work, a reputation built on graft and scholarship. Though Delores had more than four triumphs under her belt, including the Stourhead Boucher, the Fonthill Fragonard and, most spectacularly of all, a Watteau that had hung mislabelled in the staff canteen of the Rijksmuseum, these were now forgotten. She would be forever known as the numbskull felled by *The Improbability of Love*.

Perhaps, all those years ago, she should have accepted Lord Walreddon's proposal. She would now be the Lady of a Manor, living in dilapidated grandeur with a cacophony of children and ageing black Labradors. But Delores's first and only love was art. She believed in the transformative power of beauty. Being with Johnny Walreddon made her feel desperately bored; standing before a Titian reduced her to tears of sweet delight. Like a monk drawn to the priesthood, she had put aside (most) earthly pleasures in the pursuit of a higher realm.

The failure to recognise the importance of the work, coupled with the mania surrounding its sale, represented for Delores not just a loss of face but also a loss of faith. She did not want to be part of a profession where art and money had become inextricably linked, where spirituality and beauty were mere footnotes. Now even Delores looked at canvases wondering what each was worth. Her beloved paintings had become another tradable commodity. Even worse, this rarefied subject with its own special language and codes had become demystified: only yesterday she had heard two yobs in a café discussing the relative merits of Boucher and Fragonard. Delores was no longer a high priestess of high art, she was just another lonely spinster living in a rented apartment.

Delores wept for those wasted years of study, the hours spent reading monographs and lectures, the holidays stuck in subterranean libraries. She cried for the pictures that had passed through her hands that could, if she had been more financially astute, have kept her in perennial splendour and comfort. She sobbed for her unconceived children and the other life she might have enjoyed. She was devastated that her younger self had lacked the foresight or wisdom to anticipate any of these outcomes.

At exactly 7 p.m., one hour before the auction began, an expectant murmur hovered over Houghton Street as the first limousine purred towards the auction house. Lyudmila knew how to make an entrance: very slowly she released a long leg, letting it appear inch by inch out of the car. The paparazzi's bulbs exploded and had certain events not taken place, the image of Lyudmila's iconic limbs clad in black fishnets emerging from a black Bentley would have adorned the front pages of tabloid newspapers from Croydon to Kurdistan. Her fiancé, Dmitri Voldakov, who controlled 68 per cent of the world's potash and was worth several tens of billions of pounds, did not attract one flash. He didn't mind: the fewer people who knew what he looked like, the smaller the chance of assassination or kidnap. Dmitri looked up at the surrounding rooftops and was relieved to see his men stationed, armed and alert; his bodyguards, only two of whom were allowed to enter the building, were already tucked in on either side of him. Dmitri supposed that the little upstart Vlad would try and outbid him tonight. Let him try, he thought.

"Lyudmila, Lyudmila!" the photographers called out. Lyudmila turned to the left and right, her face arranged in a perfect pout.

Two dazzlingly white, customised Range Rovers, each pulsating in time with booming rap music, drew up to the front entrance.

A whisper snaked through the expectant crowd. "Mr. Power Dub-Box. Power Dub-Box."

A brace of large bodyguards dressed in black suits with conspicuous earpieces jumped out of the first car and ran to the second. As the door opened, the street vibrated to the beat of Mr. M. Power Dub-Box's number-one sound: "I Is da King." The statuesque self-anointed High Priest of Rap wore jeans and a T-shirt, and was followed by three women who appeared to be naked.

"Bet they're pleased it's a warm night," Felicia said to Dawn, looking on in amazement.

"Is the last one wearing anything?" asked Dawn.

"Her bra-let is the same colour as her skin," observed Felicia.

"It isn't the top bit I am talking about," said Dawn as she snapped a picture on her phone of the woman's bare bottom disappearing into the auction house.

"What a great pleasure to meet you, Mr. M. Power Dub-Box," said Earl Beachendon, stepping forward to shake the musician's hand. He tried and failed not to look at the half-naked women beside the rapper. M. Power offered him a half-hearted high five before turning to the waiting film crews. His three female escorts arranged themselves around him like petals framing a large stamen.

"Hi there," cried Marina Ferranti, the diminutive presenter of *BBC Arts Live*, greeting M. Power Dub-Box like a long-lost friend. "Why are you here tonight?"

"I like shopping," he said.

"This is fairly high-end shopping!"

"Yep."

"Are you hoping to buy this picture?"

"Yep."

"How much will you spend?"

"What it takes."

"Would it make a good album cover?"

"No." M. Power Dub-Box looked incredulously at the presenter. Surely the BBC knew that albums were so last century? These days it was all about simultaneous viral outer-play.

"So why do you want to buy it?" Marina asked.

"I like it," he said, walking away.

Unperturbed, Marina and her TV crew circled Earl Beachendon.

"Lord Beachendon, are you surprised by the amount of attention this picture has received?"

"*The Improbability of Love* is the most significant work of art that Monachorum has had the pleasure of selling," he said.

"Many experts say that this picture is just a sketch and that the estimate is completely out of proportion to its importance," continued Marina.

"Let me answer your question with another: how does one value a work of art? It's certainly nothing to do with the weight of its paint and canvas or even the frame around it. No, the value of a work of art is set by desire: who wants to own it and how badly."

"Do you think this little painting is really worth tens of millions of pounds?"

"No, it is worth hundreds of millions."

"How can you tell?"

"I don't decide on the value. My job is to present the picture in its best light. The auction will set the price." The Earl smiled.

"Is this the first time that a painting has been marketed with a world tour, a biography, an app, its own website, a motion picture and a documentary film?" asked Marina.

"We thought it important to highlight its history using all varieties of modern technology. This is the picture that launched a movement, which changed the history of art. It also has a peerless provenance: belonging to some of history's most powerful figures. This canvas has witnessed greatness and atrocity, passion and hatred. If only it could talk."

"But it can't," Marina interjected.

"I am aware of that," the Earl replied with withering condescension. "But those with a soupçon of knowledge about the past could imagine what illustrious events, what significant personages have been associated with this exquisite jewel. The lucky new owner will become inextricably linked to that history."

Marina decided to press a little harder. "I've only spoken to one person tonight, M. Power Dub-Box, who actually likes the painting. Everyone else seems to want it for a different reason," she said. "The French Minister of Culture and his ambassador say that it is of significant national importance. The Director of the National Gallery told me that French eighteenth-century painting is under-represented in Trafalgar Square. The Takris want it for their new museum in Singapore. Steve Brent wants it for his new casino in Vegas. The list goes on and on. Do you think that loving art is irrelevant these days, that owning pictures has become another way of displaying wealth?"

"Some rather important guests are arriving. I should greet them," Beachendon said smoothly.

"One last question?" Marina called out. "How much do you hope the painting will make tonight?"

"I am confident that a new world record will be set. Now if you will excuse me . . ." Aware that he had said too much, Earl Beachendon moved quickly back to the reception line to greet the Emir and Sheikha of Alwabbi.

Half an hour later, once all the major players had arrived and been safely matched to their carers, the Earl slipped behind the two vast mahogany doors and into the inner sanctum of Monachorum's auction room. Leaning on his dark wooden podium, he surveyed the rows of empty chairs beneath him and looked over the banks of telephones lining the back of the room. This was his amphitheatre, his arena, and in exactly twenty minutes' time he would preside over one of the most ferociously fought battles in the history of art. The bidders' arsenals were full of pounds, dollars and other currencies. His only weapons were a gavel and the voice of authority. He would have to pace the assailants, draw out their best moves and keep the factions from destroying each other too quickly. Beachendon knew that when emotions ran as high as tonight, when so much more than pride and money was at stake, when gigantic egos and ancient sores sat in close proximity, much could go wrong.

He looked down at his secret black book which held his notes on all the buyers: where they were sitting and how much they were likely to bid. In the margins, the Earl made lists of the telephone bidders and those who insisted on anonymity. That afternoon, fourteen new hopefuls had registered and the Earl's colleagues had had to scramble bank references and other securities. He already had an underbidder who had guaranteed £250 million; a record was in place before the first public bid had been made. If no one bettered that price, the auctioneer would knock it down to an anonymous buyer on the telephone. Beachendon ran through a practice round, calling out imaginary bids from empty chairs and unmanned phone lines. "Seventy million, eighty million two hundred thousand, ninety million three hundred thousand, one hundred million four hundred thousand. The highest bid is on the phone. No, it's on the floor. Now it's with you, sir. Two hundred and fifty million, five hundred thousand." Later, each bid would be simultaneously translated into dollars, euros, yen, renminbi, rupees and rupiah, and flashed on large electronic screens.

The Earl sounded calm and collected; inside he was in turmoil. A little over a century earlier, this picture had belonged to a member of his mother's family, no less than Queen Victoria; its disposal was yet another example of the inexorable decline of his noble line. Now the painting's fabulous price and its notoriety mocked Beachendon, reminding him of all that had been lost: ninety thousand acres in Wiltshire, Scotland and Ireland; swathes of the Caribbean, along with great paintings by van Dyck, Titian, Rubens, Canaletto and Leonardo. If only we had hung on to this one painting, the Earl thought sadly as he looked at the tiny canvas resting in its protective bulletproof glass case. He imagined a different life for himself, one that didn't involve the Northern Line, kowtowing to the ridiculously rich and their shoals of hangers-on, the dealers, advisors, agents, critics and experts who circled the big moneyed whales like suckerfish in the waters of the international art world. Within half an hour the floor beneath him would be swimming with those types and it would be up to Earl Beachendon to tickle out the best prices. At least, the Earl consoled himself, his personal discovery of the picture proved that although the Beachendon family had lost a fortune, they never lost their eye.

Along with the rest of the world, Beachendon wondered what the little picture would fetch. Even at its lowest estimate, it would be enough to buy a couple of mansions in Mayfair, an estate in Scotland and the Caribbean, pay off his son and heir Viscount Draycott's gambling debts, and secure decent flats for each of his six daughters, the Ladies Desdemona, Cordelia, Juliet, Beatrice, Cressida and Portia Halfpenny.

Though he was a godless man, Beachendon was a pragmatist and he offered a small prayer to the heavens.

The Earl was so lost in a private fantasy that he didn't see a young male of Chinese origin dressed as a porter examining the velvet-covered plinth. Many hours later, when the security team and police reviewed the CCTV footage, they would wonder how one individual could have pulled off such an audacious move in front of the wily Earl, the silent cameras and security guards. Most had assumed he was someone's son on work experience, one of the legions of young people paid nothing for the glory of working for a big auction house and needing something to set their CV apart. Of course, the heads of HR and security fell on their swords and resigned immediately but it was too late then. Much too late.

Chapter 1

SIX MONTHS EARLIER (11 JANUARY)

Though she often passed Bernoff and Son, Annie had never been tempted to explore the junk shop; there was something uninviting about the dirty window piled high with other people's flotsam and jetsam. The decision to go through its door that Saturday morning was made on a whim; she hoped to find a gift for the man she was sleeping with but hardly knew.

She had met Robert five weeks earlier at an "Art of Love" singles night at the Wallace Collection in Manchester Square. It was her first foray into dating since she was a teenager and she went with low expectations of meeting anyone but hoped at least to learn something about art. The flyer promised "ice-breaking lectures" and "world-class experts" on hand to discuss particular paintings. Robert caught her eye during a talk on "Passion in the Court of Louis XIV." His glance was awkward and only half-hopeful—instinctively she recognised someone else with a pulverised heart. He was nice-looking but uncared for—his hair was too long, his shirt poorly ironed and his demeanour a little battered. He was attractive in an unthreatening way. A few hours later, they kissed in a passageway behind Marylebone High Street. He had taken her number (Annie assumed out of politeness only). The following day he texted: "Dear Annie, my grandmother used to say that after a bad fall, it's important to get back into the saddle. Do you fancy a drink?" After that, Annie met Robert once or twice a week for energetic sex and desultory conversation. When Robert admitted that he was spending his birthday alone, Annie offered to cook him dinner. Against her better judgement, she struggled to keep hope at bay. Her longing to love and be loved was so strong that she overlooked her and Robert's incompatibility. At least, she thought, good solid dependable Robert, the solicitor from Crouch End whose wife had done the unforgivable and run off with his best friend, would never behave unkindly or unchivalrously.

Annie pushed the door of the shop and it opened with a reluctant shudder. In the corner there was a man, though it was hard to distinguish between his body and the armchair he was slumped in. Both were baggy and encased in brown velour. He was watching television with the sound off and Annie saw the reflection of horses racing in his spectacles.

"Are you open?" she asked.

The man waved her in, never taking his eyes from the screen. "Hurry up, close the door."

Annie shut the door gently behind her.

A telephone rang. The man snatched it up.

"Bernoff's Antiques, Reclamation and Salvage," he said

in a flat south London accent. "Ralph Bernoff speaking." His voice was surprisingly high-pitched and young. He looked fifty but was probably only thirty.

"Gaz, my old friend, you watching Channel 4? Have you seen The Ninnifer has gone out to thirty to one?" Ralph said. "I don't fucking believe it."

He paused to listen to the answer.

"Course I don't fancy that other pile of shite. It ran backwards at Haydock last week. Lend us a few quid. I know that Ninnifer is going to storm it. Please, mate."

Pause.

"What do you mean, I owe you?" Ralph said plaintively.

Pause.

"So put that on the tab. Those cunts said they'd break my legs if I didn't pay them tonight. Please, Gaz. Help me out."

Pause.

Annie edged along the back wall of the shop past the rows of oddly matched china, paperbacks with embossed covers, chipped teacups, cracked bowls, piles of plastic beads, a reproduction Victorian doll and a nest of Toby jugs. She looked nervously from the man to the door, wondering if his creditors were about to burst in.

"No one is going to buy anything," he whined into the telephone. "No one ever does. Just a load of bored Saturday-morning time-wasters," he lamented, casting a look in Annie's direction.

Picking up a Victorian brass mould shaped like a comet, Annie wondered if she could use it. Robert had been born in 1972 and she was intending to cook him a seventies-inspired dinner. Perhaps an elaborate jelly would be better than the intended rum baba? She turned the mould over—it cost £3. Rather a lot for one dinner and, besides, there was not enough time for the jelly to set. She put it back next to a china doll.

"If you're not going to lend us a monkey, make it a pony. I'll give it back with interest when I win," Ralph said.

Pause.

Gaz gave the wrong answer; Ralph slammed the phone down.

Annie walked to another table and thumbed a hardback edition of *Stalingrad*—would Robert like that? Brilliant but too depressing. She examined a box inlaid with mother of pearl. Pretty but too feminine. A few paces on she caught sight of a picture propped against the wall behind the rubber plant.

"Can I?" she mouthed to the man.

"Suit yourself." He didn't even glance up but sat slumped, staring at the television. Annie slid the picture off the filing cabinet; carrying it over to the window, she took a closer look.

"What do you know about this?" she asked.

"It's a picture."

She looked at him, trying to decide if he was stupid or rude, or both.

"Do you know the date, or who painted it?"

"No idea, it's been here for years."

"I'm looking for a present for a friend . . ." Annie hesitated. "This might amuse him."

Ralph Bernoff didn't do conversation; he was used to lonely old ladies rabbiting on about this or that. This one was a few years younger than most of his regular customers but he knew the signs; sad, single and the wrong side of twenty-five. He looked her up and down—quite nice legs but too flat on top. If she got some highlights and a short skirt, she might stand a chance.

"We share a certain interest in painting." Annie flushed, feeling his eyes on her body. "My friend," she said firmly, "might like this. It reminds me of something we saw at the Wallace Collection."

"Right." Ralph kept checking his watch and digging around in his pockets as if some change might miraculously appear.

"Do you know where it came from?"

"No idea—it came with the shop. Bought the whole place

and most of this rubbish with it. Worst decision my dad ever made." Ralph waved his hand around.

"How much is it?" Annie pulled the sleeve of her coat down and gently wiped away at the dust on the painting's surface.

"No idea. Come back Monday and my dad will tell you."

"That's too late," Annie said. "What a pity—I really like it."

Ralph snorted rudely. "There's a whole load of clobber here. Pick anything else. I'll give you a discount, being a Saturday and all that." Ralph put his little finger deep into one ear and wiggled it about with all the concentration of a violinist aiming for a high C. Annie looked away and carefully placed the painting back on the filing cabinet. Ralph looked up at the grandfather clock; it was nearly three.

"What! The Ninnifer's gone out to fifty to one, bloody hell." Ralph jumped up from his chair and stabbed a finger at the screen.

"There's nothing else quite right," Annie said. She had had enough of this rude man and his claustrophobic den.

"Bloody time-waster," Ralph muttered under his breath.

Belting her coat tightly and pulling a woollen hat down over her ears, Annie opened the door. A cold gust of air blasted into the shop and dust swirled around her face in luminous eddies. Annie took one last look at the painting. It was, even through the dust and the gloom, rather pretty. She would tell Robert about it later; it would be something to talk about in their sparsely populated conversational world. She had stepped out on to the pavement and bent down to unlock the chain on her bicycle when Ralph came bursting out of the shop, waving the painting. "Hang on. How much money do you have?" Ralph asked.

"Fifty pounds," Annie smiled apologetically.

"Five hundred quid and it's yours," Ralph said, holding out the painting.

"I haven't got anything like that kind of money," Annie said.

"What have you got?"

"I've got a hundred pounds out of the cashpoint but it has to cover dinner." She blushed slightly and moved from foot to foot.

"Give us two fifty in cash."

"I said I haven't got that." Annie was annoyed now. She put the chain in the bike's basket and started to push it down the road.

"You've got four minutes to decide, love, or the deal's off."

"I'll give you seventy-five—that's my last offer," Annie heard herself say.

Ralph hesitated and, holding out his hand, said, "Seventy-five. Give it over. Quick."

Chapter 2

I knew I'd be rescued but never thought it would take fifty years. There should have been search parties, battalions and legions. Why? Because I am priceless and I am also the masterpiece that launched a whole artistic genre. And if that isn't enough, I am considered to be the greatest, the most moving, and the most thrilling representation of love.

I was inspired by feelings of deep joy, hope and gaiety but my decorative composition masks a twisted soul drunk on the mysterious poison of despair. Unfortunately, and inadvertently, I command a wayward, erratic power over men and women—sometimes inspirational and affirming, sometimes the opposite. I am both the offspring and parent of tragedy.

Back to the present. Imagine being stuffed away in a bric-a-brac shop in the company of a lot of rattan furniture, cheap china and reproduction pictures. I would not call myself a snob but there are limits. I will not converse with pisspots or faux-pearl necklaces. *Non!* I am used to magnificence, the rustle of taffeta and *le mouffle du damask*, the flicker of candlelight, sheen of mahogany, the delicate smell of rosewater and beeswax, the crunch of gravel and the whispering of courtiers. Not a poky little room lit by bare bulbs and a greenish light straining through grime-encrusted glass. The shop's atmosphere is most damaging to my delicate canvas: fungus and mildew. Not to mention the layers of cigarette smoke and human effluvium hanging like slices of mille-feuille in the stale air.

It's not the first time I've been neglected. Human beings are a capricious lot, slaves to fancy and fashion. They are destined to be perpetual amateurs—they don't live long enough to be anything more. What can one do in a mere seventy or eighty years? During the first part of their lives, it's all haste and fornication. Thenceforward most of their efforts go into staying alive.

I am three hundred years old. As man's first paintings were made some forty thousand years ago I am a spring chicken in the panoply of art history but I like to consider myself a marinated goose in terms of experience. I've hung in pride of place in the grandest palaces and *salons* of Europe, Russia, Scandinavia and even America as the beloved possession of royalty and connoisseurs. Occasionally, and most unhappily, the whim of some new mistress or the latest critical pronouncement has led to relegation, the red card, and I have been marched off to the servants' quarters or the storage rooms.

This time was different. I was well and truly lost.

I sat at Bernoff's getting lonelier and lonelier. It is arrogant to assume human beings have the monopoly on communication—we pictures converse with like-minded objects. You try maintaining a relationship with a cake tin or a Toby jug. The latter was made in the East End of London, common as muck—it was all football, muggings and shagging. It rubs off, you know. I catch myself coming out with terribly lewd and vulgar phrases. My first language is pre-revolutionary French but I have lived in Spain, England, Russia, Germany and Italy. My once courtly vocabulary has become a frightful bastardised *Franglais* suspended between several centuries.

Still, a masterpiece develops a certain sang-froid born from a belief in the triumph of excellence. After all, what are a few decades when there are centuries ahead in which to inspire, please and inform? It was a question of patience: sooner or later someone would walk through that door and recognise my true worth. Then it happened; twice in one day. The first sighting was eerie. I never thought I would see him again. Those pale blue eyes—that darting sideways look and that huge frame hardly careworn or bent by time. I loathed him then; I loathe him now. I knew he had been looking for me for many years. For some reason he didn't buy me there and then but tucked me out of sight behind a rubber plant and a cachepot. That mistake would be his undoing.

Only a few hours passed and a woman arrived, a mere scrap of a girl, obviously poor and largely ignorant. I sensed trouble. I have developed that antenna. Fat lot of good intuition does when one can't walk or scream out loud.

It was a typical Saturday morning in Bernoff's. The old man had taken the day off and the lamentable son Ralph was tending the shop. The heinous one (a complimentary term, I can assure you) was studying the form. Apart from the odd, blousy, cheap-knickered blonde who he'd have quickly, sweatily and noisily on the filing cabinet, horse-racing was the only thing that excited him. That day a meeting at Cheltenham emanated from a small colour TV on the desk. The phone rang every few minutes. It was his "mate" Gaz. Did he fancy this one? What about the Jock? Bad run at Haydock. This went on every Saturday. Gaz got him all excited about a bay in the 3:30, name of The Ninnifer. Only problem was that Ralph had already spent his weekly at the pub. He did his normal trick, going through all the drawers, his father's coat pockets, and the petty cash box. The old man wasn't stupid; he'd cleared the lot out. Ninnifer was a dead cert, apparently. Ralph was effing and blinding. It was 2:30. He started to ring around his friends, asking if he could borrow a tenner. They knew his tricks.

There was a ding and a rattle as the front door opened. "Fucking hell," Ralph grumbled down the phone to Gaz, "another bloody time-waster." Pause. "How should I know, probably an old lady looking for a cushion for her cat." Pause. "Saturday punters never buy anything."

I watched the young woman walk between the tables, each groaning with unwanted knick-knacks. She picked up an older-looking hardback before going to another table and examining a box, quite a pretty inlaid thing. She caught sight of me, approached and moved the rubber plant slightly to one side.

"Can I?" she said to Ralph.

"Suit yourself." He didn't even look up. Very gently, the young woman slid me off the filing cabinet, away from the potted plants, and walked me over towards the window. I can't see too well these days: two layers of varnish and chain-smoking have left my surface more than a little murky. She looked at me hard, really hard. It's a long time since I've been admired properly. I must admit I enjoyed it. I looked over at her fingers. No ring. I might have known. Either a slattern or some desperate *"jeune fille à marier"*; it was odds on that she was broke so I was not too worried at that moment.

I was placed back next to the potted plant and gave a tiny shiver of relief. She left the shop. Suddenly Ralph jumped up, snatched me off the shelf and ran out into the road towards the girl. She didn't really want me. I willed her not to buy me. There was some cursory haggling and then she fished around in her bag: out came an old compact, a notebook, two sets of keys, some lip salve, a mobile phone, a lidless pen, a half-eaten chocolate bar and scraps of paper. Finally she produced a tatty leather wallet bulging with receipts and photographs. She counted out the money, a paltry pittance: the utter shame.

What was I thinking? You may well ask. I was not jumping for joy, that's for sure. There was no love lost between Ralph Bernoff and me. I was fed up with the fag smoke, the company, the television, but I had got used to it and it was safe. I knew nothing about this scrappy girl. Or the birthday boy. Who knows what they were like? What they might be into.

I had a little dream. One day the door would open, the bell would tinkle tinkle and an earnest-looking man would enter. He'd be dressed in a soft tweed suit and sport those half-moon gold glasses. His eyes would fix on my surface and he would know. Within days other men, handlers, would appear with dainty white gloves and carefully lift me on to a red velvet cushion. Taken by armed guard to a special place, a gallery, all mahogany walls and plush carpets, I would sit in state, receiving experts while they pronounced and exclaimed. I would be gently cleaned and put in a decent frame. Best of all, I would be reunited with some of my master's other works.

As usual I had no say over what happened next, for ever the victim of human whimsy.

Ralph stuffed me into a polythene bag, handed me to the girl, and hot-footed it in the direction of the local bookie's. I could hear the girl's teeth chattering slightly as she put me into the front-loaded wicker basket of her bicycle. It was raining gently. Cold splats landed on clear plastic, making it even harder to see. The chain on her bicycle was released, she mounted and off we went, riding against an icy wind. It was a new experience being among these growling, grinding, and screeching flat-sided monsters. They roared past, sucking us into a damp slipstream towards vast black wheels. She rode the bike as Peter the Great liked to gallop his horse, no thought for anyone else, fast, arrogantly, without fear. I have survived many situations but have not been so jiggled and jostled since that journey across the Pyrenees when Philip and Isabella were sacked from the Escorial and their greatest works were loaded on to the backs of mules and sent to safety.

After ten minutes of weaving through traffic, bumping into watery holes, horns bleating, men shouting, dogs barking, an endless cacophony, we arrived at a market set in a lane about thirty feet long lined with wooden tables covered with stripy awnings, glittering in the damp air and piled high with produce. Some stalls still had the remnants of Christmas lights and decorations. The air of fake cheer hung over the place like a cheap perfume.

"Nice Christmas, darling?" one asked. "Did you go to the Caribbean?"

"I stayed here and cooked a turkey for a friend," the girl answered, choosing some tomatoes carefully.

"Want to keep me warm tonight?" another called out.

The girl did not answer.

"There's an Arctic wind coming—you might regret it."

"These tomatoes are a little wintry," she said, trying to deflect their banter.

"It's January, my angel, in case you hadn't noticed." The man guffawed.

She was known and liked in the market. Two traders asked her out. One gave her a free bag of oranges. Most called her Annie. The lack of a moniker or title was inauspicious. One has rarely been owned by a person of no class or standing. I am not a snob; my master was hardly well-born, but a title suggests reassuring things like wealth, breeding and security. I have yet to meet a queen named Annie.

She spent ages picking through fruit and vegetables, feeling and smelling them, making sure each was perfect. She spent more time choosing a potato than she had *moi*. She enquired after the provenance of everything—did the stallholder know where they came from or when they were harvested? One suspects that they indulged her only because she was fair of face. At the butcher's, she deliberated over a fillet of beef but could only afford a cut called bavette, which I now understand is tasty and cheap.

At least the girl didn't put the meat, the potatoes or other consumables in my plastic bag; one should be thankful for small mercies. The stallholders put a few things aside for her. I had to admit I quite liked her. She had a pleasant breathy voice caused by sucking in a lot of air before talking. She had never been taught to breathe from her diaphragm and the shallow breaths made me think she was prone to panic attacks. Her accent was classless, definitely English, and at least she spoke in rounded sentences rather than that awful shorthand I had to put up with at Bernoff's. She had that terrible modern habit of letting words tumble over each other in the race to finish a sentence.

Eventually I was pedalled back to her residence. How we made it I don't know; it was bumpy, noisy; more than once an automobile screeched to a halt to avoid a collision. She was chided for dangerous cycling. She seemed oblivious. One was worried.

We stopped and she opened the front door. Imagine my disappointment when there were no servants to greet her, not even an aged retainer. A very bad omen. Up and up we climbed. I counted two, three, four and then five floors. Let me immediately disavow you of the romantic idea that artists like garrets. Poppycock. Artists are like anyone else—they want the grandest rooms. By the time you get to the eaves, where the servants live, the skirting boards can be as little as three inches high and the ceilings slanted and low. That was the first thing I looked at when the girl fished me out of the plastic bag. It was bad news; someone of very low social standing had bought me. As I'll explain again and again, my survival depends on good circumstances; wars, famine, poverty, weather, fashion and other acts of godlessness terrify one.

Propped up on a rickety wooden table I was able to get a good look at my new home. The room ran the length and breadth of the house and was painted a vulgar yellow. The ceiling was low; you couldn't have hung a major Rubens up there, Veronese would have had to be folded into eighths. There were windows on three sides (sunlight for us paintings is another terrible hazard). Behind a partition (you could not call it a separate room) I glimpsed an unmade bed. One side had been slept in; the other was still quite neat. She obviously lived alone. I noticed that the mattress rested on planks and bricks. On a packing crate by the messy side there were piles of books. Though my vision was distorted badly, each and every tome seemed to be about food.

There was no art to keep me company. At least there were no signs of a child; I cannot abide children. Once the dauphin, that miserable son and heir of Louis XIV, a pudding of a child, a flat-footed numbskull, had a tantrum and threw a ball at *moi*! As far as I am concerned, children should neither be seen nor heard.

At the other end of the room there was an alcove with cooking equipment: a white metal box with dials, a stainless-steel sink under a window facing out over the rooftops. Either side were shelves stacked untidily with pots, pans and china. Two old earthenware jugs contained a forest of cooking utensils, knives and forks. Small cupboards either side of the white box held a variety of packets and dry stores. There were few ornaments: a decorative but deeply ordinary chipped china jug with wilting flowers, a framed poster of a movie, *Isabella and Ferdinand*, and a worn-out teddy bear with one eye and a red bandana around its neck. The floor was wooden, painted white but heavily scuffed and a blue-and-white rug was placed before two small armchairs with blankets thrown over their backs. On another wooden pallet there was some kind of fern in a terracotta pot.

As she unpacked the shopping, I was able to get a clearer look at my new mistress. She was a slight thing; no more than five foot four. She wore dreadful clothes, those slouchy, pocketed trousers and a jumper, inexpertly darned at the elbows with bright pink thread. On her feet was a pair of pale brown boots with a wedged heel. She had marvellously pale skin and a cloud of dark auburn curls framing her face in a most fetching way. A little later she made a warm drink and sat looking intently at me and I was able to see her better. The girl was not a classical beauty, no Mona Lisa or Venus de Milo, but she had something, a certain *je ne sais quoi*. Large green almond-shaped eyes, flawlessly arched eyebrows, white teeth slightly chipped in the middle to form a baby triangle. Her mouth was slightly too wide but a good deep plum red. Her skin was so pale that it glowed like a soft marble. A fraction too long in the face, which gave her a rather charming, serious, pensive look. Then she smiled. "Cor blimey," as the earthenware boys used to say. "*Mon dieu,*" to quote old Nicolas Poussin. My saviour, I had to admit, was really lovely looking, *une belle pépée*.

"I wonder what your story is?" She spoke to me in a way I haven't been spoken to for a long time. My craquelure shone with pleasure. "I wish I could see you better. Is it age or dirt? There's something so touching about the man lying on the grass staring in wonder at the dancing woman. She's not that interested in him, is she? She's looking at us looking at her and hardly knows or cares what he thinks. She is capable of inspiring great love, isn't she? Where are they? It looks like a clearing in a wood. But the sun is coming from stage left, a beautiful dappled light. Is that a ghost in the corner? Or is it a cloud?"

What could I say? She has the eye. The heart. She may be bog poor but she *knows*, doesn't she? She can feel and sense my greatness. Like anyone, I need to be loved and admired.

She looked at the clock on the wall and jumped up, chiding herself. There was work to be done. It was clearly an occasion. She reached in the back of a cupboard and brought out a large white sheet. Not linen or damask. Placing it on the table, she smoothed the edges down carefully. Fishing some

knives and forks out of a pot she wiped them on the underside of the tablecloth. Pretty slovenly, you'll agree. Taking four
small enamel cups from the shelf, she arranged posies of paper
whites in each. Marie Antoinette was partial to narcissi—it
took me back. Two wine glasses were polished and placed
opposite each other at either end of the table. Taking some
pink napkins and wrapping each in scarlet ribbons, she placed
them in between the knives and forks at a jaunty angle. What
is wrong with the young? What is wrong with classical arrangements and doing things correctly? Still, it had a creative touch
and looked festive. I had to give her that.

Taking the beef out of a bag, she rubbed powders into its
surface, placed it in a bowl under a cloth. Then she went off
into the little side room and soon I heard the noise of water. As
she stepped out of the bath I saw flashes of naked pale flesh—
long honey-coloured limbs that would have seen off a Titian,
let me tell you. Velázquez's Rokeby Venus would have had
conniptions if she'd seen this competition.

I watched her dress. She chose a white silk shirt and purple
velvet trousers, worn at the knees and patched on one flank.
What is wrong with a nice dress? She twisted and tamed her
long hair into a knot and secured it with a chopstick. What is
wrong with a brooch? Still, she looked better.

I have had the odd spell in a banqueting hall, state rooms
and boudoirs (*ooh la la*, the stories I could tell you—the sex
lives of kings and queens) but I have never ever been consigned to a kitchen or seen a *domestique* at work. It was, one
must admit, enjoyable watching her; she cooked as if she were
conducting an orchestra, except that in the place of a baton
there were glinting knives and wooden spoons. Her hands
flew like swooping swallows sweeping over saucepans and a
heavy wooden board. Vegetables were sliced into narrow juli-
ennes and the eggs whisked in stiff peaks. My girl kept one
eye trained on her sauces, teasing, stirring and occasionally
sprinkling a pinch of salt or some finely chopped herbs. Even-

tually something frothy and glossy was teased out of eggs and spooned on to slivers of ruby-coloured beef.

My erstwhile mistress, Marie Antoinette, used to employ scores of pastry chefs; there was a girl just to watch a gâteau rise. Her remark about letting them eat cake was taken entirely out of context. It was a form of flattery. So what if there wasn't bread? Cake was more delicious. It was a little preposterous in the circumstances, I admit, but things were different then.

Placing candles on all the hard surfaces around the room, on the window ledges, a side table, on the mantelpiece and in the hearth, Annie lit them one by one and flicked off the lights. Outside, dusk was falling and there was only the faintest orange glow of the street lights coming through the window.

Whoever my girl was waiting for was late. Then later. She couldn't settle. She rearranged the knives and forks. She opened the bottle of wine and poured herself a glass. And another. She opened and closed a book. I lost count of how many times she went to the window and squinted down at the street below.

My master was just the same waiting for "her" to come. She was always late, if she turned up at all. My master would try to paint, taking up a brush and standing before his easel. You could see him attempting to regain concentration but he would dash between his palette, the stairs and the window.

The girl looked at her watch. She paced. Frequently she picked up the telephone and started to press the numbers, and stopped. She poured a third glass of wine and then a fourth. In the candlelight I could see a flush in her cheeks, an added glitter in her eye. She rummaged around in a drawer and pulled out a packet of cigarettes. My heart sank. I didn't have her down as a smoker. She lit one and drew the smoke deep into her lungs. Coughing wildly, she threw the stub into the empty hearth. The candles had burnt low. One or two had even gone out. Her guest was not coming. I didn't need three hundred years' experience to work that out.

She stood in the middle of the room and started to sway from side to side. Her legs began to move and her arms came out beside her and it was as if she were pushing air away. An awful mournful groaning wail came out of her mouth, gently at first but rising to an animalistic howl. As the noise grew louder, her movements sped up and soon she was moving and twisting like a young sapling in a high wind. I stared, transfixed. As she danced, her shadow whipped around in the candlelight and spun off the walls. Faster and faster she went, with her hair flicking this way and that, spinning around and around as if her head were going to fall off. Flashes of light caught on her bangles and reflected in the whites of her eyes. Her breathing became more and more intense. Then she stopped as suddenly as she'd started and sank to her knees, resting her head on the floor. I heard this strange and eerie sound, like wind whistling under a door or a child playing an oboe. I realised it was her. Crying. It was a heart-rending noise. I had heard it once before, from my master, when "she" told him she would never marry him.

The girl lay on the floor rocking from side to side, still clutching her knees or putting her arms over the back of her head. She cried until the soft light of dawn broke over the rooftops and a lone bird started to sing.

Chapter 3

Annie woke in the late afternoon and, opening one eye, watched the rays of a setting sun creep through the window, across her bed, turning the white counterpane a golden red. If I don't move, she thought, perhaps my head will hurt less. She ran her tongue over the roof of her mouth—it tasted furry and metallic. She checked her phone—it was already four o'clock and there were no missed calls, no emails, no texts. At least there were only a few more hours of Sunday, she thought, stumbling towards the bathroom. She stood in front of the basin mirror; her reflection mocked her. No wonder he didn't show up, no wonder they all leave you, she decided, staring back at her lank hair, bloodshot puffy eyes and mottled complexion. Who in their right mind would want you? Running the tap until the water was biting cold, she splashed her face. Using her elbow, she coaxed the last squirt of toothpaste out of its tube and brushed vigorously.

She saw the picture in the mirror, propped up on the chest of drawers. It was both inanimate and mocking. What was I thinking? £75? Insanity. Pull yourself together or check into an asylum. First thing tomorrow I will take it back, put Robert behind me and kick Desmond even further into the deep recesses of my memory. Brushing her teeth with renewed vigour, Annie made, not for the first time, various vows; number one on the list was chastity. She would cancel her subscription to the "Art of Love" dating agency, remove her ad from all lonely hearts columns and accept that she was a happily single woman. Number two: she would stop drinking; she was clearly about to turn into her mother. Number three: from now on she would only eat healthy foods and cut out caffeine and sugar. Her mind and body needed a pleasant shock. Yes, a fresh start. Use negative experiences to catapult one into positive change. Number four: stop being so self-critical.

Her body cried out for carbohydrates to mop up the hangover. Spotting the remains of last night's dinner on the table, she decided to delay the new resolutions until Monday morning. Perhaps it will taste better cold, she thought, spooning lumps of potato dauphinoise and a sliver of bavette into her mouth. He would have left me if he had eaten this, she thought, picking a bit of hardened beef out of her teeth. She ate it quickly, reasoning that speed would cover up quality.

Robert must have heard back from his wife: the longed-for reconciliation. All he ever wanted was to be reunited with her and their children—he had made that clear from the start. She should try and feel happy for him; Robert had been a body to put between her and Desmond.

Taking her small battered silver coffee pot from the cupboard, Annie unscrewed the lid, filled the lower part with water and carefully spooned freshly ground coffee into the upper section. The threads of the join between the two halves had worn thin and had to be turned tightly to prevent boiling water from bubbling out of the sides. Desmond had often told her to get another or, better still, to stop drinking coffee. It was bad for her, he claimed. He didn't want "his love" to damage her health. To appease him, Annie kept her coffee habit in check and the old pot was pushed to the back of the cupboard. When she left, it was one of the few items she had brought to London from Tavistock. It made the cut only because it was not stained with his memory.

There had only been sixteen years of life before Desmond and then another fourteen with him. Her whole adulthood spent with one person. Until their separation twelve months earlier, he had been her only lover, her best friend and her business partner.

Did she know how lucky they were, Desmond used to ask every single morning, to have found each other? Did she realise that most mere mortals didn't find true love; they just stumbled around compromising and making do? I am the luckiest man alive, he told her every night.

The coffee pot began to gurgle, steam and boiling water pushed through the coffee grounds, staining the water black and scenting the air. Annie lifted up the lid to check on its progress. A drop of boiling coffee spat on to her cheek. She jumped back and wiped her face with the back of her hand. Where were those cooling tears when you needed them?

What was Desmond doing now? Only a few months ago they would have been sitting at the kitchen table reading the papers while listening to Dylan or Neil Young. You could set your watch by his habits. Sundays always started with a familiar run that took them down the River Tavey, past the bridge at Grenofen and along the top of Lady's Hill; first one home got the first shower. Normally Desmond won; of the two, Annie was the natural athlete, but Desmond's long legs gave him an advantage. After ablutions and breakfast they got back into bed and made lazy love until lunchtime. Could you run with a small baby? Annie wondered.

The coffee pot made a final gurgle. This time Annie was

careful. Wrapping a cloth around the handle, she poured the steaming thick black liquid into a cup. Blowing on the surface to cool it down, she walked over to the window and looked out. A ginger cat picked its way over a ledge, a streak of colour in the grey cityscape. The rooftops of Hammersmith, the sludgy layers of colour, were so unlike the view over the treetops to Dartmoor with its shades of green flecked with red and yellow apples yielding to the soft browns and oranges of autumn, constantly moving in the breeze. Watching the cat threading his way around the chimney of the next-door house, Annie thought about the barn owl that nested in the solid wooden box she had made seven years earlier and placed in a tree near their house in Devon. Was he still there? Had the moorland ponies, desperate for something to eat in the barren winter months, broken through the fence again and destroyed the sleeping hydrangea? Here in Hammersmith, the only wildlife she saw were pigeons, a mangy fox with a straggly tail and the odd mouse.

She wondered who lived in their old house now. She had asked the agent not to tell her—just put 50 per cent after fees into her account. Her only instruction was to get the transaction done as quickly as possible. She would stay abroad until it was all sorted.

In the distance Annie could see the first lights on the Westway beginning to pop on, the tungsten flickering as dusk faded. In the street below, a man and a woman were having an argument; a few blocks away a car alarm whined insistently. The coffee was cool enough to drink but so thick and bitter she could only take tiny sips. Would it cut through her hangover and break through the heavy fug of stale red wine? At least her headache dulled the pain of rejection. It had been stupid to think that it would have worked with Robert.

She looked over at the picture. It mocked her. The absurdity of her actions made her smile and she began to laugh. A slow chuckle at first, followed by a guffaw. Blowing a bomb on a dirty old painting for some bloke you met at a speed-dating party in a London museum? What next? You are a lunatic, Annie McDee, a genuine 100 per cent loon. She wondered idly if the owner's horse had won. What was it called, the Ninny? Ninnifer, or something like that.

The caffeine was starting to kick in, the familiar jittery feeling, the slight nervousness, her heart pounding. Perhaps she should try and run it out? There would be no one on the streets. Maybe she should call a friend. Reconnect with the past. She knew many friends were hurt by her silence and wondered why Annie never returned their emails. A whole year had passed since her life had imploded. To her old friends, Annie's life sounded rather glamorous: six months in India and now a job working as a chef for Carlo Spinetti, a well-respected film director in London. During their rare conversations, her best friend Megan would tell Annie how lucky she was not to be stuck in a provincial town waiting for the kids to come home from school, how she had broken out of the cycle of washing and cooking and baking. Annie found herself agreeing in a gay tinselly voice that she hardly recognised. Yes, she said, it's great. I feel like I am living every single second, really living it. I have been born again, given a second chance to reinvent myself. I am uncompromisingly me.

She wanted her friends to cut through the play-acting to ask what she was doing so far away from home, so cut off from everything familiar. Once or twice she nearly told Megan. But Annie didn't know where or how to start her story. I live alone in a rented flat at the unfashionable end of the Uxbridge Road. I go to work every morning on the Central Line. I work late most nights because there is nothing to come home to. Whole weekends can pass without me speaking to another living soul. Although my job sounds glamorous, the reality is quite different. If I am lucky, I get to make a bowl of pasta or chop salad. Mostly I make endless lattes and wipe surfaces. I am so bored that I volunteer for every menial, extraneous chore—I am the office drudge. My wages are so paltry that by the time I have paid the rent and the other basics, there is enough left over for a bit of a night out every third week—alone, of course. I joined a few dating agencies and have had the odd encounter but none have led to anything. My employer is a highly talented, lecherous Italian film director, but since I have worked for him we have been "in development," which means he has long lunches out of the office and afternoons spent in bed with his latest young mistress.

If I died here in my studio flat on a Friday night, no one would notice until my employer wanted a restaurant booked or his dry-cleaning collected. In Devon I used to walk into the local pub and know half the locals; here I don't even know the people who live in my building.

How do I tell my old friends the truth?

For someone else, it could be a great life: interesting, exciting and relatively free of worry. The problem is that it doesn't happen to be the life I want. It isn't the way I planned it. Somehow the scripts got muddled up. I, Annie, am supposed to be living in a little village outside Tavistock with the love of my life, running a company that we set up together. Somehow or other I got ejected out of my story halfway through and ended up in another person's life; I don't want to be here a second longer. I am too old, too scared for this existence. It's meant for a younger, braver kind of person.

How do I tell my friends that loneliness stalks my every move and a feeling of desolation presses down on my heart? My grief is not like a cloud or an atmosphere: it has an actual physical weight and a presence. Sometimes it assumes the shape of a heavy blanket, or tiny weights suspended from every finger, lobe and eyelash; or it can be a boulder or a suitcase needing to be pushed or dragged.

Finishing the last dregs of coffee, Annie wondered how to fill the next few hours. Normally on Sundays she went to the launderette. She liked the companionship, the noise, the chatter of Magda, the Polish manageress who had, after only three years in London, morphed into a proper English grouch.

"This country going to fucking dogs. Pound is worth no shlotti. Education rubbish. Strikes everywhere. National-Health-No-Service, I call it. I will go back home to Poland, proper country, and good values. You want iron or just fold?"

If only I hadn't done the washing on Wednesday, Annie thought.

Sometimes, if the weekend seemed too empty, Annie took a ride on the number 27 bus from Shepherd's Bush to Chalk Farm, passing through London's cultural bandwidths: wealthy Holland Park, bankers' Notting Hill, bohemian Bayswater, Irish Paddington and all the way up the Marylebone Road through Camden. These rides were cheaper than going to movies and it was generally far more satisfying to invent histories for the passing people and fellow passengers. Once she had a pedicure at the local nail salon just to have a conversation; however, the girl working on her feet was Vietnamese with limited English, and the woman in the adjacent seat spoke on her mobile phone throughout her treatment.

A few roads away there was an alley. Behind a row of bins, out of the parking warden's jurisdiction, a man lived in his car. It was a small white Ford Escort and the man, probably an East European, had made curtains out of discarded newspapers and broken the passenger seat to make a flat bed. When Annie walked past on her way to work he'd be asleep, wrapped in an old rug. She tried not to think where he washed. Sometimes she left a sandwich or an apple on his bonnet. She wondered if these gestures came from true compassion or if she was just relieved to find someone worse off than herself.

Annie bought a book of London walks and criss-crossed the city, exploring different areas and small shops and pubs. There were always free talks and concerts or cut-price movies, but the lonelier she got, the less adventurous she became.

Putting on her thick overcoat, Annie slipped her front-door keys in her pocket and left the studio flat. In the communal well of the building, some of her neighbours' children were playing with a Tonka truck and an old Barbie doll. They looked at her with disinterest. She thought about smiling but could not be bothered; besides, the movement might crack her dry, stretched skin. Outside the cold was bitter and she took shallow timid gulps of air and drew her coat around her, wishing that she had changed her ballet pumps for something tougher. Walking towards her in a neat row were four youths, their hoodies pulled over their faces. Were they going to mug her? She wanted to warn them that the only thing in her pockets was despair and about seventy-five pence. Just before they collided, the phalanx of boys split, leaving the centre of the pavement clear.

"Hi," one said gently. "Cold, isn't it?"

"Yes," Annie said. "Very."

They can tell, Annie thought, I am not even worth mugging.

Walking along her street towards the Uxbridge Road, she peered down into brightly lit basements, at couples and families, children sitting, heads bowed over homework; their mothers at the sinks, a father at a computer. She tried and failed to imagine herself with a husband, some children. Happy family lives seemed to belong to others. On the Goldhawk Road, black sacks of rubbish lay in heaps waiting to be collected. A discarded television set was abandoned next to a high-heeled red stiletto. An Asian man was closing up his shop, wrapped tightly in a scarf, hat and sheepskin coat, struggling with the heavy padlocks and iron shutters. A stray dog fell in with Annie, walking companionably beside her until he spotted a young boy holding a steaming Cornish pasty.

Through a window she saw a couple lying on a sofa watching an old movie, limbs entangled. Next door, six young friends were still at lunch, three empty bottles of wine and dirty plates pushed away, laughing at a shared memory or an odd remark. How did people get together, create unions, and fall in love? Had she lost the ability to connect with others? Was loneliness going to be her constant friend and lover? Could she make a life with it? She walked on through the market, empty now apart from a fox foraging among the discarded crates and unwanted food smeared by footsteps into the tarmac. Even though it was cold, the street smelled fetid and cloying. Annie walked briskly towards the river in search of a breeze.

She saw the flashing lights before she turned into the narrow street. In the dusk the blue strobes made the small white terraced houses otherworldly, like a scene from a sci-fi movie. Walking towards the fire engine and the police cars, she recognised the row of shops where she had bought her picture. Twenty steps on, she realised that her junk shop was nothing more than a charred shell. The fire had taken place many hours earlier, only the faintest plumes of smoke drifted from the charred embers and the firemen stood around drinking cups of tea. Annie's only thought was where and how was she going to return the picture. Suddenly all she wanted was to get rid of that two-dimensional albatross whose acquisition seemed to epitomise her wrong-headed, wilful and frankly self-destructive life decisions.

The area around the shop was cordoned off by plastic tape. A policewoman stood guard by the entrance eyeing up a few children on bikes who were discussing the fire.

"Probably burnt a whole family alive."

"We'll watch the news later to find out what happened."

"Do you think it will be on the BBC?"

"Look it up on Twitter—much quicker."

Annie walked up to the policewoman. "What happened?"

"We are investigating the causes of the fire."

"Did the man leave a forwarding address? Somewhere he could be reached?" Annie asked. She had to find Mr. Bernoff and get a refund.

"Do you know the deceased?" The policewoman suddenly looked interested.

"The deceased? Oh my God, you mean he's dead?" Annie looked at the embers and shuddered.

"Perhaps you would like to come and make a statement." The policewoman lifted the plastic tape to let Annie through.

"I don't know him but I bought something here yesterday. A picture. I wanted to bring it back. I changed my mind." Annie could not believe this turn of events. £75—next time she would get a match to burn the cash; it would save a lot of time. Damn Robert and his ex-wife. Damn her own impetuousness.

Half an hour later, having disappointed the inspector with her lack of knowledge or insight, Annie walked back towards home with the words arson, homicide, murder and motive ringing in her ears. She was stunned by the apparent randomness of the crime and her proximity to the event. A mere six hours after she had left the shop, someone had barged in, tied up the shopkeeper, doused the interior with petrol and thrown a burning rag soaked in petrol into its midst. The whole place had gone up like a tinderbox. Old stuff, even bric-a-brac, burned quickly. It was unfortunate that the neighbouring shops had shut early. No one heard his screams or the crackle of the demented fire until it was too late. Annie pulled her overcoat close around her. Abandoning the thought of a bracing river walk, she continued home, her own self-pitying thoughts kicking into perspective.

Her mobile rang—a blocked number. It was bound to be a salesman—a disappointment for both.

"Miss McDee?"

"Yes . . . ," Annie said hesitantly.

"This is Paddington Green police station. We have a woman here who says she's your mother. She has said a lot of things tonight, some more fantastical than others." The man sounded weary.

Annie stopped in the middle of the road and looked up to the sky. Her hangover, forgotten in the drama of the fire, came roaring back. "Does she have any ID?" she asked.

"Nothing. Do you want a physical description?"

"Yes," said Annie, though she knew it was her mother. There had been many similar calls.

"So she's about five feet five, peroxide blonde-haired, slim, smartly dressed, good-looking. Small tattoo of a bird on her arm and a large black eye."

"Is there bail?" she asked.

"No, and we are keen to free up the cell."

"What state is she in?"

"Sobering up, slowly."

"I'll come and get her."

Annie knew she should leave Evie there—rescuing never worked, for long.

She went into a small café and bought a cup of tea and a doughnut, fortification for the hours to come. She was certain what lay ahead. Her mother would go through predictable cycles of denial, anger, recrimination, and depression. Annie would have to listen, to console, to cajole. Her mother would stay with Annie for a while before disappearing one day without warning.

This time I won't go, Annie thought, taking a sip of the scalding-hot tea. But she knew she would; they only had each other.

This is what happens for wishing I wasn't lonely: some divine and appalling joke.

The last time Annie heard from Evie she had moved to Oswestry and was training to be a shiatsu masseur. "Have finally found my calling," the postcard said. Annie had not got excited. She studied the photograph cursorily. The woolly sheep crouched at the bottom of a snowbound valley did not inspire confidence. Every time Evie moved she believed it would provide the answer: a new place, a new start. Annie had been to eleven schools between the ages of five and sixteen. But no matter how many times they crossed England, the demon drink always caught up with them.

Dragging herself out of the café, Annie walked down to Shepherd's Bush and into the underground. The train swayed on its tracks, taking Annie east past the gypsy camp, a milk factory and a riding school, where it crossed under a motorway and ran between a rail track and a canal. An empty beer can at her feet rolled backwards and forwards, the plaintive song of thin tin on a corrugated floor. She pressed her face against the cold dirty window and, looking up, saw a skein of geese circling above. Below the train was a wasteland of scrub and dirt. The vista was made from grey on grey: grey sky, grey buildings, grey upholstery, and grey concrete holding up a grey motorway. The light was too flat; there were no shadows to make it interesting, nothing to tempt the eye or spirit.

She got out of the train at Royal Oak and walked along the Harrow Road towards Paddington. Reaching a large roundabout she realised she had no idea where the police station was. A man was pushing a child in a buggy twenty yards ahead. Annie ran up to him. He looked drunk with fatigue; the child slept soundly. He pointed north. Walking on past two tower blocks and a busy intersection she saw a church, a perfect Georgian gem, set in a small garden of gravestones and statues. Beyond it, the grim façade of the police station.

Once inside the station Annie filled out various forms, handed over her driving licence and was clicked through a turnstile to an inner sanctum. The place stank of disinfectant and vomit. In the background someone banged on their cell door; another person, a man (she thought), moaned.

"Are you here for Mrs. Eve McDee?" a tired-looking officer asked.

Annie nodded.

"A few more forms to fill out." He handed her a clipboard with some paperwork attached. Annie was familiar with the questions; it was not the first time.

"I am the direct descendant of Colonel Sir Cospatrick Ninian Dunbar Drummond of Durn." Annie's mother's voice rang out from somewhere behind a locked door.

"Quite a character, isn't she?" said the policeman.

Annie was unsure what to put under known address. Where was Evie living?

"He seized the Bital Wadi Akarit Ridge, the final barrier our army had to cross to reach the southern end of the Tunisian plain. Cospatrick led his platoon up a vital spur."

"The duty officer said that she was too drunk to remember her own name but she's been spouting all this history for hours."

Annie, after some consideration, filled in her own address.

"She's got an extraordinary memory."

"My family is descended from the Earls of Moray."

"Oh shut it," shouted an irritated voice.

"Be careful, in the seventeenth century we were in charge of the eradication of banditry, we purged the Borders of malefactors, robbers and brigands."

"Someone put a sock in her mouth," another voice shouted.

"Is any of this true?" the policeman asked Annie.

"No—she's half Irish, half West Country. Grew up in Wiltshire, grandparents were pig farmers," Annie replied phlegmatically. "She'll start singing soon."

As if on cue, the hesitant notes of "Carrickfergus" drifted from the cells to the front desk. "*I wish I had you down in Carrickfergus, only four nights in Ballygrand, I would swim over the deepest oceans, to long ago.*"

"Is she always like this?" he asked.

"On a good day." Annie smiled.

As a child she would never let someone speak badly about her mother. She defended Evie passionately, hoping to convince herself and those around her that the latest round of drinking was a mere aberration. For much of the time, Evie had been a wonderful mother: fun, anarchic and loving. Younger than all the other parents, Evie was often mistaken for a sixth-former or a relief teacher, and Annie was proud when the fathers turned to look at her or the older girls copied her hairstyles and make-up. Without a father or long-term boy-friend, mother and daughter were a team: they danced in the moonlight; took buses to nowhere; sang entire Elvis Presley albums; baked extravagant cakes and ate them in bed while watching classic movies. But early on Annie had learned to spot the danger signals—more cigarettes than usual; music played at full volume; a restless pacing around the home; her mother's patience thinning until the terrible moment it went snap. It was a life built on a faultline or next to a volcano, and there was no way to know when the next fissure would appear, when the top would blow. During those times, Annie was sent out of the house and told to find her way to school by following children in identical uniforms. Calls from hospitals and police stations were not unusual; if anything these were a relief—it meant Evie was still alive. The moment she dreaded was the doorbell ringing unexpectedly: "We have some bad news." Annie had imagined this scene over and over again.

Annie sat down on one of the hard chairs in the reception area to wait for Evie. The walls were covered with friendly Neighbourhood Watch posters. The faint sounds of Radio 1 drifted out from one of the offices. Maybe, Annie thought, it will be different this time. Perhaps Evie had finally reached rock bottom. She shook herself and snuffed out the rays of hope. It was a ridiculous thought after all these years.

"Oh it's you," Evie said to Annie in mock surprise as the policemen brought her out.

"Hello, Mum, let's go now," said Annie.

Evie looked terrible. Her pale yellow trouser suit was stained and her left eye looked like a swollen, blue plum.

"It's been awful, darling." Evie began to cry. "I didn't mean to, but it was the anniversary of Daddy's death and—" Annie went over to her mother and put her arms around her.

"It's okay, Mum, don't worry. Let's go home and get you cleaned up. Where's your bag?"

"Bloody bastard stole it. Now he's pressing charges. It's a conspiracy." Evie shot a furious look at the sergeant.

"The publican said she came in with nothing, started abusing him when he wouldn't serve her and then she smashed a mirror."

"If the Earls of Moray could hear you; you're no better than those miscreants in the cells. Annie, they locked me up," Evie said plaintively.

"Time to go now." Annie steered her firmly towards the door.

"Where's the car?" Evie looked up and down the Edgware Road expectantly.

"We're going on the tube."

"Doesn't he give you a car? I thought that was the whole point of working in films: private planes and limousines."

"In Hollywood, maybe. Come on, the walk will do you good."

"My heel's broken, I can't."

"There's no other way. I've just enough cash to get us home on the tube."

"No cars. No money. Slog. Slog." Evie muttered and grumbled.

Annie walked beside her mother, wishing that she'd never come to get her. It was always the same. Tears of rage and frustration pricked her eyes. She walked faster, determined to leave Evie behind.

"Annie? Wait."

Annie heard the uneven steps break into a run.

"Don't leave me."

Annie didn't answer; she kept up a steady pace.

Evie changed tack. "I never wanted to be like this," she said, starting to cry. "I hardly touched a drop. I met a man. He left me. I got sad."

Annie turned around to see her mother standing alone in the middle of the pavement, a tired, emaciated middle-aged woman, and her heart filled with pity. Evie started to hobble towards her, one heel flapping out to the side. Annie kicked off her ballet pumps.

"Wear these, Mum."

"What about you?"

"I've got thick socks on."

"Would you do that for me? Really?" Evie said, slipping her feet into Annie's shoes. "They're lovely and warm. I do love you, Annie."

"Come on, let's go home." Annie held out her hand and Evie took it.

At the flat, Annie ran her mother a bath and laid out some clean clothes on the bed. Evie sat at the kitchen table looking around the room.

"Were you expecting someone for lunch?" The table was still set for two.

"Dinner last night. He didn't show up." Annie poured some boiling water into two cups, dunked a tea bag in both, and handed one to her mother.

"Sorry." Evie smiled sympathetically.

Annie shrugged.

"Anyone special?"

"No."

"I won't say the obvious." Evie wrapped her fingers around the mug.

"So don't."

"You need a proper man."

"Not now, Mum."

"If only you'd been more . . ." Evie stopped short.

"Your bath's ready." Annie was too tired to fight.

"Anyway, I love you for being you," said Evie, trying to make amends.

"It'll be getting cold." Annie was feeling less and less patient. She took her cup of tea and went to the window.

"You wouldn't have a hair of a dog in any of those cupboards?" Evie asked hopefully.

"No." Annie started to clear the plates away. The set table was an unwanted reminder. She grabbed the knives and forks in one hand and stuffed them, ends down, into a jug.

"Darling, you look a bit washed-out—is everything okay?"

"Everything is fine—please have a bath."

Annie filled the kettle with fresh water and plugged it into the wall.

"The thing about you, Annie, is you're determined to *Chiku*."

"*Chiku?*"

"Chinese saying—it means 'eat bitter.' Make life difficult for yourself. One day you'll be grateful for Desmond leaving you, setting you free from that drab existence. You were suffocating slowly."

Annie spun round and faced Evie, her eyes blazing. "Either get in the bath or I'm going to." Annie felt the need to put a door between them quickly.

Evie struggled to her feet and walked towards the bathroom. She stopped in front of the picture. "What's that?" she said, pointing at it.

"What does it look like?" Annie said sarcastically.

"Who's it by?"

Picking up the picture, Evie looked at it for a long time.

Going over to Annie's desk she shone the anglepoise lamp so that the light hit the centre of the painting. "Where did you get it?"

"A junk shop off the Goldhawk Road."

"It's beautiful," said Evie. "It reminds me of those lovely pictures in the Wallace Collection. Your dad used to take me there. It was always warm. We used to sit on the benches in the galleries and make up stories to go with the paintings."

"The Wallace Collection," said Annie. "How odd. That's why I bought it." Her thoughts flicked back to Robert and she flushed with fresh shame. What made her think he might stick around?

"Your dad had a favourite. I can't remember the painter's name. Flagon, Fraggin, no, Fragonard, that was it—a girl on the swing. Very like this. Really light-hearted things, musicians and parties. Your dad loved him. So unlikely, really. You'd think a motorcycle racer would go for something solid, like that Laughing Cavalier. He's there too."

"That's the painting I liked too," Annie said with a slight shiver. She knew so little about her father and what he liked. He had died when she was two; she did not even have a photograph of them together.

Turning the light slightly, Evie peered into the painting. In its glare, the dancer became animated. The yellows and golds of her dress seemed to flutter and tremble and the foliage behind her shimmered. On the floor, the young man looked up in rapt admiration.

Annie gasped. "It seems to come alive."

Evie held the picture in one hand, licked her finger and gently rubbed it over the figure of the dancer. Again, the colours shone and sparkled.

"I think it's something special," said Evie, suddenly sober. "You should go along to the Wallace. We could go."

Annie smiled. One of her mother's endearing qualities was the ability to see hope in any situation. How else had she managed to survive this long, pick herself up, dry out, find new jobs, new places to live, embark on yet another love affair?

"The bath will be stone cold by now," Annie said, taking the painting and pointing towards the door.

"I've got a feeling about it," Evie grumbled as she walked across the room. "You should never discount one of my feelings."

Chapter 4

Rebecca Winkleman, Carlo Spinetti's wife, worked with her father, Memling, at Winkleman Fine Art Ltd and hid her emotions behind a cold expression. Only her immediate family knew this was a front: Rebecca was cripplingly shy and convinced that disaster lay at each turn. Every plane she boarded was certain to crash; her deals were bound to fail; at any given moment, she was certain to be unmasked as an incompetent usurper.

Terrified of being judged or exposed as someone who had won her position through nepotism, Rebecca worked longer hours and took fewer holidays than anyone else in the company, including her father. She rehearsed facts and opinions before every meeting and lay awake most nights fretting about stray remarks or the occasional mistake. Her doctor recommended Valium, which she refused to take in case it dulled her intellect. Another suggested psychotherapy, but the thought of talking to a stranger was absolute anathema. She suffered from terrible nightmares—her screams were so loud that her bedroom was soundproofed and Carlo had moved to the room next door. About once a week she woke shaking and drenched in sweat.

Rebecca dressed to attract as little attention as possible; her clothes were plain, beautifully cut and unrevealing. By day she wore trouser suits in navy blue or black with a crisp white silk shirt. At night she opted for the simplest black cocktail dress and sensible court shoes. Her blonde hair was cut into a severe bob, her nails kept short and polished. She wore minimal jewellery: diamond stud earrings and a necklace of the finest pearls. Though she would never dream of leaving the house "without her face on," her make-up routine never extended beyond a dab of concealer, pale lipstick and a few brushes of mascara. She had inherited her father's pale blue eyes but hid them behind heavy-rimmed tortoiseshell glasses. Asked to describe her looks, Rebecca would say, after a moment's hesitation, "Ordinary"; others thought of her as being on the beautiful side of handsome.

Annie had only glimpsed her employer's wife once but she was aware of the gossip: Rebecca was seen as a woman trapped between an unfaithful husband and an overbearing father. Annie, like everyone else, assumed that it was fear of being alone and unloved that kept Rebecca with her spendthrift, philandering spouse and that Carlo, terrified of being poor, led a compromised existence as a kept man. Few guessed the real reason: the Spinettis loved each other, admittedly in an unconventional and unusual fashion, and had worked out a way to accommodate each of their peccadillos. Rebecca adored his Italian use of hyperbole, his spontaneity, carnality and his childish need to be praised, cosseted. She was delighted by the way Carlo's emotions whirled like a weather vane in a high wind so that every gust, every nuance of mood was displayed for all to see. Though his films were widely panned, Rebecca found beauty and originality in every shot. The rare occasions he entered her bedroom made up for the weeks of unrequited desire. She was fantastically proud of his aquiline profile, his curly hair, his bow-shaped mouth and perfect teeth. Above all she was a pragmatist and recognised that her workaholic tendencies were as unpalatable as his sexual proclivities. Carlo liked his wife's cool intellect, her beauty and her wild insecurities. Being the only person who could manage her panic attacks and restore her confidence made him feel omnipotent and protective. Though he was addicted to falling in love, Carlo could only indulge his fantasies knowing that Rebecca was at home, unswervingly devoted and committed. For Carlo, this solid foundation overlaid with the frisson of guilt made every dalliance pleasurable.

When the Winklemans' chef, Monsieur George, suffered a stroke, Carlo asked Annie to cover until he returned to work. Although George was Michelin-starred and Cordon Bleu–trained, Carlo assured Annie that the work was easy. Colleagues advised against the move: Rebecca was almost as hard on her employees as she was on herself.

"At least go for the interview," Carlo said. He did not need to add that his wife was making his life a misery; everyone in the office knew that.

Carlo Spinetti's film company was based in a large warehouse in Bermondsey. Like many fashionable contemporary offices, the building had been stripped to a semi-industrial finish, with the functional "guts" of the premises—the pipes, brickwork and air-conditioning ducts—left uncovered. Young production associates and runners wore a uniform of blue jeans and T-shirts. A hum of constant chatter, music and telephones bounced off the concrete open-plan floor.

Arriving at the front door of Winkleman Fine Art in Curzon Street, Annie was struck by the total contrast between the husband's and the wife's establishments. The grand eighteenth-century mansion was set back from the street and bordered by iron railings. Four stone steps, each as broad as an elephant's head, led up to polished mahogany doors. It took Annie a few moments to find a discreet brass bell. A voice asked her politely to face a security camera placed above the lintel. She gave her name and waited. Noiselessly the door swung open and she was met by a liveried doorman. Two guards stationed in a marble hallway looked her up and down, making it clear that Annie was not the usual type of visitor. The doorman led her into the first inner sanctum: a heavily carpeted drawing room with French windows overlooking an Italianate garden. The walls were lined with silk damask and hung with the finest art that Winkleman had on offer. Annie had been warned that neither Rebecca nor her father, Memling, the head of the firm, would be there to welcome her—this pleasure was reserved for important guests only. Most clients were met by one of eight permanent sales staff, which included three former museum directors. Tradesmen were sent to the back entrance. Unlike the buzzy atmosphere of Carlo Spinetti's studio, the Winkleman gallery was as quiet and gloomy as a mausoleum. Nothing to detract from the art on display.

If Annie was offered and accepted this temporary secondment, she would, like other employees, enter via the mews at the rear. The Winklemans owned every building facing and backing on to that block of Curzon Street. Four were part of Winkleman Fine Art; the other three were the family's private residences. Memling lived in one, Rebecca and her family in another and the third was for entertaining clients. There was an underground tennis court and a swimming pool for use by the family only. A retinue of eight uniformed Filipino servants saw to the cleaning. There were two chauffeurs, a resident masseuse, a full-time dog walker and a part-time tennis coach, and personal trainer.

A middle-aged woman dressed in a smart black suit, with steel-grey hair pulled into a tight chignon, her face free of make-up, came forward to greet Annie.

"I am Ms. Winkleman-Spinetti's executive assistant, Liora van Cuttersman. Please come with me."

Annie was led down a thickly carpeted passage to a small waiting area with two leather chairs separated by a low coffee table covered with art magazines. On the wall opposite was a small but exquisite painting of a Madonna and Child. Annie noticed that there was no protective glass or red rope separating the viewer from the work of art. Putting down her rucksack, she could not resist taking a closer look. The Madonna's face was flat and two-dimensional, her expression mournful and unanimated; the Christ Child looked more like a wizened old man than a baby.

"It's by Duccio—late thirteenth century," said a clipped voice.

Annie spun around to see Rebecca Winkleman-Spinetti. She was, Annie thought, extraordinary-looking. Rebecca's eyes were pools of iridescent turquoise set off by milky white skin and hair. The only other dash of colour on the moon-like face was Rebecca's surprisingly fleshy mouth, plush in a pale pink lipstick.

"It's lovely," Annie said, thinking more of Rebecca's face than the painting.

"One of the greatest works we have had the pleasure of handling," said Rebecca. Then, checking her watch, she summoned Annie into her office. "I only have a few minutes to spare."

Annie followed her through a pair of double mahogany doors and into a long, book-lined room, marvelling at Rebecca's elegant figure encased in a perfectly cut, creaseless black cashmere suit. Next to her, Annie, who was wearing baggy trousers and a duffle coat, felt like a tramp.

"Did you bring a CV?" Rebecca asked.

Annie handed over a piece of A4 paper. Rebecca glanced down and then turned the paper over, expecting to see more.

"It's short," she said.

"I spent fourteen years building up one business."

"Were you hit by the recession?"

"The business was always in good shape; the partnership foundered." Annie blushed and looked out of the window, hoping that there would be no more personal questions.

Looking at the younger woman, Rebecca wondered why she did not make more of herself—buy something decent to wear, apply some make-up. At least, she thought, my husband won't be sleeping with her; Carlo only likes the done-up types.

"Apart from night classes at the local college, your only experience with food is running a specialist cheese shop in a West Country market town?" Rebecca spoke in a clipped, high-pitched voice. Annie noticed that Rebecca's hands shook slightly, causing the paper to vibrate, and there was a tiny spasm in the muscle of her left cheek. What made this woman radiate nervousness? It certainly wasn't her.

"I am mainly self-taught," Annie admitted. "We also had a café beside the cheese shop and I made fresh food daily. Salads, sandwiches and cakes."

"Our business has to be associated with the finest quality in all things," Rebecca said.

"Everything was homemade and fresh. We had full marks on TripAdvisor," Annie said defensively. Should she tell Rebecca that regulars drove across Devon to eat her cheesecake and pies, and that a queue always formed half an hour before opening time on a Friday, bread-baking day?

Rebecca shrugged and turned her attention back to Annie's CV.

"Your only hobby is listed as cooking?"

"It's an obsession more than a hobby."

"You don't have any other interests?"

"Do you?" Annie asked. She was not being insolent; she was genuinely interested.

The faintest smile passed over Rebecca's lips. "No." She hesitated. "I suppose my whole life is art."

"So maybe we are not so different," Annie said.

Rebecca looked at the young woman with her cloud of unruly auburn hair, her duffle coat and scuffed Doc Martens and doubted that they had much in common.

"My husband speaks highly of your skills. What do you do for him?" Rebecca said.

"Honestly, not that much," Annie admitted. "I love hard work and cooking, but as Mr. Spinetti is not in production there isn't much going on. I make a lot of coffee and the odd bowl of pasta."

Rebecca checked her watch. A prospective client was due in shortly. This idea of Carlo's was hopeless: she would find a relief chef via an agency.

Turning to Annie she said. "I don't see how we can take a risk on you; there is nothing in your CV to suggest competence."

Annie winced. "I made a mistake and let my love life and work get tangled up together. It has left me in rather a bind."

Rebecca gazed at Annie thoughtfully. There was something about her predicament that inspired compassion. Anyone could make that mistake; many did. Rebecca knew that she was also too bound up with her own family. If she fell out with them, where would she turn?

A telephone rang on the desk. Rebecca snatched it up and her tone changed to polished unctuousness. She politely asked the caller several questions: "Mrs. Ankelehoff . . . Suzanne . . . how are the Bahamas? And little Tommy . . . the Duccio is on reserve to another client . . . you are, of course, one of the most important collectors we work with . . . the reserve is eighteen . . . let me talk to my father . . . send my regards to Richard." She replaced the phone quickly and dialled her assistant.

"Liora, find my father."

Annie picked up her rucksack and walked to the door. "Don't worry, I will find my own way out."

"Wait," Rebecca said, "I will take a chance on you. I've no idea why." She let out a little laugh, bemused by this unusual act of impulsiveness. "Don't let me down. Liora will show you the kitchen. We eat dinner at seven. Study the menus carefully." Rebecca waved her hand towards the door.

Annie was too surprised to respond.

"The pay is four hundred and fifty pounds per week net. No overtime. Six days a week, if necessary. Hours are erratic at best. Can you start now?"

Annie nodded—it was double her present salary, enough to quiet any misgivings.

The interview had taken less than four minutes.

Annie's new domain was a long thin galley next to the "entertaining" dining room. Opening the cupboards she found every type of kitchen equipment, most still in their protective wrappers. Annie thought of her most treasured and valuable possessions, her Japanese kitchen knives. The five sets in the Winkleman kitchen were of a quality she knew she could never afford.

She was asked to sign a confidentiality agreement, given an iris-activated password and handed a list of menus. To her dismay, Annie saw that the routine never varied. Lunch and dinner alternated between boiled and steamed fish and vegetables. The only herbs acceptable were dill and French parsley—garlic, coriander and chilli were not to be used under any circumstances; salt and pepper only sparingly. Omelettes were to be made without yolks and every meal was to be followed with stewed apple. Ingredients must be organic and, as far as possible, locally sourced. For Annie, preparing slabs of whiteness was a kind of torture. Food for her was as much about colour, smell and presentation as taste: the experience of eating should start in the eye and the nose and then erupt in the imagination. Chewing and tasting were the climax to a sensual experience.

On the nights that Memling or Rebecca ate in their respective homes, Annie was to hand the food to the Filipino servants, who would then leave it in a warmed serving hatch. She was not to address Memling Winkleman under any circumstances, was to avert her eyes if she met him in the corridor and only talk to Rebecca when spoken to. The most interesting meals she would prepare were for Memling's white husky, Tiziano, which alternated between fresh rabbit, beef and chicken mixed with raw eggs and finely sliced green vegetables.

By the third day, Annie started to compose her resignation letter even if it led to certain penury. She did not care that the fish was of peerless quality, served on Sèvres porcelain and accompanied by the finest French wines: her dream was to cook, not spend life hunched over a steamer. Part of the joy of creating a delicious meal was watching the expression on people's faces; in this job she posted her food into a hot cupboard. Her predecessor's stroke was surely induced by monotony. Late on Wednesday night Rebecca asked to see her. Annie took the resignation letter in the pocket of her starched white apron. Before she could hand it over, Rebecca told her to prepare a dinner the following week for twenty people in honour of an important American client, Melanie Appledore. The aim of the evening was to introduce the collector to a painting by Caravaggio called *Judith Beheading Holofernes*, a newly discovered version or study for the well-known painting hanging in the Palazzo Barberini in Rome. Annie was told that she could break from the fish regime as long as she eschewed garlic and chilli. There were to be three courses and the first was to be served at 8 p.m. sharp. Rebecca's PA would send through a list of personal likes and allergies. Leaving her employer's office, Annie realised that the meeting had once again taken exactly four minutes.

Unable to access any of Monsieur George's records, Annie

had little idea what was expected from the "Caravaggio" dinner. The Winklemans' head butler Jesu and his wife Primrose said that the evenings started with a soup and the main course was invariably fish. The last large dinner Annie had cooked was a surprise birthday party for Desmond and fifty of their friends in Devon. He wanted mojitos, hamburgers and toasted marshmallows—"none of that fancy shit"—but Annie hoped that the banquet would win him round. It was late summer and his fortieth, and combining the theme of harvest festival and his golden years, she suspended ears of corn, dahlias and chrysanthemums from the ceiling of a friend's barn to create an inside hanging garden. Trestle tables groaned with pumpkins, apples and corn dollies, while the guests, asked to wear red or gold, sat on bales of straw. She had made vats of spicy pumpkin soup and spent all day roasting a hog under an apple tree; for pudding there was blackberry and apple crumble and thick Devonshire clotted cream. She had made a crown of barley for Desmond to wear, but he tossed it into the barbecue and nearly ruined the evening by sulking.

With little money for presents, Annie always offered to cook parties for her friends or their children. Some joked that they had more offspring or got married just to enjoy her feasts. Her parties were legendary: towering jelly mounds in vibrant colours, life-size dogs and sheep made from cake covered with realistic fur and tails fashioned from icing and marzipan. For one friend, a professor of anthropology who spent half the year in a remote village in Cambodia, Annie re-created a tribal feast. For another friend, Pernilla, who had been born in a small town north of Stockholm, Annie made a traditional Swedish dinner with blood soup, wind-dried duck, and red berries as pudding. Although every scrap was eaten Desmond said that it was the most disgusting and inedible dinner he had ever had the misfortune to sit through; little wonder that Pernilla had fled from her home country.

Annie went to look at the painting, which was already

hanging in the main vestibule of the gallery. It was an unap-
petising image: a man's throat cut, the blood spurting over a
white cloth, his life ebbing away with each heartbeat; the perpetrator, a beautiful black-haired woman, looked at the viewer
triumphantly, holding a bloody blade in her hand, watched by
a wizened old hag. Fingering her letter of resignation, Annie
decided there was little to lose by preparing a fantastical feast:
at least she would be fired for something she was proud of.

Scouring the Internet during her lunch hours, Annie found
out that between his birth in 1571 and his untimely death in
1610, Caravaggio was almost as well known for his bad behaviour as for his painting and his technique was as spontaneous
and pugnacious as his temper. Caravaggio was known to have
killed a man in a fight; little wonder then, Annie thought, that
the blood gushing out of Holofernes' neck was so convincing.
Unable to control his appetites or temper, the painter spent
most of his life on the run from the authorities. He was damned
for his "vulgarity, sacrilege, impiousness and disgust" but his
talent and "dark spirit" inflamed collectors' desires. Annie wondered how to introduce this element of danger and brio into
her menu. The painter lived in post-Renaissance Italy between
Rome, Naples, Malta and Sicily—four different regions with
distinctly different types of food.

The food that Caravaggio subsisted on—bread, scraps
of pig and cheese washed down by young local wine—was
hardly suitable for Rebecca's guests, so Annie researched the
banquets eaten by his patrons: cardinals, popes and noblemen. She found that sugar, a newly discovered commodity,
was a sign of great wealth and was used lavishly for visual
and symbolic effect, spun and twisted, or as frosting and glaz-
ing. At one dinner given by Don Ercole, the son of the Duke
of Ferrara, for a group of noblemen, a life-size sugar model of
Hercules and a lion, coloured and gilded, was commissioned
as the central table piece and flanked by miniature models of
the goddesses Venus and Cupid. Some dinners, running to ten

courses, featured pastry castles and pies filled with live birds, gilded roast chickens, swans and peacocks, roasted and then re-dressed in their plumage. Guests could wash their hands in individual fountains of orange-blossom water and a musical accompaniment punctuated each course.

Lost in research and unable to face Evie, Annie spent a third night on a camp bed in the office, washing in the galley kitchen.

The following morning Evie turned up in the front entrance of Winkleman Fine Art. She made it through the front door but the security officers were reluctant to let this bedraggled-looking woman into the inner sanctum. Annie was called from a staff meeting to front reception.

"Is there something wrong?" Annie asked, looking up at the CCTV camera and hoping that none of her colleagues would see that her mother had a swollen eye, which had turned from deep purple to a swirl of yellow tinged with apricot.

"Where have you been?" Evie said petulantly.

"Working." Annie took her mother's arm and led her firmly towards the exit.

"There's nothing in the fridge. You don't even have a TV." Evie hesitated then added, "I've come to take you out to lunch." She looked vulnerable, like a small child.

"I have so much work—I really can't."

"It's the twenty-second of January—my birthday," Evie said in a small voice. "You forgot."

"Oh, so it is," Annie responded with as much grace as she could muster.

"I want to go to the Wallace Collection." Looking left and right around the lobby to check that no one was watching, Evie opened a large plastic bag she was carrying to reveal the picture.

"Walk around the corner to the mews entrance and wait for me. I need to get my coat and purse."

A few minutes later, Annie emerged.

"Why don't we go to the National Gallery?" Annie suggested. She had no desire to return to the Wallace, the scene of the singles night where she had met Robert.

"It's my birthday and I want to go to the Wallace," Evie said.

The Wallace was a half-hour walk from the office and with luck, Annie calculated silently, she could get her mother there, give her a sandwich and be back at her desk in less than an hour. Luckily, Rebecca and her father were in Paris and not expected back before supper.

"You are wearing my best dress," said Annie, looking at her mother.

"The only decent thing you have in your wardrobe—and it's only Zara, very high street."

"It might be off the peg but it's still my only good one so please don't borrow it," Annie said crossly.

"You should have worn a scarf," Evie told her. "It's cold."

"I am not a child," said Annie, striding along the cobbled street. I was never allowed to be a child, she thought.

"Why don't you have a radio or any music system in your place?" Evie asked. "You used to listen to music all the time."

Annie had stopped listening to music. It was too evocative and she found it easier not to live with unexpected emotional stimulants. "I just haven't got round to getting one," she lied.

"It's not normal to live without music," said Evie.

They walked along Curzon Street and dipped through a tiny garden behind a church in Mount Street. Along a sheltered wall, red and white camellias were just starting to bloom and the blossoms—clinging to green branches—swayed pendulously in the breeze. Annie looked at the garish flowers and realised that her beloved Dartmoor would still be barren, brackenless and soggy. She'd loved walking at this time of year across its lunar landscape, leaning into the gusty winds that shot up the valleys from Cornwall. Many locals avoided the moor in winter; fogs as thick as wet cotton wool could descend without warning. Every year walkers got lost; some died. One rider, lost all night in freezing foggy conditions, killed and slit open his horse's stomach in desperation, hoping to find shelter inside the warm bloody guts. Two days later he was found frozen inside the animal's belly.

"You have not heard a word I've been saying, have you?" Evie tugged at her sleeve.

"I'm sorry. I was miles away."

"Did I tell you that Stanley and I have separated?" Evie said.

"Who was Stanley?"

"I thought he was different."

"You always do."

They crossed Oxford Street and turned down a small mews to avoid the lunchtime shoppers. Evie was right: Annie wished she had worn a scarf.

"What have you been doing?" Evie asked in a false, bright, conversational tone.

"I have been living in a make-believe debauched, overindulgent world of post-Renaissance banqueting."

"That beats Shepherd's Bush."

"Rebecca wants to give a dinner for clients to celebrate a painting. I am tempted to do a themed dinner, but I know that's not what she has in mind."

"You could make anything taste delicious. You have a real talent."

Annie slipped her arm through her mother's. "Unlike their last chef, I am untrained and out of practice."

Evie stopped in the street and turned to her daughter. "I dare you."

Annie laughed. It was a game that mother and daughter used to play. I dare you to eat your supper. I dare you to get dressed. I dare you to love me.

"If it goes wrong I'll lose my day job."

"Do you think a man offered a big break would worry about his day job?"

"That's hardly relevant."

"It is, Annie. You have to take a risk."

Annie stopped and turned to face her mother. "Don't you think I am longing to take risks but if I lose my job, who will fish you out of jail? Where will you go?"

Evie looked at the ground. "Are you avoiding home because I am there?"

"That has something to do with it."

Evie wiped a tear from her face. "I'd like a few more days to sort myself out. Would that be too much to ask?"

Annie felt it was far too much to ask; the thought of spending even one more night under the same roof as her mother made her feel utterly desperate.

"Mum, it's just that—"

"It's just that I am frightened and lonely and you are the only thing I have." Evie burst into tears.

Here we go, Annie thought. Back on the endless merry-go-round of solipsistic self-recrimination. Annie knew she should shake off her mother's arm and walk away; instead she took Evie's hand and steered her silently across Manchester Square and into the Wallace Collection.

"You can stay for a few days."

Evie's face lit up like a child's. "Your dad and I used to come here," she said to Annie.

"You told me."

"I was happy then."

"You told me that too." Annie marched up the grand staircase, wishing the museum had a policy of compulsory silence.

"Wait for me. I'm not as young as I used to be," said Evie, panting.

Annie didn't wait but walked ahead through the galleries. The pictures passed in a blur as she thought about possible recipes. Would they like a hippocras jelly made from gallons of wine, cinnamon, nutmeg and ginger? First recorded in the 1530s, it was created forty years before Caravaggio's birth but would perfectly match the blood spurting from Holofernes' neck. She longed to try and make one of the 250 recipes from *On honourable pleasure and health*, said to herald modern Italian cookery, collated in 1465. The author, Platina, left humorous instructions: cook for the "length of two Lord's Prayers" and cut lard to the size of dice, meat into the size of fists and stew in a "dainty broth."

"I know when you are thinking about food," said Evie, tugging at her daughter's shirt. "You get that odd faraway look. Come and look at this one—it was another of your dad's favourites."

Annie, her reverie broken, saw Evie pointing at a painting of a man with a twirly moustache and a rather supercilious smile. Moments later, her view was blocked by a group of Japanese tourists in smart trench coats. Their guide, Annie decided, was their sartorial nemesis. His shapeless suit, made from a deep-plum-coloured corduroy, patched at the elbows with different fabric, looked as if it had been made for someone larger, his father perhaps, or picked up from a charity shop. He wore a tie, an awful knitted concoction, a gift perhaps from a maiden aunt, and its knot was definitely off-centre. Annie noticed that the guide's dark hair was unbrushed, a little too long and very messy.

"Here," he explained, "is a picture by Frans Hals called *The Laughing Cavalier*." He spoke in short sentences punctuated by lots of arm movements and with such genuine enthusiasm that Annie and Evie stopped bickering and started to listen.

"As you can see, the Cavalier is neither laughing nor even smiling and he certainly isn't a cavalier," he continued. "The name was given to the picture much later in the nineteenth century, over two hundred years after it was painted in 1624. It's likely that this portrait was a betrothal gift for a young lady."

"Betrothal?" a Japanese lady questioned.

"An engagement."

"Engagement?" She was still confused. The guide fished around for the right description and happened to catch Annie's eye. Without thinking, Annie pointed to her ringless engagement finger.

Thank you, he mouthed.

"Marriage! This man would send this picture to a lovely young lady and if she liked what she saw, she would agree to marry."

This time the translation worked and the Japanese lady nodded.

Jesse looked back at the young woman with the plaited auburn hair. He thought her eyes might be green, maybe blue; they caught the light, danced with humour and understanding. He noticed a smattering of freckles on her cheekbones and wondered idly if there were more sprinkled across her breasts. He tried to guess how old she was—looking at the tiny crinkles around her eyes he guessed late twenties. Her face was slightly too long, her mouth slightly too wide for her to qualify as a classic beauty. She had an ethereal dreamy quality, as if she wasn't quite grounded but floating above earthly matters. Her clothes were eccentric—stripy trousers and a white smock—maybe she was a chef or someone who liked the garb. Her shoes, scuffed at the edges, and her handbag, the handle mended with orange string, suggested that she was not well paid, or thrifty. The woman locked eyes with his for a second too long, blushed and looked away.

Jesse felt a wave of disappointment: she wasn't interested. He turned back to his group.

"This lovely jacket is embroidered with motifs, hidden signs which at the time were symbolic of the pains and pleasures of love, including arrows, flaming cornucopias and lovers' knots and so forth," he told them. Annie pretended to look at another painting but could not resist listening to him.

"Cornucopia?" a Japanese man asked.

"It means lots of things, many symbols, much going on." The guide waved his arms about. "This painting has become one of the most famous and instantly recognised pictures in Western art. It is our male Mona Lisa."

His audience still looked confused.

"Mona Lisa?" one lady questioned.

The guide clapped his hand to his forehead. "I'm sorry. What a dolt. You probably haven't been to Paris. It's a painting in the Louvre. By Leonardo da Vinci." The guide looked back at Annie slightly desperately. She smiled back—there was something attractive about him. He held her glance for a moment. She noticed that he had tawny-coloured eyes deepset in a wide face, with high cheekbones. His hair was thick, dark and unbiddable; some falling over his face, other bits springing in the air. Annie noticed that the collar of his shirt was worn down and that the cuffs were held together by paperclips. Unused to the scrutiny of strangers, she turned away—where was Evie when she needed distraction?

She didn't have to look far. Evie had taken the painting out of the plastic bag and was comparing it to others on walls. A room attendant watched her warily as she pushed through the crowd of Japanese tourists, past the guide and held it beside the *Laughing Cavalier*. Next to the Frans Hals it looked completely out of place, the figures too whimsical and lightly painted compared to the solid cavalier. Annie saw the guide glance from Evie to the painting. At first he seemed to dismiss the canvas, but he took a second, harder look and was about to say something when Evie whipped the picture away and headed for a painting of a woman in a heavily flounced dress with one delicate silk shoe peeking out of the hem.

Annie walked over to join her mother. The plaque said

Madame de Pompadour by Boucher. Annie and Evie looked between the two paintings. There were definite similarities in the way that the paint had been lightly applied, and the foliage and composition seemed similar. Both had figures in the foreground in an Elysian setting overlooked by a statue, but the use of paint, one feathery and vibrant, and the other muted and stagey, convinced Annie that they were by different hands.

They moved on, holding their picture up to endless scenes of half-naked shepherdesses, impudent putti, and lascivious male onlookers. To Annie, these women were stripped not just of clothes but also of their dignity: they were bent into supplicant, cloying states of come-hitherness. The colours that the artist used were like the fillings of cheap chocolates: pale blues and yellows for the skies, pinks for the flesh, a riot of pastels. The two women stopped by *The Ball* by Jean-Baptiste Pater.

"I'm sure this is the painting that Carlo used as inspiration for the sets of *The Sun King*," mused Annie.

"Do they ever do anything original in film?" Evie, like many, considered film a very poor relation to the other arts.

"Bad artists copy; good artists steal," Annie said.

"Who said that?"

Annie shrugged. "A filmmaker is working in many dimensions but getting the setting right is crucial. It is no different to preparing the canvas if you're an artist or learning grammar if you're a writer. You are creating a mood, a world for the viewer to step into."

"So is this a pastiche?"

"I'm quite sure that Pater learned by copying the stuff that came before him and that his teacher was copying his master. We're all copycats," Annie said, thinking of Platina's book of recipes.

Over on the other side of the room the guide was telling his tourists about another painter, Antoine Watteau. "Here is the painter who started this whole genre known as the *fête galante*, depicting elegant figures in theatrical, historical and contemporary dress in park landscape settings," she heard him say. "Today it's known better as Rococo."

Evie marched across the room and barged through their midst carrying the picture. "Come here, Annie, and look at this!" she called out.

Annie, mortified by her mother's behaviour, edged quietly away, hoping that the guide would not associate them.

"Annie, Annie!" Evie shouted. "Come here and look at this bloke's face. It's just like the man in your painting!" Evie leant over the red rope and held Annie's picture up against the painting by Watteau.

A gallery attendant sprang out of his chair and ran towards Evie. Annie prayed silently for Evie to calm down and move on.

"Don't you think there's a striking similarity?" Evie asked the guide.

The guide looked at both paintings closely. "I can see definite similarities. He's a much-copied artist. Rightly so," he added tactfully.

"You academics are frightened of your own shadows," said Evie rudely and turned to the Japanese tourists. "What do you think? Come on, use your eyes, not your theories, like this chump."

"Madam, can I ask you to keep a respectful distance from the paintings or we will have to ask you to leave," the attendant said.

"You have eyes, can't you see?" Evie shoved the picture under his nose.

"I am here to protect the artworks."

Evie stepped over the rope and leant in towards the painting.

"Both have the same doleful expression. And it's the same statue in the background."

Evie's observations were drowned out by the noise of an alarm and the sound of running feet. Within moments guards surrounded Evie and, pulling aside the rope, took her firmly by the arms and marched her away from the paintings.

"Don't you manhandle me," she squawked. "I wasn't doing anything wrong. I am an art lover. Unlike you barbarians. Leave me alone. I'll write to my MP."

Annie saw her mother frogmarched out of the other door.

The Japanese were talking excitedly among themselves. Annie caught the guide's apologetic glance. I'm sorry, he mouthed. Annie grimaced and left the gallery with as much dignity as she could muster.

Outside the museum Evie, with the picture tucked under her arm, was entreating other visitors to change their plans. "Don't go in there—it's full of heathens. If you so much as look at a painting they try and chuck you out."

"Have you been drinking?" Annie asked, catching up with her. "You are very lucky they didn't arrest you and press charges."

"Who are they to say, just because something hangs on their walls, that anything else is crap?" Holding the picture up in front of her, Evie proclaimed, "I believe in you."

Annie sat down on the wall. Evie was following an all-too-familiar pattern. She must have had a drink just before she got to the office. The walk and fresh air rushed the alcohol through her system and the high set in near *The Laughing Cavalier*. Soon Evie would start to come down. She would cry, find another drink, get happy, withdraw and on and on, round and round.

Annie, longing for the relative calm of the Winkleman kitchen, walked away from Evie. Her mother could find her own way back to the flat.

"Excuse me," a man's voice called her. Pulling her coat around her, Annie hurried on. Surely the gallery wouldn't need to take a statement about a lone batty woman. Surely she would be able to walk away from this incident without further embarrassment.

"Miss. Please wait." The guide caught up and walked besides Annie. "I'm sorry about in there."

Annie said nothing. Her face burned with shame.

"I bought you a postcard of something that looks a lot like your painting. It's only a drawing but I think you can see the similarities," he said, holding it out for her. Annie stopped and took it but still didn't look at the guide.

"That lady had a point. The two pictures do look alike. The figures are very similar—and so is the background. If you wanted to explore it further."

Annie interrupted him before he could continue, "I'm really not interested. That thing has brought nothing but bad luck."

"If you change your mind," the guide called after her.

Annie did not look back.

Chapter 5

Barthomley Chesterfield Fitzroy St. George liked what he saw in the full-length mirror. He was sixty-nine years old but had kept his flesh taut with a nip here and a tuck there and his figure lithe with daily calisthenics. His eyes had turned a rather watery blue but his teeth were Hollywood perfect. His hair, thick and luxuriant, was mostly his own and every part of his body was exquisitely groomed and polished by a team of manicurists, facialists and masseuses. Though he could no longer be described as elfin, Barty (as most knew him) was in, as he liked to say, "frightfully good nick."

"That darling man has done a good job, don't you think?" Barty said, appraising his newly tightened jawline.

The Lady Emeline Smythe, his twenty-two-year-old social secretary, nodded.

"You look, like, really buff."

Barty smiled graciously; he had to agree.

"The sign of successful surgery," Barty continued, "is not to be told one looks young; it's to be congratulated on looking well. And it was frightfully reasonable," he added. "Less than a new car or a weekend at the Cap. Perhaps I'll get a brow lift next summer. Botox is so deadening."

"Mummy is really jealous," said Emeline. "Daddy says she has to choose between a new face or a new horse."

Em's father was sitting on an estate of ten thousand prime Lincolnshire acres. "Can't he just sell a few fields and give her both?" Barty did not understand the aristocracy's priorities.

"Daddy says all the land is in trust for my brother," Emeline replied wistfully. "He says I'd better hurry up and get married while I still have a face or I will be on the shelf without a dusting."

Silently Barty agreed with her father. Em looked adorable now—full-lipped, peachy complexion, a tiny ski-jump nose and cascading blonde hair—but those kind of looks never outlasted the first blush of youth.

"Your aunt Joanna has let herself go," Barty said. "I saw her at the Devonshires' the other night. She sat down and her bottom spread over the sofa like a ripe Brie."

"Poor Aunty Jo," Emeline said with feeling. "She never got over losing Topper."

"I thought her husband was called Charles?"

"He was—Topper was her Pekinese."

Their conversation was interrupted by the arrival of Frances, Barty's PA, brandishing a pen and a handful of stiff invitations. Frances, as broad and sturdy as a Highland pony, dressed like a matron from a public school. Her eyes swivelled in different directions but she never missed a trick and everyone, including Barty, was a little bit scared of her.

"You have four invitations for the weekend of the seventh of June—the Sheikha of Alwabbi, the Duke and Duchess of Midlothian, Elliot Slicer and the Brommages," said Frances.

"They all sound rather tiring," said Barty, sitting down on

a pale pink sofa. "Who has the best garden? I am desperate to
see a dash of colour. This winter has been so miserable, even
the hellebores are late."

Frances loomed over him, waving the invitations. Barty
closed his eyes.

"One does love roses in June. What do you think, Em?"
Barty opened one eye and looked at Emeline, whom he
employed partly because her father was the most handsome
Marquess in England but also for her supposed knowledge of
the social scene.

"There's probably not many roses in Arabia or Texas in
June. The Brommages are on their boat so I'd suggest the
Midlothians—Daddy says they have a beautiful estate."

Barty groaned loudly, "Darling! Their castle is in northern
Scotland and everything there blooms at least a month later.
Didn't your parents teach you anything?"

Emeline was mortified. "Sorry, Barty. I hate Scotland, I try
not to go there."

"Don't we all, darling, don't we all," Barty agreed.

Frances pursed her lips. "You'd better accept the Alwabbis—
with all that gas they are getting richer by the second and we
are trying to run a business."

"Don't use the word 'business,' darling. It's common,"
Barty said plaintively.

"Is it common to have food on our plates and a roof over
our heads?" Frances said in her sharpest tone.

"Whatever Frances wants," Barty said meekly.

"I will accept their Royal Highnesses on your behalf."
Frances smiled curtly and left the room.

Barty's main indulgence (though he saw it as a calling) was
his cottage orné in Regent's Park. Built for a duke's mistress
in the late eighteenth century, the White House was a perfect miniature neoclassical palace built by the architect James
"Athenian" Stuart, set in a glade in the middle of the park.
When the descendants of the Duke of Plantagenet tried to

sell their heirloom to developers, Barty fought an impassioned campaign to save it and persuaded the judge to let him purchase and restore it for the nation and, for ninety days a year, keep the staterooms open to the public. The White House gobbled money—if it wasn't the roof it was the plumbing, the boiler, the windows, the gutters or the wiring. Barty loved it with an unbridled passion and every penny of his large fees went into his pet project.

A tremendous rustling of plastic and polythene heralded the arrival of Barty's valet, Bennie. Barty adopted a different persona for each major social occasion. The more outlandish the look, the more likely he was to be "papped," and press, he claimed, was good for business. Mainly, press was good for Barty's mood; he adored being in print. Even the worst photograph, the cattiest aside, gave him pleasure. He kept large scrapbooks full of his clippings and on dark winter nights would spend contented hours reviewing past looks and parties.

Every Monday morning, he and Bennie discussed forthcoming social engagements and inappropriate outfits. Barthomley insisted that every detail should be perfectly nuanced. "Thank goodness for eBay," he'd often remark. Today, in honour of the anniversary of Elvis's first number one, they had settled on a Teddy-boy look; Bennie scoured vintage shops to find an original 1950s suit, crepe-soled shoes and a wig with a duck's-arse quiff.

"What do you think of these?" asked Bennie, holding up a maroon-coloured jacket and preposterous black wig.

"Love, love, love. The pink lapel is simply divine," Barty said, clapping his hands together, slipping into the coat and looking at himself in the three-way mirror.

"I literally am Elvis," said Barty with no apparent irony. "Darlings—I'm worried that it's too convincing. What happens if no one guesses that it's me?" he said, spinning around in front of the mirror.

"Do you think the audience at the first night of *Der Rosen-*

kavalier will think that the King decided to be reincarnated at the Royal Opera House?" Bennie reasoned.

"But do I look handsome?" Barthomley worried that the combination of a shiny black wig and his pale sixty-nine-year-old skin was unflattering.

"I'd have you!" Bennie laughed.

"Careful. I might take you up on that!" They both knew he wouldn't; Barthomley thought sex was frightfully common and best left to the young.

Even after fifty years of Barthomley being in the public eye, of being photographed with every famous person in and out of town, no one from his home of Keddlesmere had ever recognised him or got in touch. His younger self, born Reg Dunn on 14 March 1945, had left home on 14 March 1960, and never gone back. At the age of fifteen, he knew that there was no future for "queers" in Keddlesmere. Shedding his old persona like an unwanted skin, he created a new identity by stringing together the names of the villages he passed through while hitchhiking to London. Reg Dunn was dead: long live Barthomley Chesterfield Fitzroy St. George.

On his first night in the city, Barthomley was picked up by a Tory minister in the Piccadilly Circus tube station, who recommended the young man to his colleagues and from there, young Barty graduated from "The House" to the stately homes of England. "I learned at the feet of the greats," he was fond of saying. "I was on my knees; they were standing." Within five years, Barty went from rent boy to best man. It was not only that Barthomley came of age in an era where the differences between classes blurred, when it was chic to have friends from different backgrounds, but the main reason for Barty's social success was based on a simple fact: he was a life-enhancer. Whether you were stuck in a shooting butt on a Scottish moor, on a royal train in Rajasthan, or at a dowager duchess's tea party, being with Barty made everything much more fun. His unquenchable thirst for life, his ability to see the ridiculous (particularly in himself) and his genuine love of people was compulsively endearing. Barthomley Chesterfield Fitzroy St. George became known as "darling Barty" and Society's fixtures and fittings were planned around his availability. The rough edges of his accent fell away, and within a decade he was such an integral part of upper-class life that most assumed his people were titled.

But unlike his new set, Barty had no trust fund, no indulgent spinster aunts and no education to rely on, and rotating around the house parties of England, being the life and soul of every county, was exhausting. Barty longed for some independence, a pied-à-terre to escape to and a nest egg for his retirement. His career started by accident: in 1979, with the fall of the Shah of Iran, London was suddenly awash with wealthy displaced Persians with money to burn but no idea how to spend it. For a fee, he found them apartments, decorators, personal assistants and tailors. He showed them which bars and clubs to frequent and educated them in the nuances of British life. He helped his protégés throw monumentally extravagant parties. He soon found out that the higher his fee, the happier his client. The more he charged, the more secure they felt.

Barty never had a business card; he never needed a job description. He was strictly word of mouth. The rich and needy soon found him. "Think of me as part Svengali, part Henry Higgins with a dash of Cedric Montdore," he would tell people, though few got the references.

"Let's put on 'Hound Dog' and get properly into the mood," Barty said, slipping on the crepe-soled shoes. "Chop, chop, Em, crank up Spotify."

Emeline ran over to the sound system and within seconds, Elvis's voice ricocheted around the room. Barty took Emeline's hand and they started to rock and roll. While they danced, various assistants came in to ask questions.

"Barty, Mitch wants to change tailors and go to Huntsman—

someone told him they were the oldest." Milly was one of seven girls who helped Barty manage individual clients.

"Savile Row is so last century. If he wants to look like a Chow Pei that's his decision."

"Is Chow Pei a Chinese dish?"

"It's a dog—don't they teach you anything at St. Mary's Ascot?"

Amelia, who looked after the South Americans, was next in line: "Carlos Braganza's cousin has been arrested at Northolt for bringing cocaine in on his private aeroplane and wants to know if you can help?"

"Call that sweet man at the FO whom I met at Highgrove."

Diandra, who covered the Russians, was flustered. "Dmitri Voldakov wants to know if you can organise a chalet in Gstaad that sleeps thirty?"

"Tell him, of course—even if I have to build it with my bare hands."

"Pilar has sacked her decorator—can you recommend another?" Dambesi asked.

"That is her third in a month! I will have to think and get back to her later. Did any of you see M. Power Dub-Box at the Mojos last night? God he's sexy."

"I thought you were at the Swindons' last night?"

"It was a bit dull so I went on to the Mojos. Do you think the quiff is too big?"

"No, it's perfect."

"My eyeliner's running." Barty, puffing slightly, sat down again on the pink sofa.

Frances reappeared and turned down the music.

"What will the Russian think?" she asked. "Don't you think you should tone the look down before meeting this new client?"

"What Russian?"

"Vladimir Antipovsky. You are meeting him in twenty-five minutes at his new house in Berkeley Square."

"I completely forgot. I want to go to Tim's opening before the Opera."

Frances read from her notebook. "Vlad Antipovsky, forty-one years old from Smlinsk, a small town on the borders of Siberia. Controls 43 per cent of the world's tin. Estimated to be worth $8 billion and rising. No wife or known dependants. No acknowledged interests. He was another of the regime's sudden ejects."

Barty turned round to face Frances, his eyes shining with excitement. "Imagine how abject he must be feeling, and with no wife or dependants. One does love a blank canvas. Think of the potential. The transformation. It must be how Michelangelo felt when he found the perfect piece of Carrara marble: most saw a hunk of stone, he saw David. How much money did you say he has?"

"Eight billion," Frances replied.

"Pounds or dollars?" Emeline asked.

"Darling, you can be so vulgar," Barty chided.

New employees assumed that Barty's love of the newly rich was motivated by the thought of a commission; they were wrong. Barty adored his job. Each time he rescued a new client from social obscurity and cultural oblivion, Barty relived his own escape from Keddlesmere. The real thrill was not financially quantifiable as long as he made enough to keep the White House open. He often said that his business card, if he had had one, would say "Alchemist"; "I take money and ignorance and weave them into an earthly paradise."

Bennie tried to make one final adjustment to the wig but Barty was already up and heading for the door. "Take me to my Russian. Chop, chop. Hurry, hurry. Not a moment to lose."

Standing alone in his newly purchased seventeen-bedroom house in Berkeley Square, Vlad Antipovsky was immersed in a deep slough of misery. It had been exactly fifty-four days since eight men in black suits had walked into his office in

Moscow with a one-way ticket to London. He was given thirty minutes to clear his desk or risk losing his homes, businesses and freedom. A floor at the Connaught had been rented in his name until he found a house and offices. Providing Vlad did the odd favour for a nameless person, kept his nose clean and refrained from becoming involved in any political activities or comment, he would be allowed to hang on to 65 per cent of his fortune and live without fear of assassination or imprisonment. If he behaved, he could visit Courcheval for winter sports, St. Barts for winter sun and Cap d'Antibes for the month of August.

Vlad did not question their authority or intent; he did not need to. Only the day before, Anatoli Aknatova, formerly a wealthy and powerful oligarch, had been paraded on national television, emaciated and shackled, held in a tiny metal cage for the fifth consecutive year. There were other examples of men who had become too wealthy or had been heard expressing an opinion hostile to the regime. Most were not publicly imprisoned; they just disappeared. A plane crash or a heart attack served as a reminder to all about who held real power and how quickly and effectively that power could be used.

Vlad had gone straight to the airport. He had no family to take with him, no real friends to say goodbye to, but his heart and soul were rooted in Russian soil. Without his beloved motherland, her vast landscapes, her poverty and grandeur, Vlad's life lost its meaning. He had visited London a few times before and found its small scale depressing. As for European women, they were like pit ponies—all stubby-legged and grubby morals.

Arriving at the Connaught in late August, he was given an envelope with his new bank account details and stock options. To his surprise, withdrawals could be made with prior warning, with the agreement of a faceless co-signatory; however, these assets could also be removed at any moment and were conditional on Vlad staying out of Russia and growing his business by 6 per cent per annum. The new (unnamed) co-shareholders had the right to withdraw capital without notice. Vlad knew exactly who this shareholder was; there was no higher authority.

For the first twenty days, Vlad had hardly left his suite, pacing around the floor while considering his options, which were extremely limited. The only course of action was to sit it out in England and wait for a regime change. He harboured silent dreams of helping stimulate a political coup d'état. There must be enough Russian exiles to form a formidable alliance. But Vlad was too frightened to articulate his dream even privately; he suspected the others were too.

He tried to assuage his loneliness with abandoned consumption, using room service to order girls and cars and champagne. A week later he signed the lease on a new office and bought the town house on Berkeley Square. Two more weeks passed and he had slept with more girls since arriving in England than he had in his entire life. He now owned seventeen cars and employed four secretaries, a butler, two valets, a driver, three bodyguards and eleven Filipinos. But in spite of all this activity, Vlad was seriously, desperately bored. When two friends, Natalia and Stanislav, the only happy Muscovites he knew living in London, suggested he meet Barty St. George, Vlad agreed even though he had little idea what or whom to expect.

When the diminutive ageing Teddy boy arrived at his empty house, Vlad assumed it was an elaborate joke.

"They never warned me you'd be so handsome! And big. So big. Hmmmm," Barty exclaimed, rushing towards him with outstretched hands. "My dear, you are as delicious as gentleman's relish on toast." Barty smacked his lips together. "And so muscly. And tall. What are you? Six foot eight in your socks?" He walked around Vlad making appreciative noises. "Did you know I first came to this house in 1964 when it was lived in by Earl Honey. I could tell you a few stories about that evening but you are far too heterosexual to appreciate them. Bunny Honey, as we called him, hopped through his whole fortune in seven years. Must admit I helped him a little bit. The parties we used to have. Such fun."

Vlad wondered how to respond to Natalia and Stanislav's tease. Perhaps he would deliver a carload of monkeys to their country estate.

"Shall we sit down?" Barty looked around the empty room. "I see you have no furniture. We can sort that out. No curtains. Are you sleeping here?"

"Connaught," Vlad said, wondering how quickly he could escape back to the relative anonymity of his hotel suite.

"The Connaught is so ghastly—how do you bear it? Never mind, let's have a look around."

Barty rushed around the house appraising its condition and eyeing up its potential. Vlad followed him, watching in awe as the Teddy boy scribbled notes into a small leather notebook.

"You are wondering why I am here and what on earth I can do for you." Barty looked at Vlad in a kindly, avuncular way. He understood that for all his height and strength, despite the millions salted away in a local bank, the man standing beside him was scared and lonely. He was not the first exiled Russian whom Barty had helped.

"Plis spik slowly—English not good," Vlad said. He had to admit that there was something sympathetic about the strange man; he was like the doctor at the mine whose bedside manner had been honed by years of dealing with natural disasters.

"You see, old boy, there's no point having money if you don't have fun or do anything with it, is there? If you are clever about it, money can give you a life *and* more money!" Barty clapped his hands together as if to emphasise his point. "The way I see it is that you have a choice. You can spend the rest of your life living in that frightful hotel, going to Sketch and other nightclubs, and hanging out with brassy birds in jacuzzis. Take holidays in Courcheval and St. Barts. Get a bigger plane, maybe a boat or two. Your money will buy you a seat at the top table with the odd minor royal. Or you can follow my suggestions and soon presidents, prime ministers, even the odd king or queen will be asking to sit with you."

"King, queen?" Vlad was nonplussed.

Barty could see that this great thug of a Russian did not get the reference points, was not suitably impressed. Maybe Barty had found someone he could not transform, perhaps this man would never make the journey from sow's ear to silk purse, from chrysalis to butterfly. Barty felt a deep sense of ennui. Perhaps he had had enough. He was almost seventy. Retirement? Time maybe to put one's feet up, grow roses or take a young boy to the South of France for the season. The thought was tempting, but not as delicious as the challenge before him.

"Do you know my lovely clients Carbaritch and Vassonliswilli?"

Vlad's ears pricked up. Of course he knew of them. The Ukrainian miner and the Georgian smelter were legends in the Caucasus. Two men who had made a fortune in coal and steel, who had been exiled from their countries only to resurface as principal players in the world stock markets. Carbaritch was now so wealthy that he could afford to buy a film studio and a record company, the ultimate going-nowhere rich-boy stock. More importantly, Carbaritch and Vassonliswilli looked happy.

Barty saw that he had hit his target. The Russian did understand. Leaning forward he said in a conspiratorial whisper, "All my work. They were miserable no ones when they got off the plane. I made them."

"How you make them?" Vlad sounded sceptical.

"Darling, I showed them how to live. Carbaritch (I call him the black Cabbie—he is so naughty) came to London with a dowdy little wife and twenty billion. Now he has a wing at the Tate named in his honour and a top seat at Davos. We got the wife remodelled by the best surgeon in Hollywood, put her on the Dukan diet, new teeth, new jewels, and now she's lunching with Dasha."

"Vassonliswilli?"

"Ten years ago the only horse he had ever seen was a pit pony. Last year his horse won the King George VI Chase. Next year he's odds on for the Breeders' Cup. I am told that Her Majesty will ask him to join her in the Royal Box at Ascot. Not bad for a murdering gangster."

Vlad automatically checked over his shoulder. Vassonliswilli, famously, was trigger-happy, particularly with his critics.

"Rome was not built in a day; it took me a year or two."

Vlad stared out of the window at the London cityscape. A light rain was falling and all he could see was grey. Grey sky, grey lead-lined roofs, grey pigeons sheltering under grey piping. Suddenly he longed for the dramatic landscape of Siberia with its huge empty horizon and deafening winds. How could he ever make his home, his future, somewhere so small, so parochial?

"Have I upset you?" Barty asked anxiously. The big Russian looked suddenly so sad and vulnerable, shrunken inside his enormous leather jacket.

"No, thinking," Vlad said.

"Of home?" Barty asked.

"Yes." Vlad was surprised.

"I have yet to meet a Russian émigré who is not haunted by his or her mother country. When he was at the height of his fame, I used to hold a sobbing Rudolf Nureyev in my arms while he cried for Mama Russia."

Vlad looked across the room at this small eccentric Elvis impersonator; he was dressed like a joker but was far from a fool.

Barty sensed a change in the atmosphere.

"This house is fine but it's not really in the right place. Berkeley Square is passé. You want Chester Square. If God had existed he'd have made the place three times longer. Too mean that it's so short."

"Name of road that Natalia lives?" Vlad asked.

"Kensington Park Gardens, one of those stately homes on the edge of Holland Park. Aditi Singh is having a do there on Thursday. We'll go."

"Aditi?"

"Singh. Industrialist, owns half of India. He paid for the Garden Bridge across the Thames and now the Singh Bridge is one of Europe's greatest landmarks. Quite smart. We should think of something like that for you. Imagine a Vlad Antipovsky tower being for ever emblazoned on London's cityscape."

"What 'bout hobby?"

"You have three main choices. Horses, cars or art. Arabs love horses because, as you know, all racehorses can trace their lineage back to a couple of Arabian stallions. So Sheik this and that see it as a provenance kind of thing. Horses, however, are risky. Even if you get the best breeding, best trainer, best jockey, there is no guarantee of success. Damn animals are so temperamental. The ground has to be just right, they get chills, and they break things. Between you and me the social life is a bit limited. You get the occasional attractive hooray and the odd glimpse of the Queen but really it's just cold mornings, wellies and tweed; lots of hanging around for not much action."

Vlad had never liked horses much. The mine had been full of forlorn-looking animals whose skin hung like curtains off their bones and who looked at the world through eyes of liquid sorrow.

"Cars?" He liked the sound of cars. They were masculine, exciting and required no intellectual investment. Anyone could talk about a gasket or a carburettor.

"It would have to be Formula One, of course," Barty said. "You will need to buy into a team—McLaren, Fiat, you know. But if you think racing people are dreary, oh my God." Barty threw his hands up in the air. "Silverstone is like Epsom but much noisier. My idea of total horror. No, it has to be art. Art is the answer!" Barty said with great brio.

Vlad felt instantly depressed. He didn't know anything about art. Indeed, he only saw his first original image when he came to Moscow aged eighteen. It had been –24°C and to escape the cold he had wandered into the free municipal museum, a place that seemed only slightly warmer than the streets outside.

"Don't know art."

"No one does! Lots of people pretend to—make up all sorts of highfalutin rubbish about schools and movements and so forth but quite honestly it's all tosh."

"Tosh?"

"Bosh. Bunkum. Codswallop."

Vlad had never heard of any of these artists. Surely he could stick to things he did know about such as Rolls, Lamborghini or Bentley? What was wrong with something practical?

But Barty was on his feet and dancing around the room.

"Walls!" Barty exclaimed, waving his arms around. "Walls, walls, walls, lots of lovely empty walls. I see YBAs interspersed with a dash of serious abstract Impressionism."

Vlad also looked at the walls but he saw bricks and mortar, every single one was his, the fulfilment of a life's dream. The walls in his childhood home were made of plaster and plywood. Those flimsy structures, measuring twenty by twenty feet, separated families by sight but never by sound; every breath, sniffle, fight, laugh, every mood, good or bad, reverberated around the apartments. Vlad never got used to the lack of physical privacy and living in minute personal sub-spaces in the tiny two-room apartment. For him, the encroaching noise was never manageable or predictable and there had been no way to block it out, let alone anticipate when the Yaltas would have a row or Leonard would stub his toe or the Smelty twins would put on a record.

"Now, what shall we hang on them? I am feeling some contemporary art."

"No," Vlad said firmly.

"No? So how about some just-dead artists?"

"No."

"A little bit more than dead?"

"Old art. Romantic."

"Oh no, darling. It doesn't really matter what you buy, it's about what goes with it. I am trying to give you a life. Modern art equals fun, light and colour. Old art is all warm wine and cheese, thick ankles and flat shoes. The modern art world is martinis and sushi, Azzedine and Louboutin."

Vlad still had no idea what the ageing Elvis was talking about but decided to nod simply to keep him quiet.

Taking Vlad's enormous hands in his own tiny, beautifully manicured fingers, Barty looked up into the Russian's face. "We are going to have such fun. I will pick you up at six tomorrow."

Barty let go of the Russian, spun around and slipped out of the door. He was going to miss the first act of *Der Rosenkavalier*. Lady Montague would be frightfully cross—lots of extra white roses tomorrow—still Barty didn't mind: this Russian was going to be one of his greatest transformations.

Chapter 6

Let me guess what you are thinking. Girl finds picture; picture turns out to be worth a fortune. Girl (finally) finds boy with a heart. Girl sells picture, makes millions, marries boy, all live happily ever after.

Piss off. Yes, you heard, piss off, as the cake tin at Bernoff's used to say (it was decorated with Renoir's *Les Parapluies*, which explains quite a lot).

Life is not that simple.

For a start, am I a masterpiece? Are you taking my word for it? What is the definition of a masterpiece? Ultimately it is just a painting that a lot of people like. If no one can see me, how can a consensus be reached?

Perhaps I am having a good old tease. Maybe I am just an old fake. Pulling your leg, as the bootjack used to say (it was his only joke).

So it doesn't matter if I am what I say I am or not. What

matters is that you want me. You might not know you want me yet but once I have told my story, once you understand, you will all want me.

My future depends on people believing that I am worth something and need protecting. Art only survives by striking a chord in someone's heart and offering solace and reassurance. A great picture is the distillation of emotion, offering an empathetic hand across time and circumstance. A wonderful composition inspires sympathy and harmony. No wonder mortals fight to possess us.

Right now, I am worth less than £100, my absolute nadir. The sum total of admirers is two. And one of them, the old drunk, smeared my foliage in butter and animal fats.

Even so, the young guide gave me a second look. Maybe if Annie had not turned his head, he might have looked even more carefully at *moi*.

I am not ratifying this union. Look at his crumpled suit. Second-hand, I guess. The guide is not moneyed. I need prosperity; my best chance of seeing out another century is wealth. The less I get sold on, the better the roof, the longer I'll survive. We are not encouraging old corduroy. *Non*.

Let's return to the day of the museum visit. The sheer ignominy of being stuffed into a bag with three sandwiches. Thank God it was dull old Edam rather than pungent melting Cheddar or Stilton. Shocking, really. Imagine how it felt when I was produced in front of all those old acquaintances, including lesser paintings by Pater and Lancret—mere imitators of my master.

There were whispers of recognition, a gasp of collective horror when I was whipped out from the bag: if it could happen to *moi* then it could certainly happen to any of them.

I had hung with some of those pictures in a former life, including that clutch of Canalettos bought by the first Marquess of Hertford. Canaletto, as we all know, knocked out those Venetian landscapes with alarming frequency. He was a painter bedevilled by his own success—those endless canals were so prized that poor old Giovanni could never sell anything else. Imagine how boring it was painting and repainting those smelly old waterways.

I digress. It is a bad habit of mine. It comes with age and loneliness. The coffee pot at Bernoff's used to call me Pontificating Peter. I ignored the barb. I would ask you to read on or you might miss some vital plot details. You might even learn something.

Back to the Wallace. Most works of art and the furniture in that venerable institution were bought to demonstrate the wealth and superior taste of the owner. The original Hertfords didn't know about art. They didn't have to: they had wives and advisors who told them what to buy and when. Behind every great collector is an army of dealers, consultants and critics. This did not lessen my humiliation when produced like a *lapin* out of a *chapeau* and manhandled by a drunken floozy, nearly arrested, shoved back in *plastique* and bundled back out into the cold. Outside, the mother concocted a premiseless fight with the daughter and stormed off. She didn't need an excuse—the desire to drink always wins. Annie warned that this time she wouldn't get her out of the cells. We all know she will, though. Annie's urge to care for and protect her mother is as strong as Evie's need to self-obliterate.

Evie took me on a tour of various public houses where I was nearly left in the plastic bag on the bar not once but twice. Many hours later we arrived at the "home" and I was slung into a corner. One was almost nostalgic for Bernoff's. I never thought I would say that.

By the time Annie got home, the mother had passed out. Taking me carefully out of the plastic bag, she gently wiped the butter off my foliage and stared at me for a long time. One was not sure if she was thinking of a long-lost love or *moi*.

Rummaging in her bag, she brought out the Wallace postcard and held it up next to *moi*. It is a drawing rather than a painting and though it was not a study for *moi,* it was of a similar scene: delicate foliage, clothing, hairstyle and mood.

My master drew constantly and all for the love of it. In drawing he stands unsurpassed by the great masters. Ask a Rubens or a Raphael who is the most brilliant and original draftsman. Go on, check with a Rembrandt or a Titian while you're at it. Antoine is right up there. Indeed, I would say he's never been equalled when it comes to piquancy of pencilling. He had an unrivalled freedom of hand and lightness of touch. With a few flicks of red, black and white chalk, usually on grey paper, he captured the fineness of a person's profile and made their cheeks sing with purple blushes and their eyes vivid with a radiant gloss. Another incandescently brilliant effect was to run white along the side of black, adding charming radiations and illuminations. He was especially fond of drawing the backs of figures so that he might capture the *coiffures* of the period. There wasn't a lot of money to pay sitters so models had to be caught unawares, at *salons,* in the parks.

The sketches of the landscapes were done in red chalk— *pensées à la sanguine.* (This is not a national dish.) The studies of foliage and tree bark exhibit minute care and exactitude. His lightness of touch was as delicate as the brush of the petals of a flower or an alighting butterfly. An almost Impression-ist manner separates blades of grass on a flower-decked bank. From these extraordinary sketches, my master introduced dabs of paint in the lightest way, as if fragments of colour had just blown in. He painted in gold and honey and every stroke was tuned to the mood of the moment—*l'heure exquise.* His landscapes were effulgent with the brilliance of high noon, his figures represented sartorial lighthouses; his ladies shook glittering rays from their silken skirts while the slashed sleeves of cavaliers were like gleaming lanterns. His beauties had a sort of *désinvolture* (get a dictionary). My master was the poet painter of ideal daydreams; his work was as sweet and as free as breaths sent from heaven.

I like to think Annie heard or intuited all this; and my master's genius shone through the grime and varnish. For ten minutes at least her eyes flicked from the postcard to my surface, darting from the figures to the trees to the fountain.

Then she turned the postcard over and saw a number scrawled on the back, with a name, Jesse. She smiled. I was quite overcome. She is extremely pretty. Of course she won't ever call him; it simply isn't done.

Chapter 7

In her imagination, and according to the recipe (admittedly written four hundred years earlier), Annie could see and taste the tart: a perfect confection of pistachio and pears floating in a pomegranate-and-geranium-scented custard. Though she followed the instructions down to the last grain of sugar, the pudding refused to set. It was three o'clock in the morning, less than seventeen hours to go before the first guests sat down at the Winklemans' table. Annie's tears dripped freely into the mixing bowl; she was not crying for getting it wrong; she was weeping because she so desperately wanted to get it right.

In the last six days, she had not slept more than a few hours a night: fear and excitement had kept her awake. The dinner presented the perfect opportunity to create a memorable and delicious feast and also the arena to test out a secret theory. Annie believed taste and aromas had the power to transport people from the present to other places. Sometimes this was a journey to a different mood, but it was also a form of time travel. For Annie, the subtlest whiff of freshly cut grass, or the essence of pine needles, a freshly risen cheese soufflé, the scent of a rose or a rain shower on autumn leaves, conjured up past summers. For the Winklemans' dinner, she wanted to spirit the guests back to a world Caravaggio would have recognised; to leave the twenty-first century behind, if only for a few hours, and to feel their spirits and beings immersed in the late sixteenth century.

Standing in her kitchen at home, surrounded by a meagre array of china bowls and saucepans, Annie felt enveloped by despair. She was in danger of losing her job and her fantasy at the same time. Turning off the gas ring, she went to the bedroom and lay down fully clothed on her bed next to her mother and immediately fell asleep. Not long afterwards she was woken by the grinding gears of the rubbish truck in the street below and lay for a few moments, listening to the scraping of bins. Perhaps, she thought, I should tell Rebecca to find someone else or scramble to secure a proven temporary chef—London must be full of cooks for hire. After a couple more seconds, she sat bolt upright; she was not going to give in so easily.

Leaving the bedroom, she went over to the kitchen table, covered with library books and print-outs of recipes from Caravaggio's time. She had decided on the first two courses: boned baby quails poached in wine served with gnocchi in a ricotta and watercress sauce followed by roast veal adorned with beads of onions, beetroot and grapes. Pudding, Annie reasoned, needed to be light and fruity and palate-cleansing. Perhaps, she thought, thumbing through the different options, I am making this too complicated. She switched from Roman and Sicilian recipes to Naples. She considered and discounted marzipan tartlets, pastries of prunes and soured cherries, a flower salad, slices of bread soaked in milk and fried with sugar and cinnamon. In a tattered old book, she found the perfect pudding—thin slices of quince and pear poached in honey and rosewater. These fruits would not be too hard to find. Annie decided to add ruby-coloured pomegranate seeds and tiny green leaves of scented rose geranium as decoration. Looking at the clock, she saw it was already 8 a.m. Exactly twelve hours to go till the first guest sat down. Taking out her computer, she emailed the final menu to the caligraphers who would create cards for each guest's place setting.

Septimus Ward-Thomas had a problem and as far as he could see, it was unsolvable. His institution, the National Gallery, was being asked to accept another significant reduction in their government grant while increasing both programmes and opening hours. His staff were already underpaid and overworked.

"This country is facing an unprecedented economic crisis and we have to evaluate the relative merits of food banks versus museums," said Curtis Wheeler, special advisor to the minister at the Department of Culture. "My minister is sympathetic, but without something meaty and persuasive at next week's spending review, then dot, dot, dot."

"Dot, dot, dot," Ward-Thomas said faintly.

"You're up against health and education," the special advisor said.

"Grants to the arts represent a minute proportion of overall spending."

"It's a matter of perception."

"Our visitor numbers are at an all-time high," Ward-Thomas protested.

"You are failing to reach the minority sections of the population."

"Seven million people is a big percentage."

"But is it the right percentage? Or are there too many A/Bs, foreigners and old duffers?"

The director guessed that Wheeler was about twenty-eight years old and a perfect example of the breed of ambitious young political advisors who had come straight from university to parliament, passing from quadrangle to quadrangle without a sniff at the real world.

"The problem is," Ward-Thomas said sadly, "how to justify something that is by its very nature unquantifiable. There is no machine to measure the transformative effect of beauty, or the importance of contemplation, or even the amount of happiness inspired by coming here."

As he spoke, Ward-Thomas caught a glimpse of himself in the mirror behind the advisor's head. He looked exhausted: he *was* exhausted. Feted as one of the youngest stars of his generation when he became director of the National Gallery fifteen years ago, Ward-Thomas now looked nearer seventy-five rather than his actual age of fifty-five. His once jaunty step had become leaden and his eyes were permanently bloodshot through lack of sleep. As a young curator he had been a heart-throb, with his thick thatch of blond hair, quizzical expression and his trademark red scarf thrown raffishly around his neck. Now the scarf had gone, along with most of his hair, and only a few of the bluestockings bothered to flirt with him any more.

"Your problem is that all your stuff is passé," Wheeler said, running his fingers through his modish haircut.

"Passé?" Ward-Thomas asked incredulously. How could anyone describe beautiful paintings as past it? Surely age was a cause for celebration and their survival proved that these paintings were too powerful and meaningful to disappear into obsolescence?

"I would think there is great comfort that the themes of suffering and joy recur from one generation to another," he said, wringing his hands.

"Passé is old hat," Wheeler said firmly.

"Old hat?" Ward-Thomas said, fighting back tears of frustration.

Mistaking the cause of Ward-Thomas's watery eyes, Wheeler laid a reassuring hand on the older man's arm. "You must long to be running Tate Modern. They have living artists who can explain what they are doing and why."

Ward-Thomas looked down at the pale white hand on his arm and then, raising his head, he said in a low serious voice, "We must kill modern art."

"Excuse me?" said Wheeler, removing his hand quickly.

"It was something Picasso said," explained Ward-Thomas. "He meant that once something exists it is no longer truly modern."

"I did Picasso at school," Wheeler said and laughed nervously.

"If only we still lived in the eighteenth century," Ward-Thomas lamented. "Then most of our paintings would seem frightfully modern. After all, age is just a matter of perception."

"The other thing is," said Wheeler, "the Tate's artists can be relied on to behave badly, whip up publicity, get people talking."

"I can assure you that no one behaved worse than Caravaggio," Ward-Thomas said. "He didn't just get drunk, he murdered people."

"What were his dates?" Wheeler asked, suddenly interested.

"1571 to 1610, or thereabouts."

"So the tabloids won't feature him breaking up a night-club?" Wheeler said, letting out a shout of laughter at his own joke.

"People do talk about Old Masters," Ward-Thomas protested.

"I'm not hearing it."

"Not necessarily the people you know."

"Movers and shakers, I presume?" Wheeler said with unnecessary irony.

Ward-Thomas sat back in his chair and looked out of the

window into Trafalgar Square at Nelson standing high on his column surveying London. Noises from street performers and tourists almost drowned out the traffic and a busker sang a well-known folk song with the aid of a distorted amplifier.

He wanted to tell Wheeler about the lady who had been coming to the National Gallery for over sixty years to look at one Canaletto because it reminded her of her lover, felled but not forgotten, in the Second World War. Or about the children's looks of awe when they stared up at *Whistlejacket*, the life-size painting of a horse by Stubbs. He wondered if Wheeler would believe that some visitors came simply to find a quiet contemplative space away from the tedium and stress of their everyday lives, or that others looked to these paintings as beacons of hope because they showed that the human struggle is endless and universal.

Wheeler had taken out a red notebook and pencil and looked expectantly at the director.

"When I was a young man starting out in this world, it was enough to love and know about art," Ward-Thomas said wistfully.

"You can still know and love it," Wheeler said. "But if you are expecting government funding, there are a few other boxes to tick. The minister is on your side but he needs something substantive to present, something to catch the Treasury's attention."

Ward-Thomas cast his mind back to the staff meeting and to Ayesha Sen, one of his younger colleagues, who was always proposing "trendy" ways of promoting art.

"We have an interesting programme for unmarried mothers," Ward-Thomas said, feeling slightly ashamed, as he had tried, on many occasions, to block this idea of Sen's. "We bring them in and show them lots of Madonna and Child paintings; it helps to remove the stigma."

"How do they react?"

"Fine, as long as they get free tea and biscuits at the end."

"I will put that on your form," said Wheeler, writing in his notebook.

"There is also the young offenders' club—they get shipped in from Feltham and shown some of our tougher works, things by Caravaggio or Rubens. It makes them feel less stigmatised." Ward-Thomas did not add that this was yet another one of Sen's ideas.

"I'm liking this," Wheeler said. Finally a story was emerging, something he could tell his minister, who found describing the merits of art or museums nearly impossible: for him they were places to hide from the rain, like big bus shelters.

"I've got it!" Wheeler said, jumping up and striding around the room. "Why don't you install free Wi-Fi and then every student in London will flock here: your numbers will go through the roof."

Ward-Thomas imagined the floors of his beautiful gallery strewn with gum-chewing students checking email accounts and Skyping their friends. His heart sank.

Instead he heard himself say, "We are opening late on Friday nights to encourage young people to meet and mingle." Ward-Thomas didn't add that he had been utterly opposed to Sen's latest initiative.

"Meet and mingle nights! Love it." Wheeler wrote that down too. "Maybe the minister will come—as you've read in the *Daily Mail*, he's single now."

"I don't read the *Mail*," Ward-Thomas said.

For the first time during their entire conversation, Wheeler looked truly interested.

"You can't be serious? It's everyone's guilty pleasure."

"Mine is custard creams," Ward-Thomas said.

Curtis Wheeler put the lid back on his pen and placed it in his inside pocket. "Better go and write my report. Never know, might see you at Meet and Mingle."

Ward-Thomas smiled wanly and rose to shake the young man's hand.

After Wheeler left, Ward-Thomas sat down heavily in his chair and placed his head in his hands. To be made director of the world's most perfectly formed collection of Old Masters had been the fulfilment of his dreams, but he had not anticipated that this glorious, illustrious appointment would come with so many unexpected and unwelcome additions. Looking at his watch, he saw that it was already midday. In less than one hour he was due to show a group of American collectors around, followed by a meeting with his finance committee, followed by a meeting with his senior staff. Later that night there was a dinner with London's most important dealers in Old Master paintings, Rebecca and Memling Winkleman, in honour of the American collector Melanie Appledore.

His sense of deep ennui was interrupted by a knock on the door.

"Come in," he said.

"Got a mo?" It was Ayesha Sen, reeking with ambition. "I've got an idea."

Without waiting to hear it, Ward-Thomas looked Sen up and down and said, "Ayesha, I have one piece of advice for you. Be careful what you wish for. Be very careful."

Less than half a mile away in Houghton Street, in the boardroom of Monachorum auction house, at an emergency meeting of the board of directors, Earl Beachendon was trying to account for the recent significant losses. The boardroom had mahogany floors, walls made from marble. An ornate ceiling was balanced on massive mahogany fluted Doric columns. Every whisper echoed slightly; each raised voice reverberated like a shotgun. This morning the cacophony of crossness emanating from the board seemed to drill into the Earl's temples. Taking a clean white handkerchief from his top pocket, he wiped it over his glistening balding head, trying to smooth the little hair he had left. The Earl had one of those unfortunate pink complexions that took on a high colour at times of embarrassment or exertion. Glancing down at the highly polished surface of the mahogany table, he saw his face was already cherry red.

"Why did you guarantee those prices?" Abel Mount, the chairman of the board, asked, shaking his head in disbelief. Formerly head of the Stock Exchange, Mount had a penchant for port and a nose that had come to look like a piece of Stilton cheese, which he stroked when annoyed.

"Every other auction house in London, Paris and New York was after his collection. Apart from the Lloyd Webbers, Harry Danes has the finest group of pre-Raphaelite pictures in private hands." Beachendon shifted uncomfortably in his chair.

"What happened to your underbidders? It's hardly a secret that every important sale has a guarantor."

"I was let down by the Qataris at the last minute." Earl Beachendon felt a tiny trickle of sweat work its way down the back of his neck towards his spine.

"But to go ahead and promise the vendors the top estimate plus ten per cent!" Mount said, stroking his proboscis with some force.

"The week before, a Burne-Jones sold for double its estimate," Beachendon protested.

"James, I am not going to tell you how to do your job," said Rachel Westcott-Smith, leaning across the table. All twelve board members knew that she was about to do just that. Westcott-Smith, an American hedge-fund manager with $17 billion under management, had recently bought 10 per cent of Monachorum. "But you know the rules: we never ever take foolish risks. That was an insane gamble," she said.

The trickle of sweat had turned into a small stream and Beachendon wondered if it had soaked through his shirt and into his jacket.

"It is extremely hard to secure these pre-eminent collections without some kind of guarantee," said Beachendon. "The heirs of the estate had been offered estimate plus eight per cent by Denham's."

"Had they, or were they bluffing?" Rachel snapped.

Beachendon had to admit that he had not checked the offer.

"The problem is, James, we have gone from holding the top spot as the most profitable and long-established auction house in London to being a one-hundred-and-fifty-year-old institution teetering on the edge of bankruptcy. We have handled thousands of estates, sales, auctions and so forth, and, thanks to your catastrophic misjudgement, we are now three hundred million pounds in debt."

"That's not all. What about the three lawsuits pending regarding misattributions?" Abel Mount said.

"Actually there are four," Roger Linterman, the company lawyer, cut in. "There is Constable's *Man at Lock with Horse*, the Howard Porphyry Vases, the disputed Pieter de Hooch and the follower of Titian."

"Could you take us through these one by one please, James?" Rachel asked with icy politeness.

Beachendon wasn't sure whom he loathed most: Rachel Westcott-Smith with her G5 jet purring in anticipation at Northolt airport; Abel Mount, who was only on the board at Beachendon's own recommendation; or Roger Linterman, who was seeking promotion at any price. In addition to all this, Monachorum's competitors were upping their game. In recent months, Bratby & Sons, once a no-hope dusty little auction house, had been bought by some Russians and had been given a major facelift while their main rival, Conrad and Flight, had replaced their long-serving CEO with a guitar-playing ex-vice-president of a tech company who had trebled their profits in one season by dragging his firm into the digital age.

Beachendon knew his days were numbered. If only he could hang on long enough to get the last two daughters, the youngest Ladies Halfpennies through St. Mary's Ascot with a few qualifications.

"All these cases are unfortunate," Beachendon said, using his most urbane manner to calm the worried faces around him.

"Do you call a fake Constable unfortunate?" Rachel asked.

Beachendon looked at his shoes. "The picture had been in Tamoka Castle for at least three hundred years and the same family had once owned three Constables."

"It was an open secret that when they sold their real Constables in the 1860s they had copies made to fill the empty spaces," Rachel said. "Roger, how much are we being sued for on this one?"

"There is the thirty-million-pound sale price plus the taxes and commissions and another twenty million for personal damages and loss of face. They are also bringing an incompetence suit against the house."

"What's that?" Herman van Pampe asked.

"Basically it claims we are unfit to trade."

"Fantastic," Rachel snapped.

"Let's move on to the Howard Porphyry Vases," Abel Mount said firmly.

"This is a very unfortunate case," Beachendon admitted. "We thought we had the sole and exclusive chain of title to sell these vases." He hesitated. "It turned out that the objects were owned by the vendor's cousin. Once the sale had gone through, the cousin, who had been living in Tasmania, suddenly reappeared and has asked for the objects back."

"Where are they now?" Herman asked.

"We are not entirely sure. We have the money in the bank but the vendor took the vases home to wherever he or she lives."

"If you have the money, surely you have an address. He or she didn't just walk in with a suitcase of money. What did they go for? Four million pounds or something?" Florian Grey had sat on the board for ten years; this was the first time anyone had heard him speak.

"The transaction was done by a direct transfer from a bank in the Cayman Islands. It's not unusual."

"So this is a case of money laundering?" said Rachel.

"It would appear so."

"The police are going over every single transaction we have made over the last five years to see if we have been involved with illegal washing of funds," said Linterman.

"Now the Pieter de Hooch—that was an almost unavoidable situation," said Beachendon.

"Failing to spot a forgery is unavoidable?" Rachel asked sceptically.

"The mighty van Meegeren struck again," said Beachendon. "We are not the first or last to be duped by the world's greatest forger."

"You make it seem like it's an insignificant amount," interceded Rachel.

"Seven million is not a trifle, of course," said Beachendon, feeling a blush creeping over his fine temples, "but at least van Meegerens are worth something in their own right. We can scrape back a few hundred thousand pounds."

"The forgery has a value?" Herman asked incredulously.

"The works of a master forger are now considered important," Beachendon explained. "I have clients who hang his work with plaques that say 'So and So by So and So realised by Meter van Meegeren.'"

"This would be interesting," said Rachel, "if we were talking about a small loss, but this fake is costing us seven and a loss of face."

"Sadly true," Beachendon admitted. The sweat had definitely seeped from his shirt into his suit.

"Will you leave us for a few minutes, James?" the chairman asked Earl Beachendon.

"Yes, of course." Beachendon's heart sank; he was surely about to be fired. He thought of his long-suffering wife, his son and his lovely daughters—perhaps they would like Pimlico Academy. The holiday cottage would now go. They could sell their house in Balham and relocate to Lewisham. Tonight there was the Winkleman dinner—maybe the art dealer would offer him a job—a stipend in return for a bona fide English title on his masthead.

Barty and his friend Delores Ryan, the art historian, sat side by side in his large double bed. They often met to share gossip and Chinese food, and to catch up on television soaps. Barty wore a pink face mask, Delores an oatmeal-coloured one.

Unlike the staterooms downstairs at the White House, Barty's personal quarters, in the former servants' rooms, were spartan. Every surface was painted off-white. The curtains were made from thick cream cashmere and even the carpet from finest white Axminster wool. Barty was not a homemaker; he was hardly ever at home. His life was lived in other people's arenas. Besides, having to settle on one style of decoration or commit to a particular object was anathema to the quixotic alchemist.

"I tell you he is going to get off with her." Delores jabbed her chopstick at the television.

"Don't be so vulgar, darling," Barty remonstrated.

"Tell me about Sasha," Delores said, referring to a mutual friend.

"All she did was marry a rich man; now she's in grave danger of drowning in a sea of self-importance."

"She must be having some fun."

"God no, she's gone philanthropic and apparently is single-handedly keeping the nation's museums and hospices operational."

"John's written another book on the history of taste."

"The heart sinks. He will tell us everything we need to know about the subject and quite a bit more."

"In his review, Trichcombe Abufel unkindly called it 'a burden to the bookshelves of the London Library.'"

"What's happened to your archrival, Mr. Abufel? Is he still an art-world outcast?"

"Still plotting the downfall of Memling Winkleman. It will never happen—that family has it all sewn up," Delores said. "Tell me about the Russian. Is he really rich?"

"Staggeringly. Didn't we order duck pancakes?"

"They're under your left thigh. How many billion?"

"Eight, apparently."

"Gas or oil?"

"Tin, I think."

"Attractive?"

"If I can get rid of the leather coat."

"Not another. They all follow the Chelski man like duck-lings. What's this one into?"

"He doesn't know yet; that's my job. I'm thinking contemporary American, Cap Ferrat, the odd racehorse and a fuck-off yacht."

"I desperately need a new client," Delores said. "Please. Darling. Please. The only dealers who make any money these days are the Winklemans and that's because they are into everything."

"Winkleman, Winkleman, it's all anyone can talk about. There must be another game in town?"

"A few manage to nibble off the edges of their territory but the Winklemans always produce something better. God knows where they find the stuff."

"Aren't you on their payroll?"

"Only a miserable stipend like everyone else in the art world," Delores moaned.

"French eighteenth century is so unsexy and there's so lit-tle around. I need him to spend spend spend, not wait around till a rare Boucher comes on the market."

"I have rent to pay."

"Can you see a seventeen-stone, six-foot-eight Russian going 'Rococo'? All that delicate foliage, all those love scenes and fat little cupids? My main worry is keeping him away from cars."

"You are mean."

"He'll want sexy girls, smoky parties and cocaine, not lectures and dreary dinners."

"I'll give him a going-over." Delores ate a spring roll in the manner of a coquettish young woman.

Barty looked at his beloved, rotund fifty-nine-year-old friend. "Got to be cruel to be kind: my Russian is never going to fancy you."

"Ouch," Delores said, crestfallen.

"It's a choice, darling—cream buns or men's carrots? You choose."

"Yes, I would rather stuff it in my mouth than—" She stopped mid-sentence and shrieked, "It's eight o'clock! I am late for the Winkleman dinner."

"You've just eaten enough to feed an army," Barty exclaimed.

"That was my aperitif. Now I'm really hungry." Delores climbed off the bed, brushing the remnants of dim sum and duck off her dress. "Besides, dinner at the Winklemans' is always disgusting—boiled fish, boiled potatoes and vegetables murdered to a pulp by overcooking. No wonder Rebecca is so thin."

Delores pulled on her coat.

"The face mask," Barty said. He had been tempted not to remind her. "I can't believe you are leaving me alone."

"A night in will do you good."

"The vampires of my soul will descend." Barty, panicked by the thought of his own company, wondered who he might call.

"How do I look?" Delores smeared the last of the mask off with a damp dishcloth.

"Like a blancmange."

"Love you too." Delores undulated out of the room, down the stairs and outside to hail a cab.

. . .

Carlo Spinetti finished his evening exercises. The routine never varied: half an hour of press-ups and sun salutations. Moving to the shower, he rubbed himself briskly with rough sea salt under hot water followed by an icy-cold blast. He was fifty-four years old. Age had made him more handsome: his now heavily lined skin, etched by sunlight, had softened the cheekbones and Roman nose. "Noble" was the word the young actor Chiara had used yesterday. While filming *The Sun King*, Carlo hadn't laid one finger on his leading lady but once the picture was in the can, he lost no time spiriting her into his bed.

He had watched Chiara's face carefully as he undressed, worried that she would be appalled by a body that was beginning to look like a badly stretched canvas on a frame. Young people had no idea how flesh detaches itself from bone and muscle creeps away from sinew. He hoped her professed ecstasy hadn't been an audition for his next film.

Carlo sprayed a fine cloud of extract of lime around the bathroom and walked quickly through it; a hint of scent was enough. The thick mulberry-red carpet felt soft against his bare feet as he padded next door into the bedroom painted in black lacquer and hung with mirrored panels. The windows were draped with curtains of deep-purple velvet and the furniture was upholstered in wolf skin. The door handles were copies of lion heads from an Italian palazzo and the window blinds were printed with black-and-white stills from his films. The bed dominated the room: empire-style with feet of huge gilt tiger paws.

Rebecca had given him the room as a "present"; he would have preferred a simple white linen bed and cream-coloured walls but left matters of decoration to his wife and father-in-law. Carlo knew that behind his back Memling referred to him as "my daughter's husband." It had been accepted that their own daughter Grace would follow in her maternal family's footsteps. She was at Cambridge doing a master's degree in history of art and in three years' time would find her name over the gallery in Curzon Street.

Carlo looked at a painting of Grace by David Hockney hanging over his bed, another present from Rebecca to remind him of what mattered in life. He would, for obvious reasons, have preferred to hang Grace in a more neutral area but Carlo had no say over what hung on the walls or how long the paintings remained. He had learned never to get fond of an image: the pictures rarely stayed for long. Twice a month there were intimate dinners hosted by Rebecca and her father for prospective clients. If numbers needed balancing, Carlo was expected to turn up, to be charming and occasionally to express a well-rehearsed and entirely complimentary line about a particular work of art.

Like everyone else who lived in the Winkleman orbit, Carlo was on the family payroll in return for the odd favour. Memling used Carlo's films as a way of illegally transporting paintings around Europe. Works for sale were insinuated into the inventory of props, loaded on to trucks and shipped across the Channel. Transport lorries would often take circuitous routes to reach their locations. If the Winklemans needed paintings taken to France, Germany and Italy, the lorry might make three stops on its way to the location in Hungary. In the unlikely event of being stopped, the hapless driver would shrug and say he was only following orders. Carlo would meet the convoy at each place, ostensibly to check the sets—in actuality, he would replace a specific painting with a copy. The original would be presented to its new owner. Everyone was happy: Carlo got his movies heavily subsidised; the Winklemans made a sale; and the new owner received their work without the interminable hassle of export licences or sales taxes.

Sometimes Carlo thought of striking out independently

but knew that without the Winklemans' money he was unlikely to get a single film financed. Let the old man hate me, Carlo thought; I control the next generation. Tonight was one of those occasions that he had to show up. It was part of the unwritten contract. Chiara would have to wait a little longer. He decided to call her to keep her warm.

Hearing her husband talking on the telephone in the next-door room, Rebecca Winkleman assumed, correctly, that he was arranging to meet one of his mistresses. Occasionally she had to silence gossip with a generous present to a newspaper editor for the sake of their daughter's feelings. The case of the missing picture made Carlo's latest infidelity seem a comparatively minor issue. For reasons her father would not divulge, one lost painting by Antoine Watteau was threatening to bring down their whole empire.

Rebecca looked again at the grimy photographs taken from the CCTV footage of the girl placing the painting in her bike basket and pedalling up the Goldhawk Road. Her contacts at the police station had thoughtfully picked up the girl's route as she turned down Cathnor Road into Melina Grove and when she didn't reappear at the next camera on Batson Street, they suggested that the young lady must live or work on Greenside or Goodwin Road. Unfortunately so did about eight hundred other people and beyond establishing that the cyclist was a female with curly hair tucked into a woolly hat and slim legs in heavy Doc Martens, there were no other distinguishing features. Nevertheless, Rebecca felt that she recognised her from somewhere. Part of her training as an art expert was to log each composition and every face in every painting she ever looked at. From the age of nine, on Saturday and Sunday mornings, Memling would march his son and daughter around the National Gallery. They examined more than a thousand canvases in the museum's collection. Week in, week out, over breakfast, lunch and tea, Memling would fire questions at his children: Rebecca and Marty had to recall the composition, brushwork, iconography and pigments of selected works of art. By the age of fifteen Rebecca could correctly identify the tiniest details: which flower lay at the feet of Leonardo's *Madonna of the Rocks* or in which Canaletto a tiny washerwoman could be found. Marty could never match Rebecca's scholarship or memory but both children knew it didn't matter; Marty, the son and heir, would take over the business.

Once again Rebecca picked up one of the CCTV photographs and stared at it, hoping that it was a random buy and the picture was hanging innocently on some suburban wall where its true value and dark history would go unnoticed. Rebecca was not a woman who left anything to chance: to stack the odds in her favour she was putting every ounce of effort and resource into finding the girl and the picture.

She heard Carlo replace the phone and come into her bedroom. Stuffing the photographs in her briefcase, she felt her eyes fill with tears.

"Darling, what on earth?" Carlo went to her side.

"It's nothing." Rebecca jumped away from him and wiped her face efficiently with her pale, varnish-free nails.

"Is it your father? Is he unwell?" Carlo tried to banish the excitement from his voice.

"It's a small work issue."

Carlo looked at his wife closely and saw fear rather than sorrow.

"What can I do?" Carlo felt genuinely worried.

Rebecca started to touch up her face powder. "Here, read the notes on tonight's guests."

Carlo sat down on his wife's bed, groaning inwardly. The object of the evening was to persuade Melanie Appledore to buy a one-million-pound Caravaggio oil sketch for *Judith Beheading Holofernes*. Carlo doubted the painting would really appeal to the septuagenarian grande dame of Park Avenue who collected French decorative arts. The picture was gory even for Caravaggio and showed the moment after Judith had plunged her knife for the third time into the neck of the Assyrian general.

"Does Mrs. Appledore know that the model for Judith was probably the Roman courtesan Fillide Melandron?" Carlo asked.

"She needn't know," said Rebecca. "I hope you are not going to be difficult."

"Will eating dinner in the presence of this disturbing image create the right milieu for a sale? What are we serving? Colour-coordinated raw beef?"

"Save your jokes for your whore," said Rebecca, snapping.

Carlo looked at his wife in astonishment. She never spoke to him like this—what had happened? He made a mental note to send her flowers the following morning.

In the kitchen three floors below, Annie was overseeing the last-minute preparations. Taking a still life, another painting by Caravaggio, as inspiration, Annie had worked with a team of Carlo's set designers to transform the Winklemans' dining room. The walls were now a ruby red; heavy garlands of roses, pinks and poppies festooned the white damask cloth; the sideboards groaned with figs, plums, peaches and apples along with pyramids of vegetables, cabbages, gourds and even garlic; the guests would drink water from golden goblets and eat from the finest bone china set on golden plates.

Jesu, the Winklemans' head butler, measured the distances between the glasses and plates with a small ruler while his wife, Primrose, painted glitter on the flowers' petals to make them sparkle. Annie dotted the fruit with globules of glue to simulate drops of water, hoping no one would be tempted to eat any. Each napkin was two foot square, made of heavy monogrammed linen and arranged in the shape of a Spanish galleon. Rebecca swept into the room and looked around in astonishment.

"This is not how we do things here," she said to Annie.

"I wanted to show off the painting," Annie said quietly. She had hoped that her employer would be pleased.

"You are risking one hell of a lot on a meal," Rebecca said crisply.

Annie did not demur.

Upstairs, Carlo was doing up the last button on his shirt when Jesu appeared.

"Guests are arriving, sir. Madam has asked that you come down." Crossing the room, Jesu took the cufflinks from Carlo's palm and clipped them into the cuffs of his shirt.

"Who's here?" Carlo asked wearily.

"Very old woman and friend of very old woman." Jesu hesitated.

"What is it?"

"Mr. Memling and Ms. Rebecca are in another room. Talking alone. Not disturb."

Carlo went downstairs, wondering if this unusual behaviour was connected to Rebecca's tears. In the grey drawing room he saw the guest of honour. Carlo bowed and took Mrs. Appledore's wrist in his hand. It was hard to believe that the old lady had the strength to raise an arm so weighed down by jewels; Carlo estimated that there were several million pounds' worth of diamonds in her rings and bracelets.

"What a great pleasure to see you again," he said, letting his lips hover above Mrs. Appledore's hand.

"Carlo," she said smiling.

"What brings you to London?" Carlo said, noticing that her face had been frequently lifted and her skin was parchment-thin and as smooth as a child's.

"Shopping. I normally do London in July but the Met has such a boring season this year."

"I thought they were doing *Tosca*?" Rebecca came sweeping into the room and interrupted their conversation. "With Renée."

"Don't you just love Renée?" Mrs. Appledore cooed. "She got sick, didn't you hear?"

"It has ruined our plans." A small, dapper man in a velvet suit advanced towards Carlo with an outstretched hand. "William Carstairs the Third. Thank you for having us."

William Carstairs, the director of Mrs. Appledore's museum, doubled up as her permanent companion, calorie counter and handbag carrier.

"How are the motion pictures?" Mrs. Appledore asked Carlo. "Is there a new one?"

"*The Sun King* with Chiara Costanzia."

Mrs. Appledore looked blank. "Willy, make sure we get it for the jet."

Two more guests arrived. Rebecca made the introductions. "This is Septimus Ward-Thomas, director of the National Gallery. You must know Melanie Appledore?"

"Always a pleasure," Septimus Ward-Thomas said.

"Melanie, I am sure you already know Delores Ryan, who has just completed a new book, *Watteau's Women: The Importance of the Model in the Artist's Oeuvre.*"

"Indeed, I bought it yesterday. An important work which I look forward to reading."

"Is it true you have a Boucher on your jet?" Delores asked Mrs. Appledore.

Septimus Ward-Thomas coughed, trying to hide his intense disapproval; he hated the thought of that delicate paintwork subjected to take-offs and landings.

"I did, but little flakes of Madame de Pompadour's dress came off when we hit a turbulent patch," Mrs. Appledore confessed, "so I hung a few drawings by Lancret instead."

"A better idea," Ward-Thomas said weakly.

There was a slight hush as Memling Winkleman entered the room, flanked by his large white husky, Tiziano. Memling was over six foot but carried himself so well that many assumed he was taller. He had a huge head, an aquiline nose and a full crop of silvery hair. Though his jawline and cheekbones were obscured by slightly loose, wrinkled skin, his features could still be described as chiselled. Known in his office as "Capo," he rarely spoke except to issue instructions in almost inaudible lisping fluent English, French, Russian or German. He never bothered to say hello or goodbye but left meetings or disconnected telephones when it suited him. Tiziano rarely left his side. This dog, now five years old, was the cloned son of Raphaello and had been hand-delivered by Memling in a clinic in South Korea. Raphaello was the great-great-grandson of Leonardo, Memling's first white dog.

Arriving in England without a formal education at the age of twenty-four, Memling went on to gain a first in mathematics and two years later another one in chemistry at Cambridge, followed by a PhD in history of art at the same time as building his business. Ninety-one on his last birthday, Memling still looked fitter than most men twenty years his junior. He played tennis regularly in the indoor court under his house and walked his dog most days. He drank one or two glasses of red wine in the evening and ate only organic food. Like his daughter, and his dog, Memling had the palest blue eyes. Those fumbling to find an appropriate word to describe him often said "patrician," and commented that Mr. Winkleman looked more like an emperor than the grandson of a Frankfurt rabbi. Most assumed that his icy self-control, his inability to suffer fools or indulge any kind of emotion was a legacy of enduring two years at Auschwitz, where every other member of his family perished.

Rebecca had never met a person, including herself, who was not frightened of her exacting and domineering father. Loathing fools or loose talk, Memling took pleasure in humiliating those who were either careless or indulgent. He reserved charm for wealthy clients and with them, though never flirtatious, Memling became almost playful; but this entirely artificial charm did not last a second longer than necessary. He had never mastered the art of small talk or conversation. He refused to carry a mobile phone, read an email or watch television. He carried a small leather notebook and made copious notes on every conversation and decision in his tiny writing.

"Good evening, Memling," Mrs. Appledore said. "My, my, you are so handsome."

"You are as soignée as ever," Memling replied.

"Are you keeping up with tennis?" Mrs. Appledore said. "Your arms are so . . . so virile."

"I challenge you to a friendly match."

"I think my days of overarm serving are over, sadly."

Earl Beachendon and his wife Samantha arrived moments later, followed by the ageing rock star Johnny "Lips" Duffy, who'd been invited to try to make the evening look a little more rounded, a little less like a major selling offensive. Johnny "Lips" had once been at art school and collected British pictures. His fame had waned and these days his only public appearances were in commercials touting a new golf course or a shopping centre. He had brought his wife Karen, a former Olympic equestrienne who wore a backless gold lamé dress.

When Rebecca led her guests into the dining room there was a collective gasp at its transformation into a post-Renaissance tableau. Hanging directly opposite Mrs. Appledore's place was the Caravaggio study.

"The Doria Caravaggio sketch!" Septimus Ward-Thomas clapped his hands together. "For years I've longed to see this painting and feared it destroyed."

"It's a little bloody," Mrs. Appledore said hesitantly.

"That is great blood, magnificent bloody blood," Carlo said, unable to think of anything else. "If only I could direct blood like that."

Rebecca shot him a poisonous look; she had been appalled by the transformation of her impeccable white dining room into a tiny but perfectly formed banqueting hall. Her father walked in and looked questioningly at his daughter, who shrugged.

"Great art never shies away from difficult subjects," Ward-Thomas said tactfully. "Think of Christ on the Cross or the beheading of John the Baptist."

Mrs. Appledore nodded politely. She knew, like everyone else in the room, that the evening was about trying to sell her the picture. At her age any attention was nice, so she decided to play along.

Exactly five minutes after the first guest sat down, Annie sent out the baby quails. She had arranged leaves of lettuce and herbs to look like tufts of grass and balls of flecked gnocchi resembled eggs in nests of spun potatoes. Through the open door, Annie heard gasps of appreciative delight as each dish was placed before the guests. In most areas of her life, Annie fought away nerves but in the kitchen she felt ethereal and calm, working slowly and steadily, one eye on the clock, another on the pots and pans.

Through the open door, as she cooked, Annie could hear snatches of conversation.

"Did you hear what Gerry paid for the Richter?" a voice floated through the door.

"Twenty-five million plus taxes and commissions," another answered.

"Do they charge key money just to sit on the Board of the Met these days?"

"Stanton Holsters offered fifty million dollars and were still refused."

"Manet or Monet?" somebody asked.

"They are both correct," came the answer.

"Did you see the Velázquez show?" a woman's voice demanded.

"What was the point? All the pictures belonged to museums—there was nothing to buy."

"Felicia's got a new yacht."

"Best advice I was ever given," a man's voice rose above the others, "if it floats, fucks or flies, rent it."

Everyone laughed.

"Who'd like more wine?"

"Did you hear that the Fairleys redid their apartment for the new Koons?"

"How does it look?"

"Empty—the artist has yet to produce it."

"Guess what Norton is asking for the David?"

"My shrink says I have a bad case of FOAS: Fear of Appearing Stupid."

To his surprise, Carlo liked Mrs. Appledore. Many mistakenly assumed that her long-term position as the doyenne of New York society was founded solely on the size of her fortune. They missed the point: Mrs. Appledore had style, that elusive, indefinable, un-teachable, un-inheritable, un-purchasable quality that most could only dream of. To celebrate the opening of a new wing at the Appledore Museum, she remodelled speedboats in gold and white feathers so her guests could be ferried from Manhattan upriver in giant swans. When a society hostess fell seriously ill and was bedridden, Mrs. Appledore hired the New York Philharmonic to play outside her window. Overhearing that a craze for sorbets had swept down Park Avenue, Mrs. Appledore had the ingenious idea of making a watermelon ice and substituting the seeds with chocolate pips, and serving the confection from a faux watermelon husk made of frozen apple striped with ribbons of gold leaf. After that, New York tables groaned with increasingly elaborate concoctions until Mrs. Appledore won "the battle of the frozen puddings" by serving a sorbet made from Château Lafite 1929. Profligate? Yes. Unbeatable? No. Her generosity was legendary: staying with the Duke of Denbighshire, she presented His Grace with Goya's drawing of his ancestor, the first duke. When her old friend the Maharani of Batsakpur lost an eye in a riding accident, Mrs. Appledore sent her seven eye patches, one for every day of the week, each decorated with fabulous jewels and seed pearls.

Though she and Horace never lacked money, it was Melanie's understanding of the power of cultural capital that propelled the couple into the highest echelons of society. She endowed the opera, the theatre, concert halls and museums. Using her acumen and knowledge, she created the preeminent collection of French eighteenth-century pictures and decorative arts outside France. While most collectors amassed "greatest hits" in their areas, Mrs. Appledore dug deep around her subject. In addition to masterpieces she bought drawings, etchings, books, furniture, commodes, bureaus, sconces, candelabra and even the original wooden panelling.

Entirely self-educated, Melanie knew more than most curators and art historians; she had read every monograph and visited the most obscure churches and museums from Odessa to Monmouth. Using her position as a grande dame in society, she made art a fashionable, serious and relevant subject. It was Mrs. Appledore who persuaded her friends at the White House to introduce generous tax breaks to sweeten the case for donations. Leading by example, Mrs. Appledore had given, during her lifetime, over $500 million worth of art and other chattels to her beloved museum. Her generosity was such that other museum directors frequently bemoaned their lack of a Mrs. Appledore.

She was also, as Carlo discovered over the first course, a brilliant mimic and a first-rate gossip who managed to avoid being bitchy or condescending. It was a revelation to Carlo that he could so thoroughly enjoy conversation with someone nearly four times as old as his current mistress.

In the kitchen, Annie made the final touches to her main course—interlacing the finely sliced loins of veal with brightly coloured, perfectly round, glistening balls of white, green and red baby onions, peeled grapes and miniature beetroots. Then she took a few photographs of the platter on her telephone, knowing that within fifteen minutes it would return to the kitchen decimated. Food, she decided, was like performance rather than fine art: its power was in its transience and immediacy.

As Jesu carried the steaming dish into the room, the diners broke out into spontaneous applause.

"It is almost too good to eat," Melanie said, helping herself to one grape and a finger-sized piece of meat.

"Much too good," Delores agreed, piling her plate high with veal and vegetables.

"Who is the cook?" Mrs. Appledore asked Carlo while taking a second nibble of a perfectly cooked baby beetroot.

"A woman I found—she is on loan to my wife."

"I must get her name and number."

Positioning herself just out of view, Annie peered through the serving hatch at the diners' expressions as each tentatively put a first bite into their mouth. She noticed that the conversation stopped momentarily as taste and texture erupted onto palates. Septimus Ward-Thomas put down his knife and fork and lifted his eyes to the painting.

"I am having a sensory assault," he said to no one in particular. "All I need is Beethoven to finish me right off."

Annie wanted to throw her arms around the gallery director to thank him for this unusual vote of confidence. Instead she turned her attention to poaching the quince and pear slices and hoped that the fruit would work as a balance to the rich first and second courses.

Carlo, following a stern look from his father-in-law, turned reluctantly from Mrs. Appledore to Delores Ryan.

"This food is absolutely first class," Delores said, stabbing at the meat and stuffing two whole slices of veal into her mouth.

"How's your life? Written any books recently?" Carlo asked, feigning politeness.

"Weren't you listening before? I have a new one out about Watteau's women. Promise you'll come to my little soirée?" Delores said, pushing her leg firmly against his. Her thigh was so massive that it felt like a car reversing into his leg.

"I've just finished *The Sun King*. I have high hopes for it," Carlo said, shifting towards Mrs. Appledore.

"How amusing," said Delores, sounding desperately bored. "Didn't you also do one called *The Sun Queen*? Isn't it a little repetitive?"

"Do you ever ask why painters paint the same scenes over and over again?" Carlo replied testily.

"Painting is different."

"Damn your snobbery. Both disciplines are about capturing light and beauty," Carlo said, his voice rising.

"A filmmaker is dependent on a crew, a camera and so much kit. A painter only needs his eyes, a brush and some paint."

Carlo's temper quickened. "That is such bullshit." His voice soared above the other guests. Rebecca looked nervously at her husband, fearing a row. "Look at your beloved Watteau—he rarely manages to get out of his entirely artificial sylvan glade. It's the same old drab partygoers in different frocks over and over again. I can't stand his work," Carlo shouted.

"Darling, will you be very kind and see if I left my purse upstairs?" Rebecca said firmly.

Carlo got to his feet and went out of the room, vowing never to attend another one of these dinners. Looking at his watch, he saw that it was 9:40 p.m.—soon he could slip away and into Chiara's bed. The telephone rang in the hall and without thinking he answered it.

"Pronto."

There was no one on the other end. It was the third time someone had hung up on him in one day.

"I hear the Evanses are selling up; lost a fortune in Spain when the euro went down. That means those lovely Blue Period Picassos will be on sale soon," said Johnny "Lips."

"I am so over the Blue Period," his wife called out. "Let's buy a pink one."

At the other end of the table, Ward-Thomas was talking to Rebecca.

"The other day I took a Ukrainian round the gallery and the chap kept offering money for the paintings. It's a national museum, I told him—they don't belong to me; they belong to the people of Great Britain and are definitely not for sale. So he doubled his offer—those chaps think the whole world is up for grabs," he said.

"I thought everything had a price," said Carlo, re-entering the room.

"Darling, will you swap places with Septimus? He is longing to talk to Delores about a rare attribution." She patted the seat next to her.

Like a scolded child, Carlo sat down next to his wife.

Annie looked at the clock—it was already 10 p.m.—the last hour and a half had disappeared. The noise from the dining room had risen with each bottle opened. Through the open door she saw that Rebecca's alabaster-white skin had a faint pink glow and overheard Karen Duffy telling Mrs. Appledore that riding would be very good for her pelvic floor.

Annie put the last touches on her pudding—it looked beautiful—almost translucent glistening pieces of quince and pear flecked with pomegranate seeds as red and rich as tiny rubies.

When Jesu and Primrose carried out the fruit platter, the guests claimed they could not eat another morsel. Half an hour later, all the plates and dishes were returned to the kitchen scraped clean.

Delores asked for seconds but was shouted down. Mrs. Appledore insisted that the chef come into the dining room for a round of applause; Carlo jumped to his feet and clapped loudly.

Looking around the room, Annie got her first glimpse of Memling Winkleman: there was something transfixing and unsettling about the man's intense watery blue-eyed stare. Annie made a mental note to avoid him at all costs.

As the guests left the dining room, Annie heard Mrs. Appledore tell Memling, "I might have to buy that gory picture just to remind me of this extraordinary dinner."

Chapter 8

The last guest left at midnight, but it was after 1 a.m. when Annie slipped out of the staff entrance of the Winklemans' house and into the mews behind Curzon Street. The night was cold and clear. Still wide awake, Annie decided to walk a little before catching a night bus home. The evening had been a huge success. Delores Ryan and Mrs. Appledore had both asked for her telephone number. Earl Beachendon promised to recommend her services to the board of Monachorum. Even Rebecca, famously undemonstrative and silent, had offered a clipped but sincere thank you.

Annie walked down Piccadilly and turned left into Old Bond Street, looking idly into the art gallery windows. A few weeks earlier she would have walked straight past but now she peered at each and every display with newfound interest. In one shop front she studied a painting titled *Moses with the Golden Calf* by Ludovico Carracci. Racking her brains, she tried to remember the story. Had God provided a cow as well as manna to eat or did the calf represent idolatry? To her, Moses looked racked with despair as the tablets lay in pieces around his feet and his followers shivered in the background. Annie wondered if her inability to decode the painting mattered or if it were acceptable just to like something without truly understanding its hidden messages. In the next gallery, there was an installation— four large mattresses suspended from a ceiling around a broken kettle, a dildo and a hairbrush entitled "Mama never told me there'd be days like this." To Annie, this composition was bewildering. Art, she thought, is a different language and one that she did not particularly want to learn. Overhearing the conversation at dinner, talk of skulduggery and exorbitant prices as well as the internecine rules and mores of the superrich, had only reinforced Annie's love of cooking. For just a few pounds, she could transform humble ingredients into an extraordinary experience that didn't need prior knowledge or insight or investment. Eating was an essential, sensual and communal activity requiring nothing more than taste buds and an open mind.

"Money for a cup of tea, love?" A disembodied voice emanated from a doorway. Annie jumped when a hand, followed by a face, appeared from a cardboard box. She had not noticed anyone or anything in the muddle of darkness. "Just a few quid."

Annie fished around in her pocket for some loose change and then in the bottom of her bag.

"I'm so sorry—I only have my Oyster card and a lipstick," she said apologetically.

"I don't have much use for either," the voice said.

"Goodnight," Annie said. She made a mental note to return one evening with money.

Walking on, she noticed another lumpy shape curled up in a doorway; this one was boxless but surrounded by plastic bags overspilling with possessions—Annie made out the shape of a kettle, a brush and a cup. A large fox with a long scrubby tail trotted up the road, its head low, and its gait purposeful. It passed Annie without a second glance before disappearing down the steps into the service entrance of a grand hotel.

As Annie turned down a side road and into Berkeley Square, some people spilled out of a nightclub. Three men were dressed in black tie; two young women wore tiny dresses and another man, incongruously dressed as a punk rocker, followed behind.

"Hurry up, Barty, I'm bloody freezing!" one girl shouted as her friend waved her arms to stop a taxi. Two young men cupped their hands around a match, while the third tried drunkenly to get his cigarette to light.

"You can't smoke in a taxi these days, Roddy!" shrieked Miss Pink Dress.

The punk rocker banged into Annie.

"I'm frightfully sorry," he said. "Are you okay?" His voice was slightly querulous with age and drink.

"I'm fine, thank you," Annie replied, trying to navigate her way through his friends.

Miss Tiny Golden Dress tottered up to them. "Barty, stop picking up strangers." Smiling insincerely at Annie, she pulled him away and towards the cab.

Annie walked on into Mount Street and looked longingly at a row of cabs parked outside the Connaught Hotel. If only she had the money to take one home and laughing friends to fill it up. She jumped as a couple of youth ran past, letting off a firework that whooshed and exploded above the roofline. The doorman of the hotel shouted at them half-heartedly.

One hundred feet above the pavement in the royal suite, the firework woke Vlad with a start. Since his expulsion from Russia, every bang, every sharp noise scared him. He reassured himself that he had made the necessary payments; it must be someone else getting it tonight.

Looking across the bed, Vlad saw the three other bodies, all naked, all female, all blonde, all young and all new to him. The concierge had effected their introduction, promising Vlad that they came from a reputable "house" where there was no riff-raff. He said they could organise "Oxbridge" too; Vlad wasn't sure what that meant but had said no: he just wanted "young, slim, blonde and clean."

After an energetic couple of hours, the girls had fallen asleep. Vlad, unused to having anyone else in his bed, lay there with a restless spirit, too tired to move yet too unsettled to sleep. One girl snored like a truck driver; he couldn't imagine how something so slight and pretty could make such an extraordinary noise. Her friends slept through it regardless. The sex had been good; no, better than good—the girls had known exactly what to do and fulfilled their tasks with grace and apparent enthusiasm. Unlike most of the prostitutes that Vlad had hired, their orgasms and moans of satisfaction seemed authentic. Yet for all this company, Vlad felt empty and alone. Perhaps next time he should order more girls but he knew that quenching loneliness wasn't a numbers game. Perhaps he needed a girlfriend, someone with whom he could develop a relationship. The thought made him feel even more desperate—who could possibly understand where he had come from, what this life was like? The price paid for physical freedom was emotional exile.

In an earlier life Vlad had assumed money would provide more than physical protection; it was the longed-for enabler and padding, a springboard and soft landing, a passage and lubricant. He remembered lying in his truckle bed in Smlinsk planning future comforts. Even in his wildest dreams he would never have imagined how rich he would become. The irony was that now he could not work out what to spend his billions on, let alone how to make himself happy. For all the cars, girls, boats, planes, holidays, suits, horses, he was still unable to shake off a feeling of unease and dissatisfaction. Now he saw these great gains as a large mountain with him perched alone on the top. The simplicity of his earlier anxieties, of being hungry and cold, had been replaced with more abstract terrors—of being inadequate and unlovable.

There was nothing to miss about life in Smlinsk and yet Vlad couldn't help but remember that time with nostalgia. There was a comforting simplicity: he got up, went to work, got tired, came home and went to sleep, day in and day out. He found a satisfying rhythm to the endless monotony and something else too: the knowledge that every other person in Smlinsk was in the same situation. They were all hungry, trapped and dreaming of a life elsewhere or a different future. Most would only earn enough money to buy a flagon of vodka to temporarily lift them out of the incessant daily routine, a Saturday-night reprieve.

Vlad felt one of the girls starting to stir. She opened a large blue eye and looked at him, wondering, no doubt, if she would be required to perform some sexual act. She smiled sweetly at him.

"Just going to freshen up," she said, and slithered out of the bed.

He watched her naked back as she stumbled towards the bathroom and felt a twitch of desire. So what if all this was a mercenary transaction, devoid of love and tenderness? So what if he was the necessary conduit for her to buy or enjoy the life she wanted? So what if she simulated pleasure and he gave her little? Wasn't the whole of life one kind of transaction or another? Vlad drove the earlier feelings of vulnerability out and felt his heart harden. All human relationships were based on some form of contract, some kind of exchange. Love was just an index-linked commodity, as volatile and tradable as any stock on the open market.

The girl came back. "Do you want to fool around?" she asked.

"No, talk."

"I love a chat," she said, slipping under the covers next to him. "What would you like to talk about?"

"What your name?"

"Trish."

"Vlad."

"Nice to meet you, Vlad." Trish held out a small hand. "We didn't really get a chance to introduce ourselves earlier."

"Lonely, get you?" Vlad asked.

"Do I ever get lonely?" Trish asked. "Not really, I live at home with my mum and my two sisters, a corgi, a Weimaraner and a poodle, so there's never really any time to get lonely."

"Where?"

"Epping. Where are you from?"

"Smlinsk. Siberia."

"Sounds cold." Trish snuggled with a theatrical shiver into the crook of Vlad's arm and rested her face against his chest. "Tell me about your hometown."

"Small town, big mine. Mine nearly empty now. No jobs." Vlad knew a man who murdered his grandmother so there would be more food on the table for his children.

"Sounds like Epping. They closed the Iceland factory last week. Do you have a girlfriend back home?" she asked.

"No, no one special," Vlad lied. He had only had one girl-friend, Svetlana. She would be nearly thirty now.

"There is someone, isn't there?" Trish said, poking him slightly. "I'm psycho, you see; I can tell what people are think-ing. Come on, tell me about her."

"How old are you?" Vlad asked.

"Twenty-two. Getting on. My mum was married at nine-teen. What was you doing when you was twenty-two?"

Vlad wondered whether to tell her that at her age he had already spent seven years in a mine and had murdered his first man.

"Would you kill?" he asked.

Trish thought for a minute. "I'd kill for a Burberry trench or a Mulberry handbag in pink crocodile skin."

Vlad thought about his split-second decision to kill his brother, push him down the deep shaft of the mine. Leonard had snatched first the top job and then Svetlana from Vlad in the same week. For three years Vlad watched him take home a better salary and flaunt his superior position, and his beautiful girlfriend. Sometimes he had a flashback of Leonard's startled, appalled face as he fell backwards, realising the consequences of Vlad's hefty shove. Vlad heard the thud of the body hitting the sides of the shaft and the final thunk as it crashed to the floor sixty feet below. He never once regretted killing his brother. Leonard deserved it.

"I would also love a pair of Kurt Geiger shoes," Trish continued, "but I probably wouldn't kill for them." She looked at Vlad. "You're not even listening, are you?" She gave him a gentle shove. "What would you kill for?"

"I would kill when important."

"Would you really?" she said nervously.

Vlad didn't reply. Once he had killed Leonard and found it so easy and useful, he had done it again: the wealthier he got, the further he could stay from the scene of the crime and the less chance of detection.

Looking across his suite, at the etiolated beige furniture, chosen to reflect the tastes of everyone and no one, Vlad's thoughts turned to Barty. This strange man had promised him "a life" full of colour, interests and fun. Vlad decided to retain his services; he had nothing to lose except money.

"I think you are a big softy really," said Trish, letting her fingers trail down Vlad's chest and over his stomach. "I know what will make you happy," and, getting on to her knees, she flicked her tongue over his nipples.

· · ·

Two miles away, Annie walked along the edge of Hyde Park and looking through the railings, she saw tiny spring crocuses and snowdrops peeking through the grass by the trees, bathed in the glow of street lamps. In Devon, she thought, it would be a few more weeks before any flowers appeared; London was ahead of the times in all ways.

At Marble Arch, she caught the night bus home. Thankfully, there were no revellers, no high spirits to navigate, just other tired people, each locked in their own thoughts. Annie looked down from the top deck into the inky emptiness of Hyde Park and idly counted the street lights flashing past. She wondered if she would always be a stranger in London, a stranger everywhere. Perhaps she should go back to Devon; it was her home, where she'd spent her adult life. Her exile was self-imposed but Annie knew she couldn't face seeing Desmond once, let alone every day. When their relationship ended, Annie had got on a plane to India because he would never go there. He saw it as the land of disease. He stuck to Tuscany or the Mull of Kintyre. Once she had admired his conviction, his refusal to be seduced by new ideas or faraway places, but walking through the tiny twisting streets of New Delhi, Annie understood that Desmond's world was limited by fear. He couldn't bear to step out of the known, the familiar. In Europe he could understand the rudiments of language, the coordinates of the culture, but elsewhere he was flummoxed. The same went, she began to understand, for his absolute reliance on order and routine.

The bus stopped at the top of Queensway and a group of young Asian men got on. They sat at the back of the bus talking in low urgent voices. Annie wondered where they were from. She remembered lying in her small white room in a guesthouse in New Delhi, realising that it was past nine: time to get up, have breakfast, check the headlines, go for a run, turn on the computer and set the day in progress. Instead she made a break with tradition and lay in bed, luxuriating in her sloth, letting the sounds of the city wash over her. The chatter of boys playing cricket in the street drifted up through the open window; a tea seller called out; strange bird noises rose above the honking cars and bicycle bells; a broom scraped rhythmically in the passage outside her room. Annie lay there, her mind blank and her emotions strangely abated. This abandonment of time felt almost wicked; a new and entirely foreign thought occurred to her—perhaps there were other ways to live.

She meandered around India for the next four months, whimsically deciding where to go, what to visit, when to eat and where to stay. Constant motion helped her to manage her grief, calm her emotions. Long journeys by bus or train were particularly soporific and restful—the growl of the engine, the passing landscape, snatched conversations; the bustle of human life both inside and out became a form of meditation; thoughts that were once painful floated past and refused to settle. Later, people would ask what she had seen and where she had been, but the specifics of her journey had passed like smudges. She had, of course, seen and remembered the Taj Mahal, Fatehpur Sikri, the temples of Hampi, the Ganges at Varanasi, the Red Fort in Delhi, the shoreline at Mahabalipuram but could not confidently talk about any of them. For her, the trip to India was a mental escape, a journey from herself rather than an exploration of another culture.

The bus continued on through Holland Park. From the top deck Annie could see into bedroom windows—a couple reading in bed, a man getting changed, a young girl talking on her phone. Mostly the curtains were drawn against darkness. Annie remembered the moment the email arrived. She had signed up to a walking tour in Assam when, in an Internet café, she decided to check on her account. The first email told her their house had been sold. As instructed, the agents had taken the first good offer; it was perhaps not the best price but a decent one. Her half of the money had been deposited in her account. The agents would be happy to find her another place to live—indeed there was a "delightful" maisonette in the nearby village of Aston St. Peters or a two-bedroom flat in an entirely "charming" suburb of Bristol. Clicking on the particulars, Annie failed to imagine herself in either of these places. The problem was that she failed to imagine herself anywhere but in Rose Cottage with Desmond.

She looked around the café, nothing more than a back room with two antiquated computers. Next to her was a young woman, presumably on a gap year, shouting into Skype, trying to persuade her father to advance some more money. Paper notices on the wall advertised trips to a nearby river or to a monastery. Annie wondered how long her newly realised cache of money would last and considered trying to find work locally. She knew, though, that this was unrealistic; she could not put life on hold for ever.

A new message appeared. It was from Desmond and Annie held her breath. Pushing her chair back she took a few minutes to imagine what the message might say. That he had made a terrible mistake, he missed her and loved her and needed her back home? That Liz had been run over by a bus and could she come back home and look after him? That he was really sorry about his behaviour?

> *Hi Annie,*
> *I hope you are pleased with the sale of the house.*
> *I have some wonderful news. One week ago today*
> *I became a proud father to Magnus Rory Andrew. He*
> *weighs nine pounds and has lots of blond hair like mine.*
> *Baby and mother are doing splendidly. It's been a bit of*
> *a shock but I am coping and am very proud. I hope that*
> *you can find it in your heart to be happy for me.*
>
> *Desmond*

Happy for him? Struggling to keep a torrent of tears at bay, Annie clicked the computer connection off and staggered out of the café into the damp mountain air. Walking down the tiny high street past the gift shops and guesthouses, she made her way out of the village and plunged into the forest. Earlier that day, the huge rhododendron trees dripping with red flowers, the magnolia grandiflora and paths lined with daphne bushes had seemed romantic and inviting. Now the wind shimmering through leaves and branches made an eerie sound and the night birds and tree frogs mocked her with screeching calls; be happy for me.

Annie started to cry. Where, she wondered, did all these tears come from? Were they sitting in pools inside all of us just waiting for hearts to break? Had they been there all the time, collecting behind dams of resolve, waiting to burst? Be happy for me. Did he know her? Had he ever known her? What kind of person was he? Perhaps their life had been a sham, two people living in unconnected parallel universes, each unaware of the other's dreams and fears. She replayed a particular conversation in her head. She'd told him she wanted children, his children. He said it was a deal-breaker. He would never bring a child into this wicked world; he would leave her before having a baby. Annie had fled the house and gone to Megan's to try to hide her devastation. A life without children? Was that really possible? Was he right to ask that of her, of anyone? Megan said not. Megan said she should leave before it was too late to start another relationship. Annie was nearly thirty. Time didn't wait for women, only for men. Several times over the next year she thought of leaving Desmond. Once she even packed her bags and wrote a note explaining her actions. Love held her back. She muffled her body clock under work, exercise, anything else to hand, reasoning that Desmond was her friend, her business partner, her past and future.

The light had fallen abruptly, the sun dropping like a stone over the brow of the mountain. Bathed in sudden darkness,

Annie realised that she was lost. One tree looked just like another. She couldn't be more than twenty minutes away from the village; perhaps her guesthouse would send a search party looking for her. Perhaps she would smell wood fires or hear idle chatter. She wondered whether to stay put or try and find a way out. She had been warned that the temperatures fell during the night and there were tigers and other wild animals in the forest.

Behind her was a crackle of twigs. An animal? A snake? She turned around to see a wizened old woman dressed in a long tunic holding a staff and a torch. Her face was as wrinkled as a walnut but her eyes were as shiny as newly minted copper coins. She walked right up to Annie and looked into her tear-stained face. The old lady raised two fingers and gently pressed the tips into the corners of Annie's eyes. This gesture, this tiny mark of human empathy made across cultures, religions and age, profoundly moved the younger woman. It was the moment when Annie knew with a deep sense of certainty that she wanted to live and start again. The old lady held out her hand and, with fingers entwined, led Annie back to the village.

The following day Annie booked a plane back to England. It was time to re-engage with life. Finally she had a destination and the beginnings of a plan. She had something more important too: hope. For the entire sixteen-hour bus ride to Delhi, Annie thought about where to go, what to do next. Her younger self had dreamed of a place that was all hers, that no one could take away, where the ownership wasn't shared and the front door had one key—hers. That younger self had hankered after life in London, which she imagined would offer a network of friends and events. After the mortgage on their Devon house was repaid, her share was not enough to make a down payment on even a tiny shoebox in the capital, but it could buy her a bit of time, a rental deposit, a fresh start. In Delhi, she signed up online for eleven agencies offering any kind of catering work and combed the 'net's classified ads. Before her London-bound plane took off, she had found employment as the catering assistant for Carlo Spinetti. The pay was lamentable, but it was a beginning.

The bus continued its journey past the vast silent mansions of Holland Park and into Shepherd's Bush. There were few cars; gloomy orange street lights cast pools of tepid light on to the pavement. A young man pushed his knee between the legs of a girl, who looped her arms around his neck and wrapped her legs around his waist, and he carried her across the road, looking into her smiling face. A car braked hard to miss them, the driver leant on his horn. The girl flicked a V-sign.

Getting off the bus at the corner of her road, Annie walked to her building. She climbed the stairs and let herself into the studio, where she found Evie asleep on the sofa and an empty bottle of wine at her feet. Annie covered her mother with a blanket. Tomorrow was Friday—a weekend of nothingness hung like a heavy cloud on the horizon. Worse still, she had Evie to worry about.

Looking at the clock on the kitchen wall, Annie caught sight of the Wallace postcard propped up against the fruit bowl. There was a telephone number and a name: Jesse. Above this Evie had written in heavy red pencil, "Call him. I dare you."

Chapter 9

Annie sat on the concrete walkway by the River Thames, her legs dangling over the side, and looked at the dirty brown water lapping the pockmarked mud. Debris had been left by an outgoing tide: an old trainer, a handleless frying pan and stones streaked with green algae. A dead fish floated past, bloated and tailless. Within seconds a gull hopped over the mud and pinioned it with his bright yellow beak, beady eyes looking right and left for other predators. Annie's thoughts turned to the clear-bottomed river at the end of her garden in Devon, the constant background sing-song of her former life. Were the kingfishers still nesting in the bank and had the otters had another litter of pups? She thought about the wild ponies fording the river at the end of her lane and the heron, a ghostly grey killer, waiting patiently to spear a salmon.

She and Evie had argued again that morning; the simple

act of making the bed had escalated into a vicious tirade, stray remarks flaying old wounds. Annie wondered if Evie would keep her promise and be gone by the evening. Annie laughed at herself. How many times had she heard that over the years? Too many to count. Threatened suicides, broken assurances and false proclamations sat like scars on the face of their relationship. Annie prayed for the courage to change the locks and mobile numbers, to bar her mother from her life.

Annie rang Jesse's number on an impulse. She had nothing else to do and at least someone was pleased to hear from her and happened to be free on a Saturday. She brought the picture as an alibi, something for them to talk about, and it sat beside her in a plastic bag. A weak winter sun peeked through a chink in the clouds, making the muddy flats glisten. She noticed tiny crabs scuttling and emerald-coloured weeds wrapped around rocks.

The man who walked towards her was in his early thirties, slightly long in the face with a broad infectious smile and deep-set blue eyes. He wore a crumpled linen suit, combat trainers and a faded red T-shirt with "Van Morrison" written across the front. It took Annie a moment to realise it was Jesse.

"Hello," he said, holding out his hand. It was covered in paint, so he wiped it on his trousers, leaving a yellow and green smudge, and offered his hand again. Annie shook it.

"Your suit," she said nervously. Jesse looked down.

"Damn! Bit of turps is all that's needed." He grinned. "I'm glad you have brought the picture—I thought we could go to a place near here."

Annie started to climb down off the wall. Jesse held out his hand. Annie hesitated and took it.

"Thanks. Are you a painter?"

"Painter by night; guide by day. I have a show next year and they need fourteen canvases; I'm ten short. For reasons that no one really understands, including myself, I paint variations of one field in Shropshire."

"One field?" asked Annie.

"I suppose I am trying to paint my childhood. The field is some kind of visual metaphor for memory. It's not that unusual—Delacroix became obsessed by one particular landscape, as did Constable, Bonnard and Cézanne. Not that I'm comparing myself to them," he added quickly.

Annie had heard of Constable and Cézanne but not the others.

"My brother saw my painted field—I have six brothers, I'm the youngest—he said it was nothing like the place we grew up in. Different visions. Funny thing memory, isn't it? Look, I'm talking too much. It's not far now."

Annie quite liked his soft, lilting voice.

"I had a holiday job down here once," said Jesse, pointing towards Tower Bridge. "A relief caretaker in Butler's Wharf. It was empty; the stevedores had long gone. No more deliveries of grain and flour, gold, spices, wool and wood making their way from far distant corners of the world and no more barges. In the nineteenth century there were so many boats that you could walk to the other side without getting your feet wet. Look at the Thames now, just a slip road for pleasure boats." As he talked, he swung the painting, still in its plastic bag, backwards and forwards. Every now and then he glanced at Annie; she looked so different today, hair hanging loosely over her shoulders with sunlight occasionally catching hints of red and gold. She wore a T-shirt tucked into silk combat trousers over a pair of battered but polished brown cowboy boots. In place of an overcoat she'd flung a brightly coloured blanket around her shoulders. Jesse wondered if the strings of beads round her neck were bought during exotic adventures and who those were taken with.

An elderly Citroën car backfired as it drove past. For a brief second, Annie thought it was Desmond's DS, a car he called Monty that pre-dated their relationship. Suddenly, she was flooded with thoughts of Desmond and remembered her twenty-first birthday. Desmond had borrowed a friend's apartment in Rome, two large rooms in an old palazzo overlooking the Spanish Steps. The only furniture was a bed and a grand piano; the walls and ceilings were covered in frescoes: maidens carrying water jugs, men with lyres, skipping fauns. They rented a scooter and drove up the Appian Way to a neon-lit restaurant: pasta for the gods, Desmond claimed, as dish after dish of steaming spaghetti was brought out. It was her most romantic memory. Please, Annie prayed silently, take Liz anywhere but Rome.

"All the wharfs were called after their imports," said Jesse, glancing in her direction. "Did you know that Thames means 'dark river' from the pre-Celtic *tamasa*? The same man who built most of these buildings also designed Dartmoor Prison." He knew that he was babbling but, like an incompetent, hungry fisherman, he hoped to catch a passing thought in a wide conversational net.

"When I worked here the spirit of Turner obsessed me: he spent his youth sketching the ships and barges and died looking over the river in Cheyne Walk," said Jesse. "Oh, to be able to paint like Turner." He strode along beside Annie holding an imaginary brush in his left hand, making vast sweeping strokes as if the air in front of him was a giant canvas.

Annie was hardly aware of Jesse's words. Her eyes were fixed on her own feet, brown boots padding on pavement. Like ghoulish stills from an old black-and-white movie, she imagined Desmond kissing Liz, saw his full, soft lips brush the inside shadow of her elbow; the tip of his tongue exploring her breasts. She tried to turn off the images, but the control button was jammed. Perhaps I loved him too hard, she thought.

Jesse and Annie stopped halfway across the bridge. Below a small tug boat made slow headway against a strong tide, bobbing determinedly towards Westminster. Coming the other way was a large rusty red barge; its long deck was covered in twisted bicycles, shopping trolleys and, on top of the heap, a splendidly red motorcycle. The boat's driver stood under a small plastic awning, slapping his arms against his torso to keep warm.

"Stevedores—a great word. Comes from the Saxon, *stevadax*," said Jesse. "My job at Butler's Wharf was unbelievably dull. I sat in this huge white office, with windows on three corners, just watching the tide come in and out. In and out. Relentless and magisterial. The highlight of the day was seeing what the tide left when it ran out: a spare tyre, an old bottle. Do you know the lowest suicide rates come from those who live near water? The highest is people who live near railway lines."

Oh do shut up, Jesse said to himself. He couldn't believe the amount of drivel coming from his mouth; couldn't believe the effect that this girl was having on him or, for that matter, the lack of effect he was having on her. Was this love? She hadn't spoken for the last fifteen minutes and the longer she was silent, the more idiotic he sounded. Glancing sideways, he noticed that her focus was far away. The combination of her disinterest and palpable sorrow hit him like a punch: he wanted to help her, hold her, make love to her.

Taking her arm, he led Annie across the road.

"Are you okay?" he asked. "You look so pale. Why don't we stop and get something to eat? Here, have my scarf." He wrapped his woollen scarf gently around her neck. Without thinking, he scooped her hair up over it, his fingers running around the back of her neck. She trembled slightly.

At the end of the road there was a small cafeteria called Clemmy's, painted green and red. The windows were fugged up and as Jesse pushed open the door the smell of bacon and chip fat whooshed out. Groups of men sat at Formica tables, tabloid newspapers and breakfast spread out across the swirly patterned plastic tablecloths. Annie wondered what they had been doing on a Saturday morning so far away from their families.

"Have you had breakfast?" Jesse asked, pulling out a chair for Annie to sit on. He took some mugs and two dirty plates to the counter. Annie looked around. She felt confused, removed. The men stared at her with blatant interest, a woman in their midst. She outstared them easily and they turned their attention back to the pages of their newspapers. She watched Jesse order breakfast. He was having some trouble with combinations— the number of sausages to eggs, toast to tea. He stepped back to look at the board again and knocked a large, gruff-looking man backwards. Annie sensed trouble. Knocked man seemed cross and flexed his shoulders. Jesse tapped his own head with the flat of his hand; his eyes swivelled in his head. Knocked man smiled in spite of himself.

Jesse came back carrying two mugs of tea. "The lady will bring the food, says she doesn't trust me with the plates."

Moments later a waitress appeared with two full English breakfasts. "If you want a top-up of chips, let me know," she said and then winked at Jesse.

"I could be insulted by her blatant flirting," Annie said, unpeeling gold paper from a small pat of butter. "We might be together for all she knows."

Jesse thought, I want to be. Do I have a chance? Why do you look so sad? He watched her eating, knife and fork held proud, shoulders rounded, expression fixed as she attacked the plate. Stabbing eggs with sausages, scooping up juices with chips, a touch of scarlet tomato, yellow yolk, beige mushroom lined up on a fork and slipped deftly into her mouth. She finished long before him.

"So hungry," she said. Dabs of colour appeared in her cheeks. "Missed dinner last night—very unlike me. Love food." She sat back in her chair and smiled for the first time that day.

"Same again?" he asked as a joke.

"Do you want your chips?"

He shook his head and, leaning forward, she speared four thick chips on the end of her fork. "We lived in Oxford for a few years," Annie said. "I was about ten. Mum had a boyfriend called Peter, a don." Pulling Jesse's plate nearer, she stabbed a few more chips with her fork. "He was married so we used to go to these little cafés in other parts of town, places where his wife wouldn't go. She was the posh restaurant type. This kind of food always reminds me of Peter. Food does that as much as smell, don't you think?"

Jesse nodded. Thank goodness she was finally talking; he thought he'd bored her mute. There was a tiny drip of yolk at the corner of her mouth. He longed to wipe it away with his forefinger.

"We had this routine. Every Sunday a full English and a movie. There was an arthouse cinema in Walton Street," Annie said, drawing her hand across her lips.

"What did the wife do on a Sunday?" Jesse asked.

"He never said. One of the rules of sleeping with a married man is you don't ask those kind of questions."

"Why did your mother take you on these clandestine dates?"

"I hated being left alone and we moved so often that I never made any friends."

"Did you sit together?"

"He'd buy four tickets. When the lights went down, Mum'd nip into the empty seat next to him in the row behind. It's funny. Now when I see those films again, the Fellinis and the Bergmans, I miss the squeaks, muted giggles and breathless kisses of Mum and Peter making out."

"Should you have been there?" said Jesse, feeling protective of the younger Annie.

"I saw some great movies."

"What happened to Peter?" Jesse didn't care but he wanted her to go on talking. He loved the sound of her low, slightly husky voice.

"He left," said Annie matter of factly. "They always did."

Was it bitterness or resignation in her tone? Jesse wondered. Certainly not a trace of self-pity.

"I liked him, more than most. He was clever and funny."

"Are you married?" Jesse asked.

"No." Annie was surprised at his presumptuousness. "Are you?" She didn't really care.

"Who on earth would want to marry me? I haven't got any money and even fewer prospects." He stood up and picked up the plastic bag. "We're going round the corner for another coffee."

"What's wrong with here?" Annie asked.

"I'll explain when we get there," Jesse said and held out his hand to her. Annie didn't take it.

Leaving the café, they walked the few hundred yards in silence. Jesse turned down a side street and stopped outside a silver-fronted restaurant with Le Breakfast written on the outside in flashing pink letters. The metallic ceiling was lined with neon tubes and the tables and floor were in spotless white Formica. Reeking of stale grey-fleshed meat, it was quite the nastiest place Annie had ever been to. This encounter, she thought, sliding into a red plastic booth, was definitely a mistake.

"We're not here for ambience," said Jesse, reading her mind. "The best place to look at a dirty picture is in the window seat of an aeroplane; the force of the sun at high altitude cuts through years of grime. On a dull Saturday in London this place is as good as anywhere." Fishing around in his pocket, he brought out a small flashlight. "A guide's secret tool, it beams out over five million candlepower. Can I see the picture?"

Annie pulled it out of the bag and placed it carefully on the table between them. The waitress came over. They ordered coffee. Jesse bent over the painting and ran the beam of light across its surface.

"Yes, yes," he said quietly to himself.

Annie blew on her steaming coffee and watched a group of young American backpackers translate local prices with a pocket calculator.

"Come round here," said Jesse, patting the seat beside him. "You have to imagine it without the yellow varnish." He blew his hair out of his eyes. "The torch helps, look," he said, tracing its beam along the edge of the picture and, as the light passed, colours shimmered under layers of dirt, animating the figures. Looking closely, Annie detected some kind of tension between the man and the woman—Annie could suddenly feel the man's desire, and sense the woman's disdain.

"Is that a shadow in the corner or a figure?" she said, just able to make out a white shape under a lump of discoloured varnish.

Jesse shrugged.

Suddenly Annie wanted to know about her picture. Who were the couple? Why were they there? What was happening between them? If she could prove that it wasn't just a bad copy, that it was painted by an individual with care and precision, her judgement would be proved sound. Somehow authenticating the picture meant validating herself.

"I think you might have found something wonderful," said Jesse, his eyes glowing with excitement. "Look at the way the painter has layered the paint to give the effect of light shining subtly out of it. See how he's used five dabs of colour to create that man's face, but we know exactly what he is feeling; we are him, we can almost taste his longing and his despair."

"Why assume a man painted it?" asked Annie.

"Most painters in history were men. Women weren't given the opportunity. One or two made it—Artemisia Gentileschi in the seventeenth century and Rosalba Carriera in the eighteenth—but they were the exceptions."

"So what's next? Can't we just look it up in a book?" A lump of excitement was caught in her throat. Calm down, she told herself. Things like this don't happen to people like you.

"First we have to guess the artist and when it was painted."

"I can't help you there. I know nothing about art," said Annie.

"You bought this."

"I bought it for someone else."

Jesse looked at her sharply but said nothing.

"Attribution is like detective work. Occasionally things are obvious—a slam-dunk, no contest about who did it. For less obvious works authentification requires slow painful steps. The first thing is to put a vague date to it."

"How?"

"We can tell a lot from the clothes, the hairstyles and from the paint," said Jesse, counting out some pound coins and leaving them on the table. "Shall we get out of here? This neon is stinging my eyes."

"All my senses are complaining," Annie admitted.

They walked along Tooley Street towards the underground station.

"My studio is just up that road," said Jesse.

Annie looked at him dubiously.

"Do I look like a murderer?" Jesse asked.

Jesse led them up a side street past a railway line; a train clattered over old arches converted into workshops and car garages. As they went up the road, Jesse greeted the mechanics as old friends. At the far end, he stopped by two old doors held together by a giant padlock. Outside there was a black-branched flowering tree covered with carmine-pink flowers.

"That is so lovely," said Annie.

"I am told that it comes from Japan—so how it ended up in a street in south London is anyone's guess."

"Do you know what it is called?" she asked.

"I do, as a matter of fact—*Prunus mume* 'Beni-chidori,' which translates as 'the flight of the red cranes.' It is good to find someone else who loves plants and trees."

"It's one of the things I miss most," said Annie, pausing for a few seconds. "In London, I can't tell when one season stops and another begins. Where I used to live I could tell you the date by looking at the flowers or leaves unfurling. This month I'd be waiting for the primroses and aconites."

"And then for the wild narcissi, cranesbills, bluebells and wild orchids," Jesse added.

"Followed by foxgloves," they said together and laughed.

It was the first time Jesse had seen her laugh and he loved the way she stuck her pink tongue through her small white teeth and how tiny crinkles appeared around her eyes. Taking a big key out of his pocket, Jesse unlocked the padlock and then an inner door to reveal a large wooden-floored room lined with canvases and dotted with piles of books. In the far corner there was an unmade bed and along one wall a narrow kitchen area.

"It's a little untidy," said Jesse, trying to hide some unwashed plates and other detritus. Annie sat down on a careworn chesterfield sofa made of leather with curly wisps of horsehair exploding from various parts and watched as Jesse moved quickly around the room assembling odd objects: a lamp, a couple of magnifying glasses, a glass bottle, some cotton wool. He placed them carefully on a large trestle table in the centre of the workshop. Then he took the picture gently out of the plastic bag and put it face down on a cloth in front of him.

"Have you got a coin?" said Jesse.

Annie handed him a ten-pence piece. Gently, Jesse started to work at the little nails keeping the frame in place. "You have to be so careful with these things. Sometimes the paint gets stuck to the wood. At the Wallace they pulled off a chunk of a Lancret." Slowly he lifted the frame away. The picture suddenly looked vulnerable and much smaller and Annie felt a rush of tenderness towards it. Jesse turned it over and looked along the edge.

"Come and see," he said. "There are two edges to the picture. The original painting has been laid on top of a new canvas. It's called re-lining," he explained.

"What does that mean?" asked Annie.

"Over time, the original canvas deteriorates and the paint can literally fall away. A skilled conservator can, millimetre by millimetre, peel away the old cloth leaving just the layers of paint and fix those to a new canvas or panel backing. It often goes wrong. Many pictures have been ruined this way but there aren't many alternatives: canvas degrades after a hundred years; sooner if the painter did not prepare their ground properly."

Annie ran her finger gently along the edge. "There are three ridges to this picture," she said. "Could that mean it's been relined twice?"

Jesse picked up the small torch and shone it up and down the edge of the painting. "You're right. That would make it a few hundred years old."

Annie let out a low whistle. "I think I'd better stop stuffing you in my backpack," she said to the painting.

Turning the picture over, Jesse shone his torch across the back of the canvas. "Look at this stamp; owners often leave a mark more indelible and visible than the artist's signature. It's part of the impulse to possess. There are pictures in the National Gallery and the Wallace with the Duke of Milan and Charles I's crest."

"'I was here,' kind of thing?" Annie asked.

Jesse nodded and went over to the sink. Filling a bowl with warm water, he carried it carefully back to the table. He dampened a small sponge and ran it over the surface of the painting.

"Is this really a good idea?" Annie asked nervously.

"You can often get rid of superficial dirt this way: smoke stains, everyday fug. Just like washing your hands." The yellow sponge turned a muddy brown as he rubbed gently at the picture's surface.

"Pouring water on troubled oil," Annie said softly.

"Sometimes whole figures and trees appear just by doing this, but this one is so dirty, it's made very little difference.

Now we have to get a bit tougher." He unscrewed the glass bottle, unleashing the sharp sweet smell of white spirit.

"Have you done this before?"

"On my own pictures, yes. I use it to rub out oils."

"Rub out! Stop now. You might make a hole," said Annie.

Jesse put the cotton wool down. "You're right but the alternative is to take it home, prop it up on your mantelpiece and enjoy it."

Annie searched his face for signs of sarcasm but instead she saw a kindly expression.

"I feel strangely protective about it," said Annie. "Silly, it's only a piece of cloth and oil and wood."

"Good art is affecting; that's its point." He smiled at her. "Let's consider your options. Here's a painting measuring about eighteen by twenty-four inches. The composition is lovely, a glade in a park, a dancer, a man at her feet. There are trees overhanging, sunlight coming from top left, but it's so dirty that it's difficult to make out their faces or the brushstrokes the painter used. So how do you tell who it's by or even roughly when it was painted?"

"We already know that it's a few hundred years old."

"It would be fun to narrow that down a bit, wouldn't it? It certainly looks French in style—you found that out at the Wallace by holding it up next to other works of art."

"What would that prove?"

"All artists have unique handwriting that distinguishes them. A Rembrandt horse is completely different from a van Dyck horse; a tree by Constable is totally individual and so is one by van Eyck. Your picture's trees and compositions look like a style known as *fête galante*. The problem is, though, that all great art and artists have hangers-on and copyists, so how do you tell what is the real McCoy?"

Annie wondered what he was talking about.

"I was just looking at a new book by the expert Delores Ryan called *Watteau's Women*."

"What a coincidence—I cooked for her last night."

"She is not someone one forgets, though as a mere guide, she hardly notices me. Her thesis is based on identifying the artists' models. Most painters relied on the same models so it's a kind of mix-and-match school of attribution."

"Sounds like upmarket gossip."

"Many a career has hinged on excavating the private life of artists. Most artists painted and repainted the same people. Delores has written books and curated exhibitions around the identity of sitters and she has built an enormous database around who they were and when they sat for particular artists. Show Delores a group portrait by David and she'll tell you the name of every person in it. She can cross-reference paintings and painters, find out who was sleeping with who, who got paid what. Like I said before: it's detective work."

"And if the people in my picture didn't fit her list of models?"

"She would discredit your picture."

"That sounds limited," said Annie.

"It's not just Delores," Jesse explained. "A Rembrandt is only a Rembrandt if Ernst van de Wetering and his Rembrandt Research Project endorse it. John Richardson, Picasso's old friend and biographer, could out a fake from a hundred yards."

"Is Delores the only expert in this period?"

"It's down to her or Trichcombe Abufel. His work is based on careful scholarship and provenance. He forensically examines every aspect of the painted surface and every place that picture might have hung."

"Great, let's call him."

"He's a virtual hermit, notoriously difficult to see."

"How can a picture's identity be decided by just two people?"

"Art is big business but ultimately authenticity is subjective and the only way to prove that a picture is 'right' is through circumstantial evidence. The older the painting, the harder it is to identify. Most of the time it's guesswork and for the French eighteenth century, Delores and Abufel are the most trusted guessers."

Annie looked around the studio, intrigued by this guide-cum-artist. There were stacks of books on every surface: monographs of artists, letters of artists, biographies of artists. On one wall there, he had pinned drawings and some reproductions of Old Master paintings. On an easel there was a large, mainly monochromatic painting of a meadow bound by trees on one side and a river on the other. Though unfinished and sketchy, she liked its grandeur and boldness. On another wall there was a photograph of a man and woman, arms entwined, laughing on a beach. It was in black-and-white and Annie guessed that these were his parents. She looked for signs of a girlfriend but could see none. Unlike her own spartan, sparsely furnished flat, this space, though roughly the same size, felt like somebody's home. It wasn't about the stuff or the work or the photographs, it was about an atmosphere.

She got up and walked around the sofa and looked at the thick paint-encrusted palette by the easel. "Surely science has advanced far enough to help out? Can't they analyse paint or even pick up samples of DNA?" she asked.

Jesse pointed to the black-and-white photograph of the man and the woman.

"Funny you should say that. My father was working on an ingenious scientific analysis project when he died. He thought he'd found a way of fingerprinting paint in much the same way that we fingerprint a criminal."

"What happened?"

"He rang my mother to say that he'd cracked it and was on his way home. But he never arrived. He was found the next morning under Battersea Bridge. The odd thing is that his wallet, keys, money were still in his briefcase, only his computer and notebooks were missing."

"Was it an accident?"

"The police claimed it was suicide." Jesse hesitated. "It meant they could close the case. But my father would never ever have committed suicide. He adored life. Adored my mother. Adored us. Adored his work. My guess, though I have never been able to prove it, is that there were people in the art world who were terrified of his discovery. There's a lot more money in fakes than there is in proving authenticity," said Jesse.

Annie detected a slight tremor in his voice. Turning away from her, he reached for a bottle with "turpentine" written on the outside.

"When did this happen?" she asked.

"About fifteen years ago, and then we moved to Shropshire."

"Perhaps that is what painting one field is about—trying to keep the memory of your father alive."

"You're the first person to say that out loud."

"I apologise—presumptuous of me."

"Perceptive, actually," said Jesse, taking up a piece of cotton wool in one hand. "I wish there was one person who could carry on his work, but he never explained his process to anyone. He had an assistant, Agatha, who understood it a bit, and is trying to pick up where he left off."

"Do you see much of her?"

"No, I don't. I should." Jesse picked up the bottle of turps. "Ready to glimpse into the underworld?"

Annie looked apprehensive.

"It's worth a try," he said gently.

She nodded.

"Come closer," said Jesse, tipping the bottle of turps against a swab of cotton wool. Annie held her breath as he began to rub the cotton wool over the top left-hand corner of the picture. The white spirit made a shiny lens on the dirty surface. For a brief moment they saw through the layers of brown varnish to a mass of delicate emeralds, yellows and limes. The brushstrokes danced. The drapery of the woman's dress floated in a spring breeze. Her plump bosom seemed to rise and fall under a satiny sheen. Jesse and Annie looked at each other with delight.

"Try the face," Annie whispered.

He rubbed the cotton wool gently over the woman's hair; they both bent forward expectantly. Again, as if by magic, the real picture revealed itself and her face swam through the layers of dirt. Jesse grabbed a pencil and began to sketch it on a small piece of paper.

"Look," he said, his excitement rising, "her face is made up of four major strokes—three delicate slices of pink and a dash of pale lemon. Yet in those subtle, gentle marks you get an idea of her character. She's feisty, uncompromising. You can tell, can't you, by the curve of her mouth, by the direct way she looks at you."

"Who do you think she was?" asked Annie. The white spirit began to evaporate and once again the face was obscured. Jesse shrugged.

"Shall we do him now?" she asked, pointing to the figure lying on the grass. Jesse nodded and tipped more white spirit on to a fresh piece of cotton wool. The man's face was partially hidden by a hat. Again, Jesse made a sketch, an aide memoire.

"Have you got anything stronger?" asked Annie.

Jesse laughed. "You are a funny mixture—cautious and impulsive. Ten minutes ago you were flinching at a sponge."

"So what else is in those bottles?" said Annie, ignoring the last remark.

"Acetone would be the next step."

"Nail varnish remover?"

Jesse nodded. "It can take off more than dirt. Particularly if our painter mixed varnish and paint to make a glaze; some painters were really sloppy. Watteau, for example, never bothered to prepare his canvases or clean his brushes; you get all sorts of dirt and bugs in with his paint. Turner was supposed to dilute his paint with beer."

"I still think we should have a go," urged Annie.

"It's your picture," said Jesse, nervously. "Pass me the blue bottle."

Pouring the water out of the bowl, Jesse added a few drops of acetone to some white spirit and, winding a small amount of cotton wool around an orange stick, he dipped it into the mixture. Hesitating, he straightened his shoulders and rubbed gently at the canvas. Nothing happened so he added another drop of acetone into the bowl. Again nothing. Annie noticed that tiny beads of sweat had broken out on his forehead. He added another drop, then got up and, flicking some switches, bathed the room in harsh light.

"One can't rush these things," he said, wiping his hands on his suit. In the drawer of the large bureau he found a set of magnifying lenses and strapped them on to his head. His hand shook slightly as he poured another drop of acetone into the bowl. Then he stopped. "This is too risky; I don't want to make a mistake. We could take it to Dad's friend Agatha at the National Gallery. She'd know what to do."

"Thank you for helping me," said Annie, smiling at him.

"Maybe you'd like some dinner?"

"Yes, some time that would be nice," said Annie non-committally. She wished he hadn't asked. The thought of any emotional entanglement made her feel sick. Suddenly she wanted to get away from this helpful man.

"Perhaps I could have your number?"

"I have yours!" Annie said firmly.

"I hope you call."

Annie smiled. He wasn't her type—there was no point pretending he was.

Chapter 10

"Delores Ryan called for you," said Marsha, the receptionist, to Annie. "Here's her number."

"Surely she wants to talk to Rebecca?" Annie replied.

"No, she mentioned something about cooking."

A few days later, when Rebecca and her father were abroad, Annie found herself outside Delores Ryan's apartment in Stockwell at eleven o'clock in the morning. From the outside, it was an unprepossessing, 1950s block, like so many others in that part of London, just off a main road. The communal areas were run down and Annie had to pick her way past discarded toys and a wheelless bicycle. Annie checked the address again and rang the bell hesitantly. On a whim, she had brought the picture along.

To her surprise, a maid, dressed formally in black with a white frilly apron, opened the door and led Annie along a narrow corridor. Once inside, Annie entered a different world; etchings and drawings were carefully placed on damask-covered walls. The maid's court shoes made a clack-clack on the parquet floor; Annie's trainers squeaked noisily. At the end of the passage, two double doors opened into a large, low-ceilinged room with drawn, heavy brocade curtains. The only light came from a table lamp spilling a little pool of brightness on to a leopardskin-print carpet.

"Madame Delores is at brunch," the maid said in a south London accent. "She will return shortly."

"Thanks."

The maid held out her hand. Annie stepped forward to shake it.

"Your coat," the maid said.

"I'll keep it, but thank you," said Annie, blushing, glad for the gloom around her. Taking the picture out of her rucksack, she propped it on a tapestry-backed chair.

"There's got to be another light. Can't see you properly," she said to the painting. Her eyes flicked around the room, searching for a switch or a lamp. The furniture was arranged to form little groups of tables and dainty chairs. Everything was on a small scale: slim backs balanced on finely turned legs; tabletops were piled high with books, objects and miniature boxes. There were several standard lamps with heavily fringed shades. Running her fingers around the bulbs and down the stems, Annie felt for a switch. Her hair caught in a fern, it frightened her and she jumped back, knocking a fist-sized china pug on to the ground. She held her breath. Don't break, please, she prayed, watching it bounce across the carpet and come to a halt below a golden harp. Nervously Annie examined it. She couldn't see any chips. Putting it back, she decided it would be safer to wait in one place. She tried to sit still but soon got up and picked up a book, one of many written by Delores Ryan and left in neat piles.

Annie read the blurb on the dust jacket about Watteau: "French painter (10 October 1684–18 July 1721) whose brief career spurred the revival of interest in colour and movement. He was responsible for revitalising the waning Baroque idiom that became known as Rococo." Looking at the other books by Delores in the stack, Annie saw *Watteau and the Court of Louis XIV; Watteau and Music;* and the most recent, *Watteau's Women: The Importance of the Model in the Artist's Oeuvre.*

Taking up the last book, she flicked through the pages. Delores's premise, as Jesse had explained, was to match sketches and drawings of people in each of the paintings and show how the painter had revisited the same subjects again and again. Annie was not particularly interested in this; to her it seemed obvious that an artist would repaint the same composition, or person. But she was fascinated by the preparatory drawings and how the compositions evolved before her eyes as Watteau played with different arrangements of figures, hands, glances and clothes until he found the pose that worked. Sometimes a finger moved an inch to the left or right but those tiny adjustments made all the difference to the success and strength of a composition.

As she turned the pages, Annie saw that the same woman cropped up again and again throughout his work. Turning to the foreword, Annie read. "During his short life, Antoine Watteau found little comfort in love. He was a sickly loner and a misanthrope who was never recorded as marrying. All his passions were reserved for his drawing and painting. However, in her ground-breaking new work, world-acclaimed scholar Delores Ryan shows that Watteau did form deep attachments and identifies the great love of his life as Charlotte Desmares, whose stage name was Colette." Annie read that this famous actress's career had started at the age of eight in 1690. "A renowned beauty, she became the mistress of the Duc d'Orléans, the nephew of King Louis XIV and the future

Regent of France. By association, Charlotte became one of the most influential women at court. Far more than a pretty face, Charlotte was a shrewd collector, leaving thirty-seven great works by Italian, French and Dutch masters."

Lifting her painting from the sofa, Annie placed it next to Delores's book. Flicking through the pages, she tried to match the woman in her painting with any of the reproductions before her. There were likenesses but nothing startling. Annie started on other parts of the body. On one page there was a sketch of a pair of hands resting in a lap; though Annie had trouble seeing through the heavy varnish, she thought that there were similarities in the way the sitter rested her thumb on her index finger, the long tapered fingers, the perfectly formed nails.

There was a snuffling and scuffling outside the door. Annie quickly placed the painting back on the sofa and closed the book. She realised that she had been waiting an hour. Moments later, the handle turned and two fat pugs waddled into the room, barking at Annie before sitting down on either side of a pretty padded armchair. Delores appeared moments later, huffing and puffing nearly as much as her animals. Around Delores's neck there was a confection of ruffles. These glowed white, apart from the stains of tomato and egg that had clearly strayed during the journey from fork to mouth. Delores had a large double chin, running from ear to ear, but within that blubbery frame there was a pretty, fine-featured face with bright china-blue eyes and a bee-stung mouth.

"So tell me," Delores said, kicking off a pair of kitten-heeled mules made from pink silk with gold edging, "what are Memling and Rebecca like to work for?" She had a tinkling voice, delicate, musical, quite out of proportion to her size.

"I have signed a confidentiality agreement," Annie replied.

"How dull," said Delores, looking disappointed. "I have eaten with the Winklemans for twenty years and your dinner was the first decent meal they have served. You did very well."

Annie blushed.

"Do you know anything about *fêtes galantes*?" Delores smiled condescendingly at Annie.

"Not really," Annie admitted.

"It's shorthand for the pursuits of the idle rich in the courts of Louis XIV and XV and I think it would make rather an amusing and appropriate theme for an art-world dinner, don't you think?"

Annie didn't know whether to agree or demur so she looked at one of the pugs.

"You did the Caravaggio evening so amusingly—how would you do mine?" Delores pressed.

Annie thought about her painting.

"What about creating a beautiful glade, a clearing in a wood, bowers of roses and spring flowers, a statue. The mood of the food has to be flirtatious, coquettish, light and ornate." Annie spoke quickly; her eyes shone with excitement as she thought of the evening's possibilities, of the dishes she could research and try and make.

"You are hired!" said Delores, clapping her hands together.

Annie's spirits sagged. "I would love to, but I can't. I don't have the time to do this assignment justice."

"Aren't you owed any holiday?" Delores asked. "It's to celebrate my sixtieth birthday—I want it to be a night that no one will ever forget. My friends are such a jaded lot."

Annie tried to keep her enthusiasm at bay but could not help making a suggestion. "There should be a dress code—choose one of the pictures in the Wallace—I can't remember the names," she suggested.

"You seem to know an awful lot."

"I was just reading your book."

"How much will the dinner cost?"

"It would be terribly expensive."

"Your budget is five thousand pounds."

"Five thousand pounds!" Annie could not believe what she was hearing.

"Isn't that enough? It would not include the hire of the room or the wine but would have to cover staff and sous chefs and catering equipment."

Annie shook her head in disbelief. It was more money than she had ever seen. Again Delores misunderstood the signs.

"Okay, six thousand for the food and I will pick up the tabs for the set dressing and catering equipment. Your own fee, the ingredients, and the wages of the staff will have to be taken from that."

"For how many?" asked Annie.

"Fifty, sit down. Can you do it?"

Annie nodded. It was crazy. Of course she couldn't do it. The dinner for Memling and Rebecca was a fluke.

Annie suddenly became aware that the only noise in the room was the heavy breathing and snuffling of the pugs. She looked up and saw Delores considering her thoughtfully.

"How old are you?" she asked.

"Thirty-one," Annie replied.

"No husband or children. Left it a bit late. So did I. You and I have to make our careers our lovers; work is the only thing one can rely on, isn't it?" Delores took a small gold compact out of a pocket and, flicking it open, examined her nose. "The date is the first of April, but don't make a fool out of me."

Delores looked at the door, as if she was expecting Annie to simply evaporate.

"Actually, I have brought something—would you mind looking at it?" Annie reached over to the chair and handed the painting to Delores. "I got it in a junk shop."

Delores looked at the picture propped on the chair. "Do you know how many people buy things in junk shops thinking they've discovered a masterpiece?"

"No."

"If I took even a few seriously there would be no time to write my books," Delores continued. "It's very tiring being a world expert. Let me see it." Delores held out her hand dismissively. Annie handed her the painting.

"Shall I turn on a light?"

"It's not necessary," said Delores, taking a small torch from her pocket and shining it over the picture's surface. The bright light bounced ghoulishly back on to her face. Delores spat on to the canvas and rubbed the foaming spit over the surface, muttering inaudibly, then heaved her body off the chair and waddled over to the window.

"Pull the curtain back," commanded Delores. Annie got up and drew the heavy curtain; below, two boys loitered outside a doorway, one picking his nose extravagantly. Delores spat again and this time, rubbed harder at the surface before turning to Annie.

"It's a nineteenth-century copy in the style of Watteau. They were mass-produced for the Victorians. Very few could and can afford the real thing," Delores said, crossing the room and lowering her body back into the chair.

"How can you tell just like that?" asked Annie.

"It's my life. It's what I do. Day in, day out."

"But you only looked at it for a few seconds."

"I really don't need more time," said Delores, tapping her nose. "The great Bernard Berenson once said, 'Scholarship is largely a question of accumulated experience upon which your spirit sets unconsciously.' I feel it in my gut." She handed the picture back to Annie.

Annie could not help feeling disappointed. Though it was ridiculous to think that she had found something of merit in a junk shop, there had still been a glimmer of hope, something to show for her relationship with Robert.

"Don't be upset!" said Delores. "I'll tell you what. I'll give you twenty pounds for it."

"I paid more than that."

"So you just threw away even more money! If we could buy masterpieces in junk shops, we'd be multi-billionaires."

Annie nodded sadly. Delores was right.

"You are an interesting cook and a lousy judge of art—I am a rotten cook and a brilliant connoisseur. That's the right way round. Now cheer up and toddle off, dear girl—time for my afternoon nap." Delores pointed at the door. "Send me menus in the next fortnight."

Placing the painting carefully in her rucksack, Annie walked out of the room and along the corridor. When she got to the top of the stairs she started to run, out of the apartment block, down the stone steps and along the street.

Less than two miles away, at Tate Modern, Vlad walked alone through a retrospective of the artist Damien Hirst, who, Vlad noted, was a few years older than he was. A week ago he had not heard of the Tate or Hirst, but in the last few days Barty had arranged for several experts to talk to the Russian about art and now for him to meet Ruggiero De Falacci, a dealer famous for regularly outperforming his colleagues by multiples of five. This year, when the art index had, for the first time since the last dip in 1990, fallen to −3.28 per cent, Ruggiero's clients were still up by 16 per cent.

Vlad had arrived early and walked into the first room, devoted to works by the artist done when he was in his twenties; these included brightly coloured pots, an upended hairdryer whose hot air kept a ping-pong ball bobbing happily in mid-air above it, and a messy painting of brightly coloured spots. When I was that age, Vlad thought, I was working underground in a coalmine a hundred feet deep, considering my first murder. He wondered how he would have translated that experience into art. Hirst's naïve and colourful work demonstrated that the artist had enjoyed a relatively sheltered life.

In the next rooms there were fish and a shark and a calf suspended in formaldehyde in glass tanks. Vlad shuddered, trying to imagine what his brother would look like pickled. That would be truly shocking, he thought wryly, seeing a dead man rather than a dead fish. Walking through the rooms he saw the artist try out the same ideas in different forms: life, death and spots over and over again. Vlad tried to be moved or interested in these themes, tried hard to feel and understand what Hirst was telling him. Nothing happened. Looking around at the other visitors, staring earnestly into the mouth of a shark or the back end of a cow, Vlad felt bewildered and slightly humiliated: why did these objects do so little for him? Wasn't he supposed to have some transformational, transcendental reaction? He supposed it was the poor educational system in Smlinsk or the vodka in his mother's breast milk.

Vlad decided to try harder and looked the shark straight in the mouth, willing the animal to transport him from the vast empty spaces of the Tate Modern to somewhere else. He wasn't sure what or where this other destination was supposed to be. Please, Mr. Hirst, he prayed silently, spirit me from this group of earnest bystanders, away from London, from my loneliness, away from my issues with the Office of Central Control. Reach out and tell me that you understand my difficulties and my dilemmas. Vlad imagined that he was whitebait swimming up the open jaws into the belly of mutual understanding and willed Hirst and his strange beasts to swallow his feelings. But when Vlad opened his eyes, he was still stuck in front of the torpid beast in this temple of illusion.

Vlad walked on through the exhibition. The artist, he decided, was like so many others, nothing more than a one-trick pony. Spots, flies and dead things all repackaged and rearranged in different orders, on different backgrounds and in varying formations. Still, Vlad thought, most don't have even one new idea and just dumbly follow previous generations, repeating the same patterns and mistakes over and over again. Vlad's father and grandfather had been miners and their forebears had slaved in either the feudal or the communist systems. Only one small idea set Vlad apart from his father—to get away from Smlinsk. Like Hirst, Vlad had just been repeating that same thought over and over again: everything he did, whether it was a business deal or a murder, was to put distance between himself and his hometown.

A few months ago Vlad would never have wasted hours in a gallery. Recreation was a distant dream. Only now that he had great swathes of time could he begin to have hobbies. This was why art was such an incalculable luxury: it sent out a message saying, "I have time to subcontract all the menial, dull chores out to others; I waste hours in idle contemplation of a piece of cloth covered in spots; I am an art lover; I am time-rich. I can mooch about in a sea of pickled sharks."

Pushing through some plastic doors, Vlad found himself in an artificially heated room where live butterflies feasted before dying. He looked around at the endless circle of life and how, once dead, broken corpses were stuck to large canvases on the wall. Again Vlad thought about his brother. Instead of butterflies he saw hundreds of tiny suspended Leonards. Feeling panic rise in his throat, Vlad took off his leather jacket and forced himself to breathe slowly. These were butterflies, not brothers, he told himself, pushing open a plastic door and leaving the steamy morgue for the cool of the next room.

He walked past cabinets full of medical instruments and surgical tools and into another room where the artwork was a huge blackened sun made of dead flies. Vlad thought, It takes a lot of shit and death to make a world. Suddenly he got Hirst: the man was a brilliant comedian making a joke out of life and the art world and all those who took it seriously. Vlad almost sprinted into the next room and, getting there, laughed out loud when he saw that every work of art was studded with diamonds and backed with gold leaf. For Vlad the artist's message was simple: you can encase anything, add jewels and precious metals, but it's still the same old shit. You might think you have got out of Smlinsk, you might be dressed in posh clothes and stuck in a fancy multi-million-pound house, but you're still just a turd covered in diamonds—you are still the same old Vlad.

Vlad had been so engrossed in his reverie that he failed to spot Ruggiero De Falacci shadowing him through the rooms. As he came to a stop beside a gold-plated vitrine filled with cigarette stubs, the man sidled up to him.

"Clearly you are a person of exceptional discernment and intellectual capabilities," Ruggiero said in a slightly breathy but appreciative voice.

"What?" said Vlad.

"I was watching you look at the art and saw that you totally understood what the artist is saying." The advisor's tone was honeyed.

"I get it," said Vlad.

"Ruggiero De Falacci at your service," said the man, bowing slightly. "Barty has told me so much about you."

"Expensive?" Vlad asked, looking around him.

"Exceedingly," Ruggiero purred mellifluously.

"Get me that one," said Vlad, pointing to the fly heap. "More diamonds. More gold."

"These are one-off artworks," Ruggiero said. "Mr. Hirst doesn't do commissions."

"Tell him name price."

"I will do my very best. Perhaps Damien will make an exception."

Ruggiero tried to keep the smile from his face. That Barty was a clever weasel, worth every cent of his large commission.

Vlad walked out of the Tate and slid into the rear seat of his new pale blue Maybach.

Staying south of the river, the car passed Lambeth Palace and turned over the bridge opposite the Houses of Parliament. Looking out of the window, Vlad had to admit that though London was not Moscow, it was a beautiful city. But all pleasant thoughts evaporated as the traffic slowed to a crawl. Money could buy him a smart car and a chauffeur but it couldn't clear the roads. In Moscow every person worth anything had police outriders to clear the way. London, Vlad thought, is so backward. Thirty minutes passed and they were only just on Pall Mall.

"There is a demo, sir," said the chauffeur to Vlad, who sat in the back looking out of the window. "Complaining about Israel, most likely."

"Late," said Vlad, tapping his Rolex impatiently.

"Doing my best, sir."

Vlad stared out of the window at the angry youths waving placards. "Out of Settlements," "Not your promised land, our homeland." Where was his homeland now? Was it here in England? In Smlinsk? Or somewhere in between? Could he go back again? Vlad knew he could never go back. He had seen too much, done too much. He had lost the ability to talk to the people he grew up with but had yet to learn how to talk to anyone else.

In the last few weeks, Barty had insinuated himself into every aspect of Vlad's life; finding the Russian a smart group of friends, a larger house and a better tailor. There were intensive English lessons and "improving" events. Barty was "preposterous" and "outlandish" but he was also amusing, irreverent and fantastically useful. Last night they had started at a drinks party at Downing Street where, following a donation to party funds, Vlad met the prime minister and his chancellor; later, they caught the first act of *Tosca* at the Opera House, missing the rest to attend Paris Hilton's launch of a new shampoo, and then went to M. Power Dub's for dinner. The evening ended with a visit to one club called the Box and another called Lulu's. For Vlad, the evening was like sitting on a carousel, spinning round and round, getting dizzier and dizzier.

Half an hour later, in the far corner of the Zianni restaurant in London's Brook Street, Vlad sat down opposite another émigré, Dmitri Voldakov. Although he was only a year older than Vlad, Dmitri had become his mentor since arriving in London and it was a huge relief to talk in his native tongue. Like Vlad, Dmitri had been summoned one afternoon to the Office of Central Control and offered two exit strategies: the left door led to prison, the right to the airport. Dmitri chose London because he liked soccer and it had the most advantageous tax system.

A waiter approached their table and shook out Vlad's napkin with the flourish of a matador approaching a ten-ton bull.

"We will have truffles in scrambled eggs to start, lobster pasta for main course. Château Latour 1960 to drink," Dmitri told the waiter. Then he told Vlad in Russian to take the batteries out of his phones. "These things act like microphones to the authorities." He also insisted on covering the glasses with napkins. New technology meant lasers beamed from space could listen in to any conversation via convex materials.

After knocking back a few glasses of wine and deliberating upon the latest Chelsea matches, Vlad gathered up his courage to ask his friend's advice.

"I have a problem," he confessed.

"No worries—I have good doctor," Dmitri said, patting Vlad on the arm.

"Not that kind. Money," said Vlad.

"Can't be!" Dmitri knew that Vlad's tin mines were producing millions of dollars of metal a month.

Vlad looked around the restaurant to make sure that they were not overheard. "How to make the weekly payments."

"Ah. Yes," Dmitri said, tapping his nose. Like Vlad, he had to pay at least 30 per cent of his income to the Leader to guarantee his safety. Only last week, a fellow countryman who had fallen behind on his dues was found face down in St. Katharine's Docks.

Since 9/11 and anti-terrorism initiatives, transferring large sums of money from Britain had become increasingly difficult. Transferring money directly into Russia attracted too much unwanted attention.

Lowering his voice to a whisper, Dmitri told Vlad, "Alternate stocks and shares with art or jewels. Make drop at the safe house."

Vlad was about to ask for more details when an astonishingly beautiful woman sashayed towards their table. The whole restaurant fell into a silent appreciative hush. Next to the Europeans in the room, she looked like a thoroughbred horse let loose in a field of Shetland ponies.

"Lyudmila." Dmitri rose to kiss the apparition on her cheek. "Meet Vlad, a recent arrival."

Vlad could only nod. He felt a stab of disappointment upon seeing an enormous diamond on her third finger.

"Lyudmila is my fiancée," Dmitri said firmly.

Lyudmila smiled sweetly at Vlad. "See you around," she said and returned to her table of friends. Vlad saw that she had dropped her handkerchief on the floor and, pretending to tie up his shoelace, he bent down and placed the scented linen discreetly in his pocket.

"She was my art advisor," Dmitri said.

"Art?" said Vlad. If he bought art would he also find a Lyudmila?

"Barty set me up with her. He said that I needed a hobby and an advisor. I was not sure, until I saw her. Barty is a fucking genius."

Vlad nodded in agreement.

"She is also a genius," Dmitri said. "She made me buy an Andy Warhol for twenty-five million dollars last month; I was offered fifty million this morning. I will make a drop next week. Gold is far too volatile and rather heavy."

"I am also going to buy art," Vlad said.

Dmitri took hold of Vlad's wrist and squeezed it hard, hard enough to convince Vlad that the next piece of advice was not friendly.

"My friend, remember that I have monopoly on Damien Hirst, Andy Warhol, late Picasso—I have forty-four in storage waiting to give Leader. You can have rest," said Dmitri and then let go of Vlad's wrist.

Vlad shifted uncomfortably in his seat, thinking of a certain piece made of dead flies and diamonds, which he had already decided was a perfect metaphor for the regime back home. The Leader could hardly complain: after all, it was art. Dmitri, Vlad reasoned, need never know.

Neither man realised that the beautiful woman sitting at the adjacent table had a camera concealed in her earring. A few days later Dmitri received a package containing footage of Vlad purloining the handkerchief and a copy of a commission note for a new work by a certain artist. Dmitri interpreted these as declarations of war: he was in no doubt who would win.

Chapter 11

Hello.
I am still here.
And let's not forget that I am the hero of this story.
And far more interesting than food.
And longer lasting than love.
I am still here.
Moi.

Chapter 12

J esse walked along the Thames from his studio to his friend Larissa's apartment in Battersea. It was a crisp evening, the temperature hovered just above freezing, and the street lights cast wavy shadows on the water. Normally Jesse loved this walk but since meeting Annie he felt little enthusiasm for anything. Instead of racing from work to his studio, he had taken to sitting in the corner of pubs or catching early-evening movies. Unable to concentrate on much, his thoughts rarely strayed far from Annie, where she was, what she might be doing. Her absence smothered anything in his present.

Until meeting her, Jesse had taken a laissez-faire approach to romance; allowing women to pick him out, he'd had a succession of pleasant if domineering girlfriends who had decided, for reasons Jesse could never really understand, that he was a suitable consort. Sooner or later each had become frustrated with his ambivalence and inability to commit.

"What planet are you on these days?" Larissa Newcombe had called out two days earlier when he entered the Wallace Museum staff room. "Is your mind accompanying your body?"

"What? Sorry?" Jesse forced himself to stop thinking about Annie and back into the present.

Larissa burst out laughing. "You see. You're not really here." She patted the sofa beside her and Jesse sat down heavily. He liked Larissa, who swept through life swathed in brightly coloured silks, with feathers in her hair and heavy jewellery clanking from her wrists and neck, navigating the art world like a ship in full sail followed by a flotilla of admirers who'd read her many papers or books and who signed up to her lectures and attended her courses. Her subject, the depiction of music and musical instruments in seventeenth- and eighteenth-century art, was rarefied but Larissa's enthusiasm was boundless and infectious.

"You look like someone stepped on your mandolin. What's happened?"

"Nothing, that's the problem," Jesse said wearily.

"A woman!" Larissa clapped her hands together in delight. She had just submitted a lengthy piece on the use of tambours in Mannerist paintings and was ready for a little light relief. "Spare no detail," she commanded.

"That's the problem," Jesse admitted miserably. "There is no detail, there's nothing to report." He poured out details of every encounter, text message, cup of coffee and meaningful look. "She walked into the Frans Hals room, I looked up and straight into her face and I was lost. I didn't know where or who I was, as if she and I were the only figures in a featureless, noiseless room. I felt like Alice falling down the rabbit hole, but I am still falling, waiting to come out of the other side."

To his relief, Larissa didn't laugh. She could tell from the smudges below his eyes and the slight tremor in his voice that he was bewitched and clueless.

"How many texts have you sent her today?"

"Four."

"Yesterday?"

"Five."

"When did she last respond?"

"Two days ago. She said she would go to the British Museum as I suggested."

"The British Museum?"

"She found a picture in a junk shop. I offered to help her find out who it was by."

"Ingenious, using the picture as a hook to see her again."

"It's a nice picture," Jesse said shamefacedly.

"I have stooped to far worse ploys in the name of love," Larissa said. She pushed her chair back and, standing up, clapped her hands together. "The painting is going to have to play Cupid," she pronounced with satisfaction.

She insisted they plot over a decent bottle of wine and supper. Although they had been friends for many years, it was the first time Jesse had been to Larissa's home. He brought a bunch of narcissi, small, pale yellow and deliciously scented, which she put into a small jug and on to the table.

Jesse looked around. The tiny space was full of her collection of musical instruments, a cornucopia of strange-shaped drums, pipes and lyres. As she gathered the ingredients for dinner together, Larissa explained that a lute from Rome made an entirely different sound from one from Flanders and why the world's most beautiful violins came from one village, Cremona. Jesse momentarily forgot about Annie as he heard how Larissa matched the different instruments to particular kinds of music, a painstaking process of searching contemporary inventories, diaries and accounts.

Jesse sat on a bar stool while Larissa cooked. She flung the ingredients together in the same way as she dressed, extravagant dashes of colour and textures mixed together.

"Annie is a cook," Jesse said. "You should meet her." His voice, shot with excitement, rose slightly.

"I'd like to, very much," Larissa said. "She must be rather extraordinary to have this effect on you. In four years I have never seen you so bowled over."

"Knocked out, more like," Jesse said.

"One of the good things about falling in love," Larissa commented, "is that it makes you open and vulnerable; you end up in unexpected places."

"Like here?" Jesse laughed.

Later, sitting by her small three-bar electric fire, Larissa urged him to adopt a lighter but more tactical approach. The painting was a perfect foil for romance. He should present it as an opportunity for two people locked together into a common purpose, a quest against the odds. Solving the riddle of the painting would lead them on an adventure to different places and demand a variety of skills. Through their attempts to uncover the identity of the artist, Annie and Jesse would create shared experiences, which love needs to thrive. It didn't matter, Larissa argued, whether the picture was a masterpiece or a cheap reproduction, what mattered was that it became a cypher for seduction. Even if one expert discredited the work immediately, there was always another person's opinion to seek and another avenue to explore. That was the glorious thing about art: its value was entirely subjective.

It was nearly midnight when Jesse left and though the temperature had dropped to below freezing, he felt warmed by hope and good food. In his hand he held a piece of paper on which he and Larissa had plotted ways to see Annie again, all tied up with the steps necessary to authenticate her painting. The pubs had disgorged their last drinkers and the restaurants had shut, leaving the pavements free for Jesse and the odd dog walker. He wondered how surprised Agatha would be to hear from him after all these years and whether she'd agree to see Jesse, a strange girl and a small canvas. Jesse had, until now, studiously avoided any painful or avoidable reminders of his father and this included visiting the National Gallery, even though he missed some of the paintings as much as absent friends. Two of his worlds were about to collide.

Had Jesse looked up, at that moment, and into the back seat of the large black Mercedes travelling at speed down the Embankment, he would have seen Rebecca Winkleman driving home from a fundraiser at Battersea Power Station. Sponsored by Credit Russe, the evening was in aid of Breast Cancer Awareness and, for Rebecca, it had been a waste of time.

The seated dinner was held in the main atrium. Throughout dinner there had been an aerial bombardment of acrobats suspended from silk ropes and a display of indoor fireworks. Rebecca had sat next to a hedge-fund manager and opposite his art dealer. "I have made as much money off my art as off gilts," he informed Rebecca, never thinking to ask what she did or if she knew about art. Saul Franklin, his dealer, tried to put the manager right. "Freddie, you must know of Rebecca Winkleman of Winkleman Fine Art, a world-renowned connoisseur of Old Master paintings?"

Freddie Hedge Fund ignored him. "How much is my Richter worth these days, Saul?"

"Twenty-two million, Freddie."

"Did you hear that, lady? That's what I call a return. How much did I pay for it Saul?"

"Eight million," Saul said wearily.

"What about my Warhol?"

"You paid eleven and it's worth eighteen."

"Can you get me any more like that?"

"I offered you a car crash last week."

"It might upset the kids. Can you get me a Chairman Mao?"

On Rebecca's other side was a member of the British aristocracy who had a title, a dwindling fortune and a disproportionate sense of his own importance.

"That man," Lord Clifton said, nodding at Freddie Webb, "is the kind who has to buy his own furniture."

Hoping that the noble lord might want to dispose of his family's last good picture, a Goya, Rebecca tried hard to engage him in conversation, but she knew as little about breeding Herefordshire cattle as he did about de Hooch or Canaletto.

It was a long, tedious evening. Dinner wasn't served until 10 p.m., followed by interminable speeches with the director praising the generosity of Credit Russe and various benefactors, including Freddie Webb. Rebecca could think of little apart from Memling's missing picture. Her father refused to let her enlist their network of spies and informants: the search had to be kept secret. The art world is so small, he reasoned, that sooner or later the culprit would surface. Rebecca again thought of her father's tremulous voice, his refusal to fully explain the reasons for wanting the picture back so urgently. Memling left his daughter in no doubt that unless it was recovered, their livelihood was in peril.

It was midnight before Rebecca managed to get away. She hadn't drunk or eaten much and though it was late, she could fit in a few hours' work. Slipping out of the grand hall, she hurried down the broad staircase to freedom. As her car sped through London, Rebecca tried to imagine what her father was hiding. Perhaps as a younger man he was involved in a dealing ring, like the one which had bought a Duccio di Buoninsegna Madonna and Child for a few thousand and sold it to the National Gallery for £140,000. Or was it the work of a forger and would humiliate or discredit Memling? One by one Rebecca considered and discounted these theories. Nothing quite made sense.

As her car pulled up outside the rear entrance to the office, Rebecca saw a figure slip out of the back door, unlock a bicycle and pull on a woollen cap.

"Who is that?" Rebecca asked her driver.

"Looks like your chef, Annie, madam," Ellis replied. "She often works late."

Peering through the tinted windows at Annie's disappearing figure, Rebecca knew for certain that this was the person
in the CCTV footage, the one who had bought the picture.
Rebecca shivered—it had to be more than an extraordinary
coincidence. No wonder her father was frightened: it took a
sophisticated and determined enemy to mastermind an infil-
tration of their business.

Ellis opened the door and held out a hand.

"Are you all right, madam?" he asked. "You look very pale."

Rebecca took his hand. Her legs felt weak and her heart
was beating. The same girl had worked for her husband, for
her, had even eavesdropped on a private dinner. What bug-
ging devices had she secreted in the Winkleman household?
What had she already found out?

"Madam? Can I get you something?" Ellis asked with
concern.

"No, thank you, Ellis. It is under control," said Rebecca,
trying to stay calm. She walked briskly to the back door and,
punching in the code, let herself into the building. Closing the
door behind her, she leant against the wall to steady herself.
Her next moves were crucial and she wondered whether to
pack up the chef's belongings or call the police. No, Rebecca
thought, much better to keep her enemy close at hand. She
went straight to her office bureau, opened the secret drawer
and checked to make sure her pistol was loaded.

Chapter 13

I imagine my horror at the latest turn of events: the young man has found a restorer. The mere mention of the word sends shivers through my paintwork. The atrocities committed in the name of restoration; look no further than a certain Velázquez in London or a Leonardo in Paris. I am so delicate that whole swathes of my composition could disintegrate in the wrong hands. Though my patina is smeared with layers of soot, candle smuts, human effluents, tobacco smoke and varnish, the prospect of a restorer let loose with bottles of noxious spirits fills me full of quaking, mind-blowing terror. I long to be in sparkling mint condition again; I am frightened that during the process, I will literally fall to pieces.

My conception was hurried, urgent and magnificent: my master was desperate to catch the feeling of first love, the thrill of emotion. I was painted at top speed with dirty brushes and a mixture of oils, ointments, alcohol and even paint intended for walls. If you look closely at my skyline you'll see a tiny fly embedded in the top left-hand corner. It was buzzing around that afternoon in 1702 and had (in my opinion) the good fortune to be immortalised, embalmed in my albumin and impasto. My master created that wild, vibrant shimmering foliage by mixing a slosh of wine, chicken soup and oil paint. Sometimes he used his fingers, other times a brush, a palette knife or even his sleeve in his urgent mission to capture in paint his orgasm of desire.

I digress. Back to that afternoon. We were met by a woman at a side entrance of the National Gallery. Whippet-thin, straight-backed, grey-haired with heavy-rimmed glasses, she wore plain clothes in the dowdiest way, with no spark or sartorial imagination. I hoped that she approached her work with the same lack of self. So many restorers are *artistes manqués*, believing they can improve on an artist's work. The woman—her name is Agatha—greeted Jesse like a long-lost friend, holding him tight to her scrawny chest. He was polite and didn't struggle. My mistress looked the other way, clearly a little embarrassed.

"You look more like your father than ever," said Agatha, wiping a tear from the corner of her eye. "David, his father, and I worked together for nearly twenty years," she told my mistress.

What was Annie supposed to say to that? How nice? How interesting? She smiled nervously.

"Now come upstairs," said Agatha. "I'll make you tea; we can chat and you can show me the surprise."

Annie looked longingly towards the closed door.

One was relieved not to walk through the main collection and be sneered at by old friends. Away from the public areas, the place is a real rabbit warren. Agatha led us at breakneck speed down twisty corridors into a cavernous groaning lift and up another narrow staircase. Suddenly, we were in the eaves above Trafalgar Square, in a huge room lit by a north-facing skylight. Along one wall there were shelves lined with glass jars filled with different pigments. On a large table, brushes stood to attention in metal pots. The floor was painted black and across it were easels and palettes and pigments, lights, cameras and other paraphernalia. I suppose it was a kind of studio. You see, my master didn't have a place or assistants to keep his paints or brushes in order. Indeed, he never had a fixed abode—for long, anyway. His restless spirit always moved him onwards. Most pictures left his studio soon after they were completed.

He had three protectors: his dealer, Monsieur Julienne; his principal collector, the stupendously wealthy Pierre Crozat; and his biographer the Comte de Caylus. All three gave him lodgings in return for drawings. Dirty old Caylus (a wealthy, seasoned traveller who had the temerity and bad taste to write a nasty biography of my master) liked pictures of naked women in naughty poses, so he employed lots of models for my master to paint. But Antoine was a libertine more in spirit than in action. Indeed, he was so shy he could hardly order a glass of wine without collapsing into palpitations.

As a character, he was both scathing and nervous—not, one has to admit, an endearing combination. Though he received no formal education he was an intellectual, wonderfully well read and thoughtful. Aside from drawing and painting, reading and music were his twin passions. The only thing he disliked deeply was himself. Those assuming that a modicum of success might have soothed his critical soul and inflated his self-esteem are wrong. He was even more sickened and self-disgusted. Night after night he would lie sobbing beneath paintings by Rubens and Titian, lamenting his lack of ability, his cack-handed attempts to measure up to his heroes.

A slightly lesser shade of fury was levelled at the importunate who disturbed his labours. I remember one incident when a miniaturist who had acquired a small oil stopped by the studio to ask Antoine to fix some "minor imperfection" in the cloudscape. My master looked from the miniaturist to the composition and asked for clarification. "Where exactly do you find it lacking?" he asked.

The miniaturist pointed to the top left-hand corner. Without pausing, my master took some cleaning fluid and erased the whole canvas, save for the offending cloud. "Perhaps you will be happier now," he said, shoving the offender and the ruined work out on to the street.

Where was I? I get a little lost. So would you if you were three hundred years old.

Agatha, the restorer, and Jesse chatted on about his dead father and how much she missed him. Officially they were colleagues but any damn popinjay could see she loved him; history doesn't relate if the feelings were returned. They bored on with endless reminiscences, each as scintillating as a wet sponge on a cold winter's day. Annie gave up looking interested and wandered around looking at other paintings. Finally they came to me.

Agatha shone a strong light on my surface before placing a strange contraption, huge magnifying goggles, on her head. Then, taking a wedge of cotton wool, she gently (I'll admit she was gentle) rubbed it over my surface.

"Where did you find this?" she said, turning to Annie.

"In a junk shop."

"Poor beauty," the restorer said, turning me over and examining my back.

It is not the first time a human has spent more time looking at my "other side." As we have established, there are all manner of interesting clues to be found there, including the age of my canvas, the stamps of those who have owned labels, dealers' descriptions, and so forth.

"It has been relined three or four times," Agatha said.

Jesse nodded. "So someone thought it was worth enough to do that?"

Agatha nodded. "It implies value. Or a sentimental attachment."

Taking a torch and magnifying glass, she shone it on my surface.

"There's one area here where we can see the quality of the work through the layers of dirt," she said, looking closely at the top right-hand corner of the picture. Taking another, stronger light, she passed the beam backwards and forwards over the foliage. "I am really interested in the fineness of painting of the leaves and in this patch of silk on her dress."

Putting on another pair of magnifying goggles, she stared even harder at the clump of bushes.

"If I am not mistaken that white smudge in the corner is a figure."

"I thought it was a cloud," Annie said, peering behind the foliage.

"It's a man dressed all in white. In fact, if my hunch is right, it could be Pierrot."

"Pierre who?" Annie asked.

Leaning back in her chair, Agatha said, "A character made famous in the late sixteenth century by the Italian *commedia dell'arte*. Sometimes Pierrot was portrayed as a wise clown or a buffoon, but he was always the innocent."

"Why would anyone put a clown into a love scene?" Annie asked.

"Pierrot was also the hapless and unsuccessful rival to Arlequin for the love of Columbine."

"So rather than being a painting about love on a summer's day, this might be saying the very opposite? It could be that all-too-familiar tale of its cruelty?" Annie said.

"Or just love's unlikeliness," Jesse added, gazing wistfully at Annie.

"The first and most famous Pierrot was by Antoine Watteau, done in about 1718 and now in the Louvre. It's a character so full of pathos and melancholia, so twisted with sadness, that most find it moving rather than ridiculous."

"I like the picture much more now that I see its darker side," Annie said.

"All good works of art are about complexity and emotion," Jesse said. "That's their power. They say something that we can't quite put into words."

"You remind me of your father when you talk like that," Agatha said, fighting away tears.

Jesse gave Agatha an awkward hug before steering the conversation back to *moi*.

"Why have so many generations painted this figure?" he asked, peering at the painting.

"Pierrot has become a universal symbol. From Cocteau to Picasso, Hockney . . ."

"Juan Gris," Jesse offered.

"Sickert," Agatha replied.

"Matisse," Jesse batted back.

"Modigliani."

"Max Beckmann."

"Chagall." Jesse laughed. "What about Paul Klee?"

"I love his *Head of a Young Pierrot*," Agatha agreed.

"How does it help us?" said Annie. She was feeling lost and slightly irritated by their sparring.

"At the time of your picture, there were only twenty artists painting Pierrot. Watteau was probably the first and best and then there were his followers Lancret and Pater."

"We could go to Paris to see the most famous version. It's in the Louvre," Jesse said to Annie.

"Perhaps," Annie said with little enthusiasm.

She did not need to go to France. I was the first.

The restorer picked me up and walked over to a side door, gesturing for Annie and Jesse to follow. The room was small and windowless, painted entirely black. When the restorer closed the door behind her, we were all stuck inside this tiny airless box.

"Are either of you claustrophobic?" she asked.

"Not yet," Annie said nervously.

Agatha picked up a large black lamp. "Annie, hold the picture up, please," Agatha asked. "Jesse, can you turn the main light off?"

We were plunged into immediate darkness. What on earth was the woman thinking? She flicked a switch and her contraption spluttered out a harsh violet-coloured light.

"Infrared light helps us to see through layers of paint," Agatha explained to Annie, "and most importantly, different campaigns."

"Campaigns?" Annie blinked. I could see she felt uncomfortable trapped in these strange circumstances. I could sympathise.

"It's the term given to the different times that a painting has been worked on or altered. Ultraviolet light is adjacent to visible light but it has a shorter wavelength. It helps me see gradations in surface and texture."

She passed the beam over my surface, moving the light backwards and forwards.

"Can you see there are tiny fluorescent dabs and flecks around the woman's face and again in this back corner?" she asked.

"How odd, why is it just on her face and not on his?" Annie asked, peering into my midst.

What they did not know yet was that my master had painted another face over *her* face at a later date. It was his way of managing rejection. He could not bear to part with her; he could not cope with seeing her. Like a thorn buried in his psyche, her memory was never expunged but it was, at least, hidden. The face on top belonged to a prostitute; it was as near to a joke as my master got.

"What is even odder is that the overpaint is barely discernible—it must have been done shortly after the original painting," said Agatha. "There have been occasions when people have altered faces to make the picture more commercial. The dealer Duveen made pictures more Hollywood-friendly by asking his restorer to make the Hoppners more like Joan Crawford, and Romneys like Douglas Fairbanks."

She moved to the top left-hand corner. "This campaign is clearer—you can see that someone retouched this part—a rather heavy restorer's hand—see how the paint sits here in a great clump—quite unlike the quality of painting in other areas. This is an absolutely fascinating case."

I could not agree more.

"Jesse, can you put the lights back on, please." Agatha flicked off her torch and led us back to the main studio.

"What do you think?" Annie asked her.

Agatha leaned back in her chair. "The main problem is the overpaint and old varnish. Removing it is highly perilous. Sometimes chipping and scraping at the topcoat takes off the underneath with it. But," Agatha said gently, "you have found something interesting. I don't know what, but I can confirm that it is old, that beneath these layers of grime and varnish, I think there is something fine, very fine. Would you let me keep it for a little while? I can work on it during the evenings."

My canvas shrank in horror. Work on it? What the hell does that mean? My mistress can't leave me here with all these bottles of acetone and other noxious chemicals.

"What will you do to it?" Annie asked.

"I would like to do a test on a small piece of the canvas, probably the top left corner. Working very slowly and gently, I'll take the grime and dirt off and see what's underneath it."

"I haven't got any money to pay you," Annie said.

"I would refuse payment. The painting has brought Jesse back into my life—I am very grateful for that." Agatha leant over and hugged him.

I am almost touched but most of all, I am scared—one slip and it is ruination.

I try and calm my feelings—vibrations are bad for my

canvas. At least I will be kept in a museum. Might even get some decent conversation. Across the room there's a great big Veronese—all stripped down—looking jolly dejected, if you ask me. Placed on an easel is a rather exquisite Grossart and most excitingly of all, I think I caught sight of a Giorgione lying on a table. My master adored Giorgione, utterly adored him.

"I will almost miss it," Annie said, holding me up.

"You won't have time to. This has to be a joint effort. I need information about who painted this painting and when. The more I know about the artist, the more accurate I can be. Different centuries and countries produce different types of paint and materials. It would help hugely to have an idea of when and where it was painted."

"Delores Ryan said it was a cheap copy," said Annie.

"You never told me that." Jesse looked at her, surprised.

"I forgot."

"Experts are not always right," said Agatha. "It is such fun proving them wrong," Agatha said firmly. "Jesse will make you a sketch. My hunch is this picture is approximately two hundred and fifty to three hundred years old. You've already taken it to the Wallace and seen similarities with those paintings, so it's likely to be French or Flemish." Agatha walked around the table in the centre of the room, talking out loud. "It could be a clever forgery," she said pensively. "But, I've yet to see a forger go to quite so much trouble with relining a canvas or quite so brilliantly coat it in layers of soot and smoke."

"We will take it to the British Museum together," Jesse said.

"Why?" Annie asked.

"You can go alone, of course," Jesse said, reddening.

"I didn't mean that—you talked about the British Museum before—why there?"

"They hold the British collection of drawings and etchings—you should start with the *catalogue raisonné*," Agatha said. "Those are inventories of someone's work normally captured around the time of their life in etchings. The British Museum

also has an almost unrivalled collection of drawings and etchings dating back from the early Renaissance."

Annie sat down heavily on the chair. "This still seems like
searching for a miracle in a haystack," she said.

"We don't have to go any further," Agatha said gently.
"I have lots of other work to get on with," she said, waving
her hand around her studio. "It's your choice, your picture."
Taking a piece of paper from a drawer, she started to write
some names down. "Start with Watteau, then Lancret, Pater,
Boucher and Fragonard. If they don't yield results, I will think
of others."

I could see what Annie was thinking—part of her was aghast
at this wild goose chase into an impenetrable world of arcane
practices. At the same time, though, her interest was piqued;
she wanted to find out how it worked. Most of all she wanted
me to be "good." Somehow my value and her self-esteem had
become entangled. If she discovered a lost masterpiece she
would become a person of taste and judgement.

In spite of myself I suddenly wanted this Agatha woman
to work on me. I wanted to be restored to the pantheon of
the greats, to take my rightful place with my friends, hang
on a damask wall, be talked about in hushed reverent tones,
be loved and admired and studied for who I really am. I also
wanted Annie to bathe in my glory and for her to be happy. It
is bizarre that after three hundred years I was getting properly
fond of an owner. Age was making me daft.

I watched her looking from me to Jesse to Agatha. There
was a short but intense silence until her face suddenly cracked
into a huge smile.

"Why not? Why on earth not!"

One must admit, one was quite pleased.

Chapter 14

For the third time in a week, Rebecca cancelled lunch and told Annie to leave her kitchen until further notice: she was to keep her phone on and not stray more than one hour from Winkleman Fine Art. Over the last fortnight, for reasons that none understood, Rebecca had become increasingly suspicious and untrusting of all her staff. Extra CCTV cameras were placed in the offices, access to the company's database was restricted and security guards were stationed in corridors and by the vaults. Rebecca was the first in and last out every day; all her routine meetings were cancelled and a permanent "do not disturb" sign was fixed to her door. Wanting to offer support, Annie knocked and offered to make her employer a cup of tea. "If you have time to make tea, you are not doing your job properly," Rebecca snapped. It never occurred to Annie that any of these measures were con-

nected to her, let alone to her painting; after all, she was just a
temporary chef, a woman of no importance.

Walking at a brisk pace, it took Annie ten minutes to get
from her office to the London Library. Winkleman Fine Art
had a corporate membership and for Annie, this was the best
perk of her new job. Hurrying down Berkeley Street, crossing
Piccadilly and cutting through an arcade, Annie dodged the
tourists and slipped down a side street into St. James's Square.
The library was an oasis of calm and contemplation. Annie
hung up her coat and made her way up the grand staircase
through a side door and climbed up the metal stairs and right
along a long row of books until she came to the section marked
Miscellaneous/Food. It was her fourth visit in the last ten days.

At the start of her research for Delores's dinner, Annie concentrated mainly on menus and how to prepare them, but the
food was only part of the story. French courtly life revolved
around protocol, intrigue, written and unwritten laws, and
the state banquet was simply another battlefield, the scene of
deadly strategies, mines and booby-traps, presided over by the
king. Careers were made and lost during a single course. The
more she found out, the greater the detail Annie wanted to
present. Though she could not reconstruct the nuances and
even the dangers inherent in courtly dining at Versailles, she
longed to re-create the mood and sense of occasion.

At Versailles there had been over two thousand workers
in the royal kitchens; Delores would have one, untrained. In
the Royal Courts, banquets divided into several services of
between two and eight courses: hors d'oeuvres, soups, main
dishes, puddings and fruit. How many should she prepare?
By the time Louis retired at 11:30 p.m., he would have eaten
some twenty to thirty platters, after which he would pocket
the candied fruit and nibble on a boiled egg as he made his
way to bed. Could she replicate this aura of opulence and
grandiosity? One great china service, used daily at court, was

often worth as much as a house in Mayfair. Annie knew that she could not simply present similar dishes; an air of pomp and ceremony mixed with anticipation were essential ingredients. For the royal courtiers these evenings were fraught; up to five hundred people attended and where you were placed indicated where you were in the king's hierarchy of favourites. Being placed in the wrong seat was a form of public humiliation. Those placed below the salt were not worth knowing. As she walked on, Annie wondered how to create an evening that was not simply a clever pastiche.

During Louis's reign there were cast-iron instructions accompanying every meal. These rules were part of the display of power and wealth. Turning to another tome, Annie saw that the king sat in the middle of a long rectangular table. Some guests and even members of the public assembled on the edges of the room, watching but not necessarily eating. A few would be asked to sit at the short sides of the king's table where they would not interrupt the king's sightline or the waiters. Annie smiled, imagining that Delores would enjoy this power play.

The most dangerous part of eating was not the danger of a faux pas, but the sheer quantity of food. Louis XIV's sister-in-law, born Princess Palatine, recorded, "He could eat four plates of soup, a whole pheasant, a partridge, a large plate of salad, two slices of ham, mutton *au jus* with garlic, a plate of pastry, all followed by fruit and hard-boiled eggs." The ingredients were sourced from the corners of Louis's kingdom: oysters from St. Malo and Cancale, lobsters from Normandy; vegetables from the royal gardens at Versailles; truffles from Italy; game from the hills and forests all over France. Astonishingly, Louis lived till the age of seventy-seven.

Annie began to worry how to afford the food. At the outset, Delores's budget of £6,000 seemed overly generous, but that was before she learned about recipes involving foie gras, wild salmon, oysters, salads sprinkled with gold leaf, fresh langoustine, puréed chestnut soup sprinkled with truffles, bisque of shellfish. A meal fit for a king was an investment rather than a luxury. She also knew that she would have to buy ingredients for the practice runs; she had £6,000 left from the sale of the house in Devon but was loath to break into her emergency fund.

Looking at her telephone, Annie saw that two hours had passed. There was no message yet from Rebecca, no instructions about dinner. There was enough food in the fridge for four people and providing the Winklemans were not expecting any guests, Annie only needed an hour to poach the fish and steam the vegetables. Feeling she wanted a break, she left the library and wandered away from St. James's Square, direction unknown. A sharp breeze whipped around the corner. Shivering, Annie pulled her hat further down. A girl jogged past, personal stereo in one hand, water bottle in the other. A middle-aged woman and her child came past on micro scooters, the mother breathing hard, a tight skirt restricting her movements. It started to rain, pendulous drops at first and then, without warning, a steady downpour. People ran for cover into doorways, shaking water from coats, wiping wet faces, cheerful despite sudden meteorological adversity. A young man dabbed at a raindrop halfway up his lit cigarette. Two ladies, in from the country, took out plastic headscarves from gold-clasped, shiny black handbags. A group of schoolgirls using schoolbooks as umbrellas ran laughing towards a bus stop. The scene was pure twenty-first century but Annie was still lost in the court of Louis XIV and preparations for Delores's dinner. She walked quickly, her thoughts flitting from recipes to table settings. Were geese a poor substitute for a recipe that called for six white swans? How high could she build a pyramid of profiteroles?

A cyclist speeding recklessly along the pavement towards her snapped Annie back into the present. Jumping to one side, she stumbled and a glint of silver caught her eye. It was a Greek drachma, a collector's piece now, surely. Wasn't it good luck to find a single penny, like being shat on by a bird? Pocketing the drachma, she walked on through bouncing droplets of rain. The deluge cleared the pavements. She had London to herself while pigeons and pedestrians sheltered from the storm. Water seeped through the hole in her shoe; her sock squelched. If Delores's dinner was on the first of April, less than six weeks away, what was in season at that time? Annie rued her ignorance, her lack of formal training. Should she serve things that were out of season, flown from distant parts of the world? In Louis's time, with no means of refrigeration and limited systems of transport, this would have been out of the question. But then, if Annie was to cook authentically, she should let some meat and fowl go off slightly and drown the rotting taste with pepper, nutmeg and available spices.

The rain stopped as abruptly as it had started, leaving the streets as dark and shiny as patent leather. Annie had wandered into an unfamiliar part of town and she was suddenly hungry and cold. Feeling around in the bottom of her pocket she pulled out three pound coins and the drachma. What was that going to buy? How long would a café owner let her sit nursing a single cup of coffee? She caught sight of herself in a shop window: dark hair plastered to her pale face, her eyes heavily ringed.

Memories of the previous night's encounter flooded back and she smarted with shame and self-disgust. Annie had sworn not to attend any more singles nights, but with Evie still at home, she needed to get out. She'd met the man by Holbein's *Ambassadors* at the National Gallery's "Meet and Mingle." They had both been trying to find the hidden skull in the painting's lower ground; their heads knocked together by accident. He thought they were the same age, twenty-five. Annie was secretly, pathetically grateful for his mistake.

He was German and handsome, kind of, amusing, sort of,

with a heavy sense of humour and a two-day growth of stubble. She'd agreed to go back to his flat, telling herself that it was for one glass of wine only. But the truth was that she felt desperately lonely. She hoped making love might exorcise memories, even though she knew that strange bodies and casual encounters offered only fleeting comfort. Rising from the German's bed at six that morning, she had gone straight to the office. Rebecca was already at work and, meeting her in the corridor, looked her up and down. She knows, Annie thought, blushing deeply and hurrying to the washrooms.

Annie found herself in Coptic Street. One of her mother's lovers, an expert on Ethiopian Coptic churches, had promised to take them to Lalibela to see monasteries cut out of rock. The first of many broken promises. At the end of the road there was a small coffee shop with steamy windows and desultory Valentine's Day decorations—a couple of strings of tinsel and a curling paper heart. Peering in, seeing that all the seats were taken, she walked on. She turned the corner and came face to face with an imposing façade in a courtyard bound by iron railings. Though more than twenty years had passed since her last visit as a schoolgirl, Annie recognised the British Museum's portico.

When Agatha and Jesse had suggested searching the British Museum's drawing collection, Annie had not seen the point. If you had no idea what you were looking for, how could you find anything? Three weeks ago she would have jumped at any kind of distraction; now her life was full with Rebecca and Carlo, her mother and Delores's dinner. Even sorrow had been confined to a smaller space. I don't have time to go to museums on mad hunts, she thought. She checked her watch. It was 2:15 p.m. on a Thursday afternoon. Empty hours stretched ahead. I am like the old lady in the nursery rhyme, she thought—swallowing the spider to catch the fly, swallowing the bird to catch the spider—perhaps displacement activity will kill me too.

Walking up the sweeping stone steps, past the information desk, through the grey lobby and into a huge inner courtyard, she realised her younger self would not have recognised the British Museum. In its centre was a circular building made from honey-coloured stone with a wrap-around staircase; floors were made of white marble slabs and the vast domed ceiling was made of thousands of latticed panels of opaque glass, reminiscent of a giant fly's eye. At the café in the corner she bought a bowl of soup and a hunk of bread and sat on the floor above a heating grill, watching the passers-by. This was, she decided, the place to bring uncertainty and not feel out of place. Most clutched guidebooks and printed maps and looked overwhelmed as they walked through the vast space or clustered near the ticket booths or outside souvenir shops.

Warmed by soup and blasts of central heating, Annie walked up the stairs and through the Egyptian department past bandaged mummies lying in open caskets. Schoolchildren pressed their faces against the protective glass cases. Assyrians, Phoenicians, Etruscans, living two or three thousand years earlier. How many generations ago? How many great-grandfathers? How many begetters? Annie felt strangely comforted by the feeling of being so utterly insignificant, so dwarfed by time.

She stopped by a pocket-sized, jade-coloured glass bottle. Its handle was as delicate as a sparrow's leg; its glass was translucent like a dragonfly's wing. The notice said that it dated from 3200 B.C. Annie was amazed. How had it survived? As a prized collector's item? Accidental good fortune? She turned back to the notice. "This extraordinary piece was found in a casket in Mesopotamia where it had been for four thousand years." Christ, Annie thought, what a miserable life: all time, no action. Imagine seeing nothing but the inside of a box. No one-night stands, no lunatic directors, no drunken mothers, no broken hearts, no ghastly mistakes or small triumphs— just a lot of accumulated seconds, hours, decades, millennia. Her thoughts turned to Desmond and, for the first time in

over a year, her stomach did not lurch. Then she realised that
the large weight, a permanent fixture on her heart, had less-
ened. Perhaps the shattering of her former life was some kind
of blessing: at least now she existed on her terms. This new
sojourn being alone (she hoped it would be very brief) was a
kind of second act, a different movement, however miserable
and uncomfortable. She might even find her way through this
muddle to a finale. Looking back at the jade bottle, Annie felt
a sudden inexplicable trickle of hope.

She walked on through the cavernous rooms to the east
wing of the museum where a small sign announced the drawing study room. Annie showed her driving licence to a young
man at a turnstile and walked into a long barrel-ceilinged
room. At one end there was a high window. The walls were
lined with glass-fronted mahogany bookcases on two storeys,
accessible by a gallery. Large desks ran from one end to the
other. In the middle a small exhibition space showed items
from the collection. Annie looked in wonder at a Picasso drawing, a priapic satyr with a ravishing young woman. Had it been
a photograph, Annie reasoned, it would have been banned.
Her favourite was a Jim Dine of a single plait hanging down
a girl's back. It was a literal and evocative image, reminding
Annie of the terror of first days of term: whom would she be sitting next door to? Would the teacher like her? Will they tease
me for having a red biro? What if they notice that my shoes
have holes in the soles?

Agatha had suggested, "Start with the works of Antoine
Watteau." Annie felt a slight twinge of guilt, knowing that
Jesse wanted to be there with her. She remembered Evie's
adage: "Just because someone loves you, you don't have to
love them back." She wondered if the whole world was caught
on a merry-go-round of unrequited love.

In one corner there were huge, leather-bound catalogues.
Searching under "W," Annie found twenty entries under Watteau, divided into printed matter and original drawings. She

filled in a form and took it to the librarian. "Find a seat and we will bring them to you," said the young woman behind the desk.

Annie found an empty table towards the back of the room next to two men who were examining drawings taken from a box labelled "Hogarth." Annie looked over their shoulders and though the images were hundreds of years old she knew at a glance exactly what each person had been like; Hogarth had found the essence of his subjects' characters with only a few flicks of pencil and smudges of a finger: the self-important little man with his barrel chest, bandy legs and air of supercil-iousness; the woman in a maid's dress, her sideways knowing glance crackling with intent; the two boys bent over a bird with a broken wing, clearly not set on fixing the creature or putting it out of its misery. Until recently Annie had thought that paintings were about capturing likeness and that only the cognoscenti could understand hidden meanings and arcane symbolism. Jesse had helped her to understand that an instinc-tive emotional response was equally valid.

While Annie waited for her items to appear she tried to imagine the lives of fellow readers. Who was the pretty young woman holding a magnifying glass over a man's portrait? How about the severely dressed spinster writing notes surrounded by Picasso's more pornographic images? What were the school-girl and her father discussing in such urgent whispers? Was it really the pastoral landscape laid out before them? Look-ing around the room, Annie liked the aura of seriousness and contemplation.

After fifteen minutes, the librarian brought out a box and a pair of white gloves. Annie put on the gloves and carefully opened the folio. They are letting me hold three-hundred-year-old drawings, she thought as she looked down at the head of a woman. There's no one hovering at my side. No protec-tive covering. No CCTV cameras spying. The first drawing she held was done in the same red, black and white chalk that she had seen in Delores's book. Reaching into her handbag she took out Jesse's sketches taken from her painting and laid them on the desk, looking for a resemblance between her image and a drawing entitled *Les Agréments de l'été*, of a girl on a swing. To Annie's untrained eye, all the people in Watteau's drawings looked similar and artificial: regular-featured, nicely proportioned, ample-bosomed, with delicately turned ankles.

Inevitably, her thoughts strayed back to Delores's dinner and a recipe she had studied for crayfish in a Sauternes sauce. Concentrate, Annie chided herself, and turning back to the job in hand, she tried to imagine, as Jesse had suggested, that this was a crime scene and she was a detective looking for clues. Perhaps, Annie thought, the features of a face aren't the things we recognise. Closing her eyes, she thought about Jesse, trying to capture the way his nose and mouth sat in relation to his ears, his hair. She could picture parts but failed to render the whole. She started again; thick brown hair, summerblue eyes with dark edging. Six-foot-ish. Slight freckling on his cheeks. Long thin hands. Narrow face, high cheekbones. But physical attributes didn't conjure up the essence of a person. Putting herself back into the café, she tried to remember his mannerisms, the way he brushed his fringe out of his eyes with a quick swipe, or rested his chin on clasped hands. That soft, deep voice. She remembered his eyes most: always moving, searching, running over her face, scanning. Perhaps this was the clue to art detection: don't look for the whole thing, look for an aura, a suggestion; try to find the artist's character in the drawings.

The stare of a stranger pricked Annie out of her reverie. She felt the eyes on her before she saw the man watching her intently from a few tables away. He was elderly and foppishly dressed with a spotty cravat and a velvet frock coat, his silvery lank hair framing a face as pointed as an anvil. A magnificent chain looped from his coat pocket to a button on the opposite side and hanging dead centre was an open-faced fob watch. Annie met his stare with as much hostility as she could muster. The man looked back with hard dark brown eyes and a thin-lipped smile of acknowledgement. Annie ignored this and returned to her research.

The librarian placed a second folio of drawings on Annie's desk. It was a heavy green-leather box with gold tooling and she opened the cover carefully. The first drawing was markedly different: a portrait crackling with individuality. The woman looked straight at Annie with a cool but amused stare. Annie smiled back at her. There was an inscription, "*Charlotte: la plus belle des fleurs ne dure qu'un matin.*" What was that about? The most beautiful flower *ne dure . . . un matin*, *morning*. *Ne dure, ne dure*, she repeated to herself. Endure? Duration? Last, that must be it. "Beautiful flowers don't last the morning." There must be a story here. She placed Jesse's sketch next to the drawing and called up the photograph of her picture on her telephone. It was definitely not the same person. Pity, she liked Charlotte's face, her vivacity. Annie wondered if this was the same woman she had read about in Delores's book, the love of Watteau's life. The other women in his drawings lacked Charlotte's intensity. The next image was the head of a man, a self-portrait: Watteau. Annie studied it carefully. His features were distinct, a long-faced man with oval heavy-lidded eyes and a full mouth. In his left hand he held a brush and in the right a piece of parchment. His clothes were rather splendid; the coat was edged in fur; the waistcoat had pearl buttons. His hair was long and curly. The expression on his face was deeply melancholic and disappointed, as if the world consistently let him down. The kind of person who would emit little involuntary groans and sighs as he went about his daily work.

Leafing through other drawings she found portraits of the artist from every different angle. Was he a narcissist or too poor to hire a model? His depictions of women were rather bland, as if he wasn't particularly interested in their characters, but then Annie came across another drawing of the beautiful Charlotte. Again the artist's energy and excitement fizzed out of the composition. Annie wondered what had happened to the girl—were she and the painter lovers? She was fairly sure he wasn't enamoured with any of his other subjects, or at least none that she'd come across so far.

The library assistant brought over another huge book, volume two of the *catalogue raisonné* of Watteau's work: pages and pages of prints copied from original paintings. As she turned the pages, Annie saw more and more bucolic, highly mannered scenes of courtly love and artifice, and her impression of the artist became increasingly dismissive. How could anyone be seduced by these endless social events, these overdressed figurines being serenaded by a succession of musicians? They reminded Annie of the party for Carlo's most recent premiere, where the overindulged chased the underdressed. Annie had watched guests engaged in desperate rounds of bonhomie and back-slapping while secretly plotting the downfall of friends and foes alike. Some were there for love of movies; most were panning for gold. Perhaps, Annie thought, these mannered, artificial human transactions were exactly what Watteau was painting. The behaviour in the courts of famous film directors and fabulous monarchs was probably similar, all kowtowing to a potentate in the hope of securing favours. Perhaps Watteau was trying to imbue these scenes with irony and pathos. She wondered if he had been born poor or wealthy, if he was a natural libertine. Did he feel as unsettled as she had done overhearing snatches of conversation at the Winklemans' dinner party?

Turning the page, Annie saw a print after a painting called

The Embarkation to the Isle of Cythera, which showed couples getting on to a boat. At first glance it was a bucolic scene, with fat little angels cartwheeling with apparent joy through a summer sky. Looking more closely, Annie saw hints of trouble ahead: the couples looked away from each other; there was a dead tree in the foreground and dark clouds were massing over distant snowy peaks.

Annie did not see the anvil-faced man get up from his chair and slip into the seat next to her.

"Excuse me, but those of us who appreciate Watteau are few and far between," he said silkily, peering over at Jesse's sketch. "What have you got there? May I?" Without waiting for a response he picked up the drawing and stared at it, his eyes devouring every pencil mark.

"Did you do this?" he asked.

"A friend made a copy of a painting for me."

"Where is this painting?" he asked. Annie detected a catch of excitement in his voice.

"Why do you want to know?"

"I love Watteau's work," he said, pronouncing the artist's name in a heavy French accent with a "V" rather than a "W" at the beginning.

"How do you know it's by him?" said Annie.

Without asking, he took her phone and looked hard at the photograph of the painting. Annie took it back firmly.

"I've been looking for this for a long time," said Anvil Face, pushing back in his chair and looking thoughtfully at Annie. "Where did you get the painting?"

"A junk shop," said Annie, thinking him extremely presumptuous and more than a little creepy. She took the sketch from him and folded it in half.

"Why did you think it might be by Watteau?" he asked.

"I didn't and I don't," Annie replied. "A friend suggested it could be, and," she hesitated, "I thought I would do some sleuthing."

She could hardly tell this stranger that she was lonely and needed to escape from her mother.

Anvil Face cleared his throat. "I would really like to see your painting," he said.

Annie closed the book and did up her rucksack.

"Before you go, just look at this." The man walked over to his desk, only a few feet away, picked up the large book he had been studying and brought it back to Annie. He flicked carefully through several pages.

"*Voilà*," he said with great flourish, pointing to an engraving. "The first volume of Julienne's catalogue, *Le Recueil Julienne*, published by the artist's dear friend and sometime dealer. As you can see, there is a very definite likeness between your sketch and this engraving. Q.E.D."

Annie looked again at the reproduction. Though it was in black and white, there was a clear resemblance. That strange white cloud on the left was, as Agatha suspected, a downcast clown who appeared to have been kicked out of a charming glade by the dainty foot of the woman. Behind her there was a classical fountain and a nymph astride a column laughing.

"It's not the same painting. The lady in mine has a different face," Annie said.

"There is a reason for that," said Anvil Face.

"Which is?"

"Bring me the painting and I will tell you a very interesting story."

Annie looked back at the engraving and at the title of the picture. "*L'improbabilité d'amour* faithfully engraved by Benoit Audran the Younger in 1731." Anvil Face translated for her, "*The Improbability of Love*."

Annie almost laughed.

"There are three hundred attributed paintings in Julienne's catalogue," he said, "but only a hundred survive or are known about. I have found ten missing pictures so far. To find this one would make me and a lot of other people happy."

"Isn't that what Delores Ryan does?" Annie asked.

The man sneered. "Miss Ryan can only sniff out things covered in chocolate."

Annie smiled, in spite of herself.

"So, when are you going to show me your little picture?" he asked.

Suddenly Annie wanted to get away from this rarefied room, this strange man with his pointy beard and chiselled features. She wanted to be the anonymous Annie McDee, free and inconspicuous on the streets of London.

She pulled on her coat and slung the bag over her shoulder. "I've got to go; I'm in a hurry," she said.

"My name is Trichcombe Abufel. You need me, my dear, much more than I need you."

The name jogged something in her memory but Annie could not place it.

"You have heard of me," Abufel said thoughtfully.

Annie started walking towards the door.

"Listen, miss," Abufel said as he followed her. Several readers looked up, annoyed by the chatter. "Your picture is probably nothing more than a cheap copy but there is an outside chance that it is not."

Annie walked out of the reading room and down the long corridor. To her irritation Abufel was still at her side.

"There is only one expert in the world whose opinion counts and that is me. I would suggest you stop walking and listen." Abufel was slightly out of breath. Annie didn't stop. She had had enough of being told when to stop, when to start, like a child's toy.

"You clearly have no idea what you have, so I will give you a clue or two. When you have solved these I suspect you will be only too eager to get in touch for help finishing the riddle."

Annie stopped and turned around. She wanted to shout some obscenity at the man but her interest had been piqued.

Abufel smiled triumphantly, revealing stubby yellowing teeth and rather grey gums.

"The first clue is King Louis XV, the second is Catherine the Great and the third is Queen Victoria. See if you can join the dots."

He bowed slightly. "Trichcombe Abufel, Fine Art Consultant, 11D Lansdowne Crescent, W11. I look forward to seeing you in less hurried circumstances." Smiling, he turned back towards the drawings room.

Annie marched on. "Like bloody hell," she said under her breath. "Like bloody hell."

Walking away from the museum, once again Annie felt the heavy cloak of loneliness settle on her shoulders. Looking at her phone, she saw it was four o'clock. Exiled from her office and her home, she felt purposeless and lost.

Annie decided to cook for her mother that night. It would be the first time in weeks that the women had spent any time together.

"It would be better with a nice claret," Evie said that evening, swallowing a small piece of duck.

"What do you think of the taste?" Annie hovered nervously by the stove. This was the ninth practice dish she had made and none so far had worked.

"It's delicious," said Evie, taking a second bite. "Who'd have thought of putting orange and chocolate with duck? It sounds rather horrible but tastes quite nice."

"So it's better than the beef with eels?"

"Anything's better than that."

"You know what I mean."

"There's a lot of sugar on your menu."

"It was a sign of great wealth," Annie said.

"Or maybe it just hid the taste of mould; I don't suppose they had fridges at Versailles."

Annie sat down next to Evie.

"Why aren't you eating?" Evie asked her.

"I've been tasting it for the last two hours—it would be wasted on me."

"You're wasting away."

"Don't eat too much; there are two more courses for you to try."

"Can't I have a drop of that cognac? It will cut through the fat."

"Mum, don't make me the policeman in this relationship," Annie said.

"I was just asking for a wee dram," said Evie plaintively.

"When has it ever been a wee dram?"

"You can't take drink away. That would leave me with nothing. Nothing," Evie said.

"What exactly is booze giving you? Friendship? Support? A living?" Annie started to fuss around the next dish, a puréed chestnut soup. On the night it would be sprinkled with truffles but for now a few sprigs of parsley would suffice. Some of the dishes that Annie intended to prepare were too expensive to practise.

"I don't see you being so happy," said Evie quietly. "I hear you crying yourself to sleep. I see you looking at your pinched, desperate face in the mirror. I am witnessing this so-called wonderful sober life and it doesn't look so damn great to me."

Annie said nothing for a bit but kept on stirring.

"You are right," she said finally. "I'm not happy and haven't been for a long time. Most of the time I have to struggle to put one foot in front of the other, drag myself out of bed and into the shower. My day job is not what I hoped it would be. This flat is not in the place I would like to live. My friends are three hundred miles away and even if I saw them tonight, I am not sure we would have anything left to talk about. But at least every decision, however wrong or muddle-headed or pointless, is my decision and not driven by some senseless liquid demon."

Evie did not answer. Turning back to her saucepan, Annie dripped a trail of cream into the molten chestnut.

Evie broke the silence. "You never told me what happened with the nice guide."

"Nothing happened," said Annie crossly.

"He never called?"

"No." Annie set the soup before her mother and waited patiently for the verdict. Evie took a tentative sip and then two more.

"This is delicious, darling," Evie said. "I have never tasted anything so fragrant, so unexpected, so delicate."

Annie clapped her hands together. "Do you really mean it?"

"Too bloody right—you have a real talent, Annie. You are a truly wonderful chef."

Going around the small table, Annie gave her mother a kiss on the cheek.

With a fragile truce in place, the two women sat, side by side, eating the soup.

"Tell me about the painting. What have you found out?" Evie asked.

Annie wanted to tell her mother about the developments concerning the painting but something held her back. Ladling a second helping of soup gently into the chipped breakfast bowl, she knew Evie would transform Agatha's cautious optimism into a major drama. Annie could imagine her mother storming into the National Gallery and demanding affidavits and paperwork in a misguided attempt to help her daughter.

"I have not had time to think about the painting; things at work have been so busy."

"I tell you it's good, I know it in my bones," Evie said, scraping out the last of the soup with her spoon.

Suddenly, Evie jumped up and ran to the window. "Look,

look at that," she said. Following her gaze, Annie saw the moon, so full and fat and white that it looked like a child's drawing, suspended over London.

"Do you remember?" Evie asked, her eyes shining.

"Of course." Annie laughed, thinking back to the times that mother and daughter had taken their clothes off, put Elvis on the tape recorder and danced under full moons in the backyards of their rented houses.

"If only we had a garden," Annie said.

"We do, an enormous one," said Evie, and opening the window wide, she began to climb out.

"Are you mad? We're five floors up. You could die," Annie cried out.

"Something much worse could happen: we could forget to live," said Evie.

Annie watched her mother's legs and then her feet disappear out of the window and then she heard a scrabbling sound above. Then her mother's trousers flew past the open window.

Minutes later, Annie had joined Evie on the roof. To her surprise it was flat and connected to the other houses; they could walk to the end of her street and back without touching a pavement. The moonlight bathed the townscape in a soft, silvery glow punctured by hundreds of dashes of lights from windows and street lamps. From here Annie could see the coordinates of her new world: from the corner shop to the tube station and across London to Winkleman Fine Art. She saw her cycle route along the edge of the park and in the distance, the London Eye, the Shard and the Gherkin, the landmarks she relied on to find her way about town. Seeing the city laid out sleepily beneath and around her made Annie less cowed by its vastness and, for the first time, she could imagine a life in the metropolis.

The opening bars of "Hound Dog," tinny through Evie's mobile phone speaker, started up and Evie, now dressed only in her bra and pants, started to dance.

"Aren't you cold?" Annie said.

"Freezing my tits off," Evie said, her teeth chattering audibly.

Annie looked at her mother with tenderness. If Evie hadn't become pregnant at sixteen, she might have finished school and had a career. Instead her talents were spoiled and wasted by an accident, a pregnancy with a boy who died two years later. Annie felt a sudden sense of responsibility towards the woman who had given up her life to look after her daughter, however cack-handedly. Now it was up to Annie to make that decision count, to make good for both of them. She felt a renewed sense of purpose, a surge of ambition; she was going to cook a dinner that people would talk about for many years to come and she was going to prove that an unknown picture was worth something.

"Come on, Annie, take your dress off," Evie said.

Annie slipped her dress off and, laughing, took her mother's hand and together they danced in the moonlight.

Chapter 15

A sense of equilibrium and calm settled over my weft and warp as I sat in the eaves of the National Gallery, bathed in a gentle north light, lulled by the hushed voices of conservators, and stimulated by wonderful conversations with major works by Diego Velázquez, Albrecht Dürer and Giovanni da Rimini; oh, the sheer unadulterated pleasure of being back among friends, some of whom I had not seen for nearly two hundred years. My *erstwhile* friend the Velázquez was pretty jumpy when they removed part of his upper ground. Admittedly it was a later addition, but Diego worried they would take a leg or an ear off with it. Meanwhile, the poor old Rimini, painted in 1300 and left for over seven hundred years of total isolation in the private vestry of a minor Roman church, had been sold by cash-strapped monks and was now in a state of shock about how much the world has changed: he spent days murmuring, *"In nomine Patris et Filii et Spiritus*

Sancti." Diego and I soon got bored of saying "Amen" in reply. Imagine if they bring a rowdy Picasso or a depressed van Gogh up here—Rimini's gold leaf will probably fall right off.

The head of the gallery, Septimus Ward-Thomas, came to look at me yesterday. He didn't dwell (he is only really interested in Spanish baroque) but assented to let Agatha work on me in her spare time.

In idle moments I think of my mistress; one does get attached. Odd, really. Diego said it was Stockholm syndrome but as I have not been to Sweden for centuries, he is clearly off his woodwork. I wonder if Annie took up the young man's suggestion about stopping at the British Museum's drawings collection?

Agatha, to give her her due, is not rushing into anything. Yesterday she took the tiniest pinprick of paint from the side of my canvas and took it along the corridor to the scientific department. Four scientists studied the results and no cleaning will begin until they have worked out exactly what kind of paint my master used. Antoine was not into preparation. In fact, and it pains me to criticise, he was inclined to sloppiness. In pursuit of rapidity of execution, he liked to paint in a hurry. Canvases require careful preparation and preparation was not my master's strong point. He was trying to get all those ideas, those feelings down. Instead of waiting for the paint to dry, he'd rub the canvas all over with *huile gras* and paint over that. The damage was increased by a certain want of cleanliness in his practice, which has affected the "constancy" of his colours and as a result, many faded. He seldom cleaned his palette and often went several days without setting it, so his paintings were filled with dust and dirt.

It's time to tell you about him, Antoine and the love of his life. My master was born in Valenciennes in 1684 to an alcoholic, abusive roofer. The humble circumstance of his birth underscores his genius. His father wanted his son to follow his own profession and seek a regular wage; Antoine knew that he had to paint. In the middle of one night he ran away to Paris. It broke his mother's heart and ruined his own health. The stupid boy chose winter to make the trek and after four days and four nights on foot, sleeping in ditches, eating only grass, he arrived in the capital with a debilitating pneumonia from which his lungs never fully recovered.

France was at its most sullen, choked by war, famine and the decrepitude of an aged, dyspeptic, embittered old monarch and the underhand bigoted rule of a power-crazed mistress, Madame de Maintenon. An ennui had settled over Parisian life, a heavy stinking fug of solipsistic oppression. Even the ceremonious court was exhausted by its own pomp. There was no gaiety or life in the arts, no spontaneity or originality. The pseudo-heroism of historical painting lay like a pretentious, weighty blanket on the merriest of souls. In the early 1700s, during the great plague of Marseilles, cannibalism and famine were the norm in the great capital. This was the backdrop to my master's life.

Let us continue a few years to 1703. Antoine was still a young man, nineteen, working for the decorative painter Claude Gillot in Paris. The pay was a pittance, barely enough to cover a carafe of wine and a loaf of bread, but as long as he had a brush in hand, he was happy enough. To make ends meet my master sat in taverns and drew in return for alms. His was a life mired by undernourishment and poverty. Working for Gillot was useful training but the older man's greatest contribution to my master's education was excursions to performances by the banned theatrical group, the *commedia dell'arte*. These events took place in backstreet taverns and the piquancy of performance was heightened by the prospect of a police raid. For most, the risk of arrest was worth taking: those wonderful actors were anarchic and lawless. Their leading man, Hippolyte, was broad, handsome and brave. Their clown, Gilles, was the fount of all jokes. Few in the troupe took anything seriously—they made fun of the ancient regime and its regulations. They laughed at love and life. Watching their performances, Antoine experienced a new lightness of spirit and a sense of optimism. In their exuberant, ebullient midst, he shook off, albeit briefly, his heavy heritage of Valenciennes, the years of war and poverty.

He took to going every night. On the fourth visit, my master saw her, Charlotte Desmares, widely acknowledged as the most beautiful girl in Paris, who joined the Italians for occasional performances. Her stage name was Colette. Putting down his brush and grabbing some chalks from his pockets, Antoine began frantically sketching this maiden as she pliéed, twirled and danced around the stage. Charlotte saw him, but she was one of those women who was so used to being watched that the sight of another young man rapt in admiration was hardly out of the ordinary.

Watteau drew till his fingers bled. Feigning an upset stomach, my master rushed back to his tiny atelier, where, taking the one canvas he owned, he started to paint. That piece of cloth, stretched between four pieces of wood, that inauspicious piece of nothingness, became *moi*.

I am the receptacle, the vessel into which all the agony and ecstasy of first love was poured. Urgency and magic, excitement, passion and terror flew from his heart to his brush. Watteau's ardour was so strong that there was no time to prepare the paint properly on the palette. Instead he flicked and mixed colours one next to the other in a frenzy of dabs and wipes— look at the trees, admire the sunlight, the pointillism, blurred edges, the informality and you will see the birth of Impressionism, though it took the rest of the world some one hundred and fifty years to catch up.

I am the representation of his impassioned, deranged, inflamed desire. I am *l'amour fou. La gloire d'amour*. I am the literal exemplification of utter mortal madness.

Hidden under the layers of varnish and overpaint, you will see that Charlotte's cap isn't uniform red—it's gold and yellow and crimson and magenta, silvering down to palest pink. Her dress is saffron—yellow grading from palest canary to golden buttercup, each delicate colour laid, splashed in minute harmony. Yellow, too, peeps through the opening in her décolletage and her skirt is hot with pale purple and soft browns. Her skin is creamy white like an opal taking reflections from light. There will never be a more beautiful painting of flesh, even among the Venetians.

There have been other painters and muses. One thinks of Rembrandt and Hendrickje, Modigliani and Jeanne Hébuterne, Dalí and Gala, Bacon and George Dyer, but I propose that it was my master's demented love for Charlotte that imbues my canvas with added unmatched fervour.

The composition was one my master returned to his whole life: the stage of love. The background is transitory and artificial, a mythical, mystical landscape adorned by figures reclining, overlooked by a statue of the goddess of love. In the middle he placed Charlotte, as proud and as graceful as a swan. Raising her delicate arms, she looks directly, fiercely, provocatively at the viewer. At her feet, the simply dressed young man just stares. With only the lightest flick of a fine brush, Antoine captures his awe as he looks up at this vision of femininity. You can taste the hope and despair, the love and lust implicit in his gaze.

If I tell you that the man's face is composed of only seven strokes of a brush you'll laugh and remonstrate that this can't be so; but that is why my master is a genius and why his star is still in the firmament of great artists nearly three hundred years after his death. He understands the alchemy of red and pink and pearly white. More importantly, he understands mankind, and he can, like great artists, translate our innermost joy and fear into something tangible.

Some say I'm only a sketch. It's true that I was executed with haste and élan. This intensity released Antoine from the past, from the teachings of dreary academics, from childish doodling, and in his hurry to capture love he had found his métier and a new way of painting. I was the canvas that launched a career. I was the painting that started a movement, the rococo.

I was painted to celebrate the wild cascades of love, the rollicking, bucking, breaking and transformative passion that inevitably gave way to miserable, constricting, overbearing disappointment.

Four days later, when the paint was hardly dry, Antoine took me back to the theatre as a present for Charlotte. Imagine this young, gawky nineteen-year-old laying open his heart. The troupe crowded around, pushing and shuffling, giggling and chattering like tiny chaffinches at a bird table. I had my first brush with death. Charlotte's rival, Hortense, was so overcome with jealousy that she ran her long nails down my canvas. A fraction harder and she'd have damaged me for ever. Shocking really. Charlotte was rather delighted. The attentions of this young painter elevated her and her cachet was upped by his gift of love.

"Give it to me," she demanded, holding out her pretty little hand. Watteau started to hand the picture over—then he hesitated. "No," he said. "It will be my present to you the day you agree to marry me. Until then, it will never leave my side." The company fell about in mirth. How could a young penniless painter compete with her lover, the Duc d'Orléans, nephew of Louis XIV? Their laughter was so intense, so heartfelt, that it brought Gillot running to see what the commotion was about. He looked from the actress to the painter and his eyes finally rested on me. The blood drained from his face; it took only a glance to realise that the younger man was by far the superior painter. Gillot, to give him his due, could not have been more gracious. "I can't teach you anything more but I can point you in the right direction." He sent my master to work with Claude Audran, an interior decorator in charge of the Palais de Luxembourg, home to wondrous works by Rubens, Veronese, Titian and Tintoretto.

The other actors begged Antoine to paint them and many would return with him to his atelier and sit for hour after hour while he immortalised them in chalk and pen and occasionally even in oil. But if you look at his great works you will always find glimpses of her—sometimes it's her face, other times it's her neck, arm, back, her foot. The essence of love for Charlotte haunts most of his paintings. Her sweet girlish visage peeps out everywhere and the spirit of his love for her, his unbridled romance, steals into all of his works.

If I were to offer a soupçon of criticism against my master it would be in the field of courtship: love is as much an art as painting or living; it requires practice, finesse, determination, humility, energy and delicacy. Like many before and since, my master became enamoured with the sweet ecstasy of unrequited passion; he saw his "problem" as not being loved, when really it was the inability to give love. He was so green behind the ears, so naïve, that he thought love arrived fully formed and complete. It never occurred to him, after that first rejection, to earn Charlotte's respect or her heart. He flounced off to his studio. I'm sorry to say that some find the agony of rejection far sweeter than the ecstasy of consummation.

To try and expunge the hussy's memory, he painted over Charlotte's face with that of another woman's. Then he added the clown, a ghostly figure in the gloaming: a Pierrot, the embodiment of pathos and derision. It was a self-portrait he returned to over and over again for the rest of his short life.

Then he changed my title. Once I was called *The Glory of Love*; after her rejection, I became *The Improbability of Love*.

So what happened next? I'll tell you the rest in good time.

Chapter 16

Your mother has called seven times in the last hour," the receptionist, Marsha, told Annie. "Something about a break-in—I couldn't really understand." She did not need to add that Evie had been drunk and slurring her words.

Annie looked at the clock—it was 3 p.m. That morning, Rebecca asked her to prepare dinner for eight and Annie had rushed across town to her preferred fishmonger to choose a line-caught cod. Hanging up her coat and placing her bag in a drawer, she dialled home. Evie was hardly coherent: Annie tried to stitch the series of events together. Her mother had only gone to the shops for a short while (probably the pub for a long drink, Annie thought), but on returning to the flat it took her a few minutes to realise that the door had been forced (probably twenty to negotiate the stairs and another fifteen to find the set of keys, Annie translated). Evie thought she had gone mad (thought? Annie nearly laughed), but although the flat was very tidy, things weren't quite the same (Were you see-ing double?). The toaster was in a different place; the bin was three feet away (How would you know?). Evie was frightened (Not as worried as I am that you still haven't left). Evie wanted Annie to come home early (In my dreams).

Annie promised to phone the police, pick up a takeaway and be back in time to watch the late evening news.

To Rebecca's consternation, the search of Annie's apartment had yielded nothing. No picture, no records or clues about a larger gang. Either buying the picture was an enormous and highly unlikely coincidence or, and this was both more likely and more frightening, Annie was part of an extremely sophisticated organisation. Knowing the art world better than most, Rebecca tried to think who had the resources and skills to set up this sting. What did they want? Rebecca was fully aware that the antipathy towards Winkleman Fine Art and her family spread beyond the art world. Many were jealous of their meteoric rise: Memling had arrived as a penniless refugee and was now worth several billion. As Jews, they were and would always be outsiders.

There was another factor that drove people mad: the Winklemans' world was hidden behind a veil of secrecy. As a private company it never published profits or losses and all employees were legally bound by non-disclosure agreements. The family never gave interviews or commented on events. They were meticulous, clever, informed, hard-working, pri-vate and utterly inscrutable. In a world largely populated by public-school types and academics, in a milieu where it was fashionable not to care about money and in an environment where long lunches and summer sojourns were the norm, the Winklemans, by applying order and discipline, easily out-stripped their competitors. Memling also had the uncanny abil-ity to find great lost works of art, known and newly discovered.

Moving like great white sharks through the choppy waters

of the international art world, Memling, Rebecca and their employees never stopped working. Their contacts and operatives ensured global information on a 24/7 basis: if a potentially interesting painting came up for auction in a minor saleroom in a godforsaken town, the Winklemans would know about it; when a family was thinking of selling a master work, the Winklemans were the first to hear. Their pockets were deep and their nerve strong; they generally got what they wanted. Over the years Memling had created an exhaustive database of collectors and their chattels, including their age and health and their likely heirs; and their fluctuating net worth was constantly reassessed. If you were an impoverished nobleman with one good Joshua Reynolds or a hedge-fund *ingénu* with a few billion in the bank, you would almost certainly hear from Winkleman on a birthday or another significant event. One story, often retold, seemed to typify Memling's way of doing business: while dining on his yacht miles from civilisation, the world's fifth richest man, Victor Klenkov, was amazed to see a tiny boat come alongside. It was an emissary sent from Memling Winkleman clutching a bottle of vintage Bollinger and a small sketch by Degas. The card read "Many happy returns on your fifty-second birthday. I look forward to meeting you one day. Memling Winkleman." At the time, Klenkov had never bought a painting; the following week he spent his £15 million on an early Degas from Winkleman Fine Art.

By employing the world's greatest scholars, the company did not have to go far for attributions. If a painting came into their gallery, there was an expert on hand to validate it. Important pictures were written up in glowing terms and really important works were granted their own monograph. Winkleman's also held the self-appointed but widely accepted right to authenticate work by certain artists.

They dealt in paintings, sculptures, reliefs, tapestries and antiquities. The one area that Winkleman avoided was dealing in contemporary art, which Memling described as "shooting

poisonous snakes with a water pistol." The company's cut-off
point was 1973, the year of Picasso's death.

In their Curzon Street gallery, the Winklemans put on
acclaimed exhibitions with accompanying catalogues of a
standard and quality that museums could only dream of. If
a favoured artist's price dipped, Memling would put a minor
work into a public auction anonymously and bid against himself to raise the hammer price to new heights. This ensured a
new benchmark, and soon after, one or two other works by the
same painter, owned by Winkleman Fine Art, would find their
way on to the market. In Winkleman's hands artists became
superstars and their works record-breakers.

For the first time in Rebecca's memory, the Winkleman
"system" was useless and yet Memling was still insisting on
eschewing outside advice. Sitting back in her leather Cor-
busier chair, Rebecca pressed the "do not disturb" button on
her telephone and, walking over to the door, triple-locked it
from the inside. She started to pace back and forth up the
forty-five-foot-long library wall lined with shelves full of artists'
monographs, around a thousand books that she had read and
studied. At the far end of the room, there was a huge elabo-
rately carved wooden fireplace by Grinling Gibbons. Above
the fireplace there was a small Raphael oil, an eighteenth-
birthday gift from her father, now worth in excess of £25 million. It was not for sale but served as a reminder to clients that
the Winklemans were in this business for other things besides
money.

Rebecca turned and walked down the other side of the
room, past the glass wall that looked out on to the main gallery. She could see out; nobody could see in. It was useful
having a vast spyhole on to their public space, a good way to
observe staff or potential clients. Rebecca knew most of the
important buyers by sight and if they wandered in, she could
be on the floor within moments to receive them. If trouble
rumbled there were well-rehearsed procedures.

Rebecca kept her eyes focused on her feet as she marched up and down the Aubusson carpet trying to make sense of her father's overwhelming interest in the painting. His refusal to tell her details was not unusual: Memling had a maniacal love of secrecy. When pressed, he claimed that the less she knew the better; ignorance was her best protection. It was also a reflection on how he treated his daughter. Rebecca was the CEO of Winkleman Fine Art in name only: Memling controlled every decision. She was there by default, appointed seven years earlier following her brother Marty's sudden death. At the time, her daughter Grace was still at day school and Rebecca worked for the firm as head of curatorial. She had done her PhD in Renaissance paintings at the Courtauld and had published four learned books on Florentine painting. No one had expected her to take over the business: she was just the daughter.

Rebecca surprised herself and her colleagues: she was better suited to running a business than hot-headed Marty. Her brother had been a brilliant dealmaker, a quality Rebecca would never possess, but she was methodical, organised and highly knowledgeable. Though not particularly liked, she was universally respected in the art world as a person of acumen and superior knowledge.

As she walked back and forth, Rebecca tried to empty her mind and concentrate solely on the picture. If Memling wouldn't tell her why it was so important, she would have to find out for herself. For once, Rebecca did not feel like bowing to her father's instructions and she questioned his judgement. She also realised for the first time in her memory that her indomitable, controlling father was vulnerable and frightened.

Checking that her door was locked, Rebecca went to the fireplace and, twisting a griffin's shield, stood back to wait for her secret safe to open. Known only to Marty, herself and Memling, this walk-in room, fourteen foot square, held particular paintings and company records, including details of every sale made and every artwork that had ever passed through the company's hands, including many that had been sold privately. Memling's records dated back to his arrival in England in 1946, shortly after his liberation from Auschwitz. Aged fifteen when the war broke out, Memling had never finished formal education but, as he told Rebecca many times, his mother was an art-school teacher who delighted in her son's enthusiasm. His treatment in the concentration camps (a period about which he never spoke) left Memling unsuited for regular work. Knowing, loving and dealing in paintings had been his only option.

Closing the door of the safe behind her, Rebecca went over to the shelves containing the vast ledgers. Measuring four foot by three, each leather-bound book was specially made for Winkleman by a firm in East Berlin. Entry after entry, in careful, legible handwriting, gave the details of all paintings sold, where they came from, the price they were bought for and how much they sold for. There were a series of annotations or cross-references detailing known provenance, scholarship and other relevant facts. More than 1,150 paintings had passed through the Winklemans' hands, most acquired in the last thirty years through auction or private sales. Studying these ledgers, Rebecca thought, would give any historian a fascinating glimpse of the art market and the history of taste. She lifted down the first book, marked 1946, and, turning over the heavy leather-bound cover, started to look through the entries. She didn't have a photograph of the missing painting, just a description and a photocopy of the Jean de Julienne catalogue entry. Measuring eighteen by twenty-four inches, painted on canvas in oil, it showed a woman teasing her lover in a glade, watched over by a clown. The date was 1703; the artist was Jean-Antoine Watteau. Carefully turning over the yellowing pages, she ran her finger over each record, looking for entries marked as French eighteenth century.

Earlier, she had checked the company's computerised database and found three paintings by Watteau that had passed through the company's hands. One had been bought about ten years earlier at auction, one in the 1970s and the third had the special classification VZW (*Vor dem Zweiten Welt-krieg*), designating a handful of paintings acquired during the Second World War. As always, Rebecca was struck by both the luck for the Winklemans and the inherent tragedy for the vendors of the VZW (pre-war) and NZW (post-war) classification. As Memling told his children, the rise of the Nazi Party in the 1930s meant many Jews wanted to leave Berlin but lacked the means of escape. Knowing that Esther Winkleman was an art lover and that her husband Ezra earned good money as a lawyer, they sold their paintings to the family. After the war, even if they survived, few ever wanted them back. "We saved many lives," Memling told his children. The NZW moniker referred to the immediate post-war period when the bottom had fallen out of the picture market. Again the Winklemans came to the rescue of poor Jews who wanted to trade paintings for food and other necessities. Our business, Memling told his children, is built on unavoidable, legitimate sadness.

Working quickly, Rebecca took down ledger after ledger looking for details of the missing picture. Her father had said the painting had left his ownership over twenty years earlier but refused to tell her when he had bought it or from whom. Rebecca combed the books up to the late 1990s but found no mention of any painting by Watteau matching the description. Rebecca was confused. Her father was a meticulous record-keeper and no detail was too small to overlook. Again she wondered why Memling was interested in a painting which he did not appear to own.

When possible, each painting was photographed as well as described. Its condition, provenance and any known publications were listed and accompanied by an original bill of sale. No wonder Marty had wanted to write about these transac-

tions: his dream was to tell the history of the demise of German
Jews via the chattels they owned. Memling had been passionately against the idea; the war and its aftermath were still far
too recent for him. It was one of the areas that father and son
clashed on. Rebecca felt a pang of longing for Marty; hardly
a day went past when she didn't miss her brother. While she
was neat, small and measured, Marty had been ebullient, vivacious and passionate. Rebecca understood art because she had
pored over attributions and history; Marty felt it: he had never
looked at a monograph or studied an underdrawing, he had
just known instinctively what was great and how the painter
had achieved his aim.

Thinking that Memling might have made a rare mistake,
Rebecca searched through the other paintings of that period,
works by Pater, Lancret, Boucher and Fragonard. Again and
again she was struck by the quality and rarity of the works that
her father had bought. If Memling had kept only a half of his
stock, they could have founded a world-class museum.

Checking her watch, Rebecca realised that two hours had
passed. She had a meeting in thirty minutes with a client visiting from Switzerland who wanted to buy a Cézanne. Picking
up a ledger from 1974, Rebecca struggled to put the heavy
book back on the shelf and, twisting her body awkwardly,
caught sight of something taped to the underside of the sill.
Putting the ledger down, she ran her hand under the shelf and
felt some masking tape holding a small exercise book in place.
Finding the torch app on her phone, Rebecca shone the light
and tentatively peeled away at the edges of the tape until she
could slide the book out without damage. Her heart leapt
when she saw Marty's familiar handwriting, the great messy
curves that had driven his teachers wild. Memling used to joke
that if his children had come back as painters, Rebecca would
have been Ingres, careful and precise, while Marty was more
late Titian, with daring and romantic strokes.

Flicking through the notebook, Rebecca became confused

by the references to about 125 paintings, including dates and notes on provenance. Why would Marty have created a separate system when Memling's worked so effectively? Next to each entry, Marty had put symbols, letters and strange annotations, none of which meant anything to her. In the front of the book, written in capitals, was an address in Berlin.

Using her phone, Rebecca photographed every page of the notebook before placing it back under the shelf. Instinctively she knew that the notebook and the missing picture were connected. Through the huge glass wall, Rebecca saw that her client had arrived and was looking at a late Turner hanging in the gallery. Picking up her telephone, she dialled her assistant.

"Liora, cancel my meetings today and tomorrow. Tell John to deal with my client."

"Can I help you with anything?" Liora asked.

"No, thank you," Rebecca said politely. Liora and everyone else in the office must never suspect that there was a problem. The business was built on a solid foundation of fear, respect and confidence.

Before leaving, Rebecca checked that the security camera trained permanently on Annie's kitchen was working. (She had installed other CCTV eyes around the office to make it seem as if everyone was being monitored.) A firm of private detectives was scrutinising every move that Annie made, as well as her phone calls and emails. Taking a permanently packed overnight bag and her passport, Rebecca slipped out of the back door of the office and hailed a passing cab. This time she would not be using the company's jet.

"Heathrow Airport," she instructed.

Barty and Vlad walked through the Chester Square house. It had already been done to the highest of specs and was bathed in endless variations of cream and beige.

"It's too hideous for words but we could make something of it," Barty trilled.

"Looks good, new," Vlad said, stepping gingerly on the snow-white wool Wilton carpet.

"No, darling. Not good. It's common," Barty said sternly.

"Common?" Vlad asked. Barty used this word liberally. In the last few hours he had proclaimed many things to be common, including loving your mother, vitamin pills, sparkling water, pashminas, nights in, nylon knickers, Mayfair, business cards, sushi, scented candles, BMWs, the South of France, Courcheval, children named after jewels or suburbs, summer holidays and, worst of all, Vlad's beloved leather jacket.

"Common is to be avoided. It's for ordinary people," Barty said, tut-tutting as he looked round the grand drawing room, which was painted off-white. "I loathe beige. It's like living in a pair of unwashed knickers. I see red, I see swagged curtains, I see velvet sofas, I see pouffes, I see a great brass chandelier, I see *Performance*, Mick and Marianne, hookah pipes, cashmere shawls and kilims," Barty said, dancing from foot to foot, his enthusiasm building with each step.

Vlad had no idea what the man was on about but had learned it was probably simpler to nod. He wondered if there were enough walls to tempt a Lyudmila kind of advisor into his life.

"We need to set the scene, create a mood."

Vlad looked around. "White good."

"No darling, white is common—do listen," Barty said, looking up at Vlad's broad torso.

"How much house?" Vlad asked, looking around. He didn't particularly like it but Barty had already dragged him round six properties. Convinced that his suite at the Connaught was bugged, increasingly paranoid about noises coming out of Moscow, Vlad was keen to have a place of his own. The security firm had assured him that this mansion, with a small mews house at the back, was eminently protectable.

"It's twenty-four million on a lovely long lease and you'll

need to spend another five decorating it," Barty said in his most soothing voice.

"OK. Let's buy."

Unable to find a meter, Beachendon had parked half a mile away from his destination in a car park under the arches. At least, he thought gloomily, no one would torch or key the paintwork. A young man in a baseball hat sat in a booth reading a comic and, without looking up, handed a parking ticket to the Earl.

"Which way is Whitechapel Road?" Beachendon asked.

"Down the street, two lefts, one right and straight on," the man replied, jerking his hand to the left.

Stepping out in the road, the Earl pulled his velvet-collared navy-blue cashmere coat around him and, transferring his keys into one trouser pocket and his telephone into the other, wondered if he should have left his wallet in the car. The surrounding buildings were a mish-mash of styles and dates; a former Victorian factory next to a seventies office block, an eighties housing development and a spanking new academy school built in wood and stainless steel. A teenager walked towards him with a dog, a weapon of destruction, on a lead. The owner had pink and purple hair, a nose ring and an attitude visible from fifty yards; the panting dog's head, white, almost triangular in shape, nodded from side to side as it walked, looking, the Earl surmised, for a shin to bite or a throat to rip. Wanting to put space between himself and his assailants, Beachendon wondered if he should cross the street; in the end he decided to brave out a confrontation with the girl and her animal. They passed without incident.

Beachendon walked on, reflecting gloomily on the ultimatum issued by the board: he had six months to find a sale or series of sales to reverse Monachorum's fortunes and put right the deficit: basically, he had been given a stay of execution.

Few, including Beachendon, believed that he would be able to source a £300 million blockbuster auction in such a short period of time. Trawling through his notebooks and database, Beachendon had come up with a list of twenty collectors or artists to visit, who might just, and it was a very long shot, be persuaded to consign their collections to a sale.

Finding Sir Patrick O'Mally's house took another twenty minutes, during which time the Earl had passed another five lethal, four-legged killers and their owners. "My earldom for a chauffeur," he thought. Fat chance: the people upstairs at Monachorum would only allow him to take the odd taxi within the M25. Fuck the cuts, the Earl thought, fuck their stinginess, and fuck Roger Linterman and co. Each week he sold paintings for tens of millions of pounds to collectors whose annual incomes were greater than the GDP of many countries. He took bids for some great but mainly mediocre works for amounts that would cover his own overdraft a thousand times over. It was his job to whip up frantic battles of desire, to create the thrill of a chase to secure a particular work, the indefensible in pursuit of the inedible, yet his proprietors insisted that he either take public transport or use his own dilapidated car, which would probably fail its MOT this year, heaping further indignity on to its cash-strapped owner.

Forcing himself back to the present, Beachendon took out a crib sheet from his pocket and went over the details of the collector Sir Patrick O'Mally's life. Born to a working-class family of Irish immigrants, O'Mally had studied art at Ruskin College in Oxford and later at the Courtauld Institute in London, where he developed a passion for German Renaissance works. Scouring the small salerooms and private collections, he was, for fifty years between 1934 and 1984, a lone enthusiast, collecting and publishing his thoughts on these artists to a small group of cognoscenti. Many years later, the market caught up with him.

For nearly thirty years, dealers, gallerists, auctioneers, collectors and museum directors had paid court to Sir Patrick, hoping to spirit even one canvas from his collection of seventy-four Old Masters, now estimated to be worth over £100 million. The largest works were on loan to leading world museums; only the smaller ones stayed at his Whitechapel house. The older Sir Patrick got, the more assiduous his admirers became. The most devoted was Memling Winkleman, who each year threw him a birthday party grander than the last. Sir Patrick never needed to sell anything: he lived comfortably off the gratuities offered by his collection's ardent, avaricious admirers. If he needed anything—a new roof, a mobile phone, a bronze turkey—all he had to do was lift the phone and there were over twenty people who considered satisfying any urge a worthwhile investment.

Sir Patrick's house was a handsome villa set back behind a wall on Whitechapel High Street. A few hundred years ago it would have been open country; now buses and lorries rattled its foundations as they made slow progress in and out of the suburbs. The last time the Earl had been to this area of town was to attend the funeral of a prominent Jewish philanthropist who had escaped the Holocaust and gone on to make a killing on the Stock Exchange. Rumoured to be worth £20 million, Manny Parkins had refused ever to leave the one-bedroom flat that the council had assigned him on his arrival in London in 1946. "Lest we forget," he told his family and friends. He was buried in one of the Jewish cemeteries hidden behind the high street in Whitechapel, his body wrapped in a white cloth, placed in a rough-hewn coffin and trundled on a wheelbarrow through the graveyard. Leaving the burial ground, the Earl bowed to Mrs. Parkins and her four sons, offering his sincere condolences.

"Don't weep for us, dear boy," she said cheerfully. "We can now move to our dream house in Epsom."

The Earl rang the doorbell and minutes later a woman in

a severe blue dress opened the door. Assuming she was the nurse or housekeeper, Beachendon smiled graciously and handed her his overcoat.

"Sir Patrick is waiting for you next door," she said pleasantly. "Tea, coffee?"

"Any chance of a sherry?" The Earl felt he had earned a snifter.

"I'll look in the kitchen," the woman said kindly. He followed her downstairs and noticed that she was not, as he might have expected, wearing sensible shoes but kitten heels edged with fur around the toe.

"Where are you from?" he asked politely.

"Lechlade," she said with a finality that did not invite any further questions.

Beachendon felt a sudden desire to rest his head on her shoulder, unburden himself, tell her about his debts, about his little Ladies Halfpennies and his son Viscount Draycott. He would confess that if Sir Patrick didn't agree to sell at least three of his pictures via Monachorum's saleroom, the Earl would almost certainly lose his job, and his beautiful children and noble wife would probably end up in sheltered housing on benefits.

"While I am looking for the sherry, you'd better go upstairs, as Patrick is waiting for you," she said. "It is at the end of the corridor on the right."

Beachendon wanted to linger a little longer in the kitchen but something about the woman's demeanour hurried him on and he followed her instructions.

Sir Patrick, who had just turned ninety-eight, was confined to a wheelchair. Though his brain and eyes were still working, his sinews and muscles had deteriorated, leaving his head inert, slumped over his left shoulder.

"Hello, Patrick," Beachendon said with gusto.

Sir Patrick didn't reply but squinted through damp pink-rimmed watery eyes.

"Must be twenty years," Beachendon said. He wondered if he should sit down and cock his head on to his shoulder so that the two men were face to face but decided instead to keep his own at a natural angle. "Very nice nurse—or is it a house-keeper?—you've got. I wish I had one of those."

Sir Patrick blinked.

"So what have you been up to?" Beachendon asked, wondering if Sir Patrick could speak these days. There was a rustle behind him and the woman returned with a tiny glass of brown liquid.

"We haven't got sherry, but I found some brandy. Will that do?" she asked.

Beachendon smiled gratefully and, taking the glass, finished it in one gulp.

"I was rereading your monograph on Jan Gossaert the other day," Beachendon said. "It remains the most balanced, illuminating and inspirational work on any artist."

Sir Patrick blinked a bit more.

"It's astonishing to recall that when you wrote it, few knew anything about Gossaert, a forgotten great master. Amazing to think that you were beating the drum for the German Renaissance when the rest of the world dismissed the movement as ugly and uncouth." Beachendon knew that he was talking too much but was unsure how to have an entirely one-sided conversation. "Nowadays everything is in fashion somewhere or other," he said gloomily.

"We like the Holbein book more," the woman piped up.

The use of "we" confused Beachendon. Was the old man channelling his thoughts through his carer?

"Of course, that monograph is splendid," Beachendon said, "but Holbein's reputation did not need the same kind of resuscitation. Thanks to his sojourn in England and his portraits of Henry VIII, we all got him." The Earl tried not to condescend to the nurse who, he assumed, knew more about catheters and bed pans than Altendorfer and Cranach.

"We don't pay much attention to fashion," the woman said, smiling sweetly.

"I would remind you," the Earl replied smoothly, "that Sir Patrick wrote a whole book about taste through the ages and the importance of provenance."

"Now in its eighteenth edition; Patrick is so clever," the woman said, looking fondly at Sir Patrick.

Beachendon felt a deep blush creeping from his heart towards his neck. It was not possible that this lovely young creature, barely older than his first-born, was somehow "involved" with the near cadaver lolling in this chair.

"We were never formally introduced," Beachendon said, holding out his hand.

"I am Josephine O'Mally, Patrick's wife," she said. "You can call me Jo."

"His wife?" Beachendon said.

"We got married last year so I suppose you could still call us newly-weds."

Beachendon looked from Sir Patrick to the woman.

"I know what you are thinking. What was it that first attracted me to the famous multi-millionaire art collector?" Jo said.

Beachendon smiled weakly.

"It was his mind," she continued. "Sir Patrick transported me from my dull little world to an imaginary state of bliss and fantasy."

"Bliss and fantasy?"

"Bliss and fantasy," Jo said firmly. "We are very happy."

Beachendon looked over to Sir Patrick and saw a tiny bubble of spit forming on his top lip as he tried to force out a word.

"Squapppppy," Sir Patrick said.

Jo went over to her husband and kissed him gently on the cheek.

"I know what else you are thinking," Jo said.

"Really?" Beachendon asked, feeling inordinately depressed.

"Spladdgeuery," Sir Patrick added.

"Could I have some more brandy?" Beachendon asked.

"Are you driving? If you are, I can't really recommend it," Jo said. "Now do tell us, to what do we owe the pleasure of your visit?"

"Purely social."

"Purely?"

"Schalteralterrigis," Sir Patrick commented.

"Sir Patrick thinks you came here to try and persuade him to sell his collection," Jo translated.

"Sclrlortifiscathy."

"Are you sure you want me to say that, darling?" Jo knelt next to her husband and gently wiped some spittle from his lower lip.

"Justhshioipoishldkhy."

"He says you cunt vultures have been circling his body for years but he's not going anywhere."

"This really is a social call," Beachendon protested.

"Crrasphoihslkenfijhnklend."

"And his mother is the Queen of Timbuktu."

"Vlskjidhsot."

"Sorry, Vladivostok."

Beachendon looked at the canvases hanging from floor to ceiling; there was a tiny Holbein of Erasmus, a study for the great work at the National Gallery; two late Brueghels; an almost perfect Lucas Cranach of a young girl; and a Mathias Grünewald of an old woman. He had heard there were sheaves of beautiful, priceless drawings upstairs in heavy mahogany chests, and another four floors of great paintings all bought for under £200 by the young Sir Patrick. Beachendon's fantasy had been to package the whole collection in one huge sale stretching over three days. Now, just when everyone thought that the old man could not survive another winter, he had gone and married a young woman who looked good for another fifty years. If the old man left his collection to his wife then decades of careful courtship by the art world's will-hunters had been totally pointless. Beachendon's bitter disappointment was tempered only by the realisation that there were others who would be even more upset by the announcement of a new Lady O'Mally.

"I can't believe the time," Beachendon said, getting to his feet and bowing slightly to Lady Jo. "I am on my way to Cambridge for a lecture and thought I would stop by," he said.

"I'll fetch your coat," Lady Jo said. "Just keep Patrick company."

Beachendon leant towards Patrick and, putting his eye close to the old man's watery pink one, he said softly, "Game, set and match to you, old boy."

"Fluckingsthelrrfff," said Sir Patrick. Beachendon detected the faintest of smiles on the old man's lips.

Lady Jo reappeared carrying Beachendon's coat. "It is so nice that someone comes just to say hello. There was one curator the other day, from an American museum, who walked in, took out his credit card and said, 'Name your price,' as if we were some sheep farmers from Glamorgan."

Beachendon put on his coat and nodded sympathetically.

"Another person tried to seduce me! He came on all strong about wanting to comfort me in that special place in a special way that my husband couldn't. I was outraged. Totally outraged."

"I can imagine."

"I nearly called the police."

Turning to Patrick, Earl Beachendon gave him a wave but the old man's eyes were firmly closed.

"It's time for his nap." Lady Jo nodded at the front door.

"My card—in case you need my services," Beachendon said, handing over his business card.

"I've got everything I want for now," Lady Jo said, smiling.

Beachendon walked back to his car. This time he hardly noticed the canine weapons of mass destruction. Stepping in a large pile of excrement, he didn't stop to scrape the shit from his shoe. What was the point? Arriving at the car park, Beachendon saw that the door was closed and bolted; on the door someone had tacked a note. "Family probz. Got to go. Soz. Back laters."

Turning around, Beachendon walked back towards White-chapel, where he hoped to find an underground station. The final dregs of a fruit and vegetable market littered the pavement. Stalls were being dismantled, boxes of unsold cabbages and apples remained piled up and the ground was strewn with discarded and damaged leaves. "Last box o' pears, yours for a fiver," a seller called out with little enthusiasm. With each step, Beachendon caught a whiff of dog shit and rotten cabbage.

How did this happen? Beachendon wondered. Forty years ago he was an eighteen-year-old buck leaving Eton and about to take a place at Oxford. Handsome, impeccably connected, he was supposed to inherit a grand title with an estate, but the chasm between expectation and reality had widened year by year as the full extent of his father's mismanagement became clear. Five weeks after the honeymoon ended, the very auction house that Beachendon now worked for had moved in and divided up his supposed inheritance into separate lots. Even his teddy bears had been catalogued under "aristocratic childhood memorabilia." His mother and he had sat in the front row of the auction, waving their hands at opportune moments to raise the bidding. Nothing dulled the sharp pain of seeing every last stick of furniture, from the Riesener desk to the servants' hip baths, knocked down to heritage hunters. The only pieces of inheritance the young Earl retained were a fob watch, a title and some basic knowledge of furniture. As companies still liked a titled person on the board, Beachendon had picked up a few non-executive directorships and a junior position at the auction house. Through hard work and tenacity, he made his way up through the ranks to be appointed chief auctioneer. Though the art business had prospered, the Earl had not. His clients had become richer and richer; his wages barely kept pace with inflation.

The one good bit of news was that Beachendon had remembered to put his Oyster card in his wallet that morning and that there was just enough credit to get him across London to his office.

Chapter 17

Standing in the shadow of the grey façade of an apartment block off Friedrichstadt in Berlin, Rebecca felt foolish. She was at the address listed in her brother's notebook but did not know why she was there or what she was looking for. In her professional life, Rebecca took pride in being a commander of facts, a marshal of dates and a serious historian whose reputation was built on measured, considered evaluation. In her personal life, she ignored her husband's peccadillos and concentrated instead on fulfilling the uxorial duties of a good wife and mother. Rebecca found comfort in regular, decent behaviour. To take a plane on a whim, to cancel important meetings and to lie about her whereabouts, was wholly out of character.

She guessed that number 14 Schwedenstrasse was built in about 1900 and was probably one of the few blocks left standing in that area after Allied bombing campaigns during the Second World War. At the time, the vast concrete edifice punctuated by hundreds of windows must have seemed impressive and modern. Now it was dwarfed on either side by high-rise buildings shooting into the air with monumental steely purpose.

Rebecca hesitated before entering the building: she sensed that after crossing the threshold, nothing would be quite the same. Her telephone rang; it was Memling. Rebecca felt a rush of relief—her father, with his inimitable sense of timing and intuition, was calling to offer the longed-for, plausible explanation.

"It's a foreign ring tone. Where are you?" Memling asked. He never bothered with pleasantries or any introduction.

Rebecca hesitated, wondering whether to tell her father the truth.

"I'm in Paris looking at what was supposed to be a Corot but is actually a clever copy." Rebecca was surprised by both the lie and the ease with which she delivered it.

"Any news of the picture?" Memling asked.

"A dead end. Everywhere." Summoning up her courage, Rebecca asked, "What is so important about this picture? If I am to help, you need to tell me."

Memling hung up.

Though his employees and family were expected to comment on any subject proffered, Memling answered questions selectively. He rarely explained or extrapolated. His instructions were well defined and precise, and most were grateful for this clarity and sense of purpose. His organisation was run as a hierarchical empire with a long gap between the leader and the next rung of management. In theory, Rebecca shared top billing and equal responsibility; in practice, she was just another employee. Memling maintained absolute control through a combination of natural authority and bullying enforced by an iron fist on all financial levers. Every bill, whether it was for a multi-million-dollar painting or a paper clip, had to be sanctioned by him.

Leaving university, the younger Rebecca railed against her father's totalitarian regime. Refusing any financial support, she lived on an academic's meagre wage in a squat in Brixton. Eight years later, aged thirty-two, she returned to the Winkleman compound with a husband and a child in tow. Her husband, Carlo, then an aspiring film director, was unable to support his family. Rebecca tried for three years to stretch her wages to cover more than rent and food but it would never extend to childcare. Under pressure from Carlo and her father, Rebecca eventually resigned from her job at the Courtauld Institute and accepted a Winkleman salary; as head of curatorial she worked closely with her brother, who was head of sales and deputy chairman. Their father did not need a job title.

With a sense of relief and failure, Rebecca had floated back into Memling's orbit and under their communal roof. Her family was assigned a house in the row on Curzon Street next to her brother Marty. There was a shared gym, staff, cars and drivers. There were offices in Paris, New York, Geneva and Beijing, and family holiday homes in Africa, St. Barts and the South of France. To live under Memling's rule was alternately luxurious and infantilising, and sometimes demoralising, but the absence of ultimate responsibility was preferable to life in the Brixtonian wilderness. Memling justified this centralised system as a way of protecting those he loved; he never saw it as controlling or domineering.

Rebecca defended her decision to go back as strictly professional. Winkleman was the pre-eminent dealer and many of the world's greatest pictures passed through the company's hands. When every scholar, dealer and curator dreamed of working for that company, why would Rebecca deny herself the opportunity? Privately, she was exhausted by penury and

relieved to be returning to a world of cosseted living, beautiful surroundings, domestic staff, wonderful clothes and first-
class travel. There was another element too. Rebecca loved
and revered her father: he was the cleverest and best informed
of men; he knew instinctively who would sell and buy; he was
fearless in decision-making and blamed only himself for any
mishaps or bad calls. Above all, he put family first. These were
the qualities that Rebecca most admired.

Putting her phone to her pocket, Rebecca stepped forward
and rang the bell to apartment 409. To her surprise it was
answered quickly.

"*Jah?*"

Rebecca spoke fluent, textbook German, though her father
rarely spoke to them in his native tongue.

"I am so sorry to bother you. My name is Rebecca Winkle–
man," she said, feeling foolish as she still had no idea why she
was there, or who she was looking for.

"Winkleman?"

"Yes."

"Come up to the fourth floor," the voice answered and a
buzzer sounded.

The entrance hall to the block of flats was pokey. A light
spluttered in the dark-panelled hallway and Rebecca's heels
clacked noisily on the liver-coloured tiled floor. There was a
small lift, probably installed in the 1950s, but Rebecca decided
to take the stairs.

Though she was fit, Rebecca was out of breath by the time
she reached the fourth floor. There were two identical long
corridors leading to the left and right. At the far end of one, she
heard a woman's voice.

"In here," it called out.

Rebecca walked towards the voice and after one hundred
feet stepped through the small hall into a living room where a
woman sat cross-legged on the floor changing her baby's nappy.

"Sorry, can't get up! I'm Olga; this is baby Britta," she said, fixing the last straps on the baby's nappy.

"Do you always let complete strangers into your apartment?" Rebecca asked, smiling.

"The magic word is Winkleman. The lady down the hall said a family of that name once lived here."

Rebecca tried to mask her astonishment—this was where her father had grown up? Memling had always said that Allied bombs had razed the Winkleman family's home.

"I am trying to find out more about my father's family," Rebecca said, looking around at the cramped quarters and trying to imagine Memling and his parents here. "Do you know anything about them?"

"Very little. The old lady said they had all perished. It's fantastic that one survived," Olga said with real enthusiasm. "You must stay and meet my husband Daniel—he will be so pleased. His grandparents were at Treblinka. Only his grandmother made it."

Rebecca smiled. She had never imagined that a kind of kinship could exist among the heirs of a great tragedy. Memling rarely spoke of his experiences during the war and yet the Holocaust mired every aspect of the family's life like a faint, dark stain. Most of her mother's family had also perished, after the war, when their boat travelling to Israel had sunk; only her mother and two others were rescued from their makeshift life raft, a piece of cargo. Knowing others her own age were living with similar ghosts made Rebecca feel less alone. Then another thought occurred: maybe some relations had survived and this trip would result in finding a family she never knew she had. Grace could become friends with cousins her own age. Growing up, Rebecca and Marty had never met any relatives from either of their parents' families.

"Have a look around—it won't take long!" Olga said cheerfully, getting to her feet and lodging Britta on her hip.

"She's beautiful," Rebecca said automatically; she'd only ever liked one baby, her own.

Rebecca walked around the apartment. It had two bedrooms, each just big enough for a small double bed, and a parlour with a large window that looked on to the street. Behind this there was a tiny kitchen whose window faced on to the triangular central well of the block.

"It is the perfect size for three people," Rebecca commented.

"It works for us but must have been squashed for the six members of the Winkleman family," Olga said. "I have seen them all lined up in this room in Danica's photo album."

"Six?" Rebecca said, trying to hide her confusion. Memling always told them he was an only child.

Olga looked empathetic. "Your father must have been trying to shield you from pain—or maybe shield himself. Daniel's grandmother was the same—she told him that only a few of her relations suffered when the whole family was wiped out. It was easier to rewrite history than accept the truth."

"Perhaps the old lady made a mistake?" Rebecca said.

"There is a decent-sized loft. Maybe your father and his brother slept up there. We use it to store old books and clothes." Olga pointed to a trap door.

"May I see it?" Rebecca assumed the Winklemans had stored all their friends' works of art in the loft. She thought back to the paintings; her father had once said there were over thirty that the Winklemans had either bought from or hidden for fellow Jews. Some of the company's greatest works, including two Veroneses, four Degas, three Corots, a Fragonard, a Tiepolo sketch and two Rembrandts came to them this way.

"If you take that pole," Olga pointed to the corner, "you can pull down the hatch and a ladder appears automatically. It's a bit stiff."

Rebecca climbed carefully up into the loft. With each step her heart felt heavier. The stairs were just wide enough for her slim frame; she could not imagine pulling a large Renaissance masterpiece up the rickety treads. Reaching the top, she found a tiny cupboard room, measuring about eight foot by five, full of the new family's belongings. Boxes and bags were neatly stacked. It would have been impossible to manoeuvre the large paintings up the retractable ladder and into this box room. Even if they took the pictures off their stretchers and out of their frames, the larger works would not have made the tight corner.

Rebecca came down the ladder slowly.

"There's not much to see," Olga said apologetically, "it's our first flat."

"How long have you been here?" Rebecca asked, hoping that Olga had met Marty.

"Only six months—the last people left some years back— it's been empty for a while."

"It's lovely," Rebecca said, trying to shake off the feeling of foreboding.

"Go and see the old lady in 411—she's very old and lonely. She has photographs from that time—there are pictures of your family."

Half an hour later, Rebecca was sitting in an even smaller apartment with ninety-six-year-old Frau Danica Goldberg.

"Of course I remember your family," she said. "We played together, but," she leaned over and looked at Rebecca hard, "they all died in the camps, except for the daughter Johanna. Johanna died afterwards when the Allies, trying to be kind, overfed the survivors: her stomach split."

Rebecca shivered; Danica put her hand on the younger woman's arm.

"It was insensitive of me to break the news in that way. I am sorry," she said.

Rebecca looked out of the window. If only she was shaking for that reason alone.

The two women sat in silence for a moment.

"There was a man who came here asking these same questions. I have his card somewhere." Heaving herself up, Danica went to the brown side table and, opening it, felt inside. Moments later she produced a business card and held it out to Rebecca.

"Here it is."

It had Marty's name and in his inimitable wild handwriting, his mobile number. Rebecca felt tears prickling the back of her eyes.

"My brother," Rebecca said.

"I knew you must be related somehow. I was so happy to meet him," Danica said, smiling broadly. "I thought the whole Winkleman family died, but no. I asked him to ask my old friend Memling to visit. But he has not as yet."

Rebecca's head spun. Why hadn't Marty told her about this visit? Was it a clue to his sudden death? Tiny beads of sweat broke to the surface of her neck and temples. Her heart clattered. No, she told herself, it was an accident. The coroner recorded "death by misadventure." Suddenly she was not so sure.

Rebecca looked at the floor—the patterned carpet swam in her tear-filled eyes. Danica patted her on the arm.

"The man that came was dark. You are so fair." Danica spoke clearly, if softly. Age had hardly diminished the power of her voice or, it seemed, her memory.

"Marty takes after my mother—she was Italian—a Jewess from Verona," she said, remembering that people often assumed she and her brother were not related.

"And you look like your father?" Danica asked.

"Uncannily, or so I am told," she said. "When did Marty come?" Her brother had died seven years and two months ago.

"Eight . . . or was it seven years ago? He asked to see photographs. Would you like to see them?"

Rebecca nodded: all she could think about was Marty. Marty sitting where she was sitting; Marty looking at the photographs; Marty falling over the railings of the Newhaven to Dieppe ferry on New Year's Day. Could he have done it on purpose? The circumstances surrounding his departure from London without luggage or a telephone call to say goodbye had always bewildered Rebecca. There had been no note, no explanation. For the first time since news of his death came through, Rebecca wondered about the cause.

Very slowly, Danica got up again and, going to a sideboard, brought out an old photograph album. "My father was a studio photographer. He had his own shop in Mitte and took beautiful formal portraits. The Nazis torched his shop and all those records. A whole generation went up in flames. Wiped out. They wanted to exterminate memories as well as lives. He also had a little Brownie, used to take pictures of the families here in Friedrichstadt. The Jewish Museum wants my book—they can have it when I die. But until then this is the only friend I have left."

"Have you got children and grandchildren?" Rebecca asked.

"I could never bring children into this world. I could not bear for others to experience it."

Rebecca went to sit beside Danica on the small couch. The lady smelled of stale urine, old cabbage and talcum powder. Rebecca wanted to run away but forced herself to stay.

The exploration of the album took a long time. Danica needed to tell the history of every now long-deceased person. After each description she added, "May they rest in peace."

As she spoke, Rebecca tried to imagine Marty sitting where she was. At over six foot tall, Marty would hardly have fitted on to the sofa. A man who hated to sit still for more than a few seconds, Marty would surely have taken the book from her hands and flicked impatiently through the pages. Rebecca felt a deep twisting ache as she thought about her brother—his ebullience, open-hearted generosity and childlike enthusiasm won him many admirers but no one, Rebecca imagined, could have loved him as she had.

"Here are all the children from the fourth floor," said the old lady, tilting the book so that Rebecca could get a proper look. She spotted the young Memling immediately—he must have been about eight and looked just like her daughter Grace. It was the first time she had seen a photograph of her father as a child. Even in a black-and-white photograph, Rebecca recognised the broad open face, pale blue eyes and shock of blond hair.

"That's him," she said to the lady.

"That's what your brother said too," Danica said thoughtfully. "That's not a Winkleman; that is Heinrich, the youngest member of the Fuchs family from 407. They were the caretakers, the only non-Jews in the building. Fritz Fuchs and his wife, I forget her name, had fallen on hard times and had no choice but to live here—he hated it. He hated us. He had lost his foot in the First World War and had been unable to find work. He was the moaning, complaining type who needed a scapegoat. Sometimes it was the Jews, most of the time it was little Heinrich. That poor child. If little Heinrich got something wrong at school or behaved badly, he was beaten and put out on the street with no clothes on."

Rebecca took a closer look at the little blond boy—had she made a mistake? "Which ones are the Winklemans?" she asked.

"They are so easy to spot." Danica laughed, pointing to two tiny girls and two even smaller boys, all with curly hair and shining dark eyes. "We used to joke that it was good they were so tiny—how else would they have fitted in that apartment?"

Rebecca was starting to feel overcome by the lady's smell; the room's walls were closing in around her.

"I need to get some air," she said.

"There's a balcony out there," Danica said, nodding to the window. "You get a view, of sorts. I will make some tea."

Stepping on to the balcony, Rebecca gulped down chilly

gusts of air and tried to steady her feelings. Had Marty burst out on to the balcony when he saw the photograph? Had his heart beaten as uncontrollably? Hot tears coursed unchecked down her cheeks—how dare Marty not tell her about this discovery? If only he were here now. Marty, who knew the answer to everything; Marty, who had always made things bearable. Wiping her tears away half-heartedly, Rebecca tried to dampen down her sense of panic and foreboding. Entering the building, she had held certain cast-iron beliefs re-enforced by her father at every major event. Again and again he had told her that family loyalty was the most important thing in the world. Family was all they had, all that was worth protecting.

The Holocaust had hovered over the family for two generations: even Grace spoke of her grandfather's terrible "wound." Standing on the balcony looking down into a tiny muddy park, Rebecca went over what she knew of Memling's history again. The young boy and his family forced into a train's carriage, a long suffocating journey and the arrival at Auschwitz. His grandmother, almost blind, had stumbled on the station platform and was beaten to death in front of her family. His mother had given up her meagre rations so that her son could eat a tiny bit more, starving to death in front of his eyes. His friends disappearing, one by one; his father taken away without explanation. Rebecca and Marty had stitched these details together over the years. On their father's arm was the tell-tale tattoo, a string of random numbers the ultimate symbol of suffering. They had seen it only a few times and felt the weight and responsibility of survival, knowing they must live life for those who did not make it and make the most of every single opportunity on behalf of those who perished.

Memling taught his children to be discreet, secretive, distant, removed—never trust anyone, assume that another attack could happen at any moment. Their whole way of life was predicated on their father being a Jew and narrowly escaping death in a concentration camp. What am I supposed to do now? Rebecca thought. What if my father is not the Holocaust survivor Memling Winkleman but a German called Heinrich Fuchs? Suppose, she felt panic rising, he was a member of the Nazi Party?

While she and Marty had not been brought up in the Orthodox tradition, being Jewish was a fundamental part of their identity, an inescapable fact. Being Jewish was akin to having an ever-present shadow that cast different shapes according to given situations. It was something she neither celebrated nor rejected but it was there, feeding her sense of identity and belonging. She was a child of Europe, one of a long line of German-Jewish teachers who had migrated centuries earlier from the Holy Lands to settle in Europe. The extermination of every member of her father's family in the Holocaust, while never discussed, played out in most areas of her life. The gaping absence of relations, of customs, of graveyards or mementos, created a black hole in her history, as significant as a highly peopled extended family. Now suddenly she was to give this up, to rethink her past and, worse still, to become allied to the very oppressor that had defined her. How could she hate the enemy of her father when she was the spawn of the enemy? Had her mother known? Why would anyone, how could anyone, create and then inhabit such an appalling lie?

Rebecca's body shook violently and she held on to the railings for support. Breathing deeply, she tried to compose herself by concentrating on the view opposite, the landscape of central Berlin on a cold February evening: the people returning from work, children playing in the tiny park. Their lives were continuing while her own had been shattered by a photograph.

"It must be cold out there. I have made some tea," Danica called through the open window.

Reluctantly Rebecca stepped back inside, wiping the last tears away.

"You are very pale. Would you like a sip of brandy? I keep some for emergencies," Danica said.

Rebecca shook her head. "Tell me more about the Winkleman family?"

"Generous, kind—their door was always open and even though they had no money, they would always share what they had."

"I thought the father was a successful lawyer?" Rebecca asked.

"He represented the poor and oppressed—he never made money. He was a truly kind-hearted man who put the welfare of others before himself and his family. She was an art teacher."

"My father said that they helped Jews escape in the 1930s by buying their pictures from them," Rebecca said, even though she already guessed that this piece of folklore was unlikely to be true.

Danica shook her head. "They had a loft—so people hid things up there—the odd painting, pieces of jewellery but mostly family mementos. You never knew when the Nazis were going to come."

"Did the Winklemans have any art?" Rebecca asked.

"Your brother asked the same questions," Danica said thoughtfully. "They had one painting. She was so proud of it. It hung above the mantelpiece in their parlour and sometimes she would tell us the story behind the work. I can still remember it today; it was of a beautiful young woman with her lover watched over by a clown. It wasn't harsh like so many contemporary works; it was a painting you could get lost in."

"It wouldn't be in any of these photographs, would it?" Rebecca asked.

The old lady flicked through her book. "Here we are." She pointed to a small black-and-white photograph of the Winkleman family standing in front of a fireplace. Behind them on the wall was a painting about eighteen inches by twenty-four. Although it was a tiny image and hard to make out any detail, Rebecca saw that it matched the description of the painting Memling was so anxious to recover.

"There were more than one hundred families living in this block," Danica said. "Many had beautiful paintings. The lower floors were owned by the richer families—those had high ceilings and larger works of art. I remember one family, the Steinbergs, who had works by Veronese, Rembrandt and I forget who else. Mrs. Winkleman used to take us on a tour sometimes and try and teach us about art."

Turning the pages of her photograph album, Danica was silent. "The Nazis didn't just take paintings, they took everything: sheets, towels, furniture, pots and pans, you name it. They stole the wealth of the rich and the poverty of the poor."

"What did they do with it all?"

"The very best was offered to Hitler. Then Göring. There was a pecking order."

Rebecca nodded.

"The regional leaders got the next lot, followed by the officers, and anything that wasn't wanted was sold in weekly auctions. Sometimes, before we got interned, we would go down to the sales to see who had bought our things. Once my mother tried to buy a coffee pot that had belonged to her grandmother. It was chipped and worn—it couldn't have been worth more than a few Marks. The auctioneer saw the yellow star on her coat and refused to sell it to her. He picked up the pot, which was made of china, and dropped it on to the floor, where it broke into a thousand pieces. I wouldn't have minded losing a valuable painting if I could have kept a book or two. Do you know that I don't even have a record of my mother or my father's handwriting? All I want is to have a glimpse of an old book, to see once more, 'To Danica, Happy Birthday with love from Mama and Papa.' Is that so much to ask? I am ninety-six years old but I have not given up hope."

Rebecca shook her head, fighting back sorrow and shame—was Memling an accomplice, was he a robber of memories? Had she and her family lived off the proceeds of these people's grief?

"Heinrich had a job working for the Führer's personal art squad," Danica said, as if reading Rebecca's mind. "One day he and some colleagues, all fancy in their black shirts and polished boots, came here and helped themselves to some paintings. You could see he was uncomfortable doing it—but it didn't stop him. We stood and watched them. Esther Winkleman wept with shame; she had taught little Heinrich what was good. She had never told him the meaning of evil."

"Did he take her picture?"

"Not during her lifetime," Danica said. "But I often wondered what happened to it after they were taken away."

Rebecca opened and closed her mouth and, unable to formulate any words, she just shrugged and hung her head.

Danica patted her hand reassuringly. "It's in the past."

Her compassion stung like a barb.

"How can you be so forgiving?" Rebecca whispered.

"I will never forgive them but I couldn't allow their cruelty to take over my entire life; that would have sealed their victory. I had to find a way of living with those memories, but I also don't want anyone to forget what happened." She looked at Rebecca fiercely. "By listening to my story you are helping me and others. People must know what occurred so that history does not repeat itself."

Turning back to the book, Danica flicked to the next page. This time it was the same apartment with the same belongings and the Watteau still hung above the fireplace, but something was missing.

"Where are the people?" Rebecca asked. "Where is the family?"

"In 1942, many families asked my father to take pictures of their empty apartments. It was as if we knew that this way of life was coming to an end. We were already non-people in the eyes of the state. Our businesses had been confiscated, our freedom severely restricted, our temples burned and looted. Perhaps we knew that soon only our ghosts would haunt these rooms, these buildings."

For a long time the two women sat in silence looking at the empty rooms captured in black-and-white images with their edges yellowed by age.

"Would you mind if I took some photographs on my iPad?"

Danica smiled. "Of course not."

"Are you certain there were no other Winkleman survivors?" she asked.

"I heard that Johanna had a child in the camp. A daughter. How come your father never tried to find her?" Danica shook her head in wonder. "People behaved strangely after the war—but most families wanted to be reunited."

"He started a new life in England." Rebecca fell back into a familiar pattern of protecting Memling. "He wanted to put the past right behind him."

Danica smiled. "At my age, the past is the only thing we have."

The two women sat side by side for a few minutes. Rebecca looked at the photographs, while Danica looked at Rebecca.

"You are not a Winkleman, are you?" the old lady asked in a kindly voice.

"Of course I am—look at my passport," Rebecca said sharply.

Danica leant over and closed the photograph album and, taking Rebecca's hands in her own gnarled fingers, she asked, "Are you a Fuchs?"

Rebecca looked up into the old lady's face. She wanted to lie, to jump up and run out, to scream, protest and shout. Different reactions and emotions raced around her head. Forcing herself to stay calm, she heard her own voice, hesitantly, say, "I don't know."

Danica looked at Rebecca for a few moments before answering and in her soft voice she said, "It doesn't matter if you are a Jew or a Gentile—what matters is doing the right thing."

Walking away from Friedrichstadt, Rebecca wanted desperately to talk to Marty. She had never imagined it was possible to miss him more. Rebecca stopped by the playground of a large secondary school and watched some students. Some played a game, others sat around and talked—they looked so confident and at ease. Rebecca tried to remember that feeling. Had she ever had it? She thought not. Would she ever feel that way again? That was an easy question to answer.

Taking out her iPad, she looked at the photos of Marty's notebook. She realised now that Marty had traced certain pictures back to Schwedenstrasse 14—these same ones that Memling claimed were part of the cache that the Winklemans had bought from their escaping Jewish friends and included a Veronese, a couple of Rembrandts and a Watteau matching the description of the missing picture. Next to this one, Marty had written a few details, including the name Antoine Watteau, the date 1703, a catalogue entry and a sale reference from 1929. She knew she had to complete her brother's quest. Marty had discovered his father's identity and had been in the process of working out how his father came by those early pictures. Was it fraud, opportunism or something worse?

Rebecca walked on past some shops but couldn't focus on their displays. If she found out that Memling was guilty of some awful crime, what would she do with that information? To expose her father was to bring down the whole Winkleman business. There was her daughter and Carlo to think of, as well as their employees, and the clients and museums that had bought work in good faith. Again, Rebecca wondered if her brother's death had been an accident; perhaps he had been unable to cope with the responsibility of exposing the lie against the impossibility of living with it. The missing painting was tangled up with her family's history—as a protagonist, a witness, a cypher. Hurrying towards her hotel, Rebecca knew that she had to find it before anyone else, including Memling.

Chapter 18

Memling Winkleman hit the tennis ball with every ounce of strength that his ninety-one-year-old body could muster.

"You are on fire today, Mr. Winkleman," his coach Dilys called out over the net, struggling to return his smash. She hit the ball too kindly to Memling's forehand and he hit it back at her stomach with such ferocity that Dilys only just managed to jump aside.

"I might be old and decrepit but don't hit condescending shots," Memling barked.

He treated his coach as he treated everyone: with a sense of overriding imperiousness. The combination of wealth, age and intelligence convinced him that he was better than other people and his sense of self-belief was so absolute that it was contagious.

Dilys held up her hands to apologise. She had been playing tennis with Memling three nights a week at 6 p.m. in his
private underground court under the Winkleman complex in
Curzon Street for nearly ten years. They played for forty-five
minutes and at exactly 6:45 p.m. he walked off without saying
goodbye. Dilys did not care—it was good money and more
challenging than her day job teaching children at a local private school.

Taking the lift from the basement to the fourth floor,
Memling walked through his bedroom, through his closet
and, tearing off his clothes, stepped into his shower. The water
started automatically, pre-set to do alternate blasts of hot and
then icy-cold water. Exactly five minutes later, he stepped
out of the shower room and glanced nervously at his mobile
telephone, hoping for a message. There was none. At a time
when he should have been enjoying his dotage, just when his
daughter's and granddaughter's futures were secure, he was
racked with fear. Everything he had built up, his life's work,
his family's future, was in peril because of one sentimental
mistake. The only solution was to find and destroy the piece of
evidence that linked Memling to aspects of a past that he had
so successfully buried. His thoughts turned to the farmhouse
in Bavaria—he had meant to burn the store to the ground on
his last visit but, unable to accept his impending mortality,
had baulked at the last minute. He made the decision to do
that by the end of the month, latest.

He dried himself and put on a navy-blue cashmere suit
and a pale blue shirt before getting back into the lift and going
down to his private dining room on the first floor. Annie had
left his supper, a piece of steamed fish, some spinach and a
half-bottle of red Bordeaux on a side table. If he was not going
out, Memling liked to eat undisturbed, with just Tiziano for
company. This evening he had no appetite and he sat looking at a Tiepolo sketch hanging on the opposite wall, con-

sidering his second great mistake: rediscovering the picture in the junk shop and not purchasing it there and then. Spotting the security camera on the wall, Memling had decided to send Ellis, his bodyguard-cum-chauffeur, one of the few people he trusted to buy the work. Finding the picture gone, Ellis attempted to frighten the shopkeeper. Unfortunately, his "little lesson" got out of hand. Now the man was dead, and the picture was still lost.

Pouring himself a second glass of wine, Memling allowed his thoughts to return to Marianna—she had promised never to sell or give the painting away, that it would remain with her always as the secret reminder of their true love. Her sudden, unexpected death had derailed her good intentions.

For the sake of his children, Memling had never left his wife Pearl for the love of his life. Not a man given to passion, or indeed many deep feelings, he had loved Marianna from the moment she walked up the aisle to marry his close friend. Turning, like the rest of the congregation, to catch a glimpse of the bride, Memling felt a shock pulsate through his body. As she walked past him, she caught his eye and he knew in that instant that the feeling was mutual.

Marianna and Memling spent five painful years denying their love, but one afternoon, meeting by chance near Claridge's hotel, they spent the first of many happy afternoons in a suite on the fourth floor. Seventeen years after her death, Memling still kept the suite on permanent hire and often returned alone to mourn her memory.

After her death, Memling wrote to her sons asking for his picture. He didn't add that he had given the priceless object to their mother as a reminder of their love. It was the only sentimental act that Memling had ever committed. Her children (none by Memling) were apologetic but admitted that they had sold all the contents of her house as a job lot to a house clearance firm. Memling had scoured the saleroom and museum catalogues for many years; he made a habit of visiting random galleries and junk shops on the weekend. It was a fluke that he found it in Bernoff's that Saturday after sixteen and a half years of searching. Why, Memling thought for the umpteenth time, had he given Marianna that painting? There were so many others and many more valuable. The answer was always the same: that painting said everything he believed but could never articulate about love. For the first sixteen years of his life, it had belonged to the only person who had shown him true, unconditional kindness. This, Memling assumed, was what love was all about. When he met Marianna, his understanding of love changed; he was, simultaneously, the impassioned happy man lying at the feet of his beloved and also the morose clown standing in the background of the picture. Being in love pitched him, moment by moment, between waves of ecstasy and misery. Like every other person, he believed his predicament was unique.

Being with Marianna was the only time Memling was granted a respite from self-disgust and shame. For those brief moments, he forgot about the naked, cold child standing outside the Berlin block of flats and about being a disgrace to his parents. Or the shame he felt creeping around the apartment block, ransacking the homes of his former friends, denuding those few survivors of their possessions. Or the indignity that came from stealing another man's identity, an indignity he deserved. There were times when Memling justified his actions to himself. Cutting the paintings from their frames in the storerooms, rolling up the canvases and hiding them in his kit bag was a way of saving great art, but he knew deep down that he was just a lucky thief.

Marianna's love ennobled Memling, made him a better person, cleansed of his crimes, while his love for her confirmed that far from being a bad person, there was goodness in that steely heart. Twenty years younger than Memling, she was supposed to outlive him and had promised to burn the painting on news of his death. Damn fate for taking her too early. Damn his stupidity for giving the painting to her in the first place.

Memling looked at his watch. It was already 7 p.m. He did not want to go to the Royal Academy opening but knew that he should be seen out and about, acting as if nothing untoward was happening. Pressing a discreet red buzzer on the wall, he gave the signal for his car and driver to pull up outside his house.

For the entire journey from Chester Square to the Royal Academy, Barty, whose trousers were far too tight, stood on the back seat of Vlad's car with his upper body poking out of the sunroof. To capture the spirit of the exhibition, "Music, Madness and Mayhem in Eighteenth-Century France," Barty had dressed as one of Louis XIV's courtiers in skin-hugging electric-yellow breeches, white silk tights and black patent shoes with shiny buckles. A frock coat made of pink damask fell to his mid-thigh and a shirt made of hundreds of tiny ruffles cascaded from his neck to his waist. Made for a child in a BBC period drama from the 1970s, the costume was several sizes too small, even though Barty wore control knickers and a corset and had refused solid food for three days. However, the *pièce de résistance* was a huge wig, two foot tall topped with a golden galleon nestling in clouds of white pomaded hair. "Borrowed it from Elton, darling," Barty would tell anyone who asked, and most who did not.

Vlad pulled the lapels of his leather coat up over his cheeks and, sinking low into the soft white sharkskin seat, hoped that no one he knew would spot them. He felt exhausted by the thought of an evening with Barty.

Bad news had just come in that afternoon from the factory in Eshbijan. A pipe had exploded on the factory floor, spraying 213 workers with molten metal. There were two fatalities, and sixty-four workers were in hospital with fourth-degree

burns. Their families' silence could be bought, suitable repa-
rations made, but if news of the accident got out, Vlad's hope
of launching his company on the London Stock Exchange
would be jeopardised. Almost as worrying was that news of
the accident reached the Leader two hours and forty-five
minutes before Vlad was informed. Clearly the powers were
embedded deep in his organisation. Vlad knew there was no
one he could trust.

"Oh, do cheer up," Barty said, catching a glimpse of the
Russian's morose face. "We are going to a party. If we don't
like it we can go on. That's the lovely thing about the art
world—there's such a gamut of choice. We can be serious in
Spitalfields, grungy in Golders Green or chic in Chelsea.
Mind you, though the venue changes, the people don't. Funny
how insular cultural life is: same old, same old."

Vlad's opinion of the art world was plummeting. In recent
weeks he had looked at several highly prized, ludicrously priced
and utterly baffling exhibitions. One artist had filled bookcases
with hundreds of tiny pots barely visible behind heavily frosted
glass, while another, a German, painted deformed upside-
down figures in a sea of squiggles. Vlad had been offered a
patch of graffiti by a dead street artist for more than the value
of his new house, or the work of a wunderkind who lacquered
flock wallpaper and sold it for hundreds of thousands. What
made the whole sales process even more bewildering was that
to buy one of these works, Vlad would have to join an exclusive waiting list, clearing time unknown. No wonder people
preferred the cash-and-carry system of the auction house. The
week before he had bought a Warhol Elvis and a Chairman
Mao at Monachorum's evening sale, hoping that the Leader
would gratefully receive the King and the Potentate.

To his surprise, the Office of Central Control liked Hirst's
fly-and-diamond paintings but rejected Chairman Mao with
a note saying, "The Leader doesn't want any reminder of

slit eyes." This was as near to a joke as the regime got and Vlad had almost laughed. Barty put the Chinaman in Vlad's new kitchen in Chester Square, saying it was "chic" to have $30 million hanging above the cooker.

Vlad's car turned through the vast ornate gates of the Royal Academy's courtyard. The façade was floodlit and the stone steps were lined with semi-naked dwarfs dressed in gold togas and holding flares. An elephant stood disconsolately to one side, ridden by a young mahout wearing an oversized turban, who was almost blue with cold. The elephant swayed slightly from left to right.

"That poor beast is everywhere this week," Barty said dismissively. "I saw him at Doris's, then at the Credit Russe bash and again at the Astors'."

Vlad followed Barty through revolving doors to the foot of a grand staircase.

"Make way, make way," Barty announced to anyone who might listen. "Meet Vlad."

A few turned curiously, but most were interested only in the business of seeing and being seen. "He's frightfully, stinky rich," Barty said in a stage whisper. "Makes Croesus look like"—he hesitated, struggling for a suitable metaphor—"like a pound store . . . yes, he makes Croesus look . . ." But, distracted by the sight of a wall of photographers, Barty instantly forgot his train of thought.

Looking around, Vlad realised that his red T-shirt offered a rare dash of colour in a sea of black and white, punctuated by an occasional yellow or pink handbag and a turquoise glove peeking from a breast pocket. The men wore unstructured suits and white T-shirts. Most of the women sported dresses cut in angular patterns, their hair was often erratically cropped and many preferred identical heavy-rimmed spectacles.

Barty's outfit delighted the paparazzi and he twirled before them in a blizzard of flashbulbs. Vlad went up the grand carpeted staircase lined with young girls holding trays of champagne. Vlad wondered why the waitresses were so often better-looking than the guests.

Worried that the Russian would tire quickly of the crowd and the paintings with their delicate courtly scenes set in orna-mental glades, Barty left the photographers and, mindful of his tight seams, carefully made his way upstairs. Looking around the first room he was delighted to see many old friends and potential conquests. Barty had a strict ratio of chat to status: only the very important got more than a few minutes; the rest got an air kiss and a few sentences.

The first person he saw was a harassed-looking Septimus Ward-Thomas of the National Gallery.

"Barty, hello," Septimus said wanly.

"You look tired, Septimus," Barty observed.

"Exhausted, actually. The department is insisting on a restructure—whatever that means."

"Bloody bureaucrats," Barty said cheerfully.

"Do you know, I am head of a major gallery but have no time to look at art? My diary is jam-packed with civil servants, union leaders, plutocrats and potential donors."

"I suspect it was ever thus, dear Septimus—van Dyck and Titian had to spend most of their lives kowtowing to their respective Charleses? Poor old Donatello could hardly pick up a chisel without Cosimo de' Medici bursting into his studio. Stiffen your upper lip."

Barty moved off in the direction of Earl Beachendon on the other side of the room. Nimbly avoiding the plump and dull daughter of a client, he greeted the auctioneer warmly.

"Barty, you look marvellous." Beachendon looked at his old friend with amused eyes.

"One tries, one tries," Barty said, smiling. "So you know I have this nice big Russian who wants to buy art."

"The whole of London is talking about nothing else," Beachendon replied truthfully. "I'm longing to meet him."

"I will let you have him next Thursday. Can you throw together a little lunch party? Pretty girls and lots of shopping opportunities."

"You could be my knight in shining armour," Beachendon said.

"There's serious competition," Barty said. Both men understood the code.

"Five per cent?" Beachendon offered.

"Call it six and we will see you next week." Barty smiled happily.

"That leaves me with next to nothing."

"OK—five and a half if he spends less than three million, rising to six per cent after that."

"Four if it's over ten million," Beachendon countered.

Barty put his hands on his hips. "You are a hard taskmaster."

Beachendon smiled. "See you on Thursday."

Spotting Delores in a far corner, Barty headed in her direction. "Why are you standing here? It's right out of the action."

Delores jerked her thumb behind her. "The canapés come out of that door. It means I am first in line."

"What am I going to do with you? If you get any fatter, I will be able to bounce you out of these doors, down Piccadilly and around St. James's Park."

"Your breeches are far too tight. I dare you to eat one crudité—I don't think those seams will hold."

"Yours will burst before mine," Barty quipped back. Spotting Mrs. Appledore across the room, he sprinted away from Delores.

"Darling, your hair. I adore the pink rinse."

"My hairdresser said it was fetching," Mrs. Appledore replied, gently tapping her curls in place.

"Can I copy you?" Barty squealed excitedly.

"Always," said Mrs. Appledore, looking rather pleased; imitation was the best form of flattery.

"You haven't noticed," Barty said, turning his chin to the left and right.

"You saw Frederick!" Mrs. Appledore clapped her hands together. "I can always spot his work. I love the way that he leaves a tiny dimple as his trademark."

Both Mrs. Appledore and Barty had recently visited the Parisian plastic surgeon Frederick Lavalle. They also loved Patrick Brown for tummies but disagreed about who did the best knee tucks. Mrs. Appledore preferred Wain Swanson in Kentucky (famous for working on thoroughbreds' tendons in his spare time), while Barty had recently discovered a "darling man" in Bangkok.

"I am looking for the last trophy painting," she said. "Do you know of any?"

"Masterpieces are so hard to find these days," Barty said.

"It's those Russians—they buy anything," said Mrs. Appledore.

"Don't forget the Qataris," Barty reminded her. "They hold the record."

"When I was a young girl, it was a buyers' market—you could have your pick of ten Titians. Now one is lucky to be offered a minor Canaletto." Mrs. Appledore had rewritten her own history so many times that even she had forgotten her youth was spent on a farm thirty miles south of Warsaw and then in a nunnery outside of Krakow.

"Thank goodness for the three Ds: Debt, Death and Divorce. Eventually good pieces will come up," Barty said.

"The museums spoil everything by buying things. It's so hard to get works of art out of national institutions," Mrs. Appledore lamented.

"Don't worry, darling, they are all so cash-strapped that it's only a matter of time before they start de-acquisitioning."

Looking over Mrs. A's shoulder, Barty watched the Sheikha of Alwabbi walk up the stairs flanked by four ladies-in-waiting and seven security officers. She was dressed in a magnificent white cashmere couture dress and kid-leather shoes with diamond-encrusted heels.

"Do you know that she has a room the size of a tennis court just for her jewels?" Barty said.

"Who? What are you talking about?" Mrs. Appledore turned to follow Barty's gaze. "Oh my God. Look at that rock. It's the Dar a Leila—it used to belong to Shah Jahan. Don't you love the way she's had it set?"

The diamond as big as a pigeon's egg hung on a rope of black pearls.

"Too chic," Barty agreed. "I'm going to introduce myself."

Moments later, bending from the waist to the floor, Barty did a deep bow before Her Highness. It was graceful but too much for the seams of his yellow breeches. Those standing behind Barty had a sudden glimpse of his scarlet silk underwear. Barty squealed. Her Highness assumed that this strange man's sudden yelp was a protestation of allegiance, not unlike the ululations that her subjects let out when a member of the Alwabbi family passed by.

Turning into the courtyard of the Royal Academy and seeing a large, living Indian elephant, Annie wondered if she had gone mad. It stood forlornly in front of the doorway, ridden by a frozen-looking boy wearing a turban.

Why the hell did I come? Annie thought, taking a glass of wine in each hand and heading up the large staircase. The email from the lonely hearts club had arrived that afternoon. "Last-minute call-up for all you lonely hearts. Come to the opening of the *fête galante* exhibition at London's Royal Academy tonight, 6:30 to 8 p.m." Not knowing how to kill the hour between finishing Memling's dinner and meeting Jesse at the National Gallery, Annie decided to attend. Perhaps an exhibition called "Music, Madness and Mayhem in Eighteenth-Century France" would provide inspiration for Delores's dinner.

Vlad, keen to escape from Barty, found himself looking idly at the paintings. Most were whimsical pastoral scenes: people dressed much like Barty, frolicking in glades. The subject matter and atmosphere were in total contrast to Vlad's former life in Siberia, and for that reason alone he quite liked the pictures.

At the end of the main room there was a single canvas of a nearly life-size clown dressed in white with the saddest expression that Vlad had ever seen. Vlad looked into the man's eyes and was shocked to realise that this inanimate Pierrot, painted nearly three hundred years before Vlad's birth, understood exactly what he was feeling. The clown radiated a feeling of loss, of being isolated in a strange country, of a life lived without purpose or meaning; above all, the clown knew how it felt to be rejected. Vlad knew this strange painted man had, like him, loved a woman who was unobtainable and was also an exile from his homeland. Vlad began to cry; great fat salty tears coursed down his face followed by involuntary sobs pressing the wind out of his ribcage. Patting his pockets, he hoped that someone, one of his many servants perhaps, had thought to put a handkerchief there. There were none, of course, and he raised his jacket towards his nose.

"Here, have this."

Through tear-filled eyes Vlad looked down and saw a delicate hand holding out a large piece of material.

"It makes me want to cry too. I know exactly how he is feeling," Annie said, handing the dishcloth that she had forgotten to take out of her work trousers to the weeping man.

Vlad wiped his eyes with the stripy material and looked at the woman dressed in black trousers, a duffle coat and Doc Martens standing beside him. She had a mane of curly auburn-coloured hair and a dusting of freckles on her nose.

"You an art advisor?" he asked, thinking of Lyudmila.

"I'm a cook," Annie said.

Though she was not blonde and was rather small, Vlad

thought there was something attractive and wonderfully tender about her.

"Do paintings always reduce you to tears?" Annie asked.

Vlad shook his head—he was beginning to feel embarrassed.

"Shall we walk round together?" Annie asked. "I don't know anyone here."

Vlad nodded and followed her into the next room. Few had strayed away from the central party and Vlad and Annie were able to look at the pictures unimpeded.

"I am beginning to really like Watteau's works," Annie said. "His characters are so real, his colours so vibrant and the compositions crackle with life."

Vlad nodded but he was looking at Annie. Could she be the one to help stave off his loneliness?

"You can almost overhear their conversations. In fact, I wonder if, viewed together, these pictures are an early version of sitcoms? Look," she said, glancing from one canvas to another, "the same people appear in different pictures." Annie pointed out a flat-faced man and a woman with an upturned nose who seemed to pop up in one painting and then in another. "Oh do look—here is the clown again, looking even more downcast."

Though his English had improved, Vlad had trouble following the conversation.

"Dinner tonight, you?" Vlad asked Annie, assuming that Barty would know the best place.

"No thank you," she said firmly.

"Please," Vlad said. Suddenly, he really wanted this woman to talk to him, and to share an evening with him.

"I have an appointment," said Annie. A few weeks ago she might have said yes. She liked the Russian's sad face, his battered demeanour and even the hideous oversized leather jacket. She was also amused that in this sea of wealthy, connected people, the only other seemingly poor and lonely person had asked her out.

. . .

Twenty minutes later, Annie was standing with Jesse and
Agatha in the National Gallery's conservation studio considering the painting. It was just after 7:45 p.m., the sky outside had turned an inky black and the room was lit by one
harsh tungsten bulb. Jesse tried to appear nonchalant and not
look at Annie too often. Since their last meeting, she had,
he decided, become more beautiful. Her hair settled like an
auburn halo around her face and her white skin seemed to
glow in the dark. Everything about her was fragile yet strong,
energetic yet wistful. In the unflattering glare of the overhead
light, he marvelled at her black lashes, the bluish hue of her
eyelids, the pink curves of her earlobes and a tiny smattering
of freckles, shaped like a crescent moon, on the back of her
left hand.

"Though it is far too soon to make pronouncements,"
Agatha told Annie, "there is good evidence to suggest that
your painting is from the early eighteenth century and is not
a copy."

"How can you be so sure?" Annie tried to swallow her
excitement.

"There are several technical tricks we use. The first is a
cleaning patch." She pointed to a piece of sky and the treetops in the top left-hand corner. Compared to the dull yellows
in the rest of the painting, this little area, about the size of a
matchbox, had sprung into life; the foliage shimmered.

"Why didn't you go further?" Annie asked.

"Even that little patch test took about fifteen hours of painstaking work," Jesse explained. "It has to be done at a snail's
pace to avoid accidental damage."

"I'm sorry—I didn't mean to sound presumptuous." Annie
blushed, feeling brash and ungrateful. This woman was working for free and in her spare time.

Agatha smiled. "As I said, this picture has brought Jesse back into my life, so it's a fair exchange."

Jesse smiled gratefully at Agatha.

"The main problem is that the original paint had been covered with successive coats of thick brown varnish. Going forward, we will have to make a decision whether to take it all off or thin it out. Although the first is easier to achieve, it can remove the old patina. Thankfully the last few people to slap on a coat or two of varnish used a mastic resin base, which is the most reversible."

Taking her torch, she beckoned for Annie to come close to the painting and, with her finger hovering over the surface, she pointed to the cleaned patch.

"Whoever did this was an extraordinarily skilled painter: just look at this foliage. Although it has all the depth and movement of a deep glade on a hot summer's day, though you can almost hear the bird song and smell the sun's warmth on the leaves, he has made the whole thing with just a few dabs of brown and reddish brown."

"But the effect is green and gold," Annie said, staring in wonder.

"He prepared a blue and white ground and then flicked the colours over," Agatha said, shining the torch over the area. "It's also possible that he used a green or brown glaze of his own. If we take off too much varnish, we could wipe away his work."

Putting down the torch, she went over to her worktable and returned with three large black-and-white photographs. Annie looked at one but could not really understand it—it was grainy and smudged but there was a ghost of a figure and a few highlights in white, visible in one corner. Looking more closely, she recognised the outline of a clown. In the next photograph, she detected the woman and her admirer. The last photograph was unreadable, to her untrained eye; a series of squares and numerals.

"You are right to look nonplussed by this one," Agatha said, smiling. "Two of the X-rays are obvious but this one is of the back of the canvas. Those odd shapes hint at significant and revealing stamps hidden under different linings."

"A bit like pass the parcel—you never know what you will find when you take off the wrapping," Jesse said, and he and Agatha laughed.

"Stamps?" Annie asked, baffled by the conversation and failing to get the joke.

"In much the same way as a farmer stamps his cows, owners like to leave a proprietary mark," Agatha explained before bringing out two photocopies of similar crests taken from a book and placing these next to the large photograph.

"This crest is undoubtedly the same insignia that Frederick the Great, King of Prussia, used but even more interestingly, this number, three hundred and twelve, is a cataloguing system that Louis XV put on pictures that entered his collection between March and September 1745."

"How on earth do you know that?" Annie asked, studying the sequence of numbers.

"A colleague's life work has been cross-referencing contemporary sales catalogues and inventories from that period. Using his research we have been able to pinpoint when works went in and out of the royal collection."

"Perhaps the gallery should start hanging paintings with their backs on show," Jesse joked.

"You might laugh but we have often discussed doing just that," Agatha said.

"What else did you discover?" Annie asked.

"There are two other numbers—here, at the bottom, two hundred and thirty-four, and in the top right-hand corner, you can just see the outline of an eighty—the latter looks a little bit like Catherine the Great's, but that would be far too exciting."

"Why?"

"It would mean that your little picture has the most interesting history or provenance of any work I have ever come across," Agatha said.

Annie, Jesse and Agatha looked at the painting. Annie thought back to the anvil-faced man at the British Museum: was this the answer to his riddle? She tried to remember the kings' and queens' names. What was it he had said? Louis, Catherine and Victoria? Annie tried to remember.

"Just imagine—you would be linked to some of the greatest rulers in history," Jesse said to Annie.

"From king to queen to Miss Annie McDee, mistress of a small flat in Shepherd's Bush, four pairs of trousers, eleven shirts, three pairs of shoes, a black dress, and a broken washing machine," Annie said, with more than a trace of irony.

"Plus a masterpiece," Jesse added.

"It partly explains why people want to own great works. It connects them to a glorious heritage and magnificent rulers," Agatha said.

Annie made a fake royal wave at Jesse, who bowed deferentially.

"Actually, there is more good news," Agatha said, producing what to Annie looked like an X-ray. Just visible among the greys were the flowing white lines of the artist's preparatory sketch.

"We used infrared reflectography on the painting and if you look closely, you can see an underdrawing."

"What does this mean?" Annie asked, confused.

"That it is highly unlikely to be a copy. Copyists don't need to work out where or how to place their figures—the original artist has done that for them."

Agatha produced a handful of photocopies of the reflectographs taken from other pictures by Watteau as comparisons.

"I don't want to raise your hopes but these images are X-rays of other paintings by Watteau and you can see certain similarities."

Annie looked closely, but to her the white marks could have been done by anyone.

"It's like spotting a person's handwriting," Jesse explained. "Different artists used different strokes and techniques."

Picking up one example, Annie thought she could detect a faint pattern beneath the pastoral scene—a shield? Or a lance? "What does this mean?" she asked.

"Watteau was often too poor to buy canvas so he painted on whatever came to hand. In this case it was the back of coach doors covered in heraldic signs. We know of another painting, *La Declaration*, that he painted over a copperplate engraving."

"He was too poor to afford a piece of canvas?" Annie asked.

"That's what we assume. We found another clue about his financial circumstances. Follow me," Agatha said, leading them through the door, along a narrow corridor and through two large doors. Beyond these were a series of rooms organised like a scientific laboratory.

The room was small and dark. There were several computers on the table and the walls were lined with shelves laden with test tubes and scientific paraphernalia. Annie looked at Jesse in amazement. She walked past the National Gallery twice a day and assumed that it was merely a repository for paintings.

Sitting at one screen was a man in a white coat, with wild grey hair and an irrepressibly cheerful expression.

"This is Dr. Frears," Agatha said.

"The lucky lady," Dr. Frears said, getting up from his computer and holding out his hand. "Most of us can only dream of walking out of a junk shop with a lovely work of art."

"Maybe it only happens to people who know nothing," Annie said wryly.

"Would you like to see what I have been studying?"

Annie nodded. In spite of her scepticism and Delores's impending dinner, these engaging people and their extraordinary expertise were capturing her imagination. She followed Dr. Frears to his computer and looked at an image of a mille-feuille gateau with layers of different-coloured cream and fruit.

"A cake?" she asked.

"This is a cross-section of a pinprick of paint taken from the side of your canvas multiplied several million times," explained Dr. Frears. "While not visible to the human eye, that little spot can tell us many stories."

Fascinated but entirely bewildered, Annie looked back at the image.

"The pigments used in your painting are identical to others in works by Antoine Watteau. What is fascinating is this tiny fragment of Prussian blue—we know that this pigment only arrived in Paris in early 1700. How your man could have afforded it is anyone's guess. In this lower section is an iron oxide that he often used and which we know came from a shop quite near to his lodgings."

Annie and Jesse leaned in to the computer to inspect the layers of gradated colour and grain.

"So, as this young man suspected," Dr. Frears nodded at Jesse, "we cannot discount that the picture was by Watteau's hand."

"Surely it proves it?" Annie said.

"Unfortunately we can't conclude that. Our work is mainly to discount rather than prove," Agatha said.

"Another absolutely fascinating discovery is here." Dr. Frears pointed to a tiny black mark. "This turns out to be part of a brush bristle."

Annie bit her lip—she wanted to giggle—what else would someone paint with?

Dr. Frears ploughed on. "There is also a trace of wine and blood and some kind of animal fat mixed in with the paint."

"Perhaps we should send his DNA to our friends at King's College?" Agatha suggested.

"So they can clone the painter?" Annie asked.

Dr. Frears smiled. "You never know!"

An hour later, in a small pub off St. James's Square, Annie and Jesse sat at the corner table drinking white wine.

"I'd love to have bought you champagne," Jesse said apologetically.

"This is lovely, thank you," Annie said.

"Here's to your painting." Jesse raised his wine glass and Annie tapped hers against his. Having a drink with him was the least she could do. There was a clock on the wall behind the bar, it was 8:30 p.m.; Annie was tired and wanted to get home.

"You must be excited about the picture," Jesse said.

"Excited? I don't understand this world. There is evidence to say that the picture is authentic. The restorer likes it and the scientist admires it. Age tests bear out. Paint tests stack up. There is even an engraving of the same work in a catalogue but yet none of this matters unless certain experts agree."

"Art is subjective," Jesse said.

"So is God."

"Isn't it comforting that beauty can't be decided by science? That it is in the eye of the beholder?" Jesse asked.

"That is too random for me."

"Isn't it like cooking—you can never quite tell how things will turn out?"

"At least there is a time frame with food—if you go on too long it spoils or burns."

"We have found out so much in a relatively short time," Jesse said. "We know that the picture is old, that it was painted at the time Watteau lived. That it was owned by some swanky people and that it isn't a copy."

"What next?"

I would like to kiss you, Jesse thought. I long to take you in my arms and brush the crossness and hurt out of your shoulders and kiss your eyelids. I want to stand next to you every minute of every day. I want to tell you how extraordinary you are to me.

Forcing these feelings aside, he said, "Let's try and prove a strong line of ownership from the present day back to the early eighteenth century and make the case far more compelling."

Annie looked across the pub at another couple sitting hand in hand looking at a holiday brochure. Something about the way that the woman leaned into the crook of the man's arm made her longing to be held almost overwhelming.

"Why?" Annie asked, forcing herself back to the present.

"Why what?" Jesse asked.

"Why are you helping me?"

"Isn't it obvious?" Jesse said. "I like you. A lot. I was hoping that you might like me enough, a little bit enough, that is, to go on seeing me."

Annie looked into her glass of wine, a feeling of panic welling up inside her. She could cope with meaningless encounters, but the prospect of real emotional involvement was terrifying.

"I don't feel the same way. I'm sorry." She stood up, pulled on her coat, rushed out of the pub and on to the street. Walking away as fast as she could, she told herself: I must not fall for anyone again, it just leads to desolation. I must not.

Jesse sat for a few moments staring into his half-drunk glass of wine, unable to understand how he had misjudged the situation so badly. While it was true that Annie had never actively encouraged him, nor had she rejected him. He didn't feel angry, just abject. Jumping up, he ran after her.

Looking up and down King Street, he caught sight of her hunched figure heading towards St. James's. Jesse sprinted down the road and caught up with Annie as she turned the corner.

"Wait, please," he said, panting, out of breath. "I am not in the habit of making declarations to women—in fact, you are the first and, if you must know, I feel like an absolute idiot pursuing you like this, but I am overwhelmed, literally, by my feelings for you—I realise that this will probably be the death knell, the final straw, but even if you walk off now, even if I have got this completely wrong, at least if you ever change your mind, you know how to find me."

With this, without giving Annie a moment to reply, he turned and walked quickly away.

Chapter 19

As you may have noticed, the young curator is in love with my mistress; thank goodness she is done with all that. She's packed up those trunks, labelled them "the past" and stored them away in the attic. I am mightily relieved, as love obliterates common sense: look back through history and consider the downright foolishness and acts of moral depravity committed in love's name. It is destructive and a waste of time. I should know, I have witnessed enough of it.

Love can, for limited periods of time, stave off boredom and hunger but let's not get carried away. Death is the only thing humans have to look forward to with any certainty.

Anyway, back to the important issue. *Moi.* Annie needs to explore my history. Why is it so important? Humans need methods of classification and reassurance: price is one indicator of value; scholarship is another. If a great brain writes convincingly on a painter or his oeuvre, its cachet is increased.

My erstwhile owner Monsieur Duveen, that impecunious dealer (who spawned today's art market), employed one of the greatest scholars of all time, Bernard Berenson, and together they whipped up storms of desirability around many works.

Value also accrues by association. As St. Augustine said, "Tell me who you walk with and I will tell you who you are." In pictorial terms, tell me who you've hung with and I'll tell you what you are worth. When a handsome, desirable young woman falls for a plain man, he suddenly becomes attractive. If a coterie pronounces on the subtleties of a great book, everyone wants to read it. As far as you, my reader, are concerned, a junk-shop owner and now a girl have owned me, so you don't think much of me. If I tell you I have been owned by kings, queens, a Holy Roman emperor, a pope, a great philosopher and a few others, you become interested.

As the decades rolled by, as I was passed from one illustrious owner to another, my value increased. Who wouldn't want to own something precious to a great emperor or king? Who wouldn't want to be linked to past glory, to monumental power? Most want their taste confirmed and ratified. Art is entirely subjective, so how soothing, how affirming it must be to share the choices of monumental figures from history. Great minds think alike.

My history is strewn with sex and love and lust and even a dead body or two. What follows is not an ascetic history lesson; it's a high-class first-degree romp. I am called, and I personify, *The Improbability of Love*. I was painted to celebrate the wild cascades of *amour*, the rollicking, bucking, breaking and transformative passion that inevitably gives way to miserable, constricting, overbearing disappointment. At first my master imbued every tiny brushstroke with unbound ardour, untrammelled desire and unquenchable lust. During the painting of the work he had to accept that his feelings were a mirage, a chimera in his mind. This is the great tragedy of love—even if you are lucky enough to stumble on it, it never lasts. Every young person believes that their case will be different; fools, damn fools.

Alors. My master never achieved either the fame or acclaim he deserved during his lifetime. Maybe if he had lived longer, been remotely interested in courtly life and had a more calculating dealer, things would have been different. However, he had the one thing that most powerful people want: creative talent. I have noticed that the moment people become rich and achieve their earthly desires they enter a painful, spiritual vacuum. Few wealthy people turn to religion. What's the point when it's easier for a camel to pass through the eye of a needle than for a rich man to get to heaven? Instead they often look to the soothing power of beauty. Art makes mortals feel closer to heaven. Look at any number of popes who filled the Vatican with Michelangelos or Berninis, or the noblemen and royalty: the Sforzas and Leonardo Da Vinci; the Medicis loved Raphael; Charles V loved Titian; Philip IV of Spain loved Velázquez, and so on. I once met a cynical painting by Courbet who said the rich bought art because they had run out of other things to spend their money on. A Corot claimed that it was copycat syndrome—just do as others do. Nothing drives men crazier than the inability to possess.

I have also observed that collectors buy for slightly different reasons: partly for investment, partly to big it up with their friends, partly to decorate, but mainly in the hope that the cloak of creativity could extend to cover their shoulders. Beauty has an intrinsic value. From the earliest Chinese dynasties, from the Pharaohs, to the Greeks and on through history, men have believed that beauty makes them better, lifts them from the morass of their sordid business deals to a higher plane.

My little theory is that at the heart of all human anxiety is the fear of loneliness. It starts with their expulsion from the womb and ends with a hole in the ground. In between it's just a desperate struggle to stave off separation anxiety using any kind of gratification—love, sex, shopping, drink, you name it.

My composition is about the fleeting, transformative respite over aloneness that love offers despite the cold certainty that this reprieve is only transitory.

You will see all these impulses played out again and again with each of my owners.

Paris was a small place in the early 1700s and when word got out that there was a painter who refused to sell a painting, it titillated the palates of all and sundry. There is nothing so desirable as the unobtainable. Though few had ever seen me, the rich and powerful sent nuncios, messengers, ambassadors and minions with gold and jewels to entice my master into selling. It became a badge of honour, an extraordinary game to try and win me. *Non*, Antoine always said. My sale could have saved him, bought a decent roof over his head, the best doctors and food. Think too of the amount of work he could have produced if he'd had a studio (he squatted in others' houses) or decent paints (he could never afford sable brushes or the best pigments). I was some kind of talisman to him. At least you embody my one great memory, he would say before weeping. He would not part with me.

I remember one afternoon in 1709: Madame de Maintenon, who had heard from her friend, Le Comte de Caylus, one of my master's patrons, that I existed, arrived at the house of Monsieur Crozat demanding to see the scoundrel painter who had refused to sell her minion a certain picture. Now Crozat, like any mere mortal, was absolutely terrified. Madame de Maintenon was the royal mistress, potentially the queen, and a royal command is a royal command. Crozat promised to do everything in his power to persuade my master to sell. My master wasn't having it. (I was a little disappointed. I wanted to look around Versailles and witness court life first-hand.) His refusal to sell had direct consequences: my master failed to gain the Prix de Rome and was rejected by the Academy. An unofficial decree went out that no one was to buy his work.

After my poor master died in abject penury in 1721 (so young, such *tristesse*, what a waste) there was a slight fight between his friends as to who should inherit *moi*. In the end, Jean de Julienne's suit prevailed on condition that he would never sell me during his lifetime. He meant it but even the best intentions get capsized on a sea of necessity. You see, Monsieur Julienne had a problem that grew month on month; between 1726 and 1735 he oversaw and financed the publication of some 495 prints in four volumes of the *catalogue raisonné* of my master's work, the same ones that Annie examined at the British Museum. It was an unprecedented commitment to a contemporary artist. Julienne, however, was not a wealthy man. He ran into financial difficulties and decided to sacrifice the jewel in his collection, *moi*, for a greater cause. There were many offers but Julienne understood that I should belong to someone fitting. Emissaries from George I, from the guardians of the young Louis XV, from two popes and a host of noblemen all came to make offers, substantial offers. He turned them all down until one long dark afternoon in 1729, when there was a knock at his door. The man before him was prostrate with grief and excitement; his tale of love and woe came tumbling out. That afternoon he had met the love of his life and somehow had to convince the lady of his passion.

Her name was the Marquise du Châtelet, Gabrielle Émilie le Tonnelier de Breteuil; he was François-Marie Arouet, better known as Voltaire, the great writer, historian, philosopher and champion of civil liberties. It was an unfortunate trick of timing that the Marquise Émilie was not only married but also pregnant. She had rejected Voltaire's advances as improper, inappropriate. The good lady was a mathematician and physicist, not given, one imagined, to entertaining wild proclamations. Voltaire loved her instantly and told her that he would wait till her confinement ended. She rolled her eyes and looked thoroughly unconvinced. "You see, Monsieur Julienne," the great man cried, "I need a message of love, something that will sit by her bed and remind her endlessly, romantically of me."

So it came to pass that I left Paris late in 1729 on a stagecoach with a designated handler. It was not my first trip away from the metropolis—we had been to London (hated it) and Valenciennes, where my master hailed from, and had made the odd trip to the countryside. I was to learn that Émilie's marriage to the Marquis Florent-Claude du Chastellet-Lomont had been arranged only four years earlier when she was just eighteen and he was thirty. Two children followed in quick succession and though she tried to prevent another, shortly before meeting Voltaire she fell pregnant again (raped, in case you were wondering). This might explain why Émilie decamped in haste to her husband's seat in north-eastern France, leaving him to ravish mistresses and prostitutes in Paris.

I admired but never warmed to Émilie. She was too serious. Her father, a minor noble and a *salonnier* in the court of Louis XIV, spotted his daughter's intellect at an early age and trained her much as one might do a monkey. Her tricks were intellectual rather than physical. By the age of twelve she was fluent in Latin, Greek, Italian and German. Her idea of fun was translating foreign languages into French. Naturally her mother was horrified by these unladylike pursuits and threatened to send Émilie to a convent. As we all know, a fierce female mind is a passion-killer. Men prefer the breast to the brain. Émilie's only suitor was the lame old marquis. Even Voltaire, writing to his friend Frederick II, said she was "a great man whose only fault was being a woman." Perhaps he was a little harsh. She could dance, play a little harpsichord and sing in tune, but these were prerequisites for any lady.

Émilie kept me by her bed. I like to think that I was the first and last thing she thought of. My magic worked. Within four years, Voltaire was her lover and installed at the family château. The old marquis didn't mind too much; he found a buxom wench without a brain cell in her head. I can't say it was my most exciting post. Voltaire and his mistress had a cerebral rather than a carnal relationship. When he stormed into her chamber, eyes aflame, nightdress akimbo, it was generally to discuss some libertarian theory or read from one of his pamphlets. While I hung around he completed 438 books, plays, letters, poems and pamphlets along with scientific and historical works. Émilie was almost as prolific: papers on kinetic energy, the science of fire, laws, algebra, and calculus. I am told that her translation of and commentary on Isaac Newton's *Principia Mathematica* is still in print.

I am not saying Voltaire was dull! Indeed he was probably my most amusing, learned and inspirational owner. Émilie, however, for all her intellectual prowess, wanted to sample eroticism. Perhaps for her it was another branch of learning or a human need but she yearned for passion, to be held, ravaged, taken from her mind into rapture. She began to take lovers, none satisfactorily (I should know—I witnessed). Voltaire did not mind; I am not sure he even noticed.

It was a sunny afternoon in 1745 when she saw *him*, the poet Jean François de Saint-Lambert; finally Émilie had found her grand project. It was a *"coup de foudre,"* instant unbridled lust. It was also totally unrequited. Émilie was not used to being thwarted. As a rich, powerful and clever woman, there were few situations she couldn't solve. It was the first time in her short life that her equations, hypotheses and theorems were rendered useless. In matters of love, the heart is illogical, the mind irrational. Émilie's problem was called Madame de Bouffleurs, better known as "The Lady of Delights," with whom Jean François was deeply, wildly, passionately in love.

Poor Émilie tried everything. Dropping handkerchiefs, a bolting horse, sweetmeats, parties, sonnets, but nothing worked. Then one day, through a veil of tears, she saw me as if for the first time. Two hours later, on the afternoon of 22 January 1745, I was dispatched to the poet's house. He understood my power but rather than keep me, he immediately presented me to the

Lady of Delights. I must say life in her bedchamber was jolly interesting. A king, a poet, a lawyer and even an abbot passed through her boudoir in the same week.

One evening, 28 February 1745, and I shall never forget this, a certain lady, Jeanne Antoinette Poisson, appeared in my new mistress's chamber. She had come for advice: how to catch a king. Introduced to Louis XV at the Royal Masked Ball on 26 February, she had tickled the monarch's fancy. Recently his third official mistress had died, creating a vacancy. This was the greatest job opportunity for any woman west of Constantinople. However, she was not the only candidate.

The Lady of Delights gave peerless advice: forget coquetry, be direct, and be passionate yet correct. Men need reassurance; they need to know that you love them. Casting her eye around the room, she lit on me and without further ado, I was handed to Jeanne Antoinette. Yet again my powers as an aphrodisiac and a Circe had been recognised. Ten days later, I was delivered to the King of France. One was pleased to finally make it into Versailles. *Naturellement*, with my powers of inspiration, it only took three weeks until Mademoiselle Poisson was proclaimed the official mistress (which, lucky her, was followed by ennoblement, estates, an apartment directly below His Majesty); the transformation of a Miss Fish to Madame de Pompadour; it was all down to *moi*.

The problem was that you could take a girl out of a bourgeois upbringing, dress her, ennoble her, lavish love and art and jewels on her, but ultimately, she was still considered not one of us—and not just at court. The French are a horribly snobby race. It was fine for the King to have powerful consorts as long as they were posh. Madame de Pompadour was and continues to be much maligned on account of her lowly birth. There were many redeeming features: she loved the arts and, despite some of her more outrageous pronouncements, had a fondness for the masses. Indeed, la Pompadour was a perfect provincial mother. That, ultimately, was her undoing: men don't want to make love to Mummy (unless they are English). After 1750, the King never again laid a finger on the lady. He installed a series of lovers in a small mansion at the Parc-aux-Cerfs. Madame de P. shrugged most of these off until the arrival of Louise O'Murphy. At the age of thirteen she had already caught the eye of Casanova, who called her "a pretty, ragged, dirty little creature." (Though I hate to give others credit, the most sensual painting in history is probably Boucher's portrait of Louise.)

Miss Louise got too big for her tiny boots and was dispatched after two years. When the little hussy left, she stole me, believing, as many at court did, that I was the magical element holding Louis and his mistress together.

My next significant journey was to Russia, to the bedroom of Catherine the Great. Suffice to say that everything you hear (apart from the horse) was true. I have never ever in all my years met a woman or a man with such appetites. Even Monsieur Casanova didn't come close. I was bought as a present by the Polish nobleman, Stanisław Poniatowski, for the Queen in 1755. Stanisław was the most important patron of the Polish Enlightenment, a purveyor of theatre, painting, literature and architecture—so, little wonder that I caught his eye. Of course their affair was doomed, although she gave him a daughter and the throne of Poland. She tired of him in 1759 and moved on to the Orlov brothers. Stanisław never married; he died of a broken heart. I would have loved to have stayed in St. Petersburg, the capital of the developed world. If so I would now be with my erstwhile friends by Leonardo, Michelangelo, Titian and co. But evil Count Orlov had other plans. He could not stand my face, could not bear to be reminded that his Empress had a past.

Once again I was on my way. Francis II, the Holy Roman Emperor, bought me as a tool of seduction for the Countess Wilhelmina von Neipperg. After sixteen children with his wife Maria Theresa, he should have put away his tool. His young mistress was as brutal and ambitious as they come. When he announced his intention to leave her, she begged for one last date, a trip to the opera. Francis fell ill during the second act; by the time his carriage reached home, the emperor was dead. Poisoned by viper juice administered via the prick of her diamond brooch.

The dainty-footed murderess sold me immediately. By a series of fortuitous circumstances, I ended up with the Count Gregory Velovitch. Now history has savagely etched his name from memory and it's a singular shame that my master or anyone else of that stature never painted him. The count was a beautiful man, with long delicate limbs, a shock of golden curly hair and eyes as black as liquorice. He was also an extremely ambitious homosexual who had set his sights on Frederick the Great, the King of Prussia.

Many assumed, wrongly, that Frederick loved men. There was one young man, many years before, Hans von Katte, but it was a cerebral, unconsummated love. After that Frederick only had one love: Watteau. Why else did Frederick build his utterly exquisite private palace at Sanssouci in the style that Watteau invented? How else can you explain that monumental paintings were kept elsewhere, in separate galleries, but in his own tiny house, he chose works by my master and his friends? Frederick accepted Count Velovitch's present with great pleasure but had the man's head cut off for suggesting a lewd and improper act.

Of course, Frederick had whippets—but that is another story, for later.

Chapter 20

Long after her employees had left, as darkness slipped like a velvet cloak over the streets of London and street lights cast golden orbs on damp streaky pavements, Rebecca locked the door to her office and spread the company ledgers on the floor. Placing the oldest records nearest the fireplace, she put each of the massive tomes in chronological order. The last time she had studied them, only a few days earlier, she had not known what to look for. Now she was hoping to find evidence to disprove rather than confirm her theories. Rebecca wanted reassurance that her father was Memling Winkleman, Holocaust survivor, upstanding Jew, legitimate picture dealer, loving father and grandfather.

For the first two hours, between 8 and 10 p.m., all the provenances checked seemed legitimate. Starting in 1940, Rebecca matched early acquisitions to invoices and felt her spirits rise until she found the Renoir, *Filles avec parapluies et chien*, bought for a thousand Marks from a family called Gandelstein. At first glance, the bill of sale seemed legitimate, but then Rebecca saw the address, Schwedenstrasse 14, and the date, 14 February 1944. Frau Danica Goldberg had told Rebecca that not one single family from Schwedenstrasse 14 had returned; all had been sent away on death trains, including every single member of the Winkleman family.

Rebecca tried to compose another story. Perhaps her father had acted as a fence, a go-between, selling his Jewish friends' paintings to Nazis, to give them the chance of escape. Rebecca liked this version, but it only bought her a few seconds' respite. Deep down she knew that explanation was improbable.

Pushing her chair back, she went over to the drinks cabinet. It was a fine Art Deco mahogany and gilt cupboard and had been presented to Memling on his seventieth birthday by a grateful client who frequented the same synagogue as the family. The client spent over £10 million a year with Winkleman Fine Art so the cabinet, hideous as it was, stayed. Part of the present was also an unlimited supply of the finest Cristal champagne. The client had died ten years ago but by then, his cabinet had become a feature of the room and, touchingly, the client, in the terms of his will, asked that Winklemans should be kept in Cristal until the day that any descendant of Memling's was no longer active in the business. Rebecca looked at the neat rows of champagne bottles. She thought about opening one but immediately dismissed the thought—there was nothing to celebrate. She needed alcohol; there must be something else. At the back of one cupboard she found a dusty, half-drunk 1962 Scottish malt. She never drank whisky and hoped that it did not go off. Pouring a large slug, she swallowed it in three large gulps. The shock of the burning alcohol on an empty stomach made her splutter.

Fortified, she returned to the vault. By 3 a.m., Rebecca had traced twenty-two paintings back to Schwedenstrasse 14. She cross-referenced her discoveries with Marty's notebook.

He had used, like Memling, the same VZW and NZW classifications but there were other initials that Rebecca did not understand: ERR or KH and a third, NC. She counted seventy references with one or another of these acronyms. Some entries had all three, others just one or two. The most common were the initials KH. Another aspect that troubled her was the whereabouts of certain paintings that Memling apparently owned but had not sold. According to Marty's notebooks there were at least a hundred; Memling must have a secret store.

Flipping between the official ledgers and Marty's notebook, Rebecca tried to match paintings acquired between January 1940 and February 1947 to legitimate provenances. Most had minimal descriptions. "Shepherd with flock" or "Allegory." Next to each was the date of purchase. The vendors were mostly called Herr Schmidt or Herr Brandt and came with job descriptions such as "nobleman" or "farmer." Rebecca continued to bargain with the evidence. At that time, a clever dealer with a modest amount of capital could pick up scores of great paintings. But where would a young man, a survivor of Auschwitz, get hold of that kind of capital?

Rebecca looked at her watch. It was now 4 a.m. Soon a pale sun would eke its way around the edges of the drawn curtains. Rebecca felt slightly faint and suddenly very tired. The office kitchen was downstairs and to get there she had to pass three security cameras and deactivate an alarm. The last thing she wanted was her father or employees asking questions about her unusual nocturnal activity. On her desk there was a box of marzipan flowers, a gift from a client. Rebecca loathed almonds but forced herself to eat. Sitting at her desk she bit into a petal and immediately chased it down with mineral water, waiting for the sugary surge of energy.

To distract herself, Rebecca typed the initials ERR into her computer's search engine. To her relief, the whole first page was devoted to the word's definition. To "err" is to be incorrect or to make a mistake. Perhaps Marty was using Google as a channel of comfort, telling her across time that Memling had done all this by accident. Biting into her second marzipan flower, Rebecca flicked on to the next page. Her eyes ran down the screen and stopped on the words *Einsatzstab Reichsleiter Rosenberg*. Putting the half-eaten sweet down on to the desk, she started to read: ERR was the abbreviation for the task-force led by Nazi Party ideologue Alfred Rosenberg, the man in charge of confiscating all cultural properties belonging to Jews. Feeling a rush of nausea, Rebecca put her hand to her mouth and vomited a combination of whisky, bile and marzipan through her fingers. The computer screen blurred and her heart thumped in her chest. "No, no, no," Rebecca crooned softly, wiping the sick with the back of her hand as she double-clicked on the link and read a short description. "Einsatzstab Reichsleiter Rosenberg (ERR) was the 'Special Task Force' engaged in the plunder of cultural valuables in Nazi-occupied countries during the Second World War, and up until October 1944, 1,418,000 railway wagons containing books and works of art (as well as 427,000 tons by ship) were transported to Germany. Many were bound for Hitler's personal collection, to be housed in Linz."

Without stopping to tidy herself up, Rebecca punched KH into the search engine. Nothing relevant came up. She followed with NC. Again nothing. Stop panicking and think, she scolded herself. Narrow the search. Calling up a site devoted to information about Nazi looted art, she scanned the documents, looking for someone or somewhere with those initials. Within minutes she had two possibilities. Could KH be Karl Haberstock, Hitler's personal art dealer, who advised the Führer on sales and helped the Nazi Party dispose of so-called degenerate art to dissolute Europeans? Reading on, Rebecca learned that Haberstock had brokered more than a hundred sales to Hitler, including *La Danse* by Watteau for 900,000 Reichsmarks, bought from the Crown Prince of Hohenzollern. Looking down the list of Haberstock's sales, Rebecca saw that another Watteau, unnamed, was also sold to Hitler for one million Reichsmarks in 1943—it was identified solely as "The Love" painting; Rebecca shuddered. Was this Memling's missing picture?

Rebecca discovered that although Haberstock was arrested and interrogated after the war, he was released and went on practising as a dealer until the late 1950s. Marty showed in his notebook entries between 1945 and 1956 that Winkleman had bought and sold forty works of art from a small Augsburg gallery identified as KH, including pictures by Rubens, Hals, Wouwerman, van Goyen and Tiepolo. Peppered through the same article were references to Neuschwanstein Castle. Was this Marty's NC? Rebecca looked at images of the fantastical fairy-tale castle perched on a Bavarian hilltop, built for the reclusive King Ludwig in the 1880s. Alfred Rosenberg chose it as the safe house to store looted art. What were the links between her father, Rosenberg, Haberstock and the castle?

Rebecca didn't know quite how long she had been sitting on the floor of her office, her thoughts careering from Marty to her father, trying to disentangle the facts from her feelings. Scores of stolen goods with fake invoices did not necessarily prove Memling was a Nazi Party member or a thief. Perhaps her father had helped these Jews by finding an unscrupulous dealer to buy their chattels when there were many who would have robbed them? Maybe he was a dupe working for Karl Haberstock, and Memling had never quite realised the part that art had played in Hitler's cultural aspirations. Besides, Haberstock had been acquitted of wrong-doing and rehabili- tated, becoming a leading light in Augsburg; the art that he had profited from financially seemed to exonerate him morally: a bequest bearing his name still hangs in the city's museum. Future generations of visitors would surely praise the family for its generosity rather than enquire how those works got into Haberstock's hands.

Rebecca imagined Marty sitting as she was now, having

discovered that their business was built on extortion. Then her heart caught in her throat: Memling's right forearm was tattooed with 887974, the number branded on his skin shortly after his arrival at Auschwitz in 1943. Though Memling rarely spoke of it himself, the potent tattoo was a reminder to all in the art world what this man had suffered. It had helped him become the dealer of choice to many wealthy Jews. Rebecca knew that her father was ruthless and determined, but would he go that far to realise his ambitions? Rebecca's thoughts flicked back to her brother's sudden death. Was it misadventure or murder? She stopped—what was she thinking? Memling had loved his son with a passion. He would never do that, would he? Rebecca felt tendrils of doubt and fear creep from her stomach to her chest and tighten around her heart. Again she went to the drawer of her desk and checked that her gun was still there and loaded.

Looking at her watch, Rebecca saw it was already 5 a.m. Sometimes Memling arrived early. She had to cover her tracks quickly. Jumping up, she started to replace the ledgers in the walk-in safe, making sure that each was returned to exactly the same place. Taking a cloth, she wiped away her fingerprints from the shelves and the spines. Next she closed the door to the safe and reset the logs, making sure that her previous two entrances were wiped from the electronic records. Ten minutes later, Rebecca slipped out of the back entrance of Winkleman's. She crouched on the step until the security camera was angled away from the door and then walked quickly up Curzon Street and into Berkeley Square; she had never felt so frightened in her life.

The streets were lit by the bluish light of dawn. Apart from the odd taxi, Rebecca had London to herself as she walked, without any direction in mind, hoping that the exercise would bring calm and clarity. Her sense of panic undid her navigation system and later she could not recall where her feet had taken her. Rebecca wondered who else, if anyone, had guessed about her father. The evidence was probably there for anyone to find, but it had suited most to turn a blind eye. The majority of Winkleman's business was legitimate: paintings were bought and sold on the open market. It was a hugely successful operation, worth in excess of £1 billion and turning over several hundreds of millions of pounds per year.

Surely, she thought, someone, an employee, a journalist or a competitor, must have suspected. How could a family from such humble origins possibly have built up a collection innocently during and immediately after the war? Did this explain why Memling kept so many people on an extended payroll, spreading his guilt and culpability like an acidic fog over the international art world? There were monthly payments to a number of "advisors" who alerted the Winklemans to potential sales or matters of relevance: a member of the aristocracy was thinking of selling; a museum's or collector's new acquisition policy, or changes in government legislation. The Winklemans' sphere of influence and patronage spread far and wide. Wealth brought legitimacy, and to bolster their reputation, the family gave generously to charities and museums. Only last week, Rebecca had signed cheques to a Holocaust Museum in Moscow and had paid for the reframing of two Old Masters in the Frick Collection in New York.

The consequences of exposing her father would reverberate through an industry and across continents. Rebecca had to accept that she too was not entirely innocent. She had used her husband's film company as a cover to export priceless works around Europe. She charged all domestic expenses to the business. She listed paintings sold at a fraction of their actual price to avoid taxation. Bringing Memling down would result in bankruptcy and shame for the entire family, their employees and associates. This was the moral dilemma her brother had faced and in his case that knowledge was fatal. Marty, Rebecca knew, could never have lived or operated under the weight of these lies.

Crouching in a doorway out of public view, Rebecca wept. She was trapped, with no way to turn. Perhaps she should, like her brother, opt out of this life. She considered running away—leaving Grace and Carlo and absconding to some far-away island. Could you run away today? Was there anywhere out of reach? She thought not. Memling still had absolute control over Rebecca's finances; he owned her house, paid her salary and her daughter's university fees. Paintings given to his daughter as gifts had their title deeds stored in the offices of offshore companies. Memling had kept his children on a tight rein by refusing to allow them any autonomy and keeping them cosseted by wealth. She used to think it was a kind of benevolent controlling impulse; now she wondered if Memling's iron-fisted control was an insurance policy: he knew his children would not survive outside the nest. Rebecca wasn't qualified to do anything else and if Memling was exposed, she knew she would never work in the art world again. She was in no doubt that Carlo would leave her. The thought of life without her husband made her cry even harder.

Wiping her eyes and smoothing down her crumpled over-coat, Rebecca squared her shoulders; she would delay any decision until she found out the extent of her father's duplicity. Strengthened by a sense of purpose and resolve, Rebecca looked left and right, trying to establish where she had walked. The street sign said EC1—she was several miles from home. A taxi came towards her, its orange light shining cheerfully. Rebecca put out her hand. Their downfall seemed suddenly inevitable but she wondered if, somehow, she could build up a case to mitigate the damage.

Chapter 21

The entrance to the meeting was through a side door of the dilapidated health and well-being centre. Built in the 1970s, the concrete pebbledash façade had worn away and the paintwork was now a rain-stained grey. Taped to the door was a piece of paper with "AA meeting" written by hand and underneath it an arrow pointing upwards, apparently to heaven. Straightening her coat and patting her hair lightly, Evie checked herself in the grimy window. Her appearance was important. She didn't want anyone to think that she was an alcoholic; she was just someone who needed a little support on occasion.

"Are you here for the meeting?" asked a young woman wearing pink trousers, a tight black jumper and a nose piercing, as she pushed past Evie and opened the door to the centre. She waited for Evie to follow her. "It's just at the end of this corridor. I'm Lottie."

Evie wondered how she had guessed.

"Your first time?" Lottie asked. "Don't be scared. We all start somewhere." She walked quickly down the linoleum-lined passage and, turning left at the end, opened another door into a large room.

"Hi, Lottie," a large middle-aged woman in a cardigan and slacks called out.

"Hello, Danni," said Lottie, giving her a big hug. "What did the doctor say last week?"

"He changed my meds—I'm now on a different kind."

"How are they working?"

"Feel a bit off, really," said Danni. She turned to Evie. "Welcome. Is this your first meeting?"

Evie nodded, forcing out a smile. She wanted to turn around and leave. She knew that she didn't belong with these people. Damn Annie for making her promise to attend an Alcoholics Anonymous meeting.

"Cup of tea?" Danni asked.

Evie nodded.

Evie took her tea and chose a chair on the outer edge of the room. Over the next half-hour about fifteen people arrived, all known to each other. The mix of age and background surprised Evie; there was a dapper black man in his seventies, wearing a well-cut suit and carrying a cane; an elderly trim woman, Patricia, dressed immaculately in pearls and a twinset. A grubby teenager arrived with a sixty-year-old in a tracksuit, and a heavily tattooed man with a snub-nosed mongrel. Bella, who intro-duced herself to Evie, must have been a model—the vestige of great beauty clung to her ageing face.

"Just listen to the similarities rather than the differences," Bella advised.

"Keep coming back; it works if you work it," Danni added.

Patricia got up and went to sit at the front of the room behind a Formica table.

"My name is Patricia and I am an alcoholic," she told the

room. Evie had to admit that her story was extraordinary but it had nothing whatsoever to do with her own problems. After Patricia had finished speaking, others took turns to talk about their own stories. Some identified with Patricia, others talked about struggles in their daily lives. Their language was peppered with slogans, "One day at a time" or "it works if you work it." Psychobabble, Evie thought crossly. At the end, five minutes was set aside for newcomers. Everyone looked expectantly at Evie who looked at her feet. Eventually, unable to endure the deafening silence, Evie spoke. "I'm Evie and I am not like any of you." She expected a mass rejection but was surprised when the whole group smiled benignly and encouragingly at her and said in unison, "Welcome, keep coming back. It works if you work it." Evie arranged her mouth in a lukewarm smile. Bloody loonies, she thought.

Nevertheless, she stayed for a cup of tea afterwards. The people were very kind and gave her leaflets and electric-pink-coloured biscuits. Evie took the newcomer's welcome pack back to the flat and left it on the table for Annie to see. Privately she knew that AA was not for her; what she needed was the love of a good man and some money. Evie only drank because she was lonely and broke.

In the good old days, Melanie Appledore thought as she handed her ticket to the man at the door, the chairman of the governors and the director would have met her at the entrance to the Royal Opera House. She still gave $100,000 a year to the institution, but these days, $100,000 didn't buy much respect, just a priority booking number and a small window of time to reserve seats for popular performances. Once upon a time she walked into the lobby and every head turned to look at her and her husband. People knew exactly who she was and the importance of her diamond (the Shimla, 30 carats), the designer of her gown and the value of her sable coat. They would whisper her name and speculate on her husband's net worth. Mrs. Appledore knew that they wondered about her humble beginnings and a former life. Many assumed she was a Jewish refugee, sent to America on Kindertransport before the war. "You know it is too painful for her to talk about," one society friend told another. Melanie did not put them right or wrong; she didn't mind being a Jew to the Jews or a goy to the rest. She knew that she was the object of fascination and occasionally of satire, but it was better to be talked about than never mentioned. Tonight it was like old times; the audience stared and whispered but Mrs. Appledore knew no-one recognised or even cared about her. Instead their attention was aimed at Barty, who had come dressed as the opera's hero Rodolfo, a struggling eighteenth-century writer.

Barty wore a pair of torn breeches with a raggedy frock coat on top. His handkerchief was made from the pages of an unpublished play (written out in best boarding-school writing by Emeline that afternoon), his shoes were mismatched, and on his head Barty wore a bright-pink silk bonnet in deference to Mimi, the opera's heroine. Lucky, Mrs. Appledore thought, they were in a box or many would complain about the hat obscuring views. As it wasn't an opening night, there were no photographers to capture his quite brilliant take on *La Bohème*, but Barty would never let sartorial standards drop. Besides, he had met his latest love, a young fashion student, one night leaving the ballet. Juan de Carlos had asked for his autograph and soon became Barty's screensaver.

Even if no one else understood who Mrs. Appledore was, Barty made a huge fuss of her. Having walked ladies to the ballet and opera for half a century, he knew every back passage, every loo and most of the attendants. Mrs. Appledore would get to her box without being jostled or pushed. They would get the best table in the Crush bar and an ice-cold bottle of champagne would be delivered to the box at the end of each act. Waiting for them in the box were Mrs. Appledore's other guests, the Duke and Duchess of Swindon. Windy Swindon (the nickname came from his ancestral home's position on top of the Marlborough Downs) and his wife Stinky (her real name was Glendora and she never smelled) were, in Barty's opinion, the dullest members of the aristocracy and that was saying something.

"What are you wearing, Barty?" Stinky asked.

"The references aren't that difficult," Barty said, pointing to the bonnet and the manuscript. "I am Rodolfo mourning Mimi."

"Who the fuck are they when they are at home?" Windy asked.

"You are about to find out," Barty said.

"Are they joining us too?" Stinky looked around.

"Rodolfo and Mimi are the hero and heroine of *La Bohème*," Mrs. Appledore said, giving Barty a warning glance.

"It's the opera you are about to see," Barty said incredulously. He often wondered how the aristocracy had survived so much longer than their brain cells.

The bell sounded and in Box 60 the party of four took their seats. Barty chose the high stool at the back, a position he liked. Although it gave an impaired view of the stage, it offered the best view of the audience. Taking his opera glasses out of his pocket, he scanned the boxes opposite and stalls for familiar faces. It was rather a poor night. Lord Beachendon was there with his tired-looking wife in an exhausted dress. She looks, Barty thought, like someone from a 1970s BBC documentary on rural gentility, one of those (probably only fifty-looking seventy-year-old) wives who had been retired to the country in a Laura Ashley smock with a couple of Labradors. Her hair, salt-and-pepper blonde, was pulled back into a velvet band and round her neck she wore the last family heirloom, three strings of good pearls. Earl Beachendon, Barty thought, looked emaciated. His old smoking jacket hung like velvet weeds from narrow, stooped shoulders. His hair, or the very little left of it, needed a trim. Both the Earl and Countess reminded Barty of party balloons left to deflate in a cupboard.

In complete contrast, the next-door box was full of over-pumped hedge-fund types who probably bought the tickets at a City auction, thinking that *Bohème* was related to Beyoncé. Dame Fiona Goldfarb was in the Royal Box (which, as Queen of the Jews and the major patron of the Opera House, she deserved); Tayassa, the eldest daughter of the Emir and Sheikha of Alwabbi, was there (probably deciding whether to build an opera house to go with their new museum) but apart from that, it was all rather déclassé, Barty thought sadly. Once you came to the opera to be seen; now one comes to escape.

The conductor took to the stand and the audience erupted into applause.

"Honestly," Barty whispered to Mrs. Appledore, "it's not like he just landed a holiday plane in the Costa del Sol—let the man prove himself."

The conductor turned to his crowd and bowed.

"Oh do get on with it," Barty said a little too loudly. Then the huge red velvet curtain swept open and the audience was transported on a wave of violins, piccolos, flutes and cellos into Rodolfo's garret, where the writer sat next to an unlit stove, with his friend, the painter Marcello, complaining about being cold and, of course, about love.

In Box 60, four pairs of eyes were fixed on the stage, but four minds were elsewhere. Barty lamented the drop in standards and how sad it was that few bothered to dress for the opera. Mrs. Appledore decided to blow the rest of her husband's foundation on one major donation, a real showstopper. Windy Swindon wondered if he should sell the grouse moor in Scotland. It wasn't worth much these days—the grouse had long since gone—but it might buy a new roof for the west wing of Swindon Hall. Stinky worried about her box-hedge blight that threatened the whole structure of the garden. What could she do to preserve the neat knot garden without box? Someone suggested yew but that took ages to grow; she had not been so worried about anything since Windy took a mistress (she was still around and turned out to be quite convenient really—Stinky was let off conjugal duties, a blessed relief).

When Mimi and Rodolfo declared their love, the music was so rousing and the sight of the diminutive tenor's arms trying to encircle the rotund soprano's girth was so alarming that everyone in Box 60 turned their attention to the stage. Mrs. Appledore began to cry; she remembered the other *Bohèmes* she and her husband had seen, at the Met, La Scala, Teatro La Fenice and the happy times they had spent before he died nearly twenty-two years previously, thus consigning her to a life of pampered peripatetic loneliness, moving between her houses in London, New York, Aspen, Paris, St. Barts, Buenos Aires, Cap Ferrat, St. Moritz and, of course, their yacht. The ever-attentive Barty noticed the three tiny tears meander down Mrs. Appledore's entirely smooth cheek and he passed her a scented handkerchief. Barty understood loneliness and, taking her tiny wizened hand, he held it for the rest of Act Two as gently as a baby swallow.

On stage the young people did what young people did: kissed and drank, fell in love and argued. The audience, most in their dotage, had to trawl the depths of their memories to remember what all that was like.

On the other side of the auditorium Earl Beachendon was not thinking about love or sex; he was worrying about money and a visit he had paid that afternoon to the world's highest-selling contemporary artist, a man formerly known as Gary Mitchell, who now went by the name of Blob. As he was over six feet tall and as etiolated as a peeled cucumber, no one understood why Gary had chosen such an unlikely sobriquet. Gary didn't explain or elaborate; as Lord Beachendon found out that morning, Gary or Blob kept words to a minimum. After two hours spent in his company, all Blob had conceded was "yes," "no" and "maybe," and on the whole only "maybe." Maybe he would consent to a selling sale/exhibition at the auction house. Maybe it would happen this year. Maybe he would split the profits 60/40 with the auction house. Maybe he would leave his dealers.

Lord Beachendon had entered Blob's house with a sense of hope and left in a state of confusion. Blob lived in an exquisite double-fronted Huguenot mansion in Spitalfields (bought for £8 million earlier that year); the Earl had been met by an astonishingly pretty assistant (an MIT graduate) and shown into a waiting area decorated with a Rembrandt (£18 million, sold by the Earl two years earlier). The interiors had been tastefully decorated (at least £250,000 per room) and the carpet was by Aubusson (mint condition, £2 million). Minutes later, Blob's PA, a knock-out in skin-tight black Lycra (double first from Cambridge), greeted him coolly but politely and apologised that Blob was running slightly late. She could offer a glass of Cristal (£290 per bottle) or a Lafite Rothschild 1961 (£450). What depressed Beachendon most was not the amount of money that Blob must have made from his art but that the artist and his set-up brought out Beachendon's basest instincts and most jealous inclinations. Like many of the clients he so despised, the Earl realised that he had become just another person who knew the price of everything and the value of nothing. He had not bothered to look at the Rembrandt or the carpet, he would not be able to taste the claret or admire the woman's brain—all he could think about was what they had cost.

Those mysterious market forces had decided that Blob was "it": the new wunderkind, the commander of great prices. His paintings, phantasmagorical, highly detailed visions of heaven and hell, sold for millions of pounds and the waiting lists were comprised of several hundred collectors. He was the first painter since Hieronymus Bosch to capture the essence of human depravity and virtuosity. Critics, in a rare case of unanimity, agreed that Blob's work reflected everything that was good and bad about contemporary society, and what was more, he was, unlike so many of his peers, a beautiful draftsman and astonishingly accomplished painter. What Lord Beachendon knew was that Blob was sitting on thousands of priceless drawings and preparatory oil sketches. If the artist could be persuaded to bring these to auction, all of Earl Beachendon's troubles would evaporate. The sale of Blob's work would cause a financial and critical sensation. All Blob had to say was yes; all Blob said was maybe.

At exactly the time that Mimi uttered her last breath at Covent Garden, Agatha sent Annie a text with an update on the picture.

"Annie. Discoloured varnish thinned: extraordinary transformation. White cloud is actually a clown! All very Watteau-esque. Further investigation and research needed. Septimus W-T wants pic out of gall. Please pick up ASAP. Best wishes, Agatha."

When the message came through, Annie was still at work waiting for an "oeuf en gelée" to set. She had placed the egg in a mould with nasturtium petals, sprigs of dill and mustard seeds but even after six attempts the result looked messy. She gave Agatha's text a cursory glance, her attention still on the recalcitrant starter: could she create an omelette, roll it up with salmon caviar and chopped steamed spinach to create three layers of colour and set that in aspic? Glancing at the clock she saw it was 10:30 p.m.—it would take an hour to get home on the bus or forty-five minutes to bicycle against a headwind.

The painting, she thought, is too much trouble. She decided to collect it, hang it in her flat and stop this pointless wild goose chase. Miraculous things like discovering lost masterpieces did not happen to women like her. Texting Agatha back, she wrote, "Thanks v much. Will come in ASAP. Best, Annie."

Chapter 22

At 5 a.m. the following morning, the alarm bell rang. Annie lay quietly running through the next couple of hours in her head. The Winklemans were having clients to lunch and had ordered sea bass followed by stewed apple. Rebecca had made it clear that there were to be no more flights of fantasy in the kitchen, only set menus. Annie hoped to find some wild bass but doubted she could find decent apples in March. Her next problem was the certain probability of wet black jeans, which had been sitting in the washing machine since late last night. Stumbling out of her bedroom into the studio room, she chided, "Hurry up, whack oven on, quick shower while it warms, no time for shaving armpits, who'll notice anyway? Black jeans nearly dry, lie on floor, pull. If not dry put them in the oven for a quick steam. Season chicken; rub butter on to skin, place breast down. Take jeans out of oven and hope they don't smell of old beef and cheese. Timer on sixty-five minutes. Call fishmonger."

"Do you know what the first sign of madness is?" Evie asked, lifting her head over the side of the sofa.

"Talking to oneself," Annie said, opening the fridge. "I'm sorry—I forgot you were here."

"Do you know what the second sign of madness is?" Evie asked, running her hands through her hair.

"Looking for hairs on the palms of your hands," Annie said, remembering an old game that mother and daughter played.

"Funny how often people fell for that, wasn't it?" Evie folded away the duvet from her makeshift bed and crossed the room.

"What are you going to do to that bird?" Evie asked as Annie lifted the skinned cooked chicken out of the fridge and placed it on the kitchen table.

Annie was not in the mood to chat; there was too much to do.

"I'm going to make it fit for a king," she said. "Fit for Queen Delores in any case."

"Who's coming over? Someone special?"

"I'm practising for the dinner; it's less than a week away. Can you move out of the way?" Evie stood in the narrow pathway between the fridge and the cooker.

"What's all that?" Evie asked, sitting on the one chair without a wobbly leg and pointing to the assortment of bowls and dishes arranged neatly on the table.

"Mum—please can you move the chair to the other side? And please don't talk, I need to concentrate."

Shuffling her chair away, Evie watched Annie as she carefully arranged her kitchen implements on a clean dishcloth. Knives went in order of length, starting with her prize possession, a Japanese Honyaki blade, so sharp that it could cut a dried piece of pasta cleanly in two. Next to these, Annie laid out wooden spoons, a measuring cup, two bowls and a pair of tweezers.

"I'm sorry—it's the first time I have done this and I'm nervous," Annie said, moving over to the hob where a small pan was simmering expectantly. Annie dropped an aubergine into the one with boiling water and set the timer for ten minutes. Taking a second saucepan from the rack, she mixed cream, a bay leaf and some peppercorns, and stirred it for five minutes. Then, after straining the liquid, she put that to one side.

"Can I ask a question?" Evie said.

"Go on," Annie said as she placed pats of butter in a saucepan and waited for them to melt. Then she stirred two tablespoons of flour in to create a smooth paste. In a separate bowl she dissolved gelatine into some boiling water and combined this with her sauce.

"How many dishes are you expected to do for this dinner?"

"Louis XIV had at least four services with up to seven different dishes in each."

"How many cooks did he have?"

Annie tasted the sauce. "About two thousand permanent staff in his kitchens and it took up to four hundred and ninety-eight people for each dinner, including a procession of fifteen officers of the household. The really fabulous dishes had guards all to themselves and specially assigned courtiers had to bow to the platters."

"There's only you," said Evie incredulously.

"I'll employ at least ten helpers and a few of Carlo's extras to give the occasion a bit of pomp and ceremony. The guy who played the court jester in his last movie is going to be the Principal Cupbearer. If anyone wants some more wine he will shout out, 'A drink for the king or queen.'"

Annie added half a sachet more gelatine and beat her sauce a little more, alternating fast and slow whisks. "I have also got the receptionist, Marsha, you remember her, to serve as the

Officer of the Kitchen—it's her job to taste the food before the guests so if I have poisoned them, she dies first."

"Terrifying," Evie said.

"I love the stakes being so high. These days food doesn't mean enough. It comes in ready-made packets—few would know how to spot a potato or a leek in a garden, let alone how to make a soup or a stew. We should learn how to respect and procure it."

Evie looked at her daughter's shining eyes. "I haven't seen you so fired up for years."

Annie turned and faced her mother. "I have finally found what I really want to do with my life, Mum. It's taken thirty-one years."

"I envy you," Evie said.

"If this dinner is a success, maybe others will follow. Perhaps I will make it as a professional chef."

Giving her saucepan a last stir she poured her cream-based béchamel sauce carefully over the chicken. The pale caramel-coloured liquid ran evenly over the bird, turning its puckered surface glossy and golden. Carefully spooning away any excess liquid, Annie put the bird back in the fridge.

"If anything does go wrong?" Evie asked.

"I shall have to fall on my sword like the chef Vatel, who failed to provide enough roast birds and fresh fish."

"Can I help?"

Annie hesitated. "It's not a good idea."

"I went to an AA meeting yesterday. I am going to change. I promise."

Annie didn't reply. There had been too many new dawns, assurances and hope spilled pointlessly, and this job was too important.

"I have let you down before but this time will be different," said Evie.

Annie didn't answer.

Most of Annie's childhood memories revolved around Evie's new beginnings and her outlandish schemes to get herself "back on track." Where the track had been or was supposed to be going was never explained, but each initiative, often a new career or moneymaking venture, was approached with conviction and gusto. Once Evie decided to become a landscape gardener and spent hours studying Reader's Digest *How To Grow* books. Even though they only had a small window box to practise on, Evie created parklands, borders, hedgerows and vistas in her mind. For several weeks, she described and Annie transcribed her mother's vision on to large pieces of scrap paper, vivified and coloured in watercolours and tacked to the walls of their council flat. Placing adverts in the local paper, in nearby garden centres and on the school noticeboard, Evie even won a job after convincing the vicar that she could transform his small backyard wilderness into a romantic, scented night garden, a place of calm and contemplation. Unfortunately, the vicar's wife, who had a smattering of horticultural knowledge, put a stop to the project when Evie told her that she was going to cover the walls in sweet-smelling, vigorous, climbing chlamydia.

Another scheme had involved breeding teacup-sized Yorkshire terriers, which would sell for £50 each. The parents, Bullseye and Bullet, were brother and sister ("No one need know"), cost £25 each and only managed to produce two pups in one year. One day Annie came home from school to be told that they had, in a tragic double accident-cum-suicide, dashed out into the road and been run over. Distraught and totally unconvinced, Annie did not speak to her mother for three weeks. Then Evie set herself up as a faith healer, then a masseuse and, finally, an aerobics instructor, but they never lived in one place long enough to build up a client base.

They travelled light. Evie had two suitcases and her vanity bag, which held a collection of significant objects, items from her past. There was a diamanté-studded tortoiseshell hair clip that had belonged to Great-Auntie Edna, a photograph of her maternal grandparents and the only thing that had belonged to her father, a copy of *Larousse Gastronomique*, the cookery book he had inherited from an aunt and whose recipes Annie had memorised by the age of thirteen. There was also the remnants of the bouquet Evie had carried on her wedding day and the photograph that Annie coveted most, a photograph of her father lying on a beach asleep, his trilby hat on his stomach, his arms splayed above his head like a small child.

These mementos were Annie's only connections with another life and a wider family. She longed to meet relations and find out if her eyes came from her father or a cousin and discover who else had auburn-coloured hair. With the absence of real people, she made up stories: Granny Josephine with her gout, quick temper and love of Chopin's polonaises; Grandpa Mortimer, who worked as a pig farmer but dreamed of being a perfumer; Aunt Alice, fed up with life on the farm, who ran away to join the local circus and is still riding elephants in Wigan. It was for these disparate relations that Annie began cooking her fantasy feasts. She imagined them all coming to visit and the food would be so delicious that they would put the past behind them, bury slights and hurts. She would have long and imaginary conversations with each, filling them in on aspects of her life.

Her guests would step out of their real lives and into another, becoming, for a few hours at least, travellers transported through time by flavour and costume to another world. Taking her admired characters in history, Annie matched food and ingredients to their particular time and interests. For Boadicea, she stuffed shanks of wild boar with nuts and dates and placed it on a bed of honey-soaked hay. She imagined preparing Elizabeth I's first potato—mashed and served with jugged hare with root vegetables braised in mead. To keep Alexander the Great's strength up on long campaigns, she smoked his fish and braised his vegetables lightly in a herb-infused broth.

Scouring local libraries, she built up a personal index of fantastical foods and settings. They always had to be based in the past, as Annie's present was consistently grim.

The timer on the cooker started to bleat insistently. Annie lifted the aubergine out and placed it, steaming, on to a plate to cool.

"Cup of tea?" Annie asked in a conciliatory tone.

Evie nodded.

"So tell me about the AA meeting."

"It was interesting."

"Interesting?"

Evie nodded. "I don't want to say too much—get our hopes up—but I have not wanted a drink since."

"You only went yesterday!"

"Mostly I think about drinking every minute of every day," Evie said quietly. "From the moment I wake up till I finally go to sleep."

"What's there to think about?" Annie said uncomprehendingly.

"Where I might get some, how to pay for it, how to not have too much, how to have enough. It sounds so mad—you couldn't understand, though, what it's like to be trapped inside the obsession."

Annie didn't reply—but she did understand. For months she had thought of nothing but Desmond, from the first moment she had woken to the last dregs of thoughts before falling asleep.

The timer went off again and Annie took the chicken out of the fridge and, setting it on the table, applied another layer of caramel sauce.

"What are you doing?" Evie asked.

"It should look like it's got a plasticky layer of béchamel on top and been sealed in a solid layer of golden caramel."

"A long process," Evie commented.

"Next week I will have eight to do. All from this kitchen."

She put the chicken back in the fridge to chill. Annie took the cooled aubergine and began to gently scoop out the flesh until only the deep-red skin remained. Taking her sharpest knife she began to cut the skin into diamond shapes. Using tweezers, she lifted each piece aside and arranged them on another plate. In the second bowl she mixed another three tablespoons of gelatine in water and one by one carefully dipped the aubergine-skin diamonds into the solution.

"Are you going to an AA meeting tonight?" Annie asked.

Evie nodded. "I want this to work."

You are not alone there, Annie thought to herself, and opened the fridge door.

She took the chicken out of the fridge and gently nudged a leg. It had set perfectly. Taking the tweezers, she carefully began to lay the diamond strips of aubergine skin in a line from one end to the other. Joining the shapes point to point, she made another line and then another until the chicken was covered in a matrix of ruby-red diamonds on a golden background.

"*Voilà,*" Annie said with great satisfaction.

"It is really beautiful."

"It was one of Louis XV's prized dishes, *poulet au jacquard.* It's supposed to look like a glorious cake."

"Where did you find the recipe?"

"In a musty old book in the London Library. Will it do?"

"I'd eat it."

Annie smiled gratefully.

Evie said, "You look lit up, different somehow."

Annie gave her mother a spontaneous hug. "I'm going to be fired if I don't get going. See you later."

Rebecca arrived at Wiltons at exactly 1 p.m. Tiziano sat outside but got to his feet when he saw her. She stroked the dog's head and went inside.

"Your father is already here, Miss Winkleman," said the

maître d', Mr. Tonks, as he took Rebecca's coat and led her to the table along the corridor hung with caricatures, past the plush red banquettes.

Memling sat in the far corner with his back to the wall reading a new sale catalogue from Monachorum.

"You look pale," he said without looking up.

"I'm fine," said Rebecca, picking up the menu. She knew every dish but hoped that concentrating on the options would calm her beating heart. It was the first time she had seen her father since her trip to Berlin.

"I have already ordered—you needn't bother," said Memling, nodding at the menu. "What do you think of this Boudin coming up next week?"

Rebecca closed the menu. Once she had found her father's insistence on ordering for her rather touching; today she found it maddening. She could feel him counting calories and cholesterol on her behalf. Did he really think his control extended to her body?

"I was never that keen on Boudin," she replied.

"As you know, dear child, a dealer should leave personal feelings out of transactions." Memling used the condescending tone of voice that transported Rebecca back immediately to her younger self. The fifty-year-old woman sitting on the velvet padded banquette turned into a young child locked for eight hours in her bedroom for failing to identify a Fragonard painting. Rebecca raised her hand to attract the attention of the waitress. The woman, middle-aged, wearing a white uniform, hurried over.

"Can I change my main course to roast beef with roast potatoes?" Rebecca asked, knowing that Memling would have ordered her a plain grilled sole.

"Certainly, madam," the waitress replied.

Rebecca thanked her and turned to her father. "The last three Boudins that have come on to the market have sold for less than their low estimates. The very best one was passed on to a minor museum in Arles. The one that is coming up next week has a doubtful provenance and is not, in my opinion, worth even a fraction of its reserve. We have two clients who might be interested in buying a Boudin but one already has a far superior painting that we sold them three years ago and the other just lost forty-five per cent of his net wealth in a bad deal in Azerbaijan. So my advice is to avoid this picture."

Memling looked at her pensively. He couldn't fault her opinion but something about her delivery made him uneasy. There was an unusual brittleness in her voice, a clipped tone that he was unused to hearing.

"Is there something the matter?" he asked.

Rebecca hesitated. She wanted to stand up and shout and ask him a hundred questions. (How could he live with himself? What kind of person could lead this double life?)

"What do you think the Munch will fetch at Monachorum's?" she said instead, changing the subject.

"I asked if something was the matter." Memling leaned towards her and almost put his hand on hers but stopped himself. It had been years since he had touched another person and probably four decades since he had shown his daughter any physical affection.

"There is nothing wrong," Rebecca said crisply.

"Is there any news on the little Watteau?" asked Memling.

Rebecca longed to tell her father about Berlin and Annie and Marty's notebook. She wanted to pose questions and hear plausible answers but for now, secrets were her only weapons. She had to know more before disclosing anything.

"Nothing at all," she said.

"We need to start alerting our contacts," Memling said.

"I thought you wanted this kept quiet?"

"Discretion is getting us nowhere; you have failed to unearth any useful information."

"So your mistake is my fault?" Rebecca snapped.

The waitress brought their food. Rebecca looked at the

plate of bloody beef and felt slightly nauseous. She never ate red meat but today she would have to force this lot down.

"Perhaps you had better tell me why this picture is particularly important?" Rebecca said, trying to keep the tremor out of her voice.

(What lies are you going to spin now? she thought.)

"It belonged to my family; it is the one link I have with them."

(It belonged to a family you stole from, whose memories you raped, whose trust you abused.)

"So why didn't you keep it close by your side?" she asked.

Memling sat very still and looked at his daughter. "There is something I never told you," he started.

Rebecca pushed her plate away. Suddenly she couldn't face the beef. Nor was she sure that she wanted to hear her father's confession. If he told her everything, would she have to act on it? If he confirmed her awful discovery, would that force her to share her knowledge with a wider audience?

"This will upset you," Memling said.

"Then don't tell me," Rebecca said.

Memling carried on. "There was a woman," he said.

"A woman?" Rebecca was confused.

(What does this have to do with the story?)

"Her name was Marianna and she was married to my friend Lionel."

"Marianna Larikson?" Rebecca remembered her parents' friend clearly. She and her husband often came on family holidays and attended most important family events. Rebecca tried to conjure up her appearance—tall with long white-blonde hair and brown eyes, always impeccably turned out, shoes matching her handbag, scarf matching her handkerchief. Now she thought of Marianna, she remembered her mother saying crossly, "Here comes her Royal Highness Queen Matchy-Matchy." Thinking back, Rebecca's mother never said mean things and this remark had been wholly out of character.

Rebecca looked at her father and to her astonishment saw that his eyes were full of tears. She had never seen him cry— even when Marty died.

"I loved her," he said.

"She's been dead for years—what are you talking about?"

"We loved each other but we didn't want to hurt your mother or Lionel or our children, so we kept it a secret. I gave her the Watteau as a token of my love. When she died, her sons sold it. I must have it back. I must." Memling banged the table so hard that other diners turned to look at him with a mixture of concern and irritation.

Rebecca, stunned, looked at her father and tried to add this new information to the shipwreck of emotions.

(What are you trying to tell me? If this were true why would you give someone you loved something so bloodstained? Is this a smokescreen, a way of trying to hide the truth?)

"You are probably thinking, why that picture? Why not anything else in our collection? Why not rubies or diamonds or pearls? Why not houses or money or islands? All those things I could have bought her. But when you see this painting, Rebecca, you will understand. More than any other work you have ever encountered, this painting captures what it means to love. I don't know if you have ever felt that—if you know what it means to have one's heart turned inside out by pure unbridled passion—but this is what I felt for Marianna. She was my reason for living. With her I was someone else, something better, not the reprehensible creature I believed myself to be."

Trying to control her emotions, Rebecca watched as her father broke the bread on his side plate into tiny pieces, and tears ran down his cheeks.

(Is this an admission of guilt? Are you about to tell me the whole stinking story? Did my mother know?)

She did not articulate any of her feelings but watched him in silence.

"Is everything all right?" the waitress asked, looking at their uneaten food.

Rebecca nodded.

"Shall I clear?"

Rebecca nodded again.

Father and daughter continued to sit there silently, staring at the centre of the table. Taking a plain white handkerchief from his pocket, Memling wiped his face.

"Find that picture, Rebecca," Memling said at last. "Do this for me."

"Oh, I will find it," she replied. "If it's the last thing I do." She stood up, folded her napkin carefully and put it on the table. "Goodbye, Father."

Memling didn't look up.

Rebecca walked out of the restaurant. To the casual observer she was a slim, smart, highly confident middle-aged woman with a sharp haircut, dressed in simple expensive clothes. Holding herself tall and keeping her eyes fixed on the door, Rebecca fought to preserve this impression. Once outside, she ran to her car and, slipping into the driver's seat, hidden from view by tinted windows, she clutched the steering wheel with both hands and screamed at her reflection in the driver's mirror.

Chapter 23

Earl Beachendon had been waiting eleven years to visit the studio of Ergon Janáček, the reclusive Czech painter whose work was the first to break through the £1 million barrier in the 1970s and smash the £10 million record the following decade. Janáček lived and worked in Crouch End, in a Georgian coach house, and painted the same seven models at exactly the same time on the same day of the week. The longest sitter had been coming for nearly fifty years and the ingénue for over seventeen. They were expected to pose for up to four hours at a time, sitting in a wooden chair under the large north-facing skylight. Janáček never spoke to them; he was far too absorbed in painting. Attacking the canvas with his hands, with large badger brushes, slapping, daubing, smearing and dolloping paint, Janáček would grunt and scream in frustration as he wrestled with his creative demons. Each portrait took at least seven years to complete; one had

taken seventeen. At the end of each session, when a thick
impasto of gloopy oil paint had been layered on to the canvas,
Janáček scraped the whole mass to the floor. Only the faintest
traces of the day's endeavours were left. Turning the canvas to
the wall, he opened the studio door and waited silently for his
sitter to leave.

This process was repeated week in and week out, year in,
year out, until one day, Janáček realised the work was complete. Only a few cognoscenti could discern a person within
the heavy impasto, the swirling mass of paint and colour.
Asked why they made such a long and exhausting commitment, the sitters seemed nonplussed by the question, as if
a motive were irrelevant. Most had been there long before
Janáček became a world-renowned figure; they had started
when the wooden chair was an old orange crate and there
had been no money even for a small blow heater. Those small
luxuries arrived later. The sitters were never paid, though all
could have used some extra cash. Occasionally they were
given presents or paintings. Pressed harder, one or two admitted that it gave them pleasure to be involved in the creative
process, even if vicariously. One or two said that the hours
spent posing represented a glorious private meditative inter-
lude in their otherwise humdrum, dull lives. Reports of his
insular, intimate world, his devoted band of models, mes-
merised critics and collectors alike.

Tucked down a side street in an insalubrious part of town,
bounded by a railway track, a busy high street and a former
brick factory, stood Janáček's small coach house. Apart from
the odd weed, the concrete passageway was clean and free of
dustbins and other detritus. The noise of a couple shouting,
heavy dub music, and a car backfiring suggested a certain kind
of neighbourhood. Beachendon sniffed as he walked down the
alley leading to Janáček's studio. The closer he got, the more
pungent the smell of oil paint. By the time he reached the
door, the smell of turps and paint was so strong that the Earl

wanted to place a silk handkerchief over his nose. He knocked loudly and moments later Janáček flung open the door. He was wearing a pair of ripped shorts, no shirt and, waving a paint-smeared hand in a theatrical gesture, stood to one side so that Beachendon could enter. Taking a gulp of London air, Beachendon stepped over the threshold and into the studio. His last pair of beautiful leather Lobb shoes stuck slightly to the floor and, looking down, Beachendon saw that the whole surface was covered in layers of old paint—indeed, it was hard to find any part of the room that was not splattered or smeared in some colour. The studio measured about twenty by twenty-four feet, and each wall was lined with canvases turned to the wall. Beachendon counted at least thirty and his head went dizzy as he translated their collective worth. All his problems would be solved by just ten of these works. He envisaged the sale: "The Great Janáček Auction."

"Would you like some tea?" Janáček asked. He had a gravelly voice and although he had lived in England for nearly sixty years had kept a thick middle-European accent.

"That would be very nice," Beachendon said, wondering if the bright yellow blob of paint on his right toe would respond to a quick rub of turps.

Janáček went over to a small kitchenette and filled the kettle from a single tap.

"There is a cup somewhere," he said, absently looking around the room.

Beachendon was feeling more than a little dizzy—possibly the effect of the paint but more probably the prospect of finally being able to solve his financial problems and save the auction house from bankruptcy.

"Where do you live?" he asked Janáček.

"Here, of course! I wouldn't want to waste any time commuting."

Beachendon looked around the room for a door.

"Do you have the flat or a house next door?"

"This is all I need. My kingdom!" Janáček waved his arms around.

"Your bed?" Beachendon's head was beginning to spin slightly.

"In the corner."

Looking around Beachendon saw a mound of rags covering a camp bed.

Janáček passed him a cup. Beachendon took it gingerly and smiled.

"So what can I do for you?" Janáček asked pleasantly.

"I was hoping I could do something for you," Beachendon replied. "As you probably know I work at Monachorum, the auction house."

Janáček smiled vaguely.

"We pride ourselves on working closely with artists, restoring their financial independence, cutting them loose from the shackles imposed by unscrupulous art dealers, helping them realise their full financial independence." Beachendon rather liked his turn of phrase and wished that he had a notebook in which to record these fine words. "You will no doubt remember the Hirst, Janáček?"

Janáček shook his head.

"Damien Hirst?"

Janáček shook his head again. "I'm sorry, but I don't get out much."

"The artist Damien Hirst?" Beachendon wondered if Janáček was teasing. The whole world surely knew about Damien Hirst, the David Beckham of art.

"I am afraid that I don't. My tastes rather stopped with Rembrandt and my true love is reserved for Titian. They had all the references I needed and I didn't bother to look further."

"What about Cézanne or Corot, Corbet or Manet?" Beachendon asked.

"We studied them at art school and they are good—yes, very good. But my interest peters out in 1669."

"Van Gogh?"

"No, as I said, Rembrandt is where it stops."

"I have sold rather a lot of Rembrandts during my career," Beachendon said weakly.

Janáček looked at the clock on the wall. "Sir, I don't want to sound rude, but I have a sitter coming in half an hour and I need to do some preparations. Please could you tell me why you have come?"

"I would like to create a spectacular auction around some of your paintings," Beachendon said, looking at the canvases propped up against the walls. "Perhaps we could choose ten together?"

"Why would I want to do that?" Janáček said in a rather bemused tone.

"To make money! You wouldn't have to pay your dealer a commission; you would get sixty per cent of all the proceeds. That would be millions more for each canvas than you get now."

Janáček looked kindly at the auctioneer. "And what would I do with that extra money?"

Beachendon looked around the room, at the chaos, the dripping tap, the damp stains, the layers of paint, the 1950s cooker, the camp bed, the old kettle, the crooked wooden chair and the torn clothes hung on nails.

"You see, Mr. Beachendon, I really have everything I need here. I am very happy in my room with my things. Having possessions is a distraction. Now if you could offer me millions of extra hours in my day I would jump at the chance of an auction. If one of my paintings could buy me an extra year of working, I would shake on your proposal this second."

"Do you mind me asking what happens to the money you make now?"

"I take out what I need per year and the rest goes into an account. On my death it will go to help the National Gallery stay open without admission charges. If I had had to pay to visit my beloved Titians, I would never have been able to paint."

"But the more money you make in your lifetime, the more you have to leave." It was Beachendon's final shot, the last card in his pack.

"That is a specious argument, based on far too many probabilities. Your auction might make money but it would also inflame curiosity. As it is I have far too many people wanting to visit me here, wasting my time with letters and requests. Two Japanese art students knocked on the door last week—how they found me I will never understand. Your auction will come with a blaze of publicity, reams of column inches, discussions and debate. Janáček, is he worth it? Janáček, who is he? Why Janáček? Though I might never hear about or read this stuff, this prurient interest will permeate my life, will encroach in some nasty unpredictable way. The man at the newsagent will put two and two together. The lady in the greengrocer's might realise that the Janáček in the papers and the Janáček in the store is one and the same. My sitters, who for the most part manage to separate the act of sitting from the process of selling, might begin to think of the process in monetary terms. So you see, sir, this auction is not for me."

"If there was a fire and all this was destroyed?" Beachendon looked at the canvases stacked around the room.

"For me, art is about the process and about the making. If this goes up in flames I can only pray that it takes me with it." Janáček clapped his hands together and strode purposefully to the door. He turned the handle and opened it. "Goodbye, Mr. Beachendon. I hope you find an artist to promote. I have nothing against those who want to make money, you know."

Beachendon squelched across the floor. His last pair of Lobb shoes were now covered in a multitude of different colours and he could see a small red streak on his left trouser leg.

As he left he paused. "Why did you agree to see me, Mr. Janáček?"

"I was very intrigued by the way you form the letter S in your handwriting. I once had a friend whose Ss slanted backwards and I wanted to see if there was any similarity between you and him."

"Was there?" Beachendon asked, stepping out of the door into the narrow alley beyond.

"No, none," Janáček said and closed the door firmly in the auctioneer's face.

Two schoolkids walked towards him. In the old days, he thought, they would have parted to let him pass but today they walked on and Beachendon stepped to the right. To block their way was to face ridicule or even a knife in the back. Beachendon thought about Janáček and his ascetic way of life. Perhaps he and the Countess could adapt to a simpler life, give up the fancy butcher, the skiing holidays, the villas in Tuscany. Perhaps they could find a one-room apartment and put the children into state schools. The problem was that Beachendon, unlike Janáček, didn't have any kind of passion, any desire to do anything really beyond getting through the day. For him, the only thing he really enjoyed was falling into a deep sleep. That was all he wanted. Waking up, taking breakfast, making a deal, having lunch, even seeing friends involved effort.

Reaching his car, Beachendon saw that someone had keyed the left flank, leaving an ugly white jagged scar on the pristine blue paint. He looked back at the two boys; one turned around and gave him the finger. For a moment Beachendon was tempted to run after them, catch them and beat their heads on the pavement till their brains spilled like red bloody sausages all over the ground. Instead, he unlocked the car, slipped into the driving seat and headed back to the office.

Chapter 24

I am back in the plastic bag—this time it's from a shop called Peter Jones and luckily Peter (whoever he might be) smells mainly of wool and paper, unlike his friend Waitrose, who stank of beef and potatoes. My mistress collected me from the gallery three days ago. I was extremely distressed to bid *au revoir* to my old friends. The other paintings, in a massive unified expression of their sadness and recognition of my importance, vibrated their surfaces as I left the building. I heard it above the noise of traffic in Trafalgar Square, the squealing of brakes, the puffs of exhaust, the slap of feet on pavement, the flap of pigeons' wings, the tinkle of water from the fountains. A collection of paintings is only as great as the sum of its parts: my departure dented the magnificence of the national collection.

Luckily, the conservator had wrapped me carefully in many layers of paper and spongy stuff. I saw her eyebrows raise a centimetre or two when Annie put me into a plastic bag. She would have fainted if she'd seen me put back in the bicycle basket. *Heureusement*, it was not raining. I was bumped through the streets at an improbable speed, lifted out, carried into her office and left in the bag on her desk in her kitchen. If I had the power of self-immolation I would have exploded there and then. The rage. You cannot imagine the rage.

Late on the second night of my plastic incarceration, something rather interesting occurred. Long after Annie had left, a woman came downstairs and started nosing around in the drawers and checking my mistress's computer accounts. Her mobile telephone rang and she started to talk about a picture. Needless to say, it turned out to be all about *moi*. And oddly I was only a few feet away. Her conversation started genially with small talk that did not come easily and she went through the questions without any intention of listening to the response. How are you, how is the family, how is business and then came the big one—"I am trying to locate a small French eighteenth-century painting, measuring about eighteen by twenty-four inches. The composition is of a woman watched by a man and clown in a glade. It is very important that I find it. Why? It's for a client who's willing to pay top dollar. Don't ask me why it means so much to him—but you know what these collectors are like. How much will he pay? How far is the moon? Oh yes, and I hear your Winkleman retainer is up for review. I do hope we can renew it."

I wanted to shout and scream and reveal my whereabouts. Here finally was someone who understood my true worth. I know what it is like to be wanted, to be tracked down, and to be adored, but there was a brittleness in her voice that began to worry me and it occurred to me her eagerness for my return did not tally with my best interests.

Later that night a penny dropped. Somehow this woman was involved with that time. The darkest hours of my long life.

So let me explain how it all happened.

. . .

After Frederick the Great I was sold to the son of Pope Pius VI. Of all my owners, the pope and his family were among the most avaricious and venal. I loathed them. The son was a brute, the father a weak, solipsistic creature who, like many others, attempted to use the arts as a whitewash for his futile and immoral life, as if beauty offered some kind of absolution. He was the first to set up a museum in the Vatican and, ironically, it was this initiative that inspired my next owner.

Art follows power. Just as soldiers hang medals from their uniforms, the rich hang paintings on their walls. Napoleon Bonaparte was the greatest looter in the history of the world. He was neither the first nor the last, but he was unquestionably the most systematic and determined. Hitler only dreamed of one museum in Linz; Napoleon laid plans for twenty-two. Hitler had Göring as his advisor; Napoleon had a man named Dominique Vivant Denon and together they organised thefts from all the palaces of Europe to ensure that theirs would become the greatest treasure house of the world. Hence, in the autumn of 1796, I found myself strapped to the back of a mule, crossing the Alps along with Raphael's *Transfiguration*. I wondered seriously about my hopes of survival. We were part of the great art exodus as Napoleon gobbled up all the great works in Ferrara, Ravenna, Rimini, Pesaro, Ancona, Loreto, and Perugia; I was on the convoy of eighty-six wagons from Bologna. It was quite fun really, being with so many great paintings and exchanging stories of what we had witnessed. It was the first time I met Jan van Eyck's *Ghent Altarpiece*, the *Apollo Belvedere*, as well as the bronze horses from San Marco (spoils from an earlier war themselves).

I remember arriving in Paris, part of a huge procession in an open carriage drawn by six horses. To add to the spectacle, there were also camels and a cage of lions. Each crate had a banner listing its contents; I was with two Correggios, nine paintings by Raphael, the Bears of Bern, and a collection of minerals and various religious relics. You see, beauty has always inspired brutality and the desire to possess, looting was always a facet of war, and art and power are constant bedfellows. Before Göring, Hitler, Napoleon and Denon, the Romans had Livy to keep records of their booty. The tombs of the Pharaohs were looted long before the invasion of Alexander the Great in 332 B.C. The Old Testament has many references to looting and pillaging. In the book of Chronicles, King Shishak of Egypt attacked Jerusalem, taking away the treasures of the Lord's temple and the royal palaces and everything including gold shields that Solomon had made.

I am not giving you a history lesson, dear reader, I just want you to understand the power of art, the depths and heights that it inspires.

Onwards with my story. Napoleon could have chosen any number of wonderful things to give to his Empress Josephine. There were tapestries, jewels, statues, paintings and all those other things that I have mentioned; he chose me. Only eighteen by twenty-four inches in size but more powerful than the great canvases of the Renaissance, more valuable to my owner than armfuls of precious jewels. (If I have time later, I will tell you the secrets of their marital bed. Let me just say that there was an animal in that relationship and it was not the tiny commander.)

Josephine was an indefatigable mistress; she could make love all night and day and could coax heroic performances out of her lovers. Napoleon was a mighty leader on the battlefield but she made him feel better than a conqueror. As we all know, though, his seed could not stick inside her. He divorced Josephine to marry a womb. My mistress's cries rang out for months, carried on the wind from her château at Malmaison to Napoleon's bedroom in Paris. Once the very personification in paint of a great love affair, I became the embodiment of a broken heart. On the afternoon of 11 January 1810, she threw me on to the fire. Luckily her maid rescued me and, secreting me beneath her capacious underskirts, smuggled me out of the château and into the rooms of a well-known dealer.

My next owner was a British king. George IV was an absolute rotter. The most ill-natured, gluttonous, self-important buffoon. For twenty years I bore witness to an incessant bacchanalian feast punctuated by days of prostrate lamentation as he tried to recover from his self-inflicted excesses. The man would down crates of wine, port, whisky and champagne and only pause to stuff his fat face with meat and potatoes. Weighing over twenty stone, he suffered from gout, arteriosclerosis, dropsy and venereal disorders. I watched him die a horrible slow convulsive death and breathed a little sigh of relief when the last breath drained from his body just after 3 a.m. on 26 June 1830.

I was sold (another four adventures all over Europe) but eventually was given by Albert to his beloved young Princess Victoria, soon to be Queen of England. Unfortunately and ignominiously I was consigned to a minor state bedroom at Buckingham Palace. I loathed London (as you already know)—the fog, the noise, the drab and dreariness. No doubt I would still be in that airless bedroom if I hadn't caught the eye of a young footman who wanted to give his true love a present before leaving for the front in 1914. His name was Thomas; hers was Ethel. He worked at the Palace and she at the Ritz. Perhaps the footman knew that his days were numbered and he would never be prosecuted for such an audacious theft, but the afternoon before he left for France, he whipped me off the wall, hid me under his coat and marched through the park to Piccadilly. Two weeks later, on 24 September 1914, he was dead, just another body in the mud and mire. Ethel wept for three weeks but found comfort in the arms of a doorman. After the war I was sold for £2 6d. No one was much interested in beauty at that time.

I will skip forward to the sale of 1929 in Berlin. Another

low moment: knocked down to a penniless Jewish lawyer as an engagement present for his beloved. They were my first Semites and perhaps my greatest fans. I looked rather strange hanging over the fireplace of their drab, brown small apartment in Berlin, but as Esther Winkleman used to say, "That painting is a window on to a better, purer world."

That so-called better, purer world never materialised. Ten years later another war broke out and things got more and more difficult for the Winklemans, who lost their jobs and were forced to wear yellow stars stitched onto their clothes. Even though the apartment was tiny, his mother and her father came to live with them. There was no money for fuel and, piece by piece, the furniture was burned to keep the family warm through the bitterly cold winter of 1940 and 1941.

I remember the boy clearly; he had the palest blue eyes and a shock of blond hair. He was not Esther and Ezra's child but he spent a lot of time in their apartment. After the war broke out, he wore a black uniform; he came by for a time, with food parcels and even some brandy.

Early in 1942, taking Ezra to one side, the pale-eyed man made an offer for me. "I can get you a million Marks for this picture," he said. "And tickets for your whole family to leave the country."

"Why would I want to do that?" Ezra asked, genuinely baffled. "This is my home and I have to wait here in case members of my family need somewhere to stay." Blackshirt begged and cajoled. Ezra and Esther would not capitulate.

The evening of 27 February 1943 is one I will never forget; a team of blackshirts came for the Winklemans. "Let us grab a few things, please," Esther said, casting a glance at me. She was dragged by her hair out of the room and down the stairs. She did not scream; she did not want to frighten her children.

The pale-eyed man returned a few days later. He came tearing into the flat and seeing it empty he sat down on the floor and cried; he knew what had happened. Then he got up, took me down from above the mantelpiece, and hid me beneath his heavy black coat. I was sold for a million Marks to his leader. Herr Hitler only saw me once; he held me in his hands and stared into my depths for nearly an hour. Then, calling the young soldier, Herr Hitler told him to hide me in a secret place, away from Göring's avaricious eyes, until the war had been won.

"Guard this with your life," he instructed.

Chapter 25

Annie conceived the dinner as a thank you to Agatha as well as a practice run for Delores's birthday party. She asked Jesse, hoping that he would take the invitation as a gesture of friendship only. In three days' time, the day before the actual party, she would go to Smithfield meat market, followed by New Covent Garden market. She would buy eighteen chickens, ten pheasants, pullets, chicken livers, ten kilos each of onions, carrots and potatoes, along with armfuls of herbs and lettuce. On the morning of the dinner, 1 April, she would be at Billingsgate Fish Market by 2 a.m., stocking up on oysters, sole, crayfish and lobster. Caviar and foie gras were on order from a separate supplier.

For the practice run, Annie could only afford to prepare certain dishes and they would drink prosecco rather than champagne. At Delores's dinner the guests would enjoy twenty courses, starting with an asparagus omelette and finishing with a tart. Tonight there would be only five. For Delores's dinner Annie would hire a small van to drive between the different destinations; for the rehearsal, she took a bus and a train to Vauxhall, walked across main roads and side streets before arriving at New Covent Garden market.

Wandering through the rows of asparagus, aubergines, cabbages, the deep greens and ruby reds, the hard and fleshy, unidentifiable foreign variations as well as familiar cottage-garden vegetables, Annie felt a stab of joy. Each variety of vegetable suggested a story, a delicious possibility, and a recipe waiting to be discovered. Looking at a tray of quinces, Annie saw them baked, stewed or grated, imagined them with pears or lamb or cheese. Looking to her right, she caught sight of a pyramid of fennel—perhaps she could meld a few bulbs into the onion soup or create a side dish with a sauce perfumed with anchovy, or just sauté the vegetable until its gentle perfume quivered about a dish of braised chicken.

Her thoughts turned to her painting and she wondered if the artist looked at pigments and bases in the same way that she thought about food: imagining the collision of different colours, the mixing of pigments and the overall end effect. For both the chef and the painter, creating tastes or scenes from an assortment of base ingredients was a way of navigating the world. She used salt, pepper, vegetables, oils, spices, herbs and meat; he used lapis, lead white, carmine, green earth, indigo, ochre, verdigris and smalt.

On one large table there was a vast dome of aubergines, all circular in shape and heavily veined in a deep red and creamy white.

"Aren't they beautiful? Like jewels," Annie said to a woman who was also looking at them.

"But when we cook them, they will turn to a grey mush," the woman replied.

Annie looked at her in amazement. How could anyone think of an aubergine in such a disparaging way.

That evening, Jesse was the first to arrive, clutching a bunch of daffodils, trying not to look too pleased to see her. He and Annie talked awkwardly about what they had been doing and events in the news, and were both relieved when Agatha arrived and Evie returned from her AA meeting. Annie gave Bellinis to Jesse and Agatha and a non-alcoholic fruit punch to her mother, and handed round some quails' eggs balanced on tiny squares of smoked salmon and home-made bread topped with a sprig of dill. At first everyone was shy; they stood in a circle in the centre of the room around a Moroccan pouffe making small talk about the picture that was propped on the mantelpiece over the fireplace.

"It needs a better frame," said Annie.

"It still looks lovely," Evie said. "I knew from the first moment I saw it that it was something special."

"What's next for it?" Agatha asked.

"Not sure really." Annie shrugged and went over to the painting. "I intend to live with it and admire it."

"I told her to take it to Christie's or one of those places— they have valuation days," Evie said, before turning to Agatha. "You work at the National Gallery, don't you? Maybe you could look at it?"

Agatha and Jesse looked at each other, realising that Annie had not told her mother about their suspicions.

"I just need to make a velouté," Annie said, heading towards the kitchen units.

Jesse followed her. "Let me help."

Annie hesitated and, smiling gratefully, handed him a bowl and a whisk. "Can you mix those up with some salt and pepper while I blanch the asparagus?"

Jesse expertly cracked the eggs with one hand into the

bowl, added two twists of pepper and a generous pinch of salt and whisked them hard. Once they had turned into a frothy golden cloud he asked for the next job.

"Can you layer that Gruyère and toast on top of the bowls of onion soup?" Annie asked, making sure that her clarified butter frothed up but didn't burn.

"Do you have some parsley I can chop?"

"Top left of the fridge in a small plastic bag."

While Annie gently sifted the flour, teaspoon by teaspoon into the butter, Jesse chopped the parsley into a fine green mist ready to sprinkle over the top of the soup.

"You can cook." Annie sounded surprised.

"My mother needed a sous chef."

"Was she a cook?"

"The best I've ever met—she can take the simplest, dullest ingredients and transform them into something delicious."

"That's the best kind," Annie agreed, folding the last of the flour into the butter.

"A roux?" Jesse asked.

"Yes, can you warm that small saucepan of stock?"

Jesse turned the heat on and, bending over the pan, sniffed. "Vegetable with mushroom?"

Annie smiled. "Very good—it's for the sole—Louis XV liked his fish drowning in mushroom-flavoured cream but I thought this was a slightly healthier option."

Annie took an omelette pan from the hanging shelf and wiped a trace of olive oil around its base. Placing it on a lit hob she waited for the pan to smoke.

"Shall I continue with the white sauce while you make the omelettes?"

Annie smiled gratefully. "I don't suppose you are free on the first of April? I am cooking this grand dinner for fifty for Delores's birthday. I have waiters and washer-uppers but would love someone who is confident in the kitchen. It's paid—about a hundred pounds for the night."

Jesse leant over the sauce, whisking hard; he didn't want Annie to see his cheeks blush red with pleasure and the face-splitting grin.

Annie read his silence the wrong way. "I'm so sorry. I should not have asked."

Jesse turned to her smiling. "I was just trying to remember what I was doing this Thursday. Actually, I think I'm free and would be delighted to help. Perhaps we should meet sometime before to go over the menus and timings? Maybe tomorrow?"

"That would be fantastic." Annie smiled gratefully.

Looking at Jesse's back as he stirred the sauce, she saw him as if for the first time. She liked the way that he navigated the cramped kitchen, moving gracefully in the small space between the stove and the fridge. She liked his rhythmic stirring, beating and whisking, the way the muscles in his wrist and his right arm flexed.

"Can you pass the asparagus?" Annie asked. Carefully, Jesse passed the uncooked spears to her. Placing them on the table, his hand accidentally brushed against hers and they both felt a tiny current pass between them. Annie looked down at his long fingers with pale freckles sprinkled over the backs of his hands. She tried to imagine his caress.

Jesse looked at Annie, at the soft pale down that started just below her right ear and ran to the nape of her long neck. Through her T-shirt he could see a shoulder blade and an elegant right arm. Would her skin feel soft beneath that T-shirt, would she shudder slightly if he ran his hand down her spine to the base of her back? Would she like the back of her neck kissed?

Annie sprinkled salt on the boiling water and tipped in the asparagus. She could hear Jesse's breath, shallow and slightly irregular. Glancing upwards she saw his mouth and almost feminine lips, pale pink, slightly parted, showing straight, white teeth. What would that mouth feel like, she wondered, as the asparagus tossed in the bubbling water.

Jesse was caught up in his own fantasy and, tasting the sauce to test for seasoning, he imagined running his tongue down between Annie's breasts towards her legs.

He continued to beat his sauce, never taking his eyes off the back of Annie's neck. Aware that his breathing was uneven and shallow, he took two deep breaths.

"I think that's probably okay," Annie said, without turning to face him.

"I got carried away—do you think it's done?" Jesse held out the saucepan.

Annie looked at the pale whipped sauce, and then, dipping a little finger into its glossy depths, she licked it slowly and looked at him.

Jesse swallowed, willing himself to stay upright, willing himself not to take her into his arms and kiss her.

"It's good," Annie said. She turned back to the asparagus and, spearing one with a sharp paring knife, decided that they were perfect, al dente. Taking the saucepan, she stepped over to the sink and drained the asparagus. The steam rose and covered her face in a gentle mist. What was she doing flirting with this man? She knew he had feelings for her—was she being unkind or had something changed?

Forcing herself back to the task in hand, Annie put a small frying pan on to the stove and, folding freshly chopped chives, thyme and parsley with a splash of cream into the batter, she gave her omelette mix a last whisk. Then Annie lined her large bowl of onion soup with wafer-thin slices of baguette covered with Gruyère, mozzarella and parmesan and placed that under the grill for a few minutes.

"Supper in five minutes exactly," she called out.

Jesse took four plates out of the oven and set them on the table.

Pouring the eggs into the smoking pan, Annie waited till tiny golden bubbles formed before gently arranging the asparagus on the batter, making acid-green chevrons against the deep-yellow base. The recipe suggested flipping the omelette over, but Annie decided to leave it flat and at the very last moment quickly chopped a ruby-red chilli and sprinkled tiny diamonds of fieriness over the surface.

During dinner she was glad that Jesse sat diagonally opposite her and it was not possible to touch him or even look at him too closely. Cutting the omelette into four pieces, Annie put each slice on a plate. There was silence as each took their first mouthful. The creamy egg, the hot chilli and al dente asparagus were in perfect harmony. Annie thought the next course was not quite right—the onions in the soup were a tiny bit sweet—but Jesse thought that they complemented the melted cheese. There was applause for the *jacquard* chicken and its checked deep-red-and-white jacket. Though Evie promised she couldn't eat another mouthful, she finished her sole Colbert in silence, not wanting to waste the collision in her mouth of soft pillowy layers of sole surrounded by bread-crumbed crust perfumed with the sauce. Agatha moaned slightly as she bit through the crispy outer layer of fish and felt the warm butter ooze into her mouth.

"This is better than . . ." She blushed a deep red when everyone laughed with her.

Later, when they had polished off a pie made with poached fruit, raisins, pine nuts and candied lemons topped with whipped sugared cream, Annie and her guests sat around the table nursing Louis's favourite, a hot chocolate, so thick that Evie ate hers with a spoon.

"Anyone who can make food taste this good should be tied to a stove," Agatha said.

"That would be my dream," Annie admitted.

Later, Annie offered Evie her bed, saying she was happy to sleep on the sofa. Secretly she wanted her mother behind the only door in the apartment so that she and Jesse could be left alone. Agatha left to catch the last train, Jesse stayed to help wash up. When the last dish was done, he gently took Annie's face between his large freckled hands and kissed her on the mouth.

"I am going to go now," he said. "But not for long."

Picking up his jacket and scarf, he let himself out of the studio and Annie listened as he took the stairs in great bounds.

Unable to sleep, Annie sat at the kitchen table and, laying her face sideways on the scrubbed wooden surface, closed her eyes and concentrated on the feeling of the grain of the wood pressing into her left cheek.

Chapter 26

Trichcombe Abufel stared out of his kitchen window and on to the communal gardens. He had bought this small attic flat thirty years earlier and watched the neighbourhood change from a diverse multicultural area to a homogenised pool of wealthy white bankers and their families. Looking down into the garden below he could see five almost identical blonde women in black shorts, starved to a pre-pubescent body weight, each Botoxed so their faces resembled smooth marble statues, doing calisthenics with a large and muscled black trainer. It was rather nice, Trichcombe thought as he stared at the dark-skinned man, to see a dab of colour. Trichcombe did not want to move from his home, but unless something changed in his professional life, penury would soon force him out of this apartment and into the suburbs. Maybe he would have to go back to Wales—he shuddered at the thought.

Wrenching himself away from the scene below, Trichcombe turned back to his desk and "the problem." Since
meeting the young woman in the British Museum and catching a glimpse of that sketch, Trichcombe had the certain feeling that "it" had been found. It had taken Trichcombe many
years to painstakingly stitch together a provenance for Watteau's great missing work, *The Improbability of Love*. Using
a combination of printed material, unpublished records, his
personal archive and data stored at national and international museums, Trichcombe established an almost unbroken
line of ownership. He knew the painting was made in 1703
in Paris and that the subject was most probably a beautiful
actress, Charlotte Desmares, who went by the stage name
of Colette. Watteau's undiluted passion for the woman was
reported in several contemporary accounts and for a period of
seven months her face popped up in nearly every sketch and
in many other oil paintings.

After Watteau's untimely tragic early death from consumption in 1721, the painting was left to his friend Jean de Julienne
and thenceforward its provenance was one of the most fascinating Trichcombe had ever uncovered. Was there another
picture owned by such a string of illustrious and interesting
patrons? Trichcombe was not, however, particularly interested
in the painting's early history or even in the work itself. It was
the period between 1929 and the present day that occupied
most of his attention. He found out that the painting had disappeared from the Royal Collection during the First World
War (possibly stolen) but had reappeared in a saleroom in Berlin in 1929, when a man called Ezra Winkleman had bought
it for fifty Marks. Trichcombe did not have to search Google
or *Who's Who*: he knew that Ezra was Memling Winkleman's
father.

In the last few days, the art world grapevine had started
buzzing with news that the Winklemans had "lost" a small
Watteau; they had called everyone whom they kept on a

retainer and though Trichcombe was perhaps the only expert who wasn't employed by the family anymore, he had fielded several calls.

Trichcombe thought back to the auburn-haired woman in the British Museum and her sketch. Some sixth sense honed by years of looking and thinking about works of art suggested that the painting was in her possession. He was fairly sure, from her reaction, that she wasn't an expert and probably didn't realise how valuable or important it was; he hoped to enlighten her long before anyone else.

Sitting at his desk, Trichcombe looked again at the photocopy of the engraving of *The Improbability of Love*. The picture was important in many ways: its subject matter, the juxtaposition of hope and despair, encapsulated the feelings of requited and unrequited love. Its lightness of touch, the speed, dexterity and apparent simplicity of its conception pointed to a new style of painting, encouraged generations of later painters to loosen up, let go and express themselves. And of course this work was also the father, mother and mistress of the Rococo movement. But above all, it was also capable of inspiring love.

Trichcombe got up and walked back into the kitchen. Below him the ladies were stretching, their trainer pausing briefly at each body to pull and push their limbs into ever more outlandish shapes. Trichcombe wasn't really watching them; he was trying to put together everything he knew and those things he couldn't explain about the Winkleman business. He was hoping that this time he had found the means for revenge.

Scholarship had taught Trichcombe many lessons but perhaps the most important was patience. He had learned to wait for information to unfold and to let clues emerge when he was least expecting them. Learning and discovering were not linear processes but webs of insane matrices, layers of disparate unconnected facts accrued over the years that would suddenly coalesce. His most important discoveries—finding the

Cimabue altarpiece in a saleroom in Pewsey, and Raphael's *Madonna of the Camellia* in the back passage of a boys' school—were part happy coincidence (being there) and part knowledge: the years of looking at other works, studying the tiny brushstrokes of each artist and, above all, knowing what was missing and where it was last seen. A scholar, Trichcombe often thought, was just a detective. He was one of the greatest.

Memling had been the first person to spot his particular talent; he retained Trichcombe on a princely salary. It was rare to find someone who combined knowledge with a single-minded passion for painting. For the first seven years, Trichcombe's apparent lack of a personal life, his willingness to work all hours, to travel at a moment's notice, was an enormous advantage. Memling sent the young man all over the world to evaluate new purchases and to root around minor salerooms. Together they became the Duveen and Berenson of their era.

Trichcombe's single-minded mania had certain disadvantages: most of Winkleman's employees worked for a salary and were happy to go home at night and to turn a blind eye to any inconsistencies. Their jobs were ultimately just the means to the end of the business of living. For Trichcombe, a man with no dependents and no outside hobbies, his job was his life, and while others took pride in their partners or children, he was dedicated to paintings, their study, their history, their provenance.

An increasingly tense situation between employer and employee finally erupted when Memling suddenly unearthed a lost work by Boucher. Memling refused to say where it had come from. For him, it was a simple, highly lucrative transaction. For Trichcombe it was essential to establish the painting's history. Staying up for seven nights in a row, Trichcombe established a history of ownership that stopped suddenly in 1943 in Berlin with a member of a family later annihilated at Auschwitz. Memling refused to say how he came by the work. Two months later a similar case appeared when Memling returned from a trip to Bavaria with a Canaletto, a Barocci and a Klimt. Again, Memling brushed aside his employee's demand for paperwork. At that time, few were interested in the morality behind restitution of works stolen during the war. Vendors and buyers were happy with vague chains of ownership. Memling liked to claim that his paintings came from "a nobleman" or "a titled lady." No one quibbled.

As time went on Trichcombe's unease grew. How could Memling consistently produce undiscovered great masterpieces from nowhere? Most had good provenances and secure chains of titles, but some had literally appeared from thin air. He was aware of the great fluidity in the art market following the war, the rock-bottom prices as owning art paled into insignificance next to rebuilding lives. But as wealth and stability increased during the 1960s, bargains and rarities were harder to come by. How then did Winkleman keep producing masterpieces?

Memling found Trichcombe's interrogations increasingly irksome. It came to a head one day in 1972 when Trichcombe saw a small painting by Watteau on Memling's desk. Measuring eighteen by twenty-four inches, it showed a couple watched over by a clown. Even Trichcombe, who had not been touched by another human being for thirty-seven years, felt the naked power of this painting. There was something so exquisitely moving and heartfelt about the look of the lover lying on the grass looking at the girl, something mournful about the clown's disposition and his long, languid face, and something so wilful and vivacious about the girl enjoying absolute power over her suitors' emotions.

Suddenly, Trichcombe had to know about this picture; it tipped his curiosity over the edge. But Memling said it was personal and not for sale, so did not concern his employee. Trichcombe persisted, and insisted on trawling through office records and chains of title. The following morning, he arrived at the office to find all his belongings in a box on the front step. The receptionist handed him an envelope containing £1,000 cash. It was not a simple dismissal: from that day onwards Memling used his considerable power to discredit Trichcombe at every corner and the scholar never succeeded in securing a senior post at a museum or as a private curator or in a gallery. He lived off minuscule earnings from his books and scholarly articles. Occasionally he discovered a drawing or an oil sketch in a provincial saleroom and sold that on but he never earned enough money to buy anything significant. As a young man, his great passion had been a love of art; for the last forty-two years, Trichcombe's driving ambition was to unmask Memling Winkleman. From the moment that he witnessed Memling with the Watteau, back in 1972, Trichcombe knew that its value to Memling was far above and beyond money and emotion. For reasons he had yet to prove, this picture was the key to his future and to Memling's downfall.

Trichcombe spent years piecing together the history of the Watteau; all he needed was to find the picture itself. He had almost given up hope until seeing images of the work at the British Museum. There was only one last piece of the jigsaw to put in place: the fate of the last owners, Memling's parents. The old Berlin sales records of 1929 had an address for the family: Trichcombe decided to go to Schwedenstrasse 14 off Friedrichstadt to see what was left.

In his newly formed office in Holborn, Vlad watched, in real time, money pouring into his current account. There was a spike in tin trades and during the morning, before he had even got out of bed, Vlad had made £67 million, bringing his week's total to £127 million. According to the terms of his exile, the Office of Central Control was to receive at least 30 per cent of any profit Vlad made. Almost in spite of his best efforts, the price of tin kept rising and Vlad had to constantly stoke the fire of Central Control's demands. In the last nine days Vlad had had to transfer £24 million anonymously into one of its many accounts. If, for any reason, he did not want to use a bank transfer (and sometimes the Leader disliked this method) or if Vlad had decided that an object was a better proxy, he had to deposit the item at the holding house in Surrey.

The week before, unable to contain his curiosity, Vlad had personally delivered a diamond the size of an eyeball to Crawley Place, Godalming, Surrey. Arriving at the outer perimeter of the estate, Vlad was greeted by three Russian men dressed in black. Asked to get out of the car, he was frisked thoroughly, his car was searched and, with a specially generated password printed on a scrap of paper, he had been allowed to proceed to the second gate. At the next gate, several hundred yards away, he was frisked again and issued with another password. This elaborate procedure was repeated four times before he reached a nondescript red-brick house with highly manicured lawns and a raked gravel drive. The wide wheels of Vlad's car, a pale blue Maybach, left ugly track marks on the neat patterns.

A disembodied female voice rang out of nowhere instructing Vlad to go to the front door. As Vlad approached it swung open. Nervously he went inside. The outer door looked normal enough but once inside, Vlad realised that he was now in an airtight metal box. I could be crushed like a tin can and no one would know, he thought. The same voice told him to stand completely still. A formation of infrared beams danced around his body. "You are being scanned," the voice told him unnecessarily. Another door opened. Vlad walked through. "Put your hand on the pad and look up," the voice instructed. He placed his hand on a sensor and turned his eye to the ceiling. A metal panel slid back and Vlad walked into another box. This one was considerably larger, nearly the size of the whole downstairs of the house.

"The bricks and windows are a shell to make this place resemble a house," the voice said, apparently reading Vlad's mind. "The British intelligence know exactly what it is, but they don't yet know how to break into it. Nor does anyone else."

"Who are you?" Vlad asked.

"The less we know about each other, the better," the voice said.

The floor beneath him trembled. Vlad stepped back quickly as a section of it slid back, revealing stairs to a basement.

"Descend."

No wonder they told me to come alone and switch cars twice on the journey here, Vlad thought. It wasn't to protect them; it was to make sure that even if my disappearance was registered, my body could never be traced. Knowing he had no choice, he went down the stairs and into a large safe.

"This is your payment box," the voice said. "Your code is known only to me and you, and it will change with each visit. Think of a series of five numbers, which must not relate to anything personal, such as year of birth, year of your mother's birth, et cetera."

Vlad thought for a moment before keying in the day of his brother's birthday, 61270.

"That corresponds to your dead brother's birthday. Can you think of another?" the voice said.

Vlad shivered slightly and then put in a random code.

A box the size of a tea crate opened in the wall.

Taking a small pouch out of his pocket, Vlad opened it and placed the diamond in the centre of the box.

"Re-enter your code now," the voice instructed.

Vlad punched in the digits and the wall safe closed.

"Once it has been verified, you will receive a notification by email. Exit from the passage to your left and find your car."

"What if I buy a large painting next week? How will it fit in there?"

"You will be given different instructions. If you buy from an auction house, we deal directly with their handlers. Private sales are managed in different ways."

"Or if I buy a house or an island?"

"We have yet to fail to process anything. That should not be your worry."

Going out of the building was as complicated as entering. Once reunited with his car, Vlad noticed that the gravel had been raked since his arrival and once again he had the minute but real satisfaction of messing up the perfect patterns.

Leaving the compound, Vlad drove for a few miles and then, pulling into a layby, he put his head on the wheel and succumbed to feelings of utter despair. How could he, week in, week out, find suitable objects to satisfy the Office of Central Control? If they didn't like the diamond, what then? He had already employed six people to help locate works of art, precious objects, estates, paintings and shares. The problem was second-guessing what his Leader wanted. Last week his leader had rejected a chalet in Gstaad on the grounds that he already owned 40 per cent of the resort. Vlad had offered an emerald through an agent that was returned. If the Leader rejected the diamond then he would be three weeks behind on his payments and saddled with goods that he didn't actually want. Vlad had no intention of going to Gstaad (he was told Courcheval was the only place to go); he had no girl to give the emerald to (though he lived in hope of capturing Lyudmila). Two weeks earlier he had bought a significant stake in a company that turned out to be already owned by the Office of Central Control. At this rate he would be personally bankrupt and in debt, and if he missed five weeks' payments, thoroughly dead.

Clutching the steering wheel hard in both hands, Vlad tried to think straight. He had to have a plan, a proper plan about how to meet these payments. He had to corner the market in something, some area that the Office of Central Control did not already own and whose value was irrefutable. He should also try to anticipate payments in advance—by buying something really valuable, Vlad would buy himself time: weeks, maybe months of unbroken sleep. The more he learned about the art world, the more confident Vlad became that he had found the ideal conduit. The problem with contemporary art was that there was an almost limitless supply and it was far too dependent on fashion. Hirst could pump out hundreds and thousands of spots, drown the market in brightly coloured circles. In the brief few days between buying a Richard Prince *Nurse* and delivering it to his faceless creditors, the artist's stock had fallen. Old Masters were a safer bet. After all, the painters were dead and this lack of supply to meet potential demand meant that their prices were unlikely to fluctuate by much. Vlad had another thought. I could manipulate the market by buying a few works by one artist, then putting one in an auction, bidding the price up wildly, setting a new benchmark and making all the others worth far more. Why had no one else thought of this? Then he realised that others had, and this probably explained the record prices at auction.

Taking his telephone, he punched Barty's number into the dial.

"Forty minutes—Chester Square," he said.

When Vlad rang, Barty was lying on a massage table having a treatment to keep any potential cellulite at bay. That cellulite was unlikely to strike a slim, sixty-nine-year-old man was irrelevant. Barty had an absolute terror of imperfection—just because it hadn't happened so far didn't mean that it could not sneak up behind him. Rolling off the table, Barty left the treatment room and padded down the corridor to the club's changing rooms. He had a lifetime free membership to this place and treatments to the value of £5,000 per annum, payment for providing introductions to his best clients.

Standing under the hot shower, Barty thought about Vlad and how their relationship was developing. He had known enough Russian émigrés to understand what they needed. He remembered the old White Russians, summarily expelled following the revolution in 1917, who had escaped to London to live out their days in genteel poverty, forever mourning the motherland. The new generation was equally wistful but hugely wealthy, providing they could stay alive. Letting the hot water pour over his head, washing away the massage oil, Barty thought compassionately about Vlad's situation. The great lummox had more money than most could even dream of spending, but he was a haunted, hunted figure. Being thousands of miles away from Central Control no longer offered safety. Wherever he was, Vlad was beholden: emotionally, financially and physically. His prison was luxurious and apparently without walls or boundaries, but he wasn't free. Barty suspected that Central Control could trace an errant employee to the furthest Tahitian island and eradicate them in a matter of seconds. Their operatives had doubtless secreted microchips under his skin while he slept, tracking devices inserted by prostitutes trained in many dark arts.

Barty would never swap places with the wealthy Russian, but he was happy to conjure up interesting ways for Vlad to spend his money.

Recently he had advised another Russian how to manage his billions. Boris Slatonov had bought an ailing football club and revived its fortunes by spending millions on new players, coaches and facilities. Luckily the team began to win and Boris found out that there was nothing that the Leader loved more than international success. Boris's next move, again with Barty's help, was to found a museum in Moscow and fill it with modern paintings. Soon the Leader was using Boris as one of his personal bankers, channelling money through him by means of the sports fields and the art world.

Looking at himself in the mirror, Barty drew a comb through his hair. Thick and silky, his tresses remained one of his best assets and were now dyed a strawberry blond. Barty thought the new hairdresser was probably his best ever, a man who resisted Barty's occasional pleas to cut it or coxcomb or Mohican or shave it. "If you want to change your style, get a wig, darling." Picking up the hairdryer, Barty began to rough-dry it—there wasn't time to do much more. Taking up his make-up pouch, he applied a touch of blusher to both cheeks before getting back into his three-piece suit (he was Steed from *The Avengers* today).

Fifteen minutes later, Barty was in a cab on his way to meet Vlad. In his left pocket was a list of all the football clubs currently on the market. In his right was a litany of forthcoming auctions. Barty had also decided that Vlad shouldn't look at contemporary works of art; although the Old Masters were rarer, more elusive and less sexy, Vlad should concentrate his efforts on the more recherché—in fact, Barty had decided to finally reward his friend Delores and steer Vlad towards French eighteenth century. The three of them would identify a charming little *"maison"* in St. Petersburg (far nicer than the horrid and deeply masculine Moscow). They would create a Musée des Beaux Arts de l'École du Dix-Huitième. Barty could see it now—it would be a mass of brocade, damask, ormolu, gilt, gold and other utter fabulousness. Unlike those great bastions of monumental concrete and neon whiteness known as modern museums, their little palace would be a place where the eye would never be allowed to rest, even for one split second. It would be a cacophony of colour and texture, it would be contra contemporary, a fashion insult; Barty and Vlad's museum would put the controversial back into culture.

Barty arrived seconds before Vlad's car glided into view. The enormous Russian looked even more disconsolate and depressed than usual. Barty slid into the seat next to him, feeling the soft sharkskin under his fingers and admiring his own reflection in the highly polished walnut dashboard for a second before he turned to Vlad.

"Cheer up, my little buttercup. I have a plan. A simply wonderful marvellous plan."

Chapter 27

Using set designers, painters and dressers whom she had met working with Carlo, Annie transformed the Amadeus Centre in Maida Vale into an eighteenth-century glade inspired by her painting. Large drapes painted with dappled foliage hung from the wraparound balcony and great branches of willow, bought that morning at New Covent Garden Market, were placed in massive clay pots. The centrepiece, a large fountain, identical to the one in her painting, its edifice covered in tiny smiling putti, was carved in Styrofoam and painted in cream. A swing hung from the ceiling and the floor was covered in AstroTurf strewn with fresh petals.

Annie set up a central table shaped like a horseshoe and covered it in heavy white damask. She had hired a grand service, in the style of Louis XV, along with twenty candelabra and thirty serving dishes from a prop company. The Winklemans' housekeeper, Primrose, and her daughter Lucinda had worked through the night sewing the heads of roses to sprigs of gypsum to make long ropes of flowers to festoon the sides and tabletops. The table's centrepiece was made from mounds of candied fruit and edible sugared mice chased by chocolate-coloured kittens. Each place setting had eight knives and forks, three spoons and seven wine glasses, plus one golden goblet to hold water. Starched linen napkins, each four foot square, had been folded into preening swans that sat on golden plates. In front of each place setting was a hand-engraved individual place card and a menu with details of the food and wine.

In one corner of the room there was a tiny stage from which a band of musicians dressed in period costume would play madrigals. From another door, when the *jacquard* chicken was served, acrobats dressed as harlequins would tumble across the glade in a performance for the diners. During one of the eight puddings, a lachrymose jester, the doppelgänger for the clown in Annie's painting, would appear with a lute and sing to the assembled guests.

Hidden from view at the back of the hall, Annie had created a makeshift kitchen. Timing was essential, and to achieve a state of perfection, there were only a few seconds to spare between dishes.

While the set dressers were putting their final touches to the glade, Jesse, the army of waiters and the second sous chef arrived. Annie was grateful that Jesse behaved like any other employee. With much of the detailed preparation done a day or two before, the main issue was to get all twenty courses to the table on time, at the right temperature and served with the correct wine. While failure might not, as it had at Versailles, have fatal consequences, a botched job would spell the end of Annie's dream. For Delores, the evening had to pass as a high point in the artistic social calendar.

Splitting her team into four groups, each assigned a sepa-rate task and area, Annie handed out printed sheets detailing the evening's events and chores. No detail was left to chance; even bathroom breaks were scheduled.

"This evening must run like a military campaign," Annie explained. "Please read this list carefully: you must know what to expect and what is expected from you. Jesse is my second-in-command so if I am busy please refer to him. Raoul is in charge of waiters, Amy will look after the cloakrooms, Ted is our sommelier and Riccardo is managing clearing and washing."

Annie looked at the twenty-two expectant faces. After weeks of meticulous planning, she felt confident and calm. She had employed professionals who knew what to do and how to manage stressful situations. Her profit on the evening was shaved to a minimum: this evening was about her future rather than her bank balance.

The first to arrive was Delores dressed as Marie Antoinette. Sheathed in layers of cream lace and purple shot satin, she reminded Annie of a vast animated sea anemone shimmying across the floor.

"Oh my," Delores said as she stepped into the bower. "I am going to cry. I must not cry. I am going to cry—what have you done, you marvellous, clever creature?"

Annie smiled and blushed root red.

Heading towards the swing, Delores looked as if she would try and nudge her bottom into the seat but to everyone's relief she was distracted by the putti-covered fountain. Soon she went behind the scenes to inspect the food. She paid close attention to each dish. Annie insisted on introducing each member of her team.

At exactly 8 p.m. the madrigals started to play and minutes later a bugler heralded the arrival of the first guest, Mrs. Appledore, who came dressed as Madame de Pompadour in a dress copied down to the last detail from the portrait by

Boucher. She had even bought a lap dog for £2,500 from Harrods' Pet Kingdom to accompany her, but the creature had whined and puked in the car and Mrs. Appledore left the animal to its fate on the street outside. Seconds later Barty arrived dressed as an eighteenth-century courtesan in a ballgown with a five-foot span embroidered with gold and tiny pearls (he had to bribe his friend at the V&A to smuggle it out of the stores for one night). The dress had been so complicated to put on that his whole office had taken the afternoon off to fit Barty into the undergarments, wooden stays and hoops. This time he had borrowed a wig made of ropes of blond curls. Sweating slightly under the weight of the hairpiece and the thickness of his ermine-edged flowing cape, Barty went immediately to the men's room to fix his make-up. Vlad arrived separately dressed in black leather trousers and jerkin with a crown on his head and a badge saying "Peter the Great." Having agreed to Barty's plan to build his baby Versailles in St. Petersburg, Barty had appointed Delores as the principal paintings advisor and, to her unmitigated delight, three significant purchases, paintings by Pater, Lancret and Boucher, had been earmarked. Thanks to the commission on these, Delores had upgraded the evening's choice of champagne from ordinary to vintage Pol Roger, the wine to premier cru.

At 8 p.m., news reached the kitchen that Rebecca could not come—last-minute urgent business in Berlin. Instead, Memling Winkleman was bringing Carlo and Rebecca's daughter, Grace. "Such a relief," Delores commented. "Rebecca would not know a good time if it bit her."

By eight thirty, most of the fifty guests had arrived. Peeking out from the kitchen area, Annie recognised Septimus Ward-Thomas, a minor royal, the ageing pop star Johnny "Lips" Duffy, and several *Hello!* magazine habitués. The Earl and

Countess Beachendon arrived dressed as courtiers. The Emir and Sheikha of Alwabbi were the only couple not to have dressed according to the theme "Rococo." The biggest surprise was Carlo and Rebecca's daughter—Annie had expected a demure twenty-one-year-old; Grace was a gothic punkess with piercings covering her nose and ears, and a tattoo of a dragon, clearly visible thanks to a backless dress, running from the nape of her neck to the top of her buttocks. Delores had placed her next to Vlad.

"Are you art advisor?" Vlad asked.

"I am anything you want me to be," Grace replied.

Memling walked in, looked around and became unsettled, though he could not quite articulate, at that moment, what was disturbing him.

The next four hours flew past for Annie as she sent each course out, one after the other—oysters, caviar, soups, quails, foie gras, *jacquard* chicken, onion soup with champagne, sole stuffed with crab meat, vegetables piled high, new potatoes the size of crocus bulbs mixed with quails' eggs, pigeons dressed like baby peacocks, feathers made from herbs captured in cages of spun sugar. The *pièce de résistance* was a boneless turkey stuffed with a boneless goose, stuffed with a boneless chicken, a boneless partridge, a quail and finally a baby snipe. As Jesse and two others carried the bird to the table and sliced it through with a miniature saw, the table erupted into applause.

"Chef! Chef!" the whole room clamoured.

Jesse ran into the makeshift kitchen. "They are calling for you, come out and take a bow."

"I can't—look at me," Annie said, knowing that her hair was protruding out of her chef's cap and that her face would be streaked with sweat and flour.

But the clapping continued and grew louder. Wiping her

hands on her apron, Annie smoothed her hair and, stepping out from behind the fountain, nervously made her way to the centre of the horseshoe table.

"Brava!" Delores struggled to her feet. "Brava!"

The other diners clapped enthusiastically.

Annie, blushing deep red, bowed. "Thank you so much—now if you don't mind, there are still eight more courses."

There was a collective groan.

"We can't eat any more," someone shouted out.

"Just a few bites!" Annie laughed, edging back towards the kitchen.

No one understood why Memling Winkleman left shortly after the Pierrot appeared, but everyone was having such a good time that they hardly noticed.

Annie had to take three more bows between courses, followed by a standing ovation at the end. Mrs. Appledore, Earl Beachendon and Johnny "Lips" asked her again to create an event for them, and the Sheikha of Alwabbi tried to hire her for the next six months.

When the guests had left, the floors had been cleaned, the tables cleared, all the plates, glasses and hired equipment packed into boxes and loaded into a van hired for the evening, ready to be returned to their owners the following morning, Jesse and Annie were finally alone. They sat side by side, cross-legged in the middle of the floor. The hall had been returned to its original state, large, slightly tatty and oddly purposeless.

"I'm glad Delores arranged a photographer," Annie said, looking around. "It all seems like an unreal dream now."

Taking Annie's hand in his, Jesse kissed its palm gently. "It was extraordinary—I was honoured to be part of it."

"You were bloody brilliant. The moment that chicken slipped off the tray—"

"And shot across the floor—"

"And threatened to knock over the fountain—"

"And you caught it like Jonny Wilkinson going for a try . . ."

They laughed together.

"And then Delores's breast jumped out of its corset while she was eating another meringue," Jesse said, laughing.

"I missed it completely. I was building a tower of profiteroles!"

"You should have seen Mrs. Appledore's face!" Jesse said, imitating her look of total horror.

"What else, what else?" Annie pleaded. "I missed so much of the action being stuck in the kitchen," she said.

"Vlad and Miss Winkleman left together—couldn't keep their hands off each other all evening."

"Rebecca will be furious—she thinks that her daughter is a Vestal Virgin," said Annie, lying back on the floor.

Jesse's heart skipped as he saw her hair fanned out like an auburn halo around her pale, beautiful face. In her makeshift kitchen, Annie had seemed powerful; now she looked so fragile and slight that he longed to take her in his arms and kiss away the violet smudges of tiredness under her eyes.

"Tell me more," Annie implored.

Forcing his mind back to the dinner, Jesse said, "Earl Beachendon looked thoroughly depressed. He and his wife had got hopelessly lost in a Maida Vale housing estate. Someone snatched his phone and her bag. Hearing that Vlad was building a new museum, he cheered up somewhat."

"Which one was his wife?"

"She looked like an animated herbaceous border."

"Oh my, the one wearing a pair of curtains?"

"That's her," Jesse said and lay on his side so that he could see Annie more clearly.

Annie felt Jesse's eyes on her but kept looking at the ceiling.

"For some reason Delores sat the Countess next to the rock star. What's his name?"

"Johnny 'Lips'."

"I could not understand what the two might have in common. Thought that was a bad call," Jesse said, and edged closer to Annie.

"And?" Annie wished Jesse would stop staring at her.

"It was a match made in heaven. They are both into breeding Arab horses and auriculas. What are the odds on that?"

"What's an arc-u-la?" Intrigued, Annie turned to face him. His sweet-smelling breath grazed her cheek. To her surprise, she did not feel claustrophobic and enjoyed looking into his face. She noticed, for the first time, that his deep-blue eyes were flecked with tiny gold and black streaks.

"Auricula—a kind of flower—lace-makers and silk-weavers went mad for it in the eighteenth century. Later someone sent a cutting to the States and Thomas Jefferson fell in love with it."

"How do you know that?"

"Eavesdropping on their conversation."

"Tell me about old man Winkleman."

"When your clown came out from behind the fountain he started to hyperventilate. Thought I might have to call an ambulance but he made his way out into the street, got into his car and was driven away."

"I noticed the spare seat but never stopped to think whose it was. Tell me about Barty—he won best outfit of the evening."

"He was a hoot. Gave the Sheikha and Vlad a long lecture about things that are common," Jesse said, noticing that a sprig of thyme was caught in her hair, a tiny speck of green among the red and golden curls. He reached over and gently pulled it away and then handed the herb to her. Their fingers touched and, taking the offering, she smelt it and then crushed it between her fingers. She felt a breath on her face and, opening her eyes, looked up to see Jesse leaning over her.

"You look so beautiful," he said. "Can I kiss you?"

Annie rolled away from him and sat up.

"I want to remember tonight for other reasons," she said.

"Of course." Jesse sprang up. "I am so sorry. It's selfish of me."

Annie also got to her feet and brushed off the dust from her trousers.

"I need to tell you a few things," she said. "But not tonight." Looking at her watch, she smiled at Jesse. "I am going to drive that van home and try and get a few hours' sleep."

Jesse smiled. "Can you drop me at a bus stop?"

"Thank you for helping tonight. I couldn't have done it without you," she said, holding out her hand.

Jesse took her hand. "You could and you will have to. Tonight was the start of your new life—I could see that—you looked so at home, so confident, so happy and clear."

"Do you really think so?"

Jesse looked at this strange, fierce, yet fragile creature and longed to take her in his arms.

"I forgot what joy felt like," Annie said, trying to find the key in the bottom of her bag. "I am beginning to understand that it was rather absent in my previous life. It probably sounds stupid but when I can persuade three different random ingredients to go together and create something delicious, I am overcome by waves of happiness."

"It's the same feeling when my painting springs to life, taking on some unaccountable, independent force—a dab of green, yellow and dash of scarlet meld to create a perfect leaf."

"Do you really think I could be a chef?"

"I don't think—I know," Jesse said with great conviction.

Annie turned to face him, her face shining.

"Thank you, that makes me very happy."

Chapter 28

J esse needs to wake up: get off the fence. Love is not only about feelings, it is about proof of feelings. He needs to find a way of showing his inamorata that her life would be immeasurably better with him. He needs to be indispensable without being controlling; inspirational without ego.

Unfortunately for him, my mistress has been so hurt that her merry little heart has shrivelled.

It was the same for my master—he never recovered from Charlotte's rejection. Gradually he detached from the world, exhausted by an imploded heart and a collapsing body. He moved constantly, from the countryside, to different apartments in Paris, and even to London for a spell. This peripatetic lifestyle was an effective way of avoiding memories of those little intimacies accrued through shared experiences: the tavern where they had met; the taste of a type of bread she had liked; the bars of a song she had sung; a nape of a neck that resembled hers. Gradually his aloofness from the world became complete: he lived alone with his illness and his dreams. His contempt for material interests increased. When his friend Caylus begged him to seek treatment for consumption in a hospital, Antoine snorted, "Isn't the worst that can happen to me the hospital? No one is refused admittance there." He did not want to be part of a club that would have him. My master died aged thirty-six. Alone.

I don't wish this pathetic outcome on anyone, let alone the lovely Annie; I just don't see love as a panacea or the grassy track connecting dark and light. I want her to prove my worth, to sell me, to set herself free financially, at least. I want her to enjoy creature comforts, to have the space and means to fulfil her dreams. I have not always brought luck to my owners: this time it must be different.

Chapter 29

After only a few hours' sleep, Annie woke full of energy and purpose. Throwing off her sheets, she went to the bathroom and stood in front of the mirror. The person who stared back at her had the same baggy, slightly watery eyes and pallid skin, but this morning Annie looked at her own reflection with tolerance and even slight compassion. The imperfections had been earned well. She could not believe that her fantasy life, her dream of becoming a chef, was edging forward and the gap between make-believe and reality was closing.

Taking a flannel, she soaked it in hot water and pressed it to her face.

"How did it go?" Evie broke into Annie's reverie.

"Amazing—it was amazing."

"Tell me everything," Evie said.

"I've got to take all the kit back now or I'll get charged," said Annie, patting her face dry.

"I'll come too." Evie turned towards the bedroom to get her clothes. "Keep you company."

"Mum, I want to be alone. Besides, look at yourself."

Evie stopped and looked in the mirror. Her bleach-blonde hair stuck up in the air. Round her eyes were smudges of make-up.

"You can be very cruel," Evie said, padding back to Annie's room and closing the door behind her.

Annie felt a twinge of guilt. The truth was that she didn't want Evie in the car, asking questions and turning the subject back to herself, where, like a needle on a scratched record, it would stay, repeating "Me, me, me."

Grabbing her bag, Annie let herself out of the flat and, taking the stairs two at a time, rushed down, out of the front door, to the rented van. To her relief it was scratch-less, even though her phone sat on the front seat, forgotten the night before. Between 3 a.m. when she returned home and now, nearly 9 a.m., there had been eight missed calls. Four were from Delores, one from Agatha, one from Jesse and two were from an unknown number. She played the first.

"Hi, Annie, it's me, Jesse—last night was amazing—simply amazing. Let's get together. Fancy a drink tonight?"

The sound of Jesse's voice sent shivers of anxiety down Annie's spine. Over the last few weeks, Annie had felt liberated from love or at least the feelings that she associated so firmly with the past. There was another exciting sensation: being free and independent; not compromising or having to consider another person's feelings. By desiring her, Jesse was imposing on her, and in rejecting him, Annie felt guilty. Being single meant being beholden to no one. Annie liked Jesse but not enough to take the risk of opening up her heart or contaminating her newfound spirit.

The next message was from Delores: "Darling. What a lovely dinner. Thank you. An absolute triumph. Clever girl. Now this is strange, but do you still have that painting you showed me all those weeks ago? Give me a call, darling."

Annie skipped on to the next messages.

"Miss Annie McDee. My name is Trichcombe Abufel. You might not remember but we met briefly in the British Museum drawings room. I urgently need to talk to you concerning that sketch."

"Miss McDee. This is Trichcombe Abufel again. It is urgent that you call me."

"Darling, Delores here. Call me. It's eight in the morning."

"Miss McDee, please telephone Trichcombe Abufel as soon as possible."

"Hi Annie, it's Agatha from the National Gallery Conservation department. I am terribly sorry to call you so early but something rather strange is happening. Could you give me a call as soon as you can?"

Annie hadn't thought much about her painting for the last few days. Wanting to hang on to the triumph of last night for a little longer, she ignored the rest of the messages and put the van into first gear.

She drove through Shepherd's Bush, passing a number of small family-run restaurants, a butcher and a chocolate shop. She had made her living from food before; she could again. Annie knew she could cook and that she had an original vision. She imagined herself surrounded by chefs, all dressed in white with her company's logo, "Foodalicious," printed on their caps and aprons, in a large open-plan kitchen with floor-to-ceiling windows looking over a kitchen garden with a glass wall separating the cooking from the planning areas. In another room, she saw a small design team poring over drawings and mood boards while at the back of the offices were storerooms where she would keep all the glasses, china and essential props needed to create her themed dinners.

Driving past the Russian Embassy to Kensington Gardens, Annie thought of different events she could offer—dinners inspired by *2001: A Space Odyssey*; the Arabian Nights; Art Deco; Modernism; Victoriana. Annie felt a shiver of excitement as she imagined how these might look and what menus she could create. She wanted this new life desperately: all that remained was how to achieve it. She would need a place to cook in, plus equipment, some PR and marketing, some temporary help, and some cash up front to buy ingredients. The traffic slowed to a standstill. Hot petrol fumes left a halo of smog around the cars. Annie put up her window to keep out the noxious air. Perhaps, until it gets going, she thought, I can keep my job working for the Winklemans. Though the job was boring, it was easy and left time to consider other things.

Her phone rang again and she turned it off and the radio up. A cherished song by Bob Dylan came on. Annie, who had been in the choir at each of her schools, started to sing "Blowin' in the Wind," but her voice came out as a croak. She had another go but again, she could not hold the tune. She cleared her throat hard but her voice still meandered over the chords. With a start, she realised that it had been months since she had last sung—even in the bath. In her former life, she had belted out songs everywhere, to everything and anyone—birds, the television, the river and her friends. Her vocal cords had ossified through lack of use. A teacher used to say "singing comes from the heart." I lost my heart and my voice, Annie thought, and now I am going to get them both back.

Trichcombe was not a religious man but as the aeroplane taxied down Berlin's Tegel runway, he prayed that God keep him alive long enough to write up his recent discoveries. In his excitement to get back to London, to his desk, his notes and his typewriter, he had forgotten to book "speedy boarding." Now he found himself in the middle seat at the back of the plane. On his left there was a young woman chewing gum in

a particularly revolting manner, occasionally blowing bright-
pink bubbles, which burst on her painted lips with a smack.
On the other side, a much pierced, fierce-looking young
skinhead wriggled and stretched in his seat with a manic
intensity. Trichcombe desperately wanted to avoid touching
bubble-gum woman but was actually scared of angering Mr.
Baader-Meinhof. Hunching his shoulders together, Trichcombe pressed his inner arms and his knees together and took
small shallow breaths.

The flight to London Gatwick took just under two hours.
Trichcombe refused anything to eat or drink but he touched
his jacket pocket repeatedly to check that his small digital camera was still in place. On its hard drive was a photograph of a
family standing in front of a fireplace. Above the fireplace was
a small painting by Watteau and standing with the family was a
small blond, blue-eyed boy.

In his other pocket was a piece of paper. One phone call
and a fantastical excuse had been all Trichcombe needed
to persuade the librarian at the British Museum to give up
the name and telephone number of the young woman with the
sketch. Trichcombe explained that he had picked up a valuable book belonging to her by mistake and he had only just
realised. Weeks had passed and she would be so worried. Oh,
he felt awful. The guilt. The remorse. Could the divine and
helpful person possibly help him? Of course it was against all
regulations. Mea culpa. In any circumstances. Thank you so
much. I am so very grateful. He had called the woman, a Miss
Annie McDee, twice from Berlin. He would call her again on
touchdown.

As the plane passed over Paris, Trichcombe wondered
which publication he would use as his portal to bring about
the absolute shame and exposure of Memling Winkleman
and his family. The *Burlington* magazine or *Apollo*, perhaps?
He remembered that these publications of high art were

probably part-owned by the Winklemans, whose tendrils of influence reached up and through tiny unexpected crevices. Perhaps, Trichcombe thought, it should be a daily newspaper, but they would want to edit his copy and insist on all sorts of fact-checks. As the plane passed over the English Channel, bubble-gum woman fell asleep and slumped in his direction. For the first time in his life Trichcombe felt a woman's head on his shoulder, her breath in his ear, simultaneously sweet and sour. What an utterly repulsive experience, he thought, prodding his elbow into her ribs. She woke up and snorted deeply. Perhaps, Trichcombe thought, I can make money too. He quickly pushed that idea out of his mind. All that mattered was revenge: the more humiliating, widespread and utterly conclusive the better.

Delores's office resembled a morgue preceding the funeral of a much-loved diva. Every surface was covered with extravagant arrangements of flowers.

"Twenty more minutes in here and we'll die of oxygen deprivation," Barty said testily. "Everyone knows that plants suck everything good out of the atmosphere."

"You've got it the wrong way round," Delores said, sniffing a large hydrangea. "During the day they create oxygen and at night they make carbon dioxide."

"How do you know that?"

Delores didn't answer. "How much do you think this lot cost?"

"More than the dinner, probably."

"Do you think I could send them back to the florists and get a refund?"

"You're bound to get found out."

"Who spent the most?"

"Who cares, darling? Let's get back to planning our museum."

Barty was sketching a picture of the grand salon in water-colours. The walls were lined in silk damask and the floors were made from inlaid wood.

"I will tell the decorator to gild everything. Ceilings, pelmets, cornices, door frames, the whole lot."

"I don't want your décor overwhelming my paintings."

"You haven't got any pictures yet. At the moment we'll be hanging you from the ceiling."

"It's not that easy to find great masterpieces. Nearly everything has been gobbled up by museums."

"Can't we waggle Vlad's chequebook at the odd curator? We know that most museums have thousands of works languishing in storage—surely they would not miss a few canvases?"

"It doesn't really work like that—not in this country, anyway."

"So let's go shopping in Europe—the poor dears are so broke they'd sell their grannies."

"I wonder if that's why Rebecca is so keen to get hold of the Watteau."

"What Watteau?" Barty asked.

"Some family heirloom has gone missing; she wants it back at any price."

"Any price? We like the sound of that."

Delores nodded. When Rebecca had called at 7 a.m., Delores assumed that the dealer was calling to apologise for failing to show up. She had not expected a rambling monologue about a missing painting. Rebecca explained that the Watteau had been stolen from Memling but they couldn't go to the police or publicise the theft in case the thieves got spooked and destroyed the work. The picture, Rebecca said, was Memling's last link with his family and of a sentimental value hard to quantify.

Rebecca described the work in great detail. It was about eighteen by twenty-four inches, an oil painting showing a girl dancing with her lover lying at her feet watched by a clown.

The painting's title was *The Improbability of Love* and it was an early work, perhaps Watteau's first great painting, and certainly the one that had launched both his career and the Rococo movement.

As Rebecca described the picture, Delores felt her breath shorten and the back of her neck and armpits prickle with sweat. Could this be the same work that she had dismissed as a fake?

"Are you listening?" Rebecca asked crossly.

"Yes, yes, I am thinking," Delores said, sitting down heavily on a chair.

"Have you heard anything about it? Has anyone mentioned it to you?" Rebecca said, trying to keep her tone casual.

"No! I have not!" Delores said a little too quickly. No one must know or suspect that she, one of the greatest living experts in French eighteenth-century art, had ever seen it. "Of course, if I do, I will tell you immediately."

Delores repeated what Rebecca had said about the missing painting, omitting any reference to Annie's visit.

"Are you thinking what I am thinking?" Barty asked as he listened to his friend.

"I am so thinking that," Delores said, clapping her hands together.

"We have found the centrepiece for our museum; let's call it the 'Museum of Love.'"

"How disgustingly sentimental."

"What if the Winklemans don't want to sell?"

"Everything has a price."

"If this one is the exception?"

"They are dealers—their *raison d'être* is dealing."

"Can you strike a deal?" Barty jumped up and clapped his hands together.

"I have to find it first," Delores said.

Barty sat down heavily. "If they can't find it how will you? They employ stringers and fixers the world over."

"I have a lead," Delores said mysteriously. She was not going to admit that she had held the painting in her hands.

Sitting on the edge of her hotel bed, Rebecca pressed her hands into the mattress and her feet hard into the floor to try and calm her shaking limbs. Too late, too late, too late, the voices in her head taunted. Too late, too late, too late. Why hadn't she taken the photograph three weeks ago when she first met Danica? It would have been so simple. Today she hadn't hesitated; the moment the old lady's back was turned, Rebecca had slipped the razor from her pocket and, nipping off the edges of the photo, had detached it from the album and placed it in her pocket. Closing the album, she had put it back on the shelf and, a few minutes later, invented an urgent reason to leave the apartment. Outside, she had taken the picture, torn it into tiny pieces and, standing next to the busy main road, released each fragment into the wind and slip- stream of passing cars and buses.

But she was too late: the old lady hadn't been able to recall or pronounce her visitor's name but she described him per- fectly: tall, pale-skinned, exquisitely dressed in a three-piece tweed suit with an extravagant knotted silk cravat held in place by a gold tie pin shaped like a bugle. He had a dome of grey shoulder-length hair, beautifully brushed; his nails were buffed to a shiny finish; his glasses lived in a crocodile-skin case tucked in an inside pocket.

"How odd that I have not had any visitors for years since your brother, and in the space of a few hours I receive you for the second time and that man," Danica told Rebecca, "and that you all are so interested in my funny old photographs. They were just snaps." She noticed that Rebecca was looking terribly pale. Could she make her a cup of sweet tea? It had been so kind to bring the flowers and chocolates.

Rebecca thought it was stupid of her father to try and destroy Trichcombe's career and stymie the connoisseur's attempts to gain acceptance in the academic world. Rebecca remembered the old adage, "Keep your friends close but your enemies closer still." Her father should have retained Trichcombe on a stipend and drip-fed him the occasional commission. She never knew the full details of the crime he had supposedly committed; now she didn't need to ask. Trichcombe must have stumbled on an aspect of Memling's past.

Getting up off the bed, Rebecca went to the window and looked down on to the street below. Her hotel was at the intersection of the former East and West Berlin overlooking the Holocaust Memorial: a grid of monumental grey uneven tombstones, arranged in labyrinthine narrowing pathways set on a slope. Only a few weeks ago she had been a proud Jew, from a family of survivors, one of those who had made it through. What was she now? Looking down at the monument below, she imagined getting lost in the long alleyways of the memorial and the headstones closing in and crushing her to death.

She drew the curtain and threw herself face down on the bed, waiting for the panic attack to take hold. But as she lay there with her face pressed against the velvet eiderdown, something unusual happened. Instead of her heart beating faster, it seemed to steady and instead of a whirl of confusion, her thoughts seemed to abate and she was left with one single idea. Why was she giving up so easily? Where was her grit, her determination? Why roll over and let fate and others pick over her life like an old carcass?

Rebecca got up, walked over to the window, threw open the curtain and looked down at the people criss-crossing the square beneath her. She imagined her father nearly seventy years earlier. He could have held up his hands and surrendered to the Allies. As a young SS officer who had purloined and confiscated works of art belonging to Jews, he was certainly guilty, on many counts. Instead he had made the decision to embrace life, to create a future, albeit dishonestly, rather than face a trial and disgrace. Would she, at the age of twenty, have had the courage and mendacity? What could she do now to salvage her family from disgrace?

Rebecca stood quietly for a few moments thinking about Memling. Whatever her father had done, she loved him and could not imagine or countenance his certain public disgrace. The thought of his face splashed across the papers, his age-mottled hands bound into cuffs, his silver head bent in a courtroom dock, was far worse than the prospect of keeping his dreadful secret. He was a monster, but he was her monster, an inextricable part of her past, present and future. She could expose him, but that would never erase him or his deeds; he was part of her DNA, her conscience, and whether she liked it or not, she had enjoyed the fruits of his deception.

Rebecca's thoughts turned to Marty and she knew with certainty that, confronted by this discovery, he had decided suicide was easier than facing the wreckage. For the first time, she was angry with her brother: why hadn't he destroyed the notebook? Did he mean her to find it, to face all this alone?

She stopped shaking and suddenly felt strong and full of purpose. All that stood between her and disaster was an art historian and a small painting. Remove them both and the status quo remained intact. What did she mean by "remove"? How far would she go to protect her family? Would she kill? To Rebecca's surprise, the thought didn't repulse her. She wouldn't have to get her own hands dirty—there were other people for that kind of thing. Rebecca looked at her clock—it was now 10:15 a.m. and if she hurried, she could make the midday flight back to London. Placing the last few things in her overnight bag, she left her room and ran down the stairs to the lobby. There was a taxi waiting at the entrance and, pushing past two waiting guests with an apologetic grimace, Rebecca took it.

"Tegel Airport, *bitte*," she told the driver.

In the coming months Rebecca would remember the

moment when she crossed some invisible line and took the decision to help Memling eradicate his past along with his years of subterfuge and dishonest dealings. She felt no guilt or remorse, simply a wave of clarity and determination.

She placed a call to her father. Dispensing with the usual pleasantries, Rebecca told Memling to meet her at 4 p.m. by the fountains in Hyde Park. Leaning back in the seat of the taxi, Rebecca smiled at her father's surprise; he was unused to his daughter issuing instructions. From now on, Rebecca realised, she was in control.

Chapter 30

Rebecca arrived at the Italian gardens twenty minutes early and, walking slowly around the fountains, remembered visits as a child. Her mother had loved this unlikely area of Hyde Park; it reminded her of home and Rome and the Villa d'Este, places from her past. Pearl Winkleman had liked to sit in the pump house and watch her children fish for imaginary catches with rods made from string dangling from sticks. Once they tired of that, she sent them to find different animals carved in marble and Portland stone on the fountains and urns. Each time the children pretended to discover anew the rams' heads, dolphins and swans: praise was hard to come by in the Winkleman family. Rebecca wondered how much her mother had known about her husband's origins, how much she had suspected.

Rebecca's relationship with her father had changed with one phone call; now she saw her father in a different light. A few days earlier, she would have seen a tall, elderly but fit man in a navy-blue cashmere overcoat, white silk scarf and highly polished shoes, carrying a silver-topped cane. She would automatically have checked her make-up in a compact mirror and smoothed her hair, worrying that even the tiniest sign of imperfection would annoy her exacting parent and invite unwanted criticism. A few days earlier she would never have dared call Memling to a meeting, let alone to one in a place so loved by her mother.

The man walking towards her was still immaculately dressed, purposeful and instantly recognisable with his shock of white hair and his large white husky padding beside him. But now, for the first time, he needed her more than she needed him; the balance of power had shifted; she held the keys to their future, his posterity. Without her complicity, his entire life's work, those years of subterfuge and deceit, would have been in vain. For seventy of his ninety-one years Memling had worked to lift his family out of penury and make them players on an international stage; the last thing he would want was for that good name and great business to be washed away in a tide of shame and scandal.

Memling was now only a hundred feet away. I could still change my mind, Rebecca thought, let everything return to normal and devolve all responsibility and ultimate decision-making to Memling. But although this idea brought a momentary flood of relief, it was too late: the house of cards on which his authority rested had come tumbling down.

"My daughter," Memling said, holding out his hands and smiling. "Your phone call made me anxious—has something happened?"

Rebecca smiled back automatically, unable to control the reflex, those years of being taught to be polite and courteous. "Shall we sit?" She bent down to pat the dog on its head; Tiziano responded grandly with a slow blink of his eyes.

"Why here?" Memling looked around in astonishment. "We have so many nicer places to choose."

Without answering, Rebecca turned and walked up the steps and into the pump house. It stank of piss and stale beer, but a breeze wafted the worst of the smells away. At one end, a tramp lay encased in an overcoat, half covered by a cardboard box. Rebecca chose the other end of the bench, way out of earshot, and sat down. Memling carefully swept an area beside her before pulling his coat around him and sitting down.

"I know everything," Rebecca said. "You are Heinrich Fuchs and you don't have a drop of Jewish blood. You are just a petty thief." Rebecca spoke quietly but clearly. To her surprise, she didn't feel like crying or shouting. She found a cool sense of purpose and calm.

Memling did not answer immediately but when he did, his voice was equally measured and clear. "Harsh words from my little princess, harsh and bitter and naïve. Is this what a devoted father deserves?"

"I have been to Schwedenstrasse 14 in Berlin and met your neighbour and childhood friend Danica Goldberg. She has photographs of you as a boy, a lovely blond Aryan child in the midst of a family called Winkleman. At what point did you decide to steal their identity, their past, their possessions and lives? Did you kill them or leave that to camp commandants?" Rebecca's words came tumbling out and she had the strangest feeling of watching each syllable float through the air and into her father's ears.

Memling sat in silence, his eyes fixed on the middle distance.

"I looked through the ledgers in the safe. You were thorough—too thorough, perhaps," Rebecca continued. "That must be your Nazi training—make clear, concise, exhaustive notes about everything." She stole a look at her father and although his face was an inscrutable mask, she noticed that the knuckles of his right hand were clenched and white. "Every picture that has come through our company was written up. Those early works appeared as if by magic, didn't they? Spiriting their way into your hands after the war. But you weren't a magician, were you? Nor were you very good at getting deals or spotting masterpieces. You were a fence, handling stolen property and passing it on. Who were you working for? Your old Nazi colleague, Karl Haberstock? Or the ones who had been put in prison but needed someone on the outside to carry on their good works? Or the ones that escaped, who were holed up in Bavaria or South America and needed a middleman?" Rebecca's voice had risen slightly in pitch and volume; she forced herself to lower it back to a whisper. "Or were you cleverer than that? Did you steal from your masters during the war, squirrel away the odd Titian, Watteau and Guardi, knowing that one day the war would end and the dead could not, would not, come back for their rightful property?"

For a long minute, Memling said nothing. Then, clearing his throat, he spoke in a quiet, measured tone. "I wanted to tell someone about all this. Your mother, your brother or you. I only built the business for our family and did not want to give any of you the responsibility of knowing how it began."

"This started long before we were born, before you met Mama, so don't try that line," Rebecca hissed at her father.

"There is so much you don't know," Memling said angrily.

"I have all day." Rebecca crossed her arms.

"I would like to have this conversation elsewhere. I would like you to do me the courtesy of allowing an old man to collect his thoughts."

"The days of you dictating terms are over. Here and now is as good a place and time as any."

Memling moved slightly as if to get up but thought better of it. Tiziano, sensing his master's discomfort, put his head on Memling's knee and was rewarded with a gentle stroke.

"My father, his father and many generations before were soldiers, always on the winning side. From 1701, we served the

Kings of Prussia and were thus part of the greatest fighting force that history has seen. My forebears never had a home or possessions—they and their families lived a soldier's life, moving from one campaign to another, from one barrack to another. The pay was not spectacular, but the pride—oh the pride in their achievements made up for everything. To be a Prussian captain, as my father and his father and those before, was to have respect and circumstance. In their society, they were more important than any merchant or businessman; they sat at tables with princes and aristocrats."

"I am not here for a history lesson," Rebecca interrupted.

"In years to come you will wish you had asked these questions; ignorance is a curse lying in wait for the younger generation, for those who forgot to ask."

Rebecca looked out across the fountains, at a child playing with a small dog.

"Did you tell this story to Marty?"

Memling winced. "I will come to Marty—let me at least tell the story in a way that makes sense to me. Give me that, will you?" Again, Tiziano, sensing his master's distress, put his head back on the old man's knee and looked from Rebecca to Memling.

Rebecca nodded.

"When the First World War was declared, there was rejoicing in my family. Years had passed since the last war and my father was bored with civilian life. He met and married my mother in 1913 and they were trying for a child, but she told me that once war was declared, all my father did was polish his spurs, his helmet, and his sword. Another man had entered their house and she was not sure that she liked this version of her husband. Of course, that war was a catastrophe for proud German soldiers, and the Treaty of Versailles cemented their humiliation. My father's foot was blown off by a landmine—he was sacked, decommissioned. Those who once cheered for his bravery and prowess now held him responsible for the downfall of the old order. His sword and helmet, his uniform and medals became symbols of shame." Memling spoke with his eyes fixed on his dog's face, slowly and gently scratching the animal under his chin. Rebecca used to think that the dog represented power, the great white husky; now she realised the animal was a kind of canine security blanket.

"The country lurched from one crisis to another, businesses closing, hyperinflation, unemployment, everything my parents had, even the small army pension, was eroded to nothing," Memling said, pulling Tiziano closer and stroking his white flank. "My parents, like many other Germans, were broke and destitute. The only job my father could find was as janitor for a block of flats inhabited by Jews. You have to understand, Rebecca, that this was the most ignominious and humiliating end for a proud soldier."

"What has that got to do with you, with us?"

"Listen and you might learn something," Memling said.

For a moment Rebecca returned to her younger self, the timid child cowed by her father.

"I don't need to listen to you, Father. I don't need to hear your stories. You may know about your family's past, but I hold its future in my hands. Be civil or I will walk away. Answer my questions or my ears are closed."

Memling nodded. He seemed smaller suddenly and Rebecca noticed that his pale blue eyes were watery—tears or age?

"I am sorry, Daughter. I wanted to explain what happened. Not so you forgive me, but perhaps so that you understand a little better. May I go on?"

Rebecca shrugged, a tacit assent.

"When I was born in 1924 my father found a childish receptacle for all his disappointments and unfulfilled dreams. Once I could walk, he had me marching up and down our tiny apartment. As soon as I could recognise shapes and colours, we studied battle plans of previous wars. My love of precision and detail comes from an older Germany. Night after night, he and his friends met to talk about their hopes for a Germany restored to her former glory. If Hitler had not come along it's just possible that Germans like my father would have imploded with the weight of their combined loss of pride. Herr Hitler rode their disappointment like a jockey rides a champion thoroughbred. He gave them hope and purpose."

"I can't listen to an apology for Hitler," Rebecca said quietly.

Memling ignored her. "Mine was a grim, strict childhood. If my bed wasn't made properly there were consequences; if I was late, I was shut out, whatever the weather; perceived rudeness was met with a swift beating. Sometimes forcing me to go without a meal was my father's way of hiding that he did not have enough money to put food on our table."

"What did your mother say?"

"Mother was so terrified of him that she acquiesced in any plan he suggested. Even if it meant holding me down while he beat me. My mother could have got a job cleaning the Jewish apartments but my father wouldn't hear of it. Anti-Semitism is as old as the Jews; Hitler didn't invent it."

Memling looked at his daughter. "Can we walk a bit? My legs are stiffening up and I can't stand the smell of this place. It would be nice for the dog too."

Rebecca stood up and held out an arm for her father. Leaning on his stick, Memling took her arm and struggled to his feet. While he could run on a tennis court, sitting for any length of time stiffened the joints in his knees and in the small of his back. The pair moved slowly down the steps and headed towards the Serpentine. Tiziano walked close by his master, frequently glancing up at the old man and then around them in case of unexpected danger.

A smart wind had blown through the early-flowering cherry trees and blossoms lay like snow across the ground. The birds, celebrating the coming of spring, sang and raced through the bushes. Clumps of early crocuses were scattered by the path and around trees, splashes of yellow on acid green. A squirrel ran across the path in front of them followed by an unbiddable terrier trying to catch it, the owner shouting in vain. Tiziano looked at the other dog but did not react. Rebecca walked while not really taking in the view. When she looked down, she saw that their three shadows walked in front of them, a man, a woman and a dog, caricatures made by a low-hanging sun. She was pleased to notice that hers looked strong and purposeful while her father's was hunched and creaky.

"Esther Winkleman was as kind as she was beautiful," Memling recalled. "She had long dark hair, almost black eyes and a permanent smile. Their apartment was full of music and laughter. When I was left out on the step at night she would come and find me, sneak me up to their place and feed me. There were six of them in a tiny three-room apartment so there was hardly room for another, nor were they rich, but they always made me welcome and shared their food. She was an art teacher at the local school and would show me books of paintings and tell me about the artists in her gentle, lisping voice. No wonder I fell in love with art. I didn't particularly like the son who was my age, Memling, but I made firm friends with him so I could be near her. There was a small library on the way home from school—we were allowed to take out one book per month. Once my father found a book on Dürer under my bed—Dürer—he was a good German, but you cannot imagine the beating."

Rebecca kicked a stone purposefully. She wanted Memling to explain the later stuff and how that happened. Sensing her irritation, Memling moved his story along.

"At first my father denounced Hitler as an uncouth yob but as his power grew, as he played on the hopes and fears of his countrymen, views changed. I was enlisted in the Hitler Youth movement and when war was declared, my father falsified my birth certificate so that I could join up early. I was tall for my age and, thanks to the Winklemans' food, I was strong.

I was just fifteen when I was conscripted. Once again Esther Winkleman saved my life: one of the Führer's dreams was to build the pre-eminent museum in Linz and fill it with the world's greatest works of art. Most of his soldiers couldn't tell a Vermeer from a van Gogh. The word went out that the Führer was looking for experts. I knew little but a lot more than most. I was chosen for the prestigious art squad, the ERR. It had incredible powers—we could stop battalions, order generals away from sites, close down bridges."

Rebecca and her father reached a small play area by the Serpentine. In the middle was a statue dedicated to Peter Pan, a tree made from metal with tiny figures crawling up the outside. Rebecca looked at Peter Pan calling to the lost boys to follow him while Wendy looked on disapprovingly. Rebecca rued the loss of her own innocence, aborted a few days earlier in Berlin. How long, she thought, can I protect Grace?

"What happened to the Winklemans?" Rebecca asked.

"For the first few years I was able to get the family food parcels and other necessities. I was, believe me, desperate to help them escape. The Watteau was their only asset and when I showed Hitler an image of the painting he offered a million Marks. I begged them to sell it and buy a safe passage out of Berlin and a new start in England or America. They refused. In 1943 I heard from my mother that the apartment had been sealed and the family had gone on holiday to visit some friends. I was hurt that they did not leave a forwarding address. It wasn't until 1944 that I found out the truth: they'd been taken to Auschwitz-Birkenau."

"At what point did you decide to strip their apartment?" Rebecca asked, trying to keep her voice even.

"My first intention was to keep their things safe—not just the Winklemans' but also all the families' in our block. I hoped that they would come home and find things as they were. Working through the night on my odd days home, I broke into the apartments and took the pictures off the walls, wrapped them and hid them in a cellar."

"No one noticed?"

"There was a lot going on at that time."

"And the Watteau?"

"There was increasing pressure on the art squad to come up with beautiful things."

"So you sold it?"

"It left my hands for a short time. Since I had showed him the image, the Führer had nagged and nagged me to bring it to him. I gave it to him in 1944; he looked at it and told me to hide it in a safe place. He planned to give it to Eva Braun as a wedding present when the war was over. Taking it out of its frame, I rolled it up and it stayed in my kitbag, close by, for the rest of the war."

"It seems odd that you would present the same gift to your own mistress—wasn't it stained by the association with Hitler?"

"There is something transformative about that painting—it captures your spirit and your heart—you'll understand when you see it, when we get it back."

"I never had you down as a sentimental fool," Rebecca said.

"There is a huge difference between sentimentality and romanticism."

Rebecca wondered why this hurt so much—was it that her father loved a woman who was not her mother? Or was it that the person who seemed so in control, her own all-powerful patriarch, revealed himself to be just another mortal? She started to walk away from her father, fighting back tears. She realised how little she knew about the man who had brought her up, whom she worked with every day of the week. Behind her she heard the tap of the cane and Memling's heavy tread as he caught up with her.

"I was nineteen when the war started, twenty-five when it ended. I had five extraordinary years travelling around Europe

looking at beautiful objects—those years were my high school
and university rolled into one. For the first time in my short
life I had more than enough to eat. I never had to kill a man; I
was insulated against most of the pain and hardship. We went
to every great house from here to Normandy, living like kings.
I drank wine from the cellars of Château Lafite and slept in
the King's bed at Vaux-le-Vicomte. I dined under the portrait
of Cosimo de' Medici and slept with the great-great-great-
granddaughter of a Borgia prince. My only task was to spot
beautiful objects. We worked with dealers and auctioneers,
connoisseurs and academics. Everywhere we went we were
assailed with suggestions. Everyone was out to make some
money from the war. In the seventy-odd years that I have been
dealing art, I have never seen a market like it. Over a million works were auctioned at Le Drouot in Paris between 1939
and 1945," he said. "I am not particularly gifted; unlike you I
can't spot a Titian from three hundred yards. I don't have your
powers of detection. I have a talent for detail—that is why you
have found me out."

"The Watteau was your undoing—if it weren't for that
painting I would never have started looking."

Memling stopped. The irony was not lost on him. Was this
Esther's act of revenge from beyond the grave? Pushing these
thoughts out of his mind, he continued with his story. "The
war ended. My bosses were executed or imprisoned. My father
killed my mother and himself, sealing up the windows and
doors of our apartment and turning on the gas. I didn't even
have a passport, only army papers. I had nothing, I was nobody
and I was shamed." He turned to face Rebecca. "If you expose
me you will inflict this shame on yourself and your family. Do
you really want, at fifty years old, to be standing where I was
at twenty-two?"

"Maybe I would rather live with a clear conscience,"
Rebecca said.

"I entertained that thought in 1945. I was standing by a

small farmhouse in Bavaria built next to a disused mine. In its cavernous depths there were hundreds of valuable pictures, objects and jewels that my squad had hidden during the war, destined for Hitler's personal collection. During the last four years, we carefully siphoned off some of the best things we captured, on the Führer's instructions, mainly to keep them from Göring. Four other people knew about the cache; three killed themselves rather than face the Nuremberg trials, one died of typhus."

"So you decided to keep it all for yourself?"

"I had no plans at that moment, apart from staying alive. I went to the farmhouse because it was the only place I could think of. Once the war had ended it was a kind of mad free-for-all with each of the winning countries trying to hoover up what was left. The Russians were like locusts: they scooped up everything and took it back to Moscow. The Americans sent over a posse of experts, the Monument Men, to try and stem the tide of all the looting and pillaging, but what could a hundred men or so do when the whole of Europe was up for grabs? We had stolen thousands and thousands of works, over twenty per cent of all Western art. Though paintings were not worth much, art was still an internationally accepted currency. You might only get a hundred dollars for a Klimt but at least it was a hundred dollars."

"When did you get the idea of impersonating Memling Winkleman?" Rebecca asked.

Memling walked slowly up the path towards the Serpentine Gallery. At the top, wheezing slightly, he answered her question. "It happened by accident. Three days after the war ended I went back to our family apartment and found the bodies of my parents. Then I ran upstairs hoping to find just one member of the Winkleman family, but they had all disappeared. On my way out, on an impulse I took some books and the library card that had belonged to Esther's son, Memling. I took various other paintings out of their frames, rolled them up, and by foot and only at night, I made my way to the farmhouse. I spent a year there living on nuts and berries, trapping small animals and birds. I became terribly thin; my hair grew long and matted. My clothes were ragged. In the autumn of 1946 a passing American platoon car spotted the smoke rising from the chimney and decided to check the building for fugitive soldiers. They caught me quickly. I would not say my name; I could not say my name. They searched the building looking for clues to my identity or for weapons—who knows. One officer found the library card—they put two and two together—I was a Jew who had escaped the death trains and had hidden out. God knows how they came up with that story—the Americans love a good story. They drove me back to Berlin, sorted out my papers, gave me a passport and offered me a new life in America. Seven weeks later I arrived in New York. In my bag were some jewels, the Watteau, a tiny Rembrandt and five hundred dollars courtesy of Uncle Sam."

"I suppose they tattooed you too," said Rebecca, her voice soaked in sarcasm.

"I had that done in a Korean parlour on the Lower East Side. By then I had found out what happened to the Winklemans—all gone. This number is Esther's—you might find it hard to believe, Daughter, but I had the tattoo done as a mark of respect, not as a shameless piece of cynicism."

Rebecca walked ahead of her father, trying to decide which aspects of his story she believed. Looking around, she saw the bridge over the Serpentine, an artificial lake made in the eighteenth century. She wondered how many knew that Harriet Westbrook, the pregnant wife of Percy Bysshe Shelley, had drowned herself there on finding out about his infidelities. Or that the Hanoverians had celebrated the anniversary of the British victory at Trafalgar there, another war where thousands lost their lives. She wondered how long it would take before the atrocities of the last war became just another faded memory or an entry in Wikipedia.

"You make your story sound so plausible, but your whole life has been one long shameless lie. You stole your dead friend's identity and dead people's possessions—you even stole their religion and brought your children up with some phony heritage. You are not a man—you are a parasite!" Rebecca turned and shouted at her father. A woman walking close by looked at them nervously and hurried on. Memling stopped and gripped the black iron railings with both hands.

"I wanted to live," he said weakly.

"Were you able to forget where it all came from?" Rebecca hissed.

"Never, but at least I provided you with some alternative."

"What about Marty?"

Memling's head hung down and his shoulders hunched. "He sent me a letter saying that he had found out. I wrote back immediately offering to turn myself in or to swallow a cyanide pill that I keep on my person at all times." Reaching into his jacket pocket, Memling took out a small silver box and, opening it, revealed a tiny blue pill sitting on a velvet cushion.

"Put it away, Father. It's not time for amateur dramatics," Rebecca said coldly.

Memling turned to face his daughter. "Your brother was my pride, my joy, and our future."

Rebecca did not contradict her father; she knew that he was speaking the truth. She knew too with some sadness that, although her father was fond of her, it was Marty whom he loved.

Tears sprang from Rebecca's eyes. "Poor Marty—he couldn't cope with having to hold the scales of justice, having to choose between right and wrong, exposing you and mortifying us."

"Believe me—I would have given up everything, gone to prison, surrendered to the authorities, Simon Wiesenthal—whatever it took to have kept him here," said Memling.

"Mama—did she know?" asked Rebecca.

"No, nor did she ever suspect."

"At least, thanks to her, I am a Jew—I haven't been sitting in synagogues all my life as a Nazi—what did that feel like, Papa? To have to pray through Holocaust Day?"

"I prayed, Rebecca, just not for the same things," said Memling, bending down and sinking his hands into his dog's fur. Tiziano turned and nuzzled his master's face. Memling did not push the animal away but let him lick his folds of skin.

"I often wondered if you loved your dogs more than any member of your family," Rebecca said.

"Will it shock you to hear that I think love is an over-rated emotion?" Memling said. "I am very fond of dogs, as I am of my children. I am particularly grateful for the dogs' unquestioning and uncomplicated affection. Do you remember, when you were children, going to the National Gallery at weekends?" Memling asked.

"Every weekend."

"Many of those great works were owned by unscrupulous and mendacious collectors—slave traders, racketeers and murderers. But when we look at those men's possessions, their Rubenses, Hogarths, Raphaels, Titians and Velázquezes today, we just see beauty."

"What has this got to do with anything?" Rebecca asked incredulously.

"I was trying to teach you about a bigger picture, about the passage of time, to look beyond individual stories," said Memling.

"Art does not have the power to eradicate sin," Rebecca said. "What strange, twisted tales you have had to tell yourself in order to justify your actions, and your dishonesty."

"I have never tried to justify anything but there are things which are greater, more long-lasting and important than myself or my family."

Rebecca steered them to a bench by a small copse. Overhead a flock of brightly coloured parakeets, escapees from a private collection perhaps, swooped and screeched as they flew between trees, flashing incongruously iridescent colours; yellows, greens, reds and blues among the gentle greens and blues of the English parkland. Memling sat down heavily and, taking out a starched white handkerchief, he wiped his face.

"What are you going to do?" he asked. "Promise me you are not going to hurt yourself. I will do anything to stop that. I will walk into the nearest police station. Name your terms." Memling's voice cracked with emotion.

Rebecca looked down and realised that the sun was setting and their shadows had disappeared. She looked at the diamond rings on her fingers, one from Carlo on their engagement, the other a present from her father when Grace was born. Her hands were already slightly wrinkled and the beginning of a liver spot was forming on her left wrist. She tried to imagine a life without her father, daughter or husband and excommunication from her milieu, the world of art. Turning her hands over, she looked at her unlined palms, her almost white skin and the sliver of a blue artery in her wrist. Her thoughts turned to Marty and his decision. Slowly she turned her hands over and looked at her rings, those bands of love and responsibility.

She looked up at her father, at his wary, anxious expression. "We have lots of work to do," she said.

Memling's shoulders slumped and he slowly let out lungs full of breath.

"What matters is that Grace inherits a clean title and fortune and that the shame and guilt stops with you. It is your dirty secret, not ours," said Rebecca.

Memling tried to keep a smile of relief from his face.

"You will write a full confession so that if anything is exposed, it is made clear that I never knew of any of this," Rebecca said.

Memling nodded.

"Trichcombe Abufel has a copy of Danica Goldberg's photograph of the Watteau," she said.

"Trichcombe?" Memling looked amazed.

"He's been trying to nail you for years," Rebecca said.

"But he was always so ineffectual," Memling said, shaking his head.

"You need to destroy all his notes, anything that he can trace back to us. If the worst comes to the worst, you will have to get rid of him."

"Get rid?" Memling looked appalled.

"Cut the crap, Papa—I know you incinerated that poor man in his antique shop trying to find the Watteau—don't try and pretend otherwise."

"That was a mistake. I asked Ellis to frighten him."

"My driver is your henchman?" Rebecca was amazed.

"He is a former policeman."

"Two incompetents," snapped Rebecca.

Memling looked at his hands. "I have underestimated you."

"You underestimate everyone," Rebecca replied.

Memling looked at her sadly—he saw now that he had overlooked his daughter, written her off for being a woman, a person of no consequence.

"You need to find that painting and get rid of it. Not hide it—destroy it," Rebecca said.

Memling winced but nodded. "I have been the victim of my own sentimentality."

"Sentimentality!" Rebecca scoffed. "Solipsistic self-regard, flagrant stupidity, greed and weakness is how I would describe it."

"I am a fool," Memling said weakly.

For a few minutes, they sat in silence.

"There isn't a museum or curator, dealer or expert who doesn't owe us something. I have called around, but now it's your turn. Get on to them. Call it in or the cash dries up. Get every dirty secret on every individual—affair, gambling debts, murky little details—you might need them," Rebecca instructed.

Memling nodded.

"There is one lead—we have to hope that it is simply a ghastly coincidence. Our temporary chef, Annie McDee, was photographed coming out of the same bric-a-brac shop and later with the right-sized parcel in her bike basket."

"She is still working with us?" Memling asked.

"Better to keep her closely observed. If she is working with others then she can be a hostage, a bargaining chip."

Memling looked thoughtfully into the distance. "Does she have access to the computers and records?"

"She has no access to our records. I double-checked all her searches and her emails—there's nothing."

"There must be something?"

"The only thing the woman thinks about is food and recipes. I have even tried to decode some in case they contained hidden messages or cyphers."

"I will send some people round to her apartment."

"I did that already. Maybe it's time to create a little damage."

Father and daughter sat side by side for a few minutes longer, both lost in thought. Checking her watch, Rebecca got up.

"What will you be doing?" Memling asked.

"Running the business as normal and keeping up appearances," Rebecca said.

"When will I see you again?" Memling asked.

"We will meet at the Italian gardens at 9 a.m. in four days' time. I will book you on to a flight to Munich tomorrow morning. There will be a car in the name of Brueghel at the Hertz desk. You will drive to the farmhouse and start a fire in the cellar."

"You want me to burn the paintings? There are Fragonards, a Leonardo, five Titians, three Monets and about seventy others. Catherine the Great's Amber Room—the greatest treasure known to anyone."

"What value do they have to us? Think, Papa. Think. They are cords around our necks."

"Can't we just leave them and hope that someone finds them one day?"

"And wait for them to put two and two together? The young man picked up in the same location in 1946? The times you have been driven there?"

Memling nodded sadly. "And if I fail in any of your tasks?"

"The next time we meet will be at your graveside," Rebecca replied.

Chapter 31

Evie sat on the side of the bed and wept. Two days had passed since Annie's triumphal dinner, but since then her daughter had avoided her. She wanted to share in Annie's triumph, not to take any credit for her success, merely to insert one small positive memory into the bank of their shared experience. The last few weeks attending AA meetings had helped Evie understand how the child Annie had been forced to live in the vortex of her compulsive world, a hapless victim of Evie's chemically enhanced or withdrawn moods. Returning from school, the child would never know which Evie was waiting behind the door. Would it be the happy-go-lucky-just-had-a-drink mother, or the nervous, fidgety let's-try-not-to-have-a-drink person? The angry withdrawing Evie, or the flat-out black-out mother? Sometimes Evie wasn't there— it would be days, occasionally weeks, before she returned, offering no explanations. No wonder Annie learned to cook; she had had to.

This morning, the weight of guilt was almost unbearable. Evie did not know how to forgive herself. Without her daughter's love what was the point in living? Evie looked back at her life, the shipwreck of dreams; it added up to so little. Half-started careers, messy relationships and a river of alcohol. Perhaps a little drink would help ease the pain of this moment? After all, booze was her friend, her constant companion. They'd had some fun together, hadn't they, her and Billy Bottle—at least she had lived, had a bit of fun. Where was the fun in Annie's sterile, lonely life? Work, work, work. Get up at the crack, slave for someone else's benefit, come home and sleep. And as for the cooking, I mean, that just proves it, doesn't it—make something that is eaten and shat out. Who says that's a more worthwhile existence? Who's judging whom now?

Evie felt the fire returning to her spirit. She got up and looked at herself in the mirror and laughed; she did look awful. She splashed cold water on her face. Surely one drink wouldn't hurt? One is too many and a thousand never enough, the mirror mocked back. Evie scrubbed at the mascara stains under her eyes, took off her clothes and ran a damp cloth under her armpits and between her legs. Never know, she said to herself, Mr. Right might come a-poking today. She looked at herself naked in the bathroom mirror. Not bad, really. Not like some of those smug bitches you see with their semi-detacheds and their second-hand sports cars. They might have a bank account but they couldn't even pull their own husbands. Evie could, mind you. She could get those titties up and out, and in a good light you couldn't see the crepey surface at all. She was only forty-seven and her stomach was flat and her legs firm. Most men said she could pass for a thirty-five-year-old. Mind you, men said just about anything at closing time.

Evie did her hair carefully, backcombing it into a springy, fluffy helmet, hiding the worst of the roots under a little gold clip. She took Annie's diamanté earrings—nothing like a bit of paste to lift the face. She made up her eyes carefully, dabbing concealer to cover the bags and a light dust of reflective powder. Then she took Annie's "best" dress and her pair of black heels. Looking at herself in the glass, Evie decided she was "outside world" ready.

Evie stopped. She had forgotten one important thing—the most important thing, perhaps. She had no money. Not even a pound. She felt a sense of rising panic. Now that the decision to drink had been taken, nothing could get in the way. She needed money. She opened the drawers and cupboards hoping to find a roll of cash; only take ten, maybe twenty, she didn't need much. Evie could not find anything—not even a handful of pennies. She felt a faint sweat rising on her temples and under her armpits.

Sitting down at the kitchen table, she tried to breathe slowly and even thought of calling her sponsor. Maybe her higher power was looking after her. Then she saw the picture—that was worth something, wasn't it? It's not like Annie even wanted it—she had told her often enough that she regretted buying the thing. If Evie took it she'd be doing her daughter a favour, wouldn't she? But where would she sell it? The pawnshop? What would they want with an old picture? Evie remembered a pub in the East End, a place where young artists went to drink—maybe she could take it there and leave it behind the bar as collateral. Kind of a brilliant idea, she thought; she wasn't selling her daughter's picture, just getting it to earn its keep. Wrapping the painting in an old jumper, Evie put it into a Sainsbury's bag, and grabbing her coat, hurried out of the flat, down the stairs. It was 11 a.m.: opening time.

I am too old to be messing around with petrol cans and flame torches, Memling thought as he sloshed the corners of the farmhouse with diesel. Once he could have lifted five-gallon cans on his own, but now he had to struggle with a single litre. Not wanting to arouse suspicion, he had driven an extra thirty kilometres to stop at different stations to buy individual cans. He had never set fire to a building before and had little idea how to ensure that it really burned. Later he would walk through the small orchard to the hillock where the trap door to the disused mine was located. He was almost too old to negotiate the steep steps down into the bunker. He had lost count how many times since the war he had come back—thirty, maybe forty. It was strange how pictures that had been almost worthless in the 1950s had come back into fashion. Once he nearly threw out a pair of late Renoirs, never believing that anyone would really want those sickly sweet rotund bathers. Today both would fetch crazy prices, Memling thought, remembering the sale of Renoir's *Au Moulin de la Galette* in 1990 for $78.1 million to the chairman of a Japanese paper manufacturing company. The new owner intended to be cremated with the painting; fortunately his company ran into serious difficulties and the Renoir was sold privately to a collector with less grandiose ideas about funeral pyres.

Memling had grown to love the pictures in the cellar. He allowed himself one last trip into the bowels of the small hillside, one last browse among the stacks. He could remember where most of them came from. That Léger had been in a Jewish collection in Paris; he had carried the Titian out of a small church near Venice; the van Loo came from an attic in Amsterdam where some Jews had tried and failed to hide it above a cupboard; a golden cup, probably by Cellini, had been found in a French château where it had been used to keep a baron's cufflinks. Memling doubted that any of the original owners had loved these pieces as much as he did. For him, these works of art represented beauty and also escape— they were the magic bridge connecting an impoverished, joyless childhood in Berlin with the luxurious, powerful position as one of the world's pre-eminent dealers. Once, Memling's name was likely to appear only on the school register; now it was engraved into the walls and architraves of the great museums of Europe, in rooms and extensions that Memling had paid for. In the Holocaust Museum in Bremen above the entrance hall there was an inscription, each letter a foot high, that read *"Opera Memlingi Winklemani in perpetuum admiranda sunt."* The deeds of Memling Winkleman should be admired for ever.

Memling had to crawl through the tangled bushes to reach the entrance to the cellar. These days even sinking down to his knees was a terrible effort. I might never get back up, he thought grimly as he shuffled slowly through the dense thorny undergrowth. Ten feet on he saw the familiar mound covered with brambles and ivy. Luckily he had remembered his heavy rubber gloves and a small crowbar. Clearing the top of the trap door he prised the door open inch by inch until he could raise it and prop it up with the wrench. Then he turned around, still on all fours, and reversed towards the hole. Until even a few years ago Memling could walk up to the trap door, lift it up with two hands and walk down the steps facing forward. Now he didn't trust either his legs or his balance. It occurred to him that he could save a lot of bother by self-immolating in the cellar and thus doing away with both the evidence and the perpetrator simultaneously. But Memling had always dreamed of a grand funeral. He had pre-booked the Liberal Jewish synagogue but was thinking of the Barry Rooms at the National Gallery or perhaps the Guildhall. He suspected that the Prime Minister would want to say a few words. No doubt the Chief Rabbi would officiate.

Memling took each step carefully—he knew there were thirty before reaching the bottom. Once he had navigated these he felt in the dark, on the brick ledges, for the torches that he left waiting. Once he thought of running a cable from the house to the cellar, but that was too detectable. Taking the flashlight, he turned it on and shone the powerful beam down a narrow corridor. He and his colleagues had chosen well and there was no hint of dampness even after recent heavy rains. After twenty paces, he arrived in the first room. Measuring twenty by twenty foot, it was stacked from floor to ceiling with paintings, each in its own crate marked with the artist; he looked at one row: Donatello, David, Degas, Daumier, Delacroix, Denis, Domenichino, van Dyck and Dürer. To think he had not even opened many of these. It was estimated that more than forty thousand works of art were still missing from Nazi looting—Memling suspected that eighty-four or maybe eighty-five remained here in the cellar; he had, over the years, sold another sixty-five. He walked through to the next room—it was even bigger—Moretti, Matisse, Martini, Matsys, Michelangelo, Nattier, Oudry and Parmigianino. Beyond that was an exquisite treasure, the Amber Room—fifty-five square yards of amber panelling backed with gold and weighing over six tons. Known as the Eighth Wonder of the World, it was made for a Prussian king at the turn of the eighteenth century. Memling had been one of the officers in charge of its freighting and shipping from St. Petersburg. He and his colleagues had worked in silence inspired by sheer wonder. It was a German masterpiece and belonged back in the fatherland. Given to Peter the Great when the two countries had been allies, it should now be taken back to its rightful home.

Memling stroked the delicate panels with the tips of his fingers. When he shone his torch on to the amber it glowed like a furnace, light dancing along the panels and bouncing off the delicate gold carving. Rescuing the Amber Room from Königsberg Castle had been the single greatest act of his life. Hearing that the store was likely to be attacked, he led a group of men to take the crates out. They had worked solidly through the night with only a few mules and a rickety cart before requisitioning a train to get the pieces across Germany to Bavaria. When news broke that Königsberg Castle had been bombed and only a few fragments of brick remained, Memling and his team decided not to speak of their successful mission—the fewer who knew, the better. Now my own daughter wants me to destroy the things that I risked my life to save, Memling thought, as he shone his torch around the store. If his life counted for anything, if he had served any purpose, it was to help preserve these great treasures for future generations.

Memling thought about the kindness of Esther Winkleman, who had taken pity on the unloved child even though he was the son of a man who hated her race and her family. She had fed him scraps off her table, had helped him learn and had inadvertently given him a skill that helped him to survive and prosper. Of course this woman could never have known that she would save another man's child rather than her own. Shining his torch on a Leonardo portrait of a young woman, yet another mistress of his patron the Duke of Milan, he thought about the Watteau, the pictorial embodiment of the few.

His tastes had evolved over the years. He liked to rearrange the works in the mine like a personal mini-museum, pulling particular paintings to the forefront of the stacks, according to his mood or situation. It seemed to Memling that great artists had the power of divination and could predict and translate even the most minor human travail. In the vast panoply of life, there were paintings to suit every predicament. No emotion, however base or delicate, had been considered too petty or panoramic. Artists' brilliance went further than compassion or empathy; masterpieces could inspire as well as reflect different emotions. As a young man, Memling had been unable to stand anything sentimental and had prized guts and gore above beauty. He had loved Caravaggio's *Judith Beheading Holofernes*, recently sold to Mrs. Appledore, as it suggested that violence, if pragmatic, was acceptable. He thought of a Claude landscape whose bucolic scene quieted a troubled mind or the Bronzino statesman whose magisterial looks inspired leadership and fortitude.

After Marty had died, Memling shut himself in the cellar for five days and five nights. He had taken water but no food and intended to die there, but his desperate spirit was rescued by a Duccio Madonna, whose sweetness of expression amid her own suffering had cajoled him back to life. When he had been in love with Marianna, Memling had pulled Renoirs and Del Sartos to the fore; sweetness emanated from those women that suited his mood. But no work ever matched up to his little Watteau—that extraordinary work embodied the agony and ecstasy of love.

By asking him to destroy the constants, the sources of joy and comfort in his life, these tender renderings of the universal human conditions, his daughter was depriving future generations of solace that he had not just enjoyed but depended on.

Looking around the cellar, Memling could not summon up the courage or barbarity to realise Rebecca's wishes. Taking his torch, he said a last goodbye to his private collection. Heaving himself up the narrow steps and out into the sunshine, he turned and closed the trap door and pulled earth, twigs and other matter over the surface, then, sinking painfully to all fours, he crawled back through the hedge and down the slope to the track.

Reaching the farmhouse, Memling took a match and set fire to a heap of rags and kindling that he piled in the centre of the room. He stood for a while watching the tiny flames lick and flicker through the debris. Going to the next room, he sloshed more petrol on to the old kitchen table and chairs and across the threadbare pre-war curtains. There was, he knew, no point at all in burning an abandoned farmhouse but at least he could pretend to Rebecca that part of her instructions had been completed. No doubt the local police would come to investigate and assume that a group of vandals had taken advantage of an empty site. Looking into the records, they would see that the house and hectares surrounding it belonged to a company registered in Buenos Aires. The police would spend many frustrating hours trying to track down the rightful owner. Memling had set up a series of shell companies, a trail that led from Buenos Aires to the Cayman Islands to Guernsey to Bermuda and back to South America. At some point, long after Memling's death, the local authorities would give up, requisition the land and sell it off. He hoped that the new owners would be delighted to discover a stash of great masterworks beneath their property. Memling's only regret was not to be present to hear the speculation regarding how the works came to be lodged in a long-disused underground mine and who, if anyone, knew about their whereabouts. As he always wore gloves to inspect his work, even the cleverest forensic scientist would be unable to match DNA samples.

Memling drove away from the house, occasionally glancing in his rear-view mirror at the plume of black smoke curling in the distance behind him. On the main road he checked to see if any other cars were coming, and once sure that no one saw his Fiat Panda pull out from the track, he turned into the road and headed back to the airport. In less than four hours he would be home. On his return, he expected to hear that the joint problems of the missing picture and that pest Trichcombe Abufel had been properly dealt with. Then he would have a large Scotch and an early night.

Though Trichcombe had not seen his nephew for nearly twenty years, he would occasionally post copies of his manuscripts to Maurice at his terraced house in Mold. It made the art historian feel better that there was a hard copy of his work safely stored in a small attic in his native Wales. He doubted that Maurice bothered to open the envelopes, but at least his nephew was kind enough to acknowledge safe receipt with a postcard. Some of Trichcombe's students laughed at these

Luddite impulses, urging him to use the Cloud or a hard drive. Trichcombe would smile and ignore their suggestions.

Today he mailed a copy of the document to Maurice by registered mail. He even telephoned Maurice to ask him to watch out for the postman. Maurice's wife Della (or was it Delia? Trichcombe could never remember) had sounded irritated. "Will I have to go out of my way to sign for it?" she asked. Trichcombe could hear her breathless tones; she had been fat on her wedding day and was probably obese by now. He imagined her struggling up the lane, pausing to catch her breath at the crossroads before heading up to the local post office, thighs chafing, droplets of sweat collecting between moist rolls of fat, bunions aching slightly.

"I would not normally ask such a humungous favour, dear Della," he said unctuously.

"Delia," she corrected.

"Delia. This is the most important document I have ever written. If something happens to me, make sure it gets to the police, my dear."

Delia nearly laughed; what would the local police force make of an ageing art historian's thoughts on a long-dead artist? She would certainly not be trying their patience with any of Trichcombe's words. Her husband's uncle was an anomaly in their family—an academic—those four short dry syllables made Delia reach for a cigarette—what kind of life was that? Buried deep in books and in the past. Life was for living—you only got one shot, as Maurice often said.

"Dahlia, dear—are you still there?" Trichcombe asked querulously.

"It's Delia. Don't worry—I'll get your package," she replied, drawing deeply on her cigarette.

Trichcombe waited until the post office van arrived and watched his copy disappear into a large grey sack. He stayed till the van had disappeared around the corner before heading back to his flat. He had waited forty-two years to wreak revenge on Memling Winkleman—forty-two long years. And now, finally, after all that painstaking and meticulous research, he had him. The fish was truly hooked. Later that day Trichcombe was meeting the editor of *Apollo*—the magazine might not have the biggest circulation, but it would get to everyone who was anyone in the art world and after that it would seep out into the wider press. Again Trichcombe decided not to send his precious research over the Internet. Better to hand it over in person.

I will probably be on the news, Trichcombe thought. Almost certainly. They were bound to give him some hackneyed sobriquet like "Nazi Hunter" rather than "Art Historian." He wondered if Delia would see it—whether she would adopt that condescending "do hurry up, old man" tone when he next called. Maybe there would be a film or even a book by him that sold more than a few hundred copies. His last work, *Les Trois Crayons d' Antoine Watteau*, had performed disappointingly, shifting only 124. Trichcombe wondered what to call this book—*The Improbability of Love*, maybe, after the painting itself. Or A *Question of Attribution? Provenance*, or what about *Nice and Nazi*—Trichcombe was so lost in thought that he didn't notice the two men waiting near the entrance to his building. Putting the key into the lock and turning it to the right, he pushed on the door and felt, to his surprise, a sharp prick in his neck. Turning, he saw a man, short, burly and dark with a hat pulled over most of his face, holding a large syringe. Trichcombe tried to cry out but from somewhere else another hand appeared with a thick cloth. Trichcombe felt strangely fuzzy, his legs gave way and the stairs came up to meet him. His last thought was of a Piero Della Francesca altarpiece, *The Flagellation of Christ*, seen in Urbino when he was twenty-one.

Chapter 32

Earl Beachendon sat alone in his small basement kitchen in Balham looking at a large damp patch on the wall; he was sure that it had got noticeably larger since the night before. Earlier in the year, it had looked small and unthreatening, the shape and size of a fifty-pence piece, but over the last few months it had grown to resemble a headless piglet leaping over a half-eaten loaf of bread. Soon, he thought gloomily, it would probably look like a carthorse stepping over a lifeboat. The Earl couldn't afford to pay a man to investigate the rising damp, let alone a builder to fix it. I wonder who will last longer, the damp patch or me, he thought.

A few months ago, the Earl still took *The Times* but that had gone along with organic eggs, Berry Brothers claret and dry-cleaning, in an endless and apparently futile attempt to prune the household budget. The Ladies Halfpennies could dispense with a whole week's allowance on new tights alone—

what was the point of buying more when they laddered immediately? As for his son, Lord Draycott—the Earl despaired of
the pimply youth ever making good. His heir should have
been born in the late eighteenth century when the Beachen-
dons had money to burn, estates to lose.

The Earl opened the fridge in search of a snack before
dinner—there were at least four hours to go before his next
meal. Staring out from the cold white abyss were four pots of
face cream, some cottage cheese and three low-fat yoghurts.
Thank goodness for business dinners, Beachendon thought
gloomily. Yesterday he had been caught purloining some
bread rolls—he didn't care if colleagues thought him greedy
as long as they didn't suspect that the fifteen little loaves stuffed
into his briefcase were intended to fill six hungry mouths
back home. "The man who could not feed his family"—
Beachendon was unable to imagine a more shaming epithet
on his tombstone. Every single one of his attempts to lure a
great collector or collection to the auction house had failed.
Without a performance-related bonus, his miserable salary
hardly covered the basic bills, let alone the nylons.

Beachendon chose a rather stale bun left over from yesterday's buffet. There was no butter but he did find some ancient
plum conserve at the back of the cupboard; it had a large coat-
ing of mould on top, enough to put off the female inhabitants
of the household. Opening the free evening paper, he turned
immediately to the obituary pages in case there were any rich
pickings to be had from the deceased: the odd estate, maybe
a Gainsborough heirloom or, if he was really lucky, a crack-
ing art collection built lovingly during a man's lifetime and
readily offloaded by the heirs. It was such a bore that people
were living longer—damn modern medicine, Beachendon
thought. Once upon a time a duke would drop off his perch
every sixty years; now the average nob was living till his late
eighties. Beachendon kept a notebook of those likely to die
soon. Once the death was reported, he would write a long,

flowery and utterly insincere letter to the relatives, inveigle himself into the funeral proceedings and hope to pick up the dispersal of assets as soon as the body was decently cold. Unfortunately these days, an awful lot of art-world vultures were circling graves. Only last week he had attended the funeral of the widow of a relatively minor abstract expressionist artist. To his astonishment he saw the heads of the major national British and American museums, three of his counterparts at auction houses, no fewer than seven dealers and, sitting by the family in the front pew, a certain solicitor from Narrahs, Shattlecock & Beavoir. Mental note to self, Beachendon thought, take the solicitor out to lunch, tea and dinner.

The only noteworthy death today was that lizardy old art historian, Trichcombe Abufel. Beachendon's eyes flicked to the end of the obituary to establish the cause of death. A heart attack. How dull. "Trichcombe Llewellyn Abufel of Mold in Wales was a distinguished art historian of the eighteenth century who wrote about the Rococo with as much panache as he wore a silk cravat," Beachendon read. That is a really silly line—what was the writer trying to do? Entirely discredit the man? "Mr. Abufel wrote several interesting books on large subjects such as *Watteau*; *Courtly Love in the Time of Louis XIV*; *The Interplay of Etchings, Drawings and Paintings* and *Les Trois Crayons d' Antoine Watteau*." What about his masterwork, his monograph of Antoine Watteau, still the standard text on the artist—didn't that get a look-in, a small mention? "Trichcombe Abufel remained resolutely independent during his long career, never taking a significant post at a major museum or a chair at any university but preferring to work alone." Utter rot, Beachendon thought; he worked closely with Memling Winkleman for ten years, bringing immense intellectual kudos to that establishment. How odd that this wasn't mentioned at all. "Abufel's contribution to academic discussion was always careful, considered and he would develop his arguments with a passionate eloquence." Beachendon wondered what his own obituary might say: "Auctioneer who brought both his family and his company to bankruptcy."

Done with the serious section, Beachendon went to the Daily Tits and Tittle-Tattle. Though he had never heard of most of the people, he couldn't resist examining some revealing bikini shots of a little-known starlet called Kelly who had "snapped" back to her pre-pregnancy body. Princess someone or other was literally fellating an ice cream. A minor royal was caught snogging her best friend's boyfriend outside a nightclub in Havana. A footballer was papped drunk the night before a major league game. Oh, to have such an interesting life, Beachendon thought.

He was about to go upstairs for his evening shower when his eye was caught by a small headline, "The Painting, the Piss Artist and the Publican." Beachendon looked at the picture of a public house in Spitalfields, The Queen's Head, and at the rotund publican holding a small painting. In a side bar there was a smudgy photograph of a dishevelled middle-aged woman being loaded into the back of a police van. Beachendon looked more closely at the painting. It was hard to tell, as the image was pixelated—it was probably some cheap copy, the kind of thing you bought in the back of a colour supplement. He read the article. A lady turns up at a bar with no money and persuades the barman to take a painting as collateral before her friend turns up to meet her. The barman, Percy Trenaman, knows a little bit about art and thinks "this is a fine work of the Baroque period" and accepts the woman's proposal. Cut to five hours later, there is no sign of a friend but there is by now a huge unpaid bar bill. Percy Trenaman's boss Phil gets back, sacks his barman on the spot and calls the police. Now the painting and the so-called Piss Artist are being kept courtesy of HM in a police cell in Paddington. "I don't care if it's a Leo-fucking-nar-do," Phil tells the reporter, "people are expected to pay for their drinks in my establishment." If only life were that simple, Earl Beachendon thought. I could take any number of old canvases to John Lewis or Waitrose or Berry Brothers. Not a bad idea, really. Putting the paper back on the table, he lifted himself painfully out of his chair and climbed the stairs to his bathroom.

Four nights after the dinner, Annie's life slipped back into a predictable form. The Winklemans had hardly been in the office and when they were there, had asked for their steamed fish to be left in the warming cupboard. Unable to face her mother's amateur dramatics, fearful that her trips to AA had stopped, Annie had slept in her galley kitchen for three nights in a row. Finally, realising she could not stay away for ever, she made her way home. At the end of her road, she decided to delay her confrontation with Evie for a little bit longer and stopped off at a pub, where she ordered a Campari and soda. It was a drink that reminded her of summer, of holidays and being young, of sitting in a piazza in Italy or on a beach in Spain, not the kind of drink you would normally take in a back room in Hammersmith on a soggy evening in April. As this week marked the start of her new life, Annie decided to have an unlikely cocktail at an unusual hour to celebrate. In a plastic bag beside her there was a new dress, the first she had bought for over six months, and a radio—part of her campaign to get her voice back.

Gazing into the pink depths of her drink, Annie thought of her former local, the Fox and Hounds in Devon, and the regulars: Ted the builder, Joe the shepherd, Ruby from the corner shop and Melanie the publican's wife. The conversation would have been comforting and circular, no need to find a beginning, middle or end when you were sure of seeing each other most nights that week—that year, probably. Tentatively she let her thoughts stray to Desmond and she visualised him in the Hounds drinking his usual, a pint of 6X with a packet of cheese and onion crisps. He would go around the room greeting the drinkers in the same way, "You all right, Joe? You all right,

Ruby?" until he had finished and then, taking his pint, he would sit in his seat near the bar; Desmond was a man to set your watch by. To her surprise Annie was able to think of him with a sense of detachment and there was something else, something new, an honesty, a realism about their relationship. She now saw that for most of her adult life she had been trapped on Planet Desmond, in a world governed by his rules, customs and sensibilities. For the younger, more fragile Annie, this had been comforting, necessary even. But as she grew older, she had begun to feel claustrophobic and stifled. By ending their relationship, she suddenly realised, Desmond had set her free to live a different kind of life, her life rather than his. Annie shook her head in wonder: Desmond had actually done her a good turn.

Taking out a notebook and pen, Annie finally started to tackle her telephone messages. There were now fifteen, two more from Delores about the painting. There were three from Jesse, each asking, in different ways, to see her again. The most surprising message was left by Agatha saying that Winkleman Fine Art was offering a ransom for a missing Watteau. Annie assumed Agatha must be mistaken.

The most exciting messages were from a journalist from the *Evening Standard* wanting to do a feature on Annie's dinners and another from Mrs. Appledore wondering if Annie could re-create the dinner at her Museum of Decorative Arts in New York the following month. Annie drained her Campari and soda in one. It was happening; Annie could hardly believe her luck.

Annie's telephone rang again—a blocked number. It was time to re-enter the real world. She answered it tentatively.

"Hello."

"Is that Miss Annie McDee?" a voice asked.

"Yes."

"This is Paddington Green police station. We have your mother here. Again." It was the same policeman who had arrested Evie on the previous occasion.

"Again?" Annie couldn't keep the weariness out of her voice.

"Could you come and collect her, please?" The police-man sounded equally weary. "You will need to bring your chequebook—the publican is keeping the painting as collat-eral for damage caused."

"What painting? What damages?" Annie asked, though she had a good idea about both.

"She swapped a picture for a few drinks, promising a friend would be along later. The friend never turned up. She got abusive, broke a mirror and a few glasses."

Annie sat back in her seat. She had enjoyed less than a week of success, and now this.

"Will you be along soon?" the policeman asked.

"No—I won't. Tell my mother she should not contact me. I have had enough of her lies and her drunkenness."

"What about the picture, the damages?" the policeman asked.

"That is between the publican and her. As far as I am con-cerned, I never want to see either again. Thank you." Annie hung up.

She expected to feel a sense of liberation—she had finally stopped enabling her mother—but there was no sense of tri-umph or relief. She just felt terribly sad. Evie had wasted her life and Annie had spent far too long worrying about her.

Picking up her bags, Annie took the empty glass to the bar. She knew that however much time and distance she put between her and Evie, she would never escape the memories, never be able to answer her telephone without a sense of dread and foreboding. Still, she had a job offer in New York. Perhaps one thing would lead to another and she would start a new life there. The thought was suddenly thrilling. She had noth-ing to keep her in London apart from a job that she did not enjoy and a flat she did not particularly like. Walking down the Uxbridge Road, Annie made a plan. She would hand in her notice and accept the job offer in New York.

The process of destroying the incriminating parts of the Winkleman archive was taking longer than Rebecca had hoped. She had bought two industrial-sized paper shredders, but with over twenty large leather-bound ledgers and sixty-nine trunks of records, and the necessity of working through the night discreetly after business hours, it meant that after four nights she had only destroyed the evidence for one year—1946. Because Memling had so consistently raided the Bavarian mine, without checking and cross-checking three different sources, Rebecca could not be sure which works had come from war stock and which had been obtained from bona fide sources. Most of the pictures were entirely legitimate, with clear records of where they had been bought, from whom, for what and with equally detailed records of their sales. A meticulous record-keeper, Memling had logged in every detail: the minor country salerooms, even the under-bidders, the auctioneer, bank accounts used, frames, and amounts spent on restoration and transport.

In a filing cabinet in the safe, she found records of all of Memling's journeys. Rebecca read that during 1946 her father had made several trips to Bavaria, three to Munich, one to Vienna and four to Buenos Aires. Was there anyone who had witnessed those trips or guessed why they had been made? She glanced at her twenty-first-birthday present, the small Raphael oil, and then to her father's gift to her on the birth of Grace, an exquisite Klimt painting now worth in excess of £12 million. Had he bought these or were they purloined as well?

Rebecca thought about the families who were desperately trying to retrieve works of art; hardly a day went by without some heartbreaking story in the newspapers. One family, the Silvermans, once wealthy and powerful burghers of Germany,

had lived out their days on benefits in Grimsby. Manny Silverman was still alive, ninety-eight, crippled by arthritis, hoping to
get just one of his family's missing paintings returned. Even the
humblest Modigliani, the least valuable of Manny Silverman's
paintings, would buy his grandchildren a tiny annuity against
the hardship of modern living. Manny had found a few possessions, two in German galleries, four in Russian museums, but
neither country was prepared to return his inheritance. The
war had ended, Rebecca realised, but the battles continued.
To her relief, she could find no claims for restitution against
pictures that her father had sold. Perhaps, Rebecca thought,
she could use the millions that they had made to help those in
need; she could launder her conscience.

It was in trying to establish the provenance of another
work, a Titian, that Rebecca had an idea. Logged in the gallery's records in 1962, it was described as *Man in Furs*. It had
no provenance and had the telltale initials KH next to it. However, in a later ledger, Rebecca found another Titian, with
identical measurements, a similar composition and with a
perfect provenance called *Man in Ermine*. Was this the same
painting under a different title? Had her father faked titles and
provenances?

Rebecca laughed—how could she have been so slow, so
naïve? Faking documents was anathema to a trained art historian such as herself, but if she was to enter the world of subterfuge and cover up one of the greatest frauds in the history
of art dealing, it was time to stop thinking like an academic
and start behaving like a criminal. Many dealers, owners and
even museums regularly amended history of ownership—she
could do the same with the Watteau and create an entirely
fictitious provenance that led people away from the gallery in
another direction. She could easily fabricate a provenance for
the painting which avoided the Second World War altogether
by falsifying documents and records to look as if the painting
had been holed up in a Scottish castle or an American robber

baron's house. Now that Trichcombe had been dealt with, his phone, computer and other records destroyed, who could ever link the painting to the young SS officer through the Berlin apartment block? Even if someone did trace Frau Goldberg, she no longer had the offending photograph in her possession. Then Rebecca had another idea. The company owned several Watteaus, all bought legitimately. All she needed was to substitute the records of one of roughly the same size and subject matter for the "Love" picture.

This time, Rebecca went to the drinks cabinet and opened a bottle of vintage Cristal; she had, finally, something to celebrate. Carrying her glass back into the strongroom, she pulled out the records relating to the family's other Watteaus. There were seventeen drawings and though none were suitable, she made a quick copy on her smartphone of their provenance. There was one large oil bought earlier that year at Sotheby's and she ruled that out, as its subject matter, a music party, was too well documented. Memling had acquired another picture in the 1970s, *Soldiers at Valenciennes*, a picture painted by a young Watteau, but this was the wrong size and subject matter. There was one more possibility, *The Rejection*, bought in 1951 and still in the company storeroom.

Rebecca looked back through *The Rejection*'s history. The Marquis de Jumblie had bought it in 1869 from a sale in Paris of the collection of the Duke of Pennant. Pennant had, in turn, bought it from Lord Cuddington, who had acquired it directly from the estate of Madame de Pompadour at Versailles. Rebecca closed the file and, holding up her glass, curtseyed to the memory of Louis's mistress. All that remained now was to destroy *The Rejection* and switch the two provenances. It seemed barbaric to burn a picture worth around £5–£8 million but a small price to preserve a family's reputation.

Rebecca's thoughts turned to Annie. Could she have known or was it really just a bizarre coincidence? Was there any way that Carlo had found out about Memling's past and sent his chef to find the incriminating evidence? Rebecca discounted this theory quickly. Her husband was heavily implicated in fraudulent activities. The other possibility was that Annie had worked this all out for herself. Reaching up to a lever arch file, Rebecca took down Annie's dossier and flicked through it. According to a hastily commissioned but apparently thorough report, Annie was just what she claimed: the adult daughter of an alcoholic, who had been unceremoniously ditched by her long-standing boyfriend and had come to London to try and create a new life. The private investigator had been through every one of her bank statements and phone records for the last five years and found no strange payments, no inexplicable numbers. It was a pathetic life, Rebecca thought. Enslaved to a man, cast out, losing your business and reduced to making your way as a chef, condemned to poaching fish day in and day out.

Looking at the CCTV pictures of Annie leaving the junk shop, a new thought crossed Rebecca's mind. She logged on to the company's own CCTV database and punched in a random day that Annie had worked. Rebecca looked at footage of Annie at her job, Annie chopping, cutting and filleting. Hitting the fast-forward button, Rebecca relived Annie's days. The woman had a work ethic, that was for sure—she only left her kitchen to go to the bathroom. Nor was she wasting hours on Google or dating sites. Rebecca fast-forwarded through the CCTV images even though she was not quite sure what she was looking for.

Then by accident, Rebecca saw Annie bringing something into work; the package was the same size as the missing picture, about eighteen by twenty-four inches and in a plastic bag. Annie put the bag on top of the kitchen counter at one end. Later the same day, Rebecca saw herself enter the kitchen and search Annie's drawers. To think the picture was right there, Rebecca thought. She spooled on through the next few days—the bag sat in the same place. The irony was not lost on Rebecca.

On the Thursday, Annie left work with the plastic bag. It proved to Rebecca that the woman had no idea of the importance of what she was carrying. Had Annie had the slightest inkling, she wouldn't have kept it so unceremoniously; if she was a professional sleuth, she would never have brought the painting into the lions' den. Rebecca heaved a sigh of relief—it was a horrible coincidence.

Rebecca realised that all she had to do was splice the CCTV footage in a different way and she could make it look as if Annie had stolen the picture from the Winkleman storeroom. Without Trichcombe's evidence and the old lady's photographs, without the records in the family archive, this work belonged legally to the Winkleman family and had been stolen from their vaults. It would be Annie's word against Memling's—a temporary cook versus the Holocaust survivor who had donated so many millions of pounds to European museums over the last decades.

What would a court deduce? That was easy. Annie would claim that she bought the painting on a whim from a junk shop. Could she explain where the junk shop was? It has since burned down, Your Honour. Really? Isn't that something of a coincidence? It does look that way, Your Honour. Where is your receipt for the painting? I never asked for one—the owner was in a hurry to get to the bookmaker's. Are you in the habit of buying presents but not asking for a receipt? Aren't you a chef in full-time employment and a former businesswoman—surely you know the importance of getting receipts for the taxman? Yes, Your Honour. The person who sold you the painting perished in the fire, didn't he? That's what the policewoman told me when I went back to the shop the next day. So you were at the crime scene the day before and on the day of the fire? It's not like that. So what is it like? It was a coincidence, Your Honour, a horrible coincidence. Is it also a horrible coincidence that there is CCTV footage of you putting a package that exactly matches the proportions of the missing painting, stuffed into a plastic bag, into your desk drawer? Your Honour, the same camera will reveal that I brought the package into the office that same morning—it had been at my house and I was taking it to the National Gallery to show to a restorer. Miss McDee, the CCTV camera does not show you coming into the building with the package. It must, Your Honour. No, it does not—all footage from the CCTV camera between 7 a.m. and 1 p.m. has been mysteriously wiped: the prosecution allege that you took the painting from the Winkleman vault during your lunch break and wiped the digital records before anyone returned. But, Your Honour, I have no idea where the CCTV camera banks are located. Access to the vault is limited only to Mr. Memling and Ms. Rebecca— no one else has the passcodes or keys.

In Rebecca's fantasy version, the judge turned to the police officer standing guard and commanded, "Take her down— fifteen years." The newspapers would have a field day—lots of censorious pieces about alcoholism. Lots of Thelma and Louise, mother-and-daughter grifters stereotyping. The more stories, the less likely the truth was to come out. Real facts would be hidden behind a smokescreen of tabloid reporting. Rebecca felt no guilt about sending an innocent woman to jail. It was survival of the fittest, ensuring Grace's future and the Winkleman bloodline. Rebecca understood the young Memling Winkleman better than he could have imagined. Another thought crossed Rebecca's mind. She should auction the picture and donate the proceeds to some Jewish cause—if it fetched enough, perhaps she could even create a museum in her mother's name—after all, she had been a Jew who had lost many relations in the Holocaust. It would not be an entirely cynical move: the Winkleman Centre for Survivors.

Looking at the clock on her desk Rebecca saw that it was

3 a.m. She must get a decent night's sleep to remain alert and clear-headed. Before turning in, she decided to walk around the block to get some air. Stepping out into the mews behind the gallery, Rebecca felt small stabs of excitement—things were going to be different, very different. For the first time in her life she did not feel frightened—instead she felt a sense of strength and purpose. Walking along Curzon Street, she looked up at a plane and realised that it was not going to fall from the sky and crush her. A taxi drove towards her and this time, the driver was not going to lose control and mow her down. She let her thoughts drift to Grace—a few days ago Rebecca had spent an entire night worrying about her daughter's affair with the Russian—now she thought of Grace's love life with a sense of detachment and even a scintilla of amusement.

As she walked, Rebecca felt a glow of purposeful determination. Until now her efforts had seemed unfocused—she had wanted to bring up her daughter and to write respected academic papers, and not get found out. From now on, her life would be devoted to ensuring that Winkleman Fine Art remained the world's pre-eminent dealers in Old Master paintings.

As Rebecca walked up New Bond Street, she caught a glimpse of herself in a plate-glass window: it was time to overhaul her appearance. Her suits and hairstyle were stuck in a previous decade and she needed to make a statement and get noticed as a woman of individuality, panache and style. Looking in one shop, she saw a sumptuous evening coat made from red velvet and gold brocade and decided to buy it. She would change her lipstick from pale pink to letter-box red and ask Grace to help her choose a new hairstyle.

At the corner of the street was the billboard for the evening paper flapping in a cool breeze. The headline caught Rebecca's attention. "The Painting, the Piss Artist and the Publican." She stopped and stared at it. There was a photograph of the missing picture. Her old fear returned for a moment—was she too late? Taking out her phone, Rebecca punched in the address of the pub and read the headlines quickly. Turning back, she hurried towards her office. Though the news potentially helped corroborate her story against Annie, there was work to be done on doctoring the footage as well as expunging certain aspects of the family's records. She would not sleep until all the evidence was gone and the picture had an entirely new and wholly plausible provenance.

Chapter 33

I have been rediscovered. One is frightfully pleased: after so many years in the wilderness, it is delicious to bathe in the hum of praise, the murmurs of approbation and the glow of appreciation. I have had a little clean and have been hastily fitted with a perfect period frame. The auctioneer, the Earl of Something or Other, is using every trick in his book, all the selling ploys, to hot up my auction, which is scheduled to take place in July, two months hence. I have teams of girls in tight-fitting suits escorting the world's collectors and museum directors to see *moi*. There are conservators examining every thread of my canvas. There are underwriters and bankers standing by, waiting to lend assistance to cash-soaked desperados longing for a piece of *moi*.

Le tout art world will be there and most are predicting a record price. Everyone knows about *mon histoire* . . . my illustrious line of owners, *Les Amants du Monde*. Suddenly, thanks to *moi*, history is fashionable. *Apparemment*, even the lowliest are parleying in shopping centres about creativity and the likes of Voltaire, Louis and Frederick are bandied about with the frequency of soap stars. It's *de rigueur* to drop the name Madame de Pompadour into casual conversation.

Septimus Ward-Thomas solved the riddle of the face when he realised that someone had painted over Charlotte's visage. You can only imagine the kerfuffle and foofaraw about whether to restore or not to restore. They even brought in psychiatrists and philosophers to debate the effect on Watteau's mind. I wanted to shout and scream: the painter has been dead for almost three hundred years.

Rebecca decided to publish the details of my lurid history. Memling, in her version, was cast as a poor Jewish boy who, unlike his entire family, narrowly escaped death in a concentration camp. Taking his mother's most prized possession, a Watteau, he had hidden out in a remote farmhouse during the war until his rescue by the Allies in 1946, where he was found clutching *moi* like some security blanket. Everyone agreed that it was far too good a story to make up. Except, of course, that somebody did.

They are fighting over the film rights.

A hairy man is making a documentary for the BBC.

The Earl has commissioned my biography—about time too—by some fancy writer, a potter who is good with words and melodrama. There will be many mistakes, of course, but gratifying nonetheless. Right now I am hanging in state in Houghton Street. I have more visitors than a dead monarch. There are queues. *Franchement*.

Next month I am to go on tour, like a campaigning general or a rock star, so they say. I will have my own aeroplane, handlers and guards. I will visit America (both coasts), the continents, Moscow, St. Petersburg, Tokyo and Beijing. No one bothers with Europe any more—it's finished. One never thought that Japan and China would get Western art. One is not always right. Once upon a time I thought Russians were barbarians. Come to think of it, I still do.

The catalogue for the sale will be as thick as a horse's rump—full of learned essays, details and photographs. There is to be a numbered collector's edition of one hundred in hardback.

The Tate, the National Gallery, the National Theatre and others, in a rare attempt at cultural harmony, are co-curating an *hommage* to *The Improbability of Love*—twenty contemporary artists, playwrights, singers and what have you of international repute are creating pieces inspired by *moi*. These works will be auctioned on the night of my great sale; the proceeds will also go to the Winkleman Centre for Survivors. Needless to say, Ms. Winkleman is taking a commission on all this. She gets 60 per cent to cover loss and damages (whatever that means).

There is one terrible blot on my landscape: my poor mistress, who is facing the rest of her life in prison on charges of theft, arson and the murder of the shopkeeper Ralph Bernoff. The "evidence," kindly provided by Ms. Winkleman, is apparently incontrovertible and includes film of Annie taken near the shop, film of the girl with the painting, witness statements, affidavits—you name it. Apparently she inveigled herself into the Winklemans' lives, got keys and passwords and stole the painting from their vaults. If I didn't know better I would be thoroughly convinced. The mother, never one to miss a drama, tried to stab herself in front of me as some kind of protest. Pretending to be a normal visitor, she took out a bread knife and started slashing at her body, screaming, "She's innocent. She's innocent." Of course the Earl loved it—more publicity, more notoriety. I heard him tell an assistant that the incident pushed my price up by another £800,000.

What is sad is that not one person has stepped forward to defend the girl. Some louse ex-lover sold a story to the newspaper about his years of terror with Annie—apparently she tried to steal his business; he had to fight to preserve it. The press found friends from Annie's primary schools who admitted there was something "funny" about the girl and her mother. The girl was always on her own—the mother never appeared at the school gates. The press worked out that Annie and Evie moved town every few months—that led to another orgy of comments on the problems of single motherhood. If there is a modern ill, a social issue, Miss McDee is suddenly a perfect example. The girl doesn't stand even half a chance. The young man, the mother and I are the only ones who remain convinced of her innocence, but can the inanimate and the unconnected triumph against vigorous and powerful opponents?

When you have been around for as long as I have, you get familiar with the tipped scales of justice. I think specifically of my master's short and tragic life; the perpetual presence of ill health, the spectre of death hanging over him and plucking him from the mortal world aged only thirty-six.

Since my master's pathetic and painful demise, I had not allowed myself a soupçon of sentimentality for any of my owners. Yet there is something about this young woman, Annie, her vulnerability, passion, the essence of her character both fragile and strong, that has insinuated itself into my weft and warp.

At least she became, even for a short time, part of a long line of extraordinary patrons and collectors, part of an illustrious cabal of great leaders, tastemakers and intellectuals. She held me in her hands. She looked into my depths. That counts for something.

Chapter 34

Jesse joined the long orderly queue of friends and family outside Holloway Prison. It was the third week he had been to visit Annie and this time he hoped she might see him. Until now she had refused any visits and was on twenty-four-hour suicide watch.

While the whole world was convinced of Annie's guilt, Jesse knew she was innocent—even the most practised liar could not have upheld that level of deception. Apart from Evie, no one else shared his conviction. He had visited the police, had solicited affidavits and statements from Agatha at the National Gallery, and even from the market traders whom Annie dealt with regularly. But the evidence against Annie was overwhelming.

Evie's grief and protestations added theatricality rather than substance. Jesse tried to explain that Annie needed to create a portrait of a troubled family life rather than overblown hysteria. Evie trying to commit suicide in front of the painting, throwing herself in front of a racehorse at Windsor or tying herself to a railing near Downing Street only added negative publicity. For a while the press gave Evie print and air time. She was the gift that kept on giving. When Evie showed reporters round Annie's destroyed apartment, most assumed she had wrecked it in a drunken stupor. Soon the press got bored with Evie's claims and few bothered even to tweet about the mother's antics.

After an hour of waiting there were only two families in front of Jesse—a woman and her three young children and an elderly, smartly dressed couple.

"Why do we have to come again?" a little girl whined.

The woman looked at Jesse sadly.

"Can I give them a sweet?" asked the older woman, opening up her bag and taking out a packet of mint humbugs.

The mother shrugged, as if she had stopped caring long ago.

"Where you from?" the boy asked, opening the sweet and dropping the wrapper on the floor.

"Jamaica," the elderly lady answered.

"My dad—my real dad—is Jamaican," the boy said proudly. "Do you see him?"

"Nah—he left her." The boy jerked his head towards his mother. "Can't blame him."

"Visitor, McDee," the warden opened the metal door and looked at Annie, who was lying on her side. "The same man, Jesse, who has come to see you every day for three weeks."

Annie did not move.

"Give the guy a break," the warden said more kindly. "You've got to get up sometime."

Annie rose. Her limbs had stiffened through lack of use. Her hair was greasy and she pushed it behind her ears. If Jesse sees me like this, she thought, it would scare him off once and for all.

She had not slept properly since arriving at HMP Holloway. It was not only the constant banging of doors, the shouting and her cellmates' incessant ramblings, it was also her recurring nightmare. It starts with Annie at home, fast asleep; someone starts banging on her door and shouting "Open up! Police! Open up!" Going to the door, she finds a man and a woman in blue uniforms.

"Miss Anne Tabitha McDee?" the man asks.

Annie nods. She is confused, sleepy.

"I am arresting you for the crimes of theft, arson and first-degree murder. Anything you do or say may be given in evidence."

In her dream, Annie laughs. There is some kind of mistake, she remonstrates, they have the wrong person. The police officers shake their heads.

"You are to come with us now."

The female officer watches Annie while she pees and dresses.

Annie is taken from a cramped cell to a windowless holding area in Holloway Prison. While she waits, visions from her life, good and bad, float in front of her like patterns in a kaleidoscope, but when she tries to remember an incident in any detail, it instantly evaporates. Occasionally Rebecca or Memling poke their faces into her dreams, laughing loudly and so closely that all she can see are the backs of their blackened throats.

A guard dumps her on to the back seat of a van whose tiny windows are heavily tinted and too high to see out of. It takes off at great speed, rolling and bucking through traffic. Annie holds on to the seat so as not to fall. She looks down at the floor and it is covered in sick—it is hers. In the yellow gloop she sees the remains of Delores's banquet. Tiny quails, lumps of pâté, eggs and twelve featherless chickens dressed in harlequin suits float around on the floor at her feet. She tries to fly out of the window into a piercingly blue summer sky but the trees' leaves are made from knives and force her back down.

Occasional noises deafen her: a baby screaming, the relentless boom-boom beat of a dub track from a nearby car, the honking of horns and screeching of brakes.

Eventually the van tips down a ramp. Annie is thrown against the end. She shakes as she walks down a long ramp and into another airless room. There are other men wearing orange bibs and twisted expressions.

"You are that woman—the murdering art-lover," they sing to a chorus from Gilbert and Sullivan.

"I am innocent, innocent," she sings back.

"Tell that to the judge and jury. Tell that to the judge and jury."

"Not guilty, not guilty."

The men chant. "A crime is a crime is a crime. You're no better than any of us."

"I don't belong here," Annie sings into darkness.

She is taken into the courtroom to be met by a wall of grimacing familiar people. Her primary-school teachers, mean girls from past playgrounds, Robert, the "one-night" German, the Winklemans and her mother.

Together they chant, "Guilty, guilty, guilty."

To her horror, the prosecution is led by Desmond, who holds a baby in the crook of his arm.

"How do you intend to plead?" the judge asks.

"Guilty, guilty, guilty," the chorus chant more loudly.

Annie looks up at the judge, hoping he will show mercy, and finds she is looking into the eyes of the doleful clown in her painting.

"Take her down," the judge cries out.

The ending is always the same.

It took Jesse a few seconds to register that the figure shuffling towards him was Annie. Her eyes were dull, limbs concave, hair dank, mood utterly listless. She had lost weight; worst of all, some life force had drained from her.

"Are you here to gloat?"

Jesse recoiled. "No, of course not."

"Mostly it's journalists who ask to see me."

"You know I am not a journalist."

Annie sat down at the Formica table facing Jesse. Around them were other families and couples, but Jesse could only see Annie. Pushing her lank hair behind her ears, she spoke in such a quiet, low voice that Jesse had to lean close to catch her words.

"I don't really understand any of this, Jesse. Even my solicitor can't be bothered to listen to my explanation. He just talks about plea-bargaining and mitigating circumstances, about deals and time for good behaviour. He tried to make me blame Evie, to say I was some kind of accomplice and she was using her drunkenness as a cover." As she spoke, Annie's fingers picked at tiny pieces of skin by bitten nails.

"I know you are not guilty," Jesse said firmly.

Annie looked up at him. "I'm not sure myself anymore. They play that CCTV footage on the news—I look weird and furtive."

"You are not guilty, Annie—you must keep reminding yourself of that."

"It would take a miracle to convince anyone else."

Jesse reached across the table to try and take her hand in his. Annie pulled it away.

"The only way to get through this is to close down—not to think about anything good or bad. Not to have memories or dreams. We are shut up for twenty-three hours a day. I am lucky to have three cellmates who are really troubled—being with them takes my mind off my situation."

Jesse nodded—he had to force himself not to come around the table and take her in his arms. He loved her now even more.

"You have to help me to help you, Annie," he said. "Please, let's go through everything to see if there is a tiny detail that might help your case. Start from the day you bought the pic-

ture: did you take the money out specially? Did you tell anyone else that you bought it? Show it to anyone? We need to
establish that you got it from that shop in the first place."

"I put it in the plastic bag in the front basket of my bike,
and went to the market—it stayed there until I got home."

"Did you tell the traders about it?"

"I was thinking about cooking dinner."

"When you got home? Did you see anyone on the stairs to
the flat?"

"No—I got stood up. The following morning Mum came
to stay. You were the next person to see it at the Wallace and
then Agatha at the National Gallery."

"Didn't you show it to Delores?"

"That is being used as evidence against me—apparently I
was trying to sell it behind the Winklemans' backs."

"What about that man Trichcombe Abufel?"

"He saw your sketch; he never saw the painting."

"You told me he left you a message."

"The day after Delores's dinner, he asked to see me
urgently; something about Berlin and an attribution."

"Did you call him back?"

Annie shook her head. "You heard that he died?"

Jesse nodded. "Larissa, a colleague and friend of mine, told
me that in his will he left all his research papers to the Courtauld, but when someone went to collect his files, nothing was
left. The hard drive on his computer was wiped."

For the first time, Annie looked up. "What are you
suggesting?"

"I asked to see his death certificate—the police had trouble
finding it."

"That doesn't prove very much," Annie said.

"When I eventually got a copy it was dated last week—he
died a month ago."

"How is this relevant?"

"I am not sure, Annie—the establishment has closed ranks.

The museums, the police, the press, the authorities have all toed some invisible line. Someone put out a story and everyone just bought it. There was no question of testing its validity—it's a done deal."

"So I am done for?" Annie's head sank back into her chest.

Jesse leant over the table and took her hands in his. She tried to pull them away but Jesse held on to them.

"As long as there is breath in my body, you have hope. I will not let them lock you away, Annie, I promise."

Many hours later, Annie lay in her bunk bed thinking about Jesse. She had underestimated him, seeing him as charming, attractive even, but somehow un-concluded, a person on his way to being fully formed. She had found his diffidence irritating and had assumed it hid an innate fecklessness. If only she had realised this was a mask and seen the real person months earlier, then she might have had a shot at love. Moments later, she dismissed these musings as mere fantasy: incarceration was warping her judgement and exhaustion was clouding her ability to judge situations. A few weeks earlier, she reminded herself, the plan had been to work in America. Now, with a criminal record, she would never get a visa even to visit America and by the time she got out of prison, Jesse would be with someone else; if she ever got out of prison.

Feeling waves of desperation well up inside her, Annie turned to her failsafe escape route and planned a banquet to celebrate her release. But today, she could not assemble the ingredients, let alone think of interesting combinations of food or people. She turned instead to a much-loved spring walk on Dartmoor. The hillsides were still scorched by sunless winter winds and only a few ferns were pressing tentative fingers out of the earth, waiting to unfurl their fronds. The banks of the lanes were covered in primroses, dandelions and early cow parsley. Scattered all over the moorland were tiny violets, like freckles of purple on brown earth. Walking through the hedgerows, she noticed alexanders, stitchwort and campion on the ground and the last vestiges of flowering blackthorn. Lying in her bunk, tracing her imaginary footsteps, Annie realised that for the first time she could remember Devon without the normal stab of pain; instead she felt glad simply to have known and loved a place so dearly.

She thought back to that random act of generosity: buying a present for a lover stricken by the loss of his wife. All her life she had tried to be good and fair. She had rescued her mother from a myriad of situations—some dangerous, some merely humiliating. She had loved a man who had tired of her. She had given up the idea of having children to please him, only to watch him father a baby with someone else. She had worked hard and conscientiously at every job and had never even stolen a paperclip. In spite of this she was caught in a trap with no prospect of escape.

Annie started to sob.

"Will you shut the fuck up," one of her cellmates grumbled.

"Sorry," Annie mumbled, pushing her face into her hard foam pillow. Even through a clean cover, she could smell other people's breath, phlegm and dirty hair, the effluents of prison living.

Only Jesse believed her, but how could one person wade against the tide of public opinion? A visit to Trichcombe's friend Larissa yielded nothing. The editor of *Apollo* had never had lunch with the art historian—it had been scheduled for the day after the heart attack. The Winklemans produced an exhibition catalogue and an invoice dating from 1929 proving that the painting was theirs. None of the market traders remembered seeing Annie the morning of the purchase, but the female police officer clearly remembered Annie at the scene of the fire asking after the man in the shop and the extent of the damage. It appeared that innocence counted for nothing.

Annie thought how much she had been looking forward to this summer, to longer days, walks by the river, picnics in the park. Most of all, though, she thought of that new life just started and now eviscerated. Even if she got out, she knew that her confidence was shattered. She had tried and failed to enter a new world. Looking up, she saw an aeroplane fly past the small barred window. Ordinary sights seemed suddenly so magisterial. What other everyday pleasures was she going to miss?

In two days' time, her little painting would be sold at auction. It was no comfort that though hundreds of pairs of eyes had looked at the canvas, she had been the only one to recognise its quality. She had read about her picture's provenance with a sense of wonder and in other circumstances perhaps she would have enjoyed the photographs of it surrounded by armed guards and lauded by the great and the good. For now, though, it was an evil talisman, bringing nothing but bad luck. She didn't care that its value was estimated to be tens, possibly hundreds of millions, or that by owning it she was automatically tied to some of the most notorious characters in history. Annie, wanting nothing to do with the picture or its stained history, had signed away any rights of ownership to the work. The further away from it, the better.

As a blanket of self-pity adjusted itself around her, Annie's spirits sank even further. Perhaps she should take her lawyer's advice, plead guilty and paint a self-portrait of a desperate, deluded woman. But then, from nowhere, Evie's voice called out. "I dare you to find a way out of this. I dare you." Annie sat up and looked around the cell for her mother. She was not there, but her words bounced off the walls. Evie was right. Annie must not give up so easily. She had to find a way through the quagmire of lies, think through every tiny possibility, every irregularity. She needed to start at the end. Why, she wondered, was Rebecca so determined to frame her for this crime? It can't be about money—the Winklemans had enough of that—they didn't need to risk being accused of embezzlement or subterfuge. Annie knew that this enmity was not directed at her personally—she was a nobody to Rebecca, simply a means to an end.

So what was it about the small canvas? Why couldn't Rebecca just claim it as rightfully hers or her father's? Why go to these ridiculous lengths? Why accuse a girl who you knew must be innocent? Rebecca was a clear and strategic thinker—there would be good reasons to set up this chain of events. The answer had to lie with the picture.

Annie sat up on her bed and started to recall all that she had learned over the past months. She now knew that every painting had a unique fingerprint, starting with the artist and his or her intentions, skills, life choices and luck. The difference between a good and a great work of art was down to an almost indistinguishable series of largely unidentifiable factors: the élan of a brushstroke; the juxtaposition of colours; the collisions in a composition and an accidental stroke or two. Like a rolling stone gathering moss, a painting gathered history, comment and appreciation, all adding to its value. In its relatively short life, Annie's little painting, all eighteen by twenty-four inches, had accrued so much admiration and history that it had become surrounded by a halo of accumulated desire, bumping its value up to dizzy heights. Somewhere in this story there were clues as to why Annie was being held. Only by unpicking this riddle could she regain her freedom.

Something had terrified Rebecca—something had caused her to invent a sequence of events that was final and brutal. Rebecca needed closure at all odds; she was set on avoiding any loopholes or ambiguities, even if it meant a perfectly innocent person being sacrificed. The innocent act of buying the picture had pitched Annie into the middle of the terrible secret that Rebecca and her father had to keep concealed.

Jesse was right: Annie had to replay every tiny conversation, examine every lead, think back to every situation to try and unearth clues. She thought back again to Trichcombe's message—he had said something about provenance and Berlin. What did this have to do with anything?

Annie felt a bubble of frustration building up within her. How could she prove her innocence stuck away in prison? She had no access to books or the Internet, no opportunity to retrace her footsteps. Was this part of Rebecca's master plan? Annie felt a shiver of fear. Rebecca must not find out that she had an accomplice on the outside. Annie had to get a message to Jesse quickly to warn him.

Jesse did not consider himself to be particularly brave or principled. He had lived life exclusively on his terms, eschewing responsibility and convention in the pursuit of his passion for painting. In some respects, he had little to show for his thirty-two years—no significant relationships, no children and no major exhibitions of his work. Jesse knew that his lack of drive and materialism frustrated his family and most of his friends; his idea of success did not tally with theirs. He did not want to be tied to a mortgage or an employment contract; he had no interest in possessions and could never understand his brothers' relentless quest to upgrade their belongings—better television, better girlfriend, better car. Jesse's job at the Wallace, combined with the odd sale of a painting, covered his basic living expenses. His possessions fitted into a couple of bags and included two suits, ten T-shirts, four pairs of trousers, a kettle, two pans, a radio, paintbrushes, paints and an easel. He neither needed nor desired anything else. This pared-down living suited him perfectly: until he met Annie McDee.

His thoughts turned to his father's supposed suicide and he wondered if he was conflating Annie's situation with the unresolved pain from his dad's death. Perhaps the past contributed to his sense of injustice, his disgust with the way aspects of the art world operated. He knew that his feelings for Annie were real. He wanted to protect her and love her. For the first time in his life he saw the point of money. Wealth did not, he realised, guarantee happiness, but it did offer a measure of security and opportunity. Before Annie was arrested, Jesse dreamed of setting her up in a professional kitchen; since her arrest, he longed to engage a leading barrister to fight her case. The only thing Jesse could offer Annie now was every waking second and an absolute conviction that she was innocent.

Convinced that Trichcombe Abufel had stumbled on information relating to the painting, and unable to think of any other lead, Jesse found the deceased art dealer's address in the telephone book, and persuaded the building's caretaker that he was an associate of Trichcombe and needed to collect a book. Arriving at 8 a.m., Jesse had woken the snub-nosed red-faced man in striped pyjamas. The caretaker was surprisingly friendly and loquacious for someone wrestled out of sleep by an insistent doorbell—he had not yet had the opportunity to talk about the art historian's death. Yes, it was sad that the old man had died after a sorry life devoid of friends, family and parties—all the old boy had done was work work work. His relations from somewhere in Wales never visited and only last night, his nephew, in a phone call to the caretaker told him to ship everything off to a sale with no reserves. They didn't want any mementos. Not even his clothes or one of those fancy cravats.

Jesse listened patiently, hoping that the caretaker would leave him alone to rummage. The apartment was on the top floor; the caretaker was sixty-plus with rattly breathing. Jesse crossed his fingers in his pocket. Half an hour later, Jesse let himself into the dead man's flat. It looked as if someone had just stepped outside: a half-finished cup of tea sat on the table; an open book sat by a chair; the bed was unmade and a pair of slippers waited expectantly for their owner. Jesse picked up the book—it was a monograph written by Trichcombe on Watteau, open on a section concerning provenances. Jesse held it up, hoping to find a scrap of paper or some explanatory notes. He went to the bedside reading table, where there was a book of Montaigne's essays and a biography of Catherine the Great. Again Jesse flicked through both in case Trichcombe had left any signs that might point him to the truth.

Walking over to the far wall, Jesse saw eight shelves crammed with books, endless monographs of artists, mostly from the Rococo and Baroque periods. It was as comprehensive as the Wallace Library and certainly better digested. Jesse wondered if he should tell one of his colleagues that these would be sold for next to nothing the following day at Lots Road Auction House. He thought about Annie's frantic message that morning— no one must connect Jesse and Annie, let alone Jesse and the painting. Her concern for him had made him happy.

Jesse pulled out all the books on Watteau, hoping again for clues about Annie's painting. But Trichcombe was a careful academic and hence would not mark his books. Occasionally there was a white piece of paper with a number and letter written in neat pencil, but if these were references, where were the corresponding file notes? Jesse went to a large cabinet in the corner—on the front were three labels—the top said "Personal," the next said "Books Completed" and the last said "Books Pending." Each of the three sliding drawers was empty. It made no sense to Jesse that a man would clear out all his notes, professional and personal, erase his computer's drive and then succumb to a fatal heart attack lying on his bed fully dressed.

Jesse went to the window and looked out over the communal garden. Below some ladies were having an exercise class with a muscled trainer in a string vest. In the far corner, two nannies chatted while their charges played in the sandpit. To the right of the sink there was a small noticeboard. On it Trichcombe had written some notes—the first said "Manuscript to Mold"; the Second said "Lunch *Apollo*; Fairy Liquid; thank you note to Larissa." Jesse took a photo of the noticeboard with his phone. Picking up the open book on Watteau, he let himself out of the flat and walked down the stairs.

The caretaker was waiting for him at the bottom.

"Here it is!" Jesse held up the book.

"That's good," the caretaker said, looking at Jesse. "A lady came here and asked me to call her if anyone came round. She was most insistent."

Jesse didn't miss a beat. "Tall, slim with short blonde hair, in her late forties?" he asked, providing a description of Rebecca Winkleman.

"That's her."

"That's my boss—she'll be so happy that I have the book."

"So I don't need to call her?" the caretaker asked.

"Oh no—I am going to the office now." Jesse tried to sound light and unconcerned. Waving at the caretaker, he slipped out of the building and, turning the corner, ran as fast as he could down the street.

Rebecca and Memling walked around the Italianate fountain in Kensington Gardens.

"Are you happy with the way things have turned out?" Memling asked, his voice tense and weary.

"I had not predicted the extent of the media circus," Rebecca admitted. She did not need to tell her father that the press interest, which showed no sign of abating, was making her nervous. She had envisaged a small conference attended by some friendly arts journalists who would listen respectfully to Memling's story. The following day Rebecca thought there might be a paragraph or two in the broadsheets, at worst a small segment on the graveyard slot of the *Today* programme.

Instead the family had been shadowed from sunup to sundown by a seemingly insatiable group of photographers and reporters. For three weeks, the story had been headline news—

the words "art" and "painting" were even splashed liberally throughout the red-top press.

"I am just concerned that this whole plan has spiralled out of control," said Memling.

"You were the person who burned the shop and its unfortunate keeper. You and your heavies should be thanking me, not berating me."

Memling looked around him to check that there was no one within earshot. "These things are better handled discreetly, not in a blaze of publicity."

"I might remind you, Father, that these things are entirely of your making—I am just trying to protect our heritage."

Father and daughter walked on in silence. Rebecca noticed that her father was lamer than usual; she often forgot he was ninety-one years old.

"There is just the documentary, the sale and then it'll all blow over."

"No documentaries." Memling had a horror of photography and film, and had refused all requests for portraiture.

"I need you to do this one."

"Why?"

"The imprimatur of television will seal our innocence," said Rebecca.

"You are like Icarus flying too close to the sun, Rebecca," Memling said, his voice rising. A passer-by looked at him curiously. "We need to keep our heads down, be discreet. You will see that sympathy soon turns to antipathy. Much better to pretend to have nothing, be nothing."

"Father—you got us into this, you are going to get us out."

Instead of being angry, Memling marvelled at Rebecca's transformation and her steely determination; in her hands, the Winkleman empire would continue and this was what he wanted most: posterity. Walking on, Memling was aware how his joints were stiffening up; this morning he had cancelled his tennis lesson and for the first time in his life, Memling felt desperately tired. Perhaps, he thought, this was nature's way of preparing the body for death, an event he looked forward to. He imagined it was like slipping into a deep anaesthetic-induced haze of eternal blankness. He had had enough earthly delights, more than most could dream of.

"Do you feel any remorse for the girl? She is looking at a lifetime behind bars." Memling didn't care about Annie's fate but wondered at his daughter's sudden brutality.

"She is a miserable specimen. Broke, single, in her thirties—her life is a kind of prison already. Anyway, once she is convicted, I'll be able to breathe," Rebecca said.

"No, Daughter—you are about to find out that you will never sleep easy again. There will always be a drip of fear that you are about to be discovered and that the whole pack of cards will come tumbling down."

"You don't seem troubled by guilt," Rebecca said to her father.

"I have had more than sixty years to learn how to manage it. You have a long way to go."

It was a warm day but Rebecca shivered and pulled her cashmere coat around her. "Have you written the letter?"

"You know I have—you, your husband and daughter are fully exonerated—none of you knew anything about my past or the pictures."

"Where is it?"

"It is in a bank vault in Switzerland—I put it there myself two days ago. The details are in my will—there are twenty-nine different vaults in four different banks. The codename for this one is Mousetrap. The password is Love, followed by Marty's birthdate backwards." Memling turned to his daughter. "I implore you one last time. We should not say any more about the case publicly. We should let the embers die down, maintain a dignified silence. It's not up to us to talk about compassion or forgiveness—we are not God or the courts—we are two duplicitous, dishonest dealers, nothing more, nothing less."

"Do the interview—it's non-negotiable. The car will pick you up at 4 p.m. and take you to the television studios." Rebecca turned and walked away.

Once again the Earl's house was full of organic treats and Berry Brothers made regular deliveries. He even threw a little dinner the night before the sale. He didn't ask his important clients to Balham (the borough probably didn't feature on their chauffeurs' sat-nav)—soirées took place in the gallery, where the Watteau hung in its specially constructed bullet-proof glass case. It was astonishing who would accept his invitation once the painting was mentioned: the Prince of Wales, the ambassadors of every important country, a few oligarchs, a few more billionaires, not to mention the deputy Prime Minister and his wife.

The Earl thought back to that cold April evening three weeks ago. He had eaten a stale bun covered in slightly mouldy jam, put on a dinner jacket and set off for his dinner in Little Venice. The Northern Line was, for once, working, as too was the dear old Victoria, but the Bakerloo ground to a halt at Edgware Road, spewing Beachendon out at one of the nastiest intersections in north-west London. He only entered Paddington Green police station to ask for directions and, to his astonishment, saw the picture propped on a ledge behind the duty officer. Were it not for the small square of cleaned canvas in the top left-hand corner, Beachendon would never have looked twice at the work. He was not the type to believe in coincidence or fate, but the whole way through an exceedingly dull dinner he could think of nothing else. Beachendon remembered the newspaper article and the telephone call only that morning from Rebecca Winkleman concerning a missing painting matching the description. On his way home, he stopped by the police station again and, using the last few hundred pounds in his current account, the Earl stood bail for Evie and persuaded her to let him take the painting home.

Arriving home Beachendon took his first long look at it. The painting was dirty but unmistakably fine. Slightly worse for wear after a few bottles of wine, the Earl insisted that the Countess get up and look at it. The Countess agreed that it was marvellous and suggested they talk about it in the morning. By 10:15 a.m. the next day, the Earl had left with the painting. By the time he arrived home at night, the painting had been declared by Monachorum's an original lost work by Jean-Antoine Watteau. The auction house was granted temporary custody until the rightful owner stepped forward. The press already had the spark of a story; it didn't take much to fan their interest. The Earl rather enjoyed the limelight and allowed *Tatler* to take a family photograph with Viscount Draycott and his daughters on the steps of their erstwhile ancestral home.

The Earl never could understand why it took the Winklemans a whole week to come forward and claim their painting. He could only assume that Rebecca wanted to wait till the publicity had died down. By the end of the week there was hardly a person in England who hadn't heard of the painter Antoine Watteau and who did not have an opinion about the case.

The Winklemans took the difficult decision to sell the picture at auction to raise money for good causes and asked the Earl to represent their interests. Just when the publicity began to abate, their cook Annie McDee was arrested and charged with theft and murder. It helped the Earl that the thief was a beautiful woman and her accomplice, her mother, was a raddled old alcoholic. The press painted the pair as a modern-day Thelma and Louise. Hollywood grandes dames and ingénues lined up to play the parts. Beachendon didn't remember that the same girl had cooked for him, twice.

Beachendon was given a promotion and a pay rise. Part of his condition for staying on was the immediate dismissal of the company lawyer, Roger Linterman, who had tried so hard to bring about his downfall.

Each time there was a lull in interest, some new, unexpected piece of information emerged. Every journalist turned art historian. The British Museum's prints and drawings room was overwhelmed by an influx of new visitors and had to restrict numbers for the first time in its history. The Wallace Collection's visitors shot up. Gradually the painting's fascinating history began to emerge. As the *Mail* declared, even Hollywood could not have dreamed up its scenario. First they found the consumptive, destitute and desolate Antoine, who had fallen for the strumpet, Charlotte, who used her admirer like a devoted lap dog, occasionally throwing him scraps of affection but generally ignoring his entreaties, his damp looks, his tragically collapsing shoulders. Three hundred years after her death, Charlotte finally received the public attention she had so longed for in her lifetime.

The descendants of Dr. Mead, the British physician who failed to cure Watteau of his TB, were traced to Guernsey, from where they issued a public apology.

Some bright hack traced the painting to Voltaire and his mistress, and from there to Madame de Pompadour. The *Daily Gossip* headlined with "Wot I Saw—The King, the Ho and the Handyman." There followed pages of lurid speculation about the lewd acts the picture had witnessed over the last three hundred years. The broadsheets, considering themselves above the gutter, ran timelines of important treaties and bills that the picture might have glimpsed. When it turned out that Frederick and Catherine the Great had owned the painting, all niceties were dispensed with. Whippets, horses, catamites, sodomites, eunuchs, virgins, and dwarfs—every known variety of deviant or deviation were trotted out.

Attendance of museums went up by 34 per cent for adults, but schools cancelled their educational trips, fearing a backlash from anti-pornography and children's rights campaigners.

Septimus Ward-Thomas, Director of the National Gallery, issued a statement: "While it is true that the gallery contains paintings of unmarried mothers (the Virgin Mary) as well as depicting violence, rape, murder, assault and other quite alarming human pursuits, these acts have been considered through the lens of an artist. We do not consider a visit to the National Gallery unsuitable for any age."

When it was revealed that the painting had been stolen from Buckingham Palace by a footman, there were further flurries of speculation. How could the royals miss something so valuable? Were they total heathens? Would the Winklemans bow down before the royals and hand the painting back? There was a silence of five days from the Palace before Her Majesty announced, "We are pleased that our painting has been rediscovered after such a long absence. We are delighted that it will be auctioned to raise money for an admirable cause." Every paper on both sides of the Atlantic and from Durban to Dar es Salaam, from Cape Wrath to the Cape of Good Hope, carried a picture of the Queen grimacing. (In fact, the photograph was taken the moment the Queen's horse was beaten at Epsom, not when she made the announcement.)

Media attention fanned the flames of avarice; it seemed everyone wanted to own *The Improbability of Love*. Monachorum fielded thousands of calls. Old-age pensioners offered their life's savings; children their pocket money "for ever"; museums, private collectors, kings, queens, Russians, Arabs, rap stars and even governments came forward to register their interest.

The Earl had never felt so popular. If only he could delay the sale by another couple of years and continue to enjoy the cases of wine, free dinners and other extravagant presents that came his way. He was also aware that it would take some skilful negotiating powers to keep everyone happy. There would only be one winner and somehow the Earl had to keep the runners-up calm. Monachorum could end up losing more than it gained if its Ultra-High-Net-Worthers felt played or hard done by.

Sifting through the time-wasters and the out-of-their-league category, Beachendon identified some likely candidates. Mrs. Appledore, an old friend of the auction house, wanted to use the millions in her husband's charitable foundation before her death. The Earl thought she could bid up to £250 million.

Ladies Halfpennies were "beyond excited" by the mention of the rap singer M. Power Dub-Box. In recent months he had stunned the art world by buying some seminally important and expensive works of art.

The Emir and Sheikha of Alwabbi had recently built a museum in their dusty Middle Eastern capital. The building— 1,227 hectares of polished marble—was the same size as Heathrow's Terminal 5. As recent arrivals in the museum world, they had found little of real importance to put in their museum. If the Alwabbis could get the Watteau it would immediately put their little kingdom on every art tourist's must-visit list. As the largest producer of the world's liquid gas, they might bid up to £1 billion, the Earl reckoned. Whether the Emir would allow his headstrong wife to go that far was anyone's guess.

Then there were the warring oligarchs whose battles had already driven up the prices of property and precious objects to unimaginable levels. The Earl had met London's newest oligarch, Vladimir Antipovsky, with Barty and it was well known that the man who controlled 43 per cent of the world's tin production would stop at nothing to outbid his arch-rival Dmitri Voldakov, who controlled 68 per cent of the Earth's potash. Both men had recently sold minority stakes in their companies, for $8 billion and $9 billion respectively. The Earl didn't dare speculate what they might spend to thwart each other.

To his amazement, there had also been calls from representatives of the French and British governments. France believed that it had a right, as Watteau was one of theirs. (The

Earl did not tell the French ambassador that Watteau was born in Valenciennes and was therefore technically Flemish.) While the British Prime Minister said the painting must remain on British soil, everyone knew the country could not afford the price tag.

As recipient of 0.2 per cent of the winning bid, the Earl was looking at a tidy nest egg for himself and his family.

"Snatched from poverty's jaws," he told the Countess. "Not a second too early."

The Countess smiled and agreed that it was really too marvellous.

Seeing Jesse lost in a fug of gloom in the Wallace staffroom, Larissa insisted he join her for dinner that night. When he arrived, she sat him on a stool by her worktop while she chopped and prepped dinner.

"Of course I know about the Watteau—you'd have to be living in Nova Scotia with your head up a polar bear's bum to have avoided it," she said, plunging a live lobster in boiling water. A terrible scream came from the pot; Jesse winced.

"Don't worry, it's just air coming out of the shell," she said cheerfully. "Can you peel those pieces of garlic, darling?" She stopped. "Or are you seeing a girlfriend later?"

Jesse shook his head.

"Great gods—wasn't the girl you liked Annie, the thief?"

Jesse winced again but nodded.

"Lucky you got out alive."

"It never really got going." Jesse decided that Larissa didn't need to know everything, for both of their sakes.

"Chop the garlic into tiny segments, please," Larissa instructed.

Jesse felt a stab of sadness—the last time he had cooked was with Annie on the night of her triumphant dinner. She had looked so happy and at ease in the makeshift kitchen, sending dishes out like neatly ordered squadrons, one after the other.

"Was Trichcombe a friend of yours?" Jesse asked, trying to keep his voice casual.

"I knew him for twenty years but he was only ever an acquaintance. Can you make mayonnaise?"

Jesse nodded. Taking an egg, he cracked it on the edge of a china bowl and separated the yolks from the whites. Then, taking the tiny segments of garlic, he crushed them into the mix.

"Do you like mustard with it?" he asked.

Larissa nodded and Jesse added half a teaspoon of mustard, a tablespoon of vinegar and some salt and pepper to the mixture. He beat these hard together before drizzling olive oil into the bowl.

"He came here for dinner a few nights before he died. Never seen him so cheerful."

"What was he working on?" Jesse asked.

"He wouldn't tell me exactly but something that would cause an absolute scandal—he kept saying 'this is going to be big, very big.' Why do you ask?"

"He called me up and kept going on about *Apollo*—I couldn't think what he meant," lied Jesse.

"I heard he was writing about Watteau." Larissa fished the lobster out of the pot and put it on a side plate. "He was going to publish a new piece of research he'd been working on—couldn't decide if it should go to the *Mail* or *Apollo*. Rather different beasts, if you ask me."

"Did he tell you what it was about?" Jesse beat the oil into the mayonnaise. He felt his face redden slightly. He had always been hopeless at subterfuge.

"Some issue of provenance, a lost painting. Bound to be wonderfully dry. Poor old Trichcombe, he was always off-beam. Never really recovered from being fired by Memling Winkleman."

Jesse stopped beating. "He was fired by Winkleman? What for?"

"Keep stirring, darling, or it will curdle," Larissa chided. "I never could get to the bottom of his dismissal. It included a non-disclosure agreement so he couldn't talk about it. In an unguarded moment Trichcombe said he discovered some skulduggery in the archives. Standard art-world conspiracy stuff. Delores said he had one drink too many and Memling flipped."

"It would be too much to hope that he sent you a copy of his manuscript for safe keeping?" Jesse asked.

"Good lord, no. He wouldn't share anything like that with anybody. He probably sent it to a PO box in Timbuktu or a relative in Mold."

"Mold?"

"Where the family comes from."

Jesse remembered the noticeboard in Abufel's flat on which the academic had written "Manuscript to Mold."

"Sit down, this pink gentleman is *à point.*" Larissa plunged the lobster into icy water and placed a salad on the table. She dipped a finger into Jesse's mayonnaise. "Not bad, not bad at all."

Jesse looked at the crustacean and his thoughts turned to Annie. Would she ever eat or cook a lobster again? Would she be able to make or taste fresh mayonnaise? He wondered what it would be like to be told that he'd never paint again, never be able to lose himself in a composition or express his ideas pictorially.

Larissa looked at Jesse closely. "What's wrong, Jesse? What have you got mixed up in?"

Jesse shook his head and swallowed. "I was just thinking how delicious dinner looked."

Putting down her knife and fork, Larissa took his hand. "Take a piece of advice from me. The art world is not some cosy little backwater; it's a cut-throat business. Beauty and the desire to possess have driven men mad for centuries. Add a hundred and twenty billion dollars annually to that equation and you have serious trouble. Think about it, Jesse—these days even a lesser work by a minor artist is worth more than most of us see in a lifetime."

Jesse nodded glumly.

"To make matters more complicated," Larissa continued, "it's a world built on reputation and the bigwigs will stop at nothing to maintain their standing—nothing. I don't know what happened between Trichcombe and the Winklemans all those years ago—frankly, I didn't want to know. When Trich came in here a few weeks ago claiming to have finally nailed 'the bastard,' I asked him to shut up. I wish I hadn't told you that I had seen him. The Winklemans' influence spreads beyond salerooms, museums, galleries and institutions; they own dealerships, stringers; they bribe the police, the press. The old man probably owns *Apollo* and the *Burlington*. He's the single biggest charitable donor, not just to the art world but also to the political parties. Trich thought he could take him on. Now he's dead—go figure. Even if I did know some-thing, Jesse, I wouldn't tell you."

Leaning across the table, Larissa looked earnestly at Jesse.

"I'm sorry you fell in love with that girl. Truly sorry. But you have to accept that even if she is innocent, she is never coming out of prison."

"She is innocent!" Jesse jumped up, red in the face.

"One woman and her impassioned boyfriend against the world? It doesn't work like that. Jesse, the best thing you can do is put the girl behind you."

"I can't."

"You don't have any choice. If she's lucky, she'll stay behind bars. Now eat your lobster and tell me about the rest of your life."

Jesse had no appetite and had to force the lobster down. He knew that Larissa spoke the truth and though it didn't frighten him personally, he was terrified for Annie. Maybe being in prison was the safest place for her. At least there, they could not kill her.

Chapter 35

It was the first time that the Rt. Hon. Barnaby Damson had been summoned to the Prime Minister's office in the Houses of Parliament. Damson waited outside while efficient private secretaries strode past, none giving him the time of day. Everyone knew that Damson's ministry was a political backwater, at best a stepping stone to greater things, at worst a place of no consequence. Once upon a time, members who were either hopeless or hopeful were sent to Northern Ireland; now they went to the Department of Culture.

After a forty minutes' wait, Damson was shown into a room the size of a tennis court. The PM sat at the very end and Damson's shoes squeaked loudly as he made his way on the parquet floor towards the stately desk.

"Bit like being called before the Provost at 'school,'" Damson remarked.

"For God's sake don't mention 'school,'" the PM hissed.

"Eton was supposed to prepare us for life, not hang a rope of guilt around our necks. Now, why are you here?" he asked crossly.

"You asked to see me."

"What for?"

Damson's hopes rose and fell simultaneously; he was not being promoted or demoted.

"Is it to explain about the painting, *The Improbability of Love*?" Damson suggested.

"Of course. Now start from the beginning. How do you pronounce the chap's name?" the PM asked.

"Watteau—it rhymes with French for boat," Damson replied.

"Boat, moat, float, John o' Groat?" said the PM, mystified.

"The French word for boat is *bateau*," Damson pointed out. He pronounced the word in a perfect French accent, "V-A-T-T-E-A-U."

"Vat—what?"

"Think of 'What Ho,'" Damson suggested.

"What Ho! He must have been Bertie Wooster's kind of painter," said the PM.

"Hilarious. What a good joke, sir," Damson said, thinking about his promotion.

"So what's the subject matter?"

"Two lovers in a woody glade."

"Is it pornographic?" the PM asked nervously.

"Not at all. I have a reproduction in my pocket." Damson took a folded piece of A4 out of his pocket.

"Art is a minefield, isn't it?" the PM said.

Damson nodded and laid the picture out on the desk. "You see, it's not rude—just a man looking at a beautiful woman."

The PM looked at the picture closely. "Not much to write home about, is it? Kind of thing Great-Aunt Maude would have liked."

"It has integrity and beauty," Damson said.

"I never liked art much," said the PM.

"Really?"

The PM got up and walked around his office. Looking out of his window he saw four distinct groups of protestors shouting about the price of bread, the failure of education, foreign policy in the Middle East and the collapse of the National Health Service. They looked insignificant on the grass rectangle, dwarfed by government buildings on two sides, the Supreme Court opposite and Westminster Abbey behind, but the PM knew that together they encapsulated the mood of the country: there were less than twelve months till the next election and his ratings had collapsed.

"I need a patriotic story. Can this picture deliver a positive message?" he said, striding around his office. "Plucky little Britain snatches the work from under the noses of foreigners. Your government has saved a great masterpiece for the nation." The PM had gone quite pink around the gills. "What do you think?"

"That is a brilliant idea."

"Thank you, Plum."

"It's Damson actually," Damson said quietly.

"What is this thing worth?" the PM asked.

"It's worth what someone is willing to pay for it. There is a market consensus that gives us a kind of guide figure." Damson thought the moment had come to educate his Prime Minister a little bit.

"For God's sake stop talking in riddles," said the PM. "How much?"

"The low estimate is one hundred and eighty million."

The PM put a hand to his chest. "One hundred and eighty million pounds? Is it painted on gold?"

"No, just plain old canvas," said Damson.

"I could buy a warhead for that. A bit of a warhead, anyway."

"It is a lot," Damson agreed. "The French are determined to buy it. I have heard they are prepared to spend up to three hundred million pounds."

"Three hundred million! That is exactly the amount of money they received to bail out another collapsing bank. Over my dead body are those frogs getting my painting."

"It is a French painting," Damson pointed out.

"It's on our bloody soil now: that makes it a British painting."

"Do we have the money?" Damson asked.

"Not exactly; well, not at all, actually. What else can we do?"

"We can refuse an export licence and hope to find a white knight willing to buy it and donate it to the country."

"Who the hell would do that?" the PM asked.

"Someone who might want an honour."

"Can we get away with an OBE?"

"I don't think so."

"Knighthood?"

"Unlikely."

"I can't give away peerages these days without every bloody select committee and newspaper going after me."

"The problem, sir, as you know," said Damson, "is that art, rather like gold, has become another kind of currency. With the euro gone to pot and the yen in free fall, many see art as a safe investment."

The PM strode around the office. He had the disconcerting habit of clicking his fingers loudly and every so often an alarmingly loud crack of knuckle broke the silence.

Damson looked out of the window at the demonstrators, who, catching sight of a figure in the window, waved their placards with gusto.

"I've made a decision," the PM said decisively. "I had better get on to MI6—tell them to sort it out."

"They can't exactly storm an auction house; we're not the Congo," Damson said nervously.

"It's highly unlikely the Congo has an auction house. Our Foreign Office, however, has a secret service."

"James Bond to the rescue!" Damson said, doing his rather fine Sean Connery impersonation.

The PM looked furious.

"That was a joke," Damson said quickly. "No idiot would think of sending in James Bond."

The PM raised his eyebrows. "Wouldn't they?" he said coldly. "Actually, that was exactly what I was thinking. Only these days James Bond is called Darren Lu—second-generation Chinese—deadly, I am told." The PM looked at his watch and sighed.

"See you later, Plum," the PM said, dismissing his minister, and turning his back.

This time Damson didn't put him right. To be remembered by the wrong name might turn out to be a blessing in disguise.

Behind the heavily guarded walls and the monumental gates made of four Ionic columns flanked with windowless walls, of the French President's official palace, the Elysée, the Council of Ministers had been called to an emergency meeting. They walked quickly through the majestic ceremonial court-yard. Though all had visited before, most were still cowed by the grandeur of the French Classical style, the exquisite wall hangings, the carefully chosen paintings and ornaments.

For once, the President did not keep his Cabinet waiting. He strode purposefully into the room, flanked by two aides.

"In two days' time in London a painting will be sold at auction."

The Minister of Culture smiled—it was he who had informed his president.

"The painting is by the French master Antoine Watteau, the founder of the Rococo movement and one of the great-est we have produced," the President told his colleagues. "For those whose art history is a little sketchy, Watteau died in 1721, the year before this palace was completed. To repatriate this picture to its country of origin and to hang it in this palace will send out the clear and deafening message that France is a country of pre-eminent cultural importance and wealth. At a time when we are suffering from the greatest economic crisis in our history, when our banks are collapsing, lines of credit are defaulting and our bonds are failing to attract takers in the markets, buying this picture will prove that France is still to be reckoned with. We are not finished. We have not even begun. We will buy the picture. Whatever the cost. *Vive la France!*" With this the President turned and left the room.

His Council of Ministers looked at each other. They were in even bigger trouble than any had suspected.

Since meeting at Delores's dinner, Vlad and Grace Spinetti-Winkleman had spent every night and most of each day together. It was the first time in a decade that Vlad had not paid for sexual intercourse.

During one of the couple's rare moments apart, Vlad asked Barty, "How do I prove love?"

"In olden days, you would have challenged someone to a fight," Barty answered.

"A fight? Who do I fight?" Vlad asked, rather confused.

"I wasn't being serious, old bean. The thing is that I have never been very good at love—hopeless, actually. You should ask someone better qualified."

Vlad became suddenly enraged and picked Barty up by the lapels of his velvet suit (today he was channelling Adam Ant and the New Romantics) and said, "This is not stupid joke. This is question. Important question. How do I prove love? Answer question."

"It's a question that's occupied many fine men's and women's minds for centuries. I am not a semiotician or a phi-losopher," said Barty, trying to wriggle out of Vlad's iron grip.

"She does not want money. Or cars, or stones or houses. She says 'just prove love.'" Vlad breathed fiery garlic into Barty's face and plonked him down on the chair again.

Barty loosened his collar and dabbed at his temple with a scented handkerchief.

"Do you need to prove it? Can't you just be together?"

"I want her to come to Russia with me. To live."

"That's a really terrible idea. You will lose everything!" Barty felt bereft; the day Vlad set one foot back on Russian soil, he would be stripped of all his assets. "What about our museum?" said Barty, plaintively.

All he had thought about recently was Vlad's building in St. Petersburg. He was not motivated for mercenary reasons; he loved the idea of creating a perfect miniature jewel that anyone could visit. Most of the houses he decorated could not even be photographed—they were secret treasures for their wealthy owners. Barty's White House, open to the public, gave him enormous pleasure. He longed to create another building that everyone could enjoy.

"Love more important than museum," Vlad said firmly.

"Why do you want to go back there and be poor?" Barty asked. "When you can live here with your money and love."

"I want my children to be Russian."

"Is she pregnant?" Barty asked.

"*Niet.*"

Barty ran his hands through his hair in despair. Heterosexual love could be so bewildering at times. Endless negotiation followed by misunderstanding, renegotiation, more misunderstanding and finally unhappiness. Much better to live life as a non-practising homosexual: that seemed remarkably clear and straightforward.

"What does Grace think about living as a penniless Siberian?"

"She says really cool."

"That it would be."

"She says she's had enough of damn shit capitalism—wants real values."

"Tell her that damn shit poverty is much, much worse than damn shit capitalism," said Barty crossly. "Honestly, I have never heard anything so silly and short-sighted."

The two men sat in silence. Both were on the brink of losing what they wanted. Suddenly Barty jumped up.

"I've got it!" he said, clapping his hands together.

Vlad raised his head slightly.

"You must buy the picture that belonged to her great-grandmother: *The Improbability* or *Impossibility* or whatever it's called *of Love*. You hang it in our, I mean, your museum in St. Petersburg."

"Great what?" Vlad was having trouble following.

"Never mind that bit. What matters is that you must buy the painting. That is the proof of love. Don't you see?"

Vlad lifted up his head. Barty could see tears shining in his eyes and starting to tip down his cheeks.

"My friend," Vlad said, and once again he picked up Barty and planted moist garlic-scented kisses on both his cheeks. "My friend. My friend."

"Easy, easy," Barty said. "There's only so much affection a man can take."

"Go now. Buy picture. Right now. We take it to Grace tonight."

"That's not really how it works, Vlad. It's an auction and you have to bid."

"Offer more."

"You can't offer more until you know what's on the table."

"Everything has price," said Vlad, getting agitated.

"You will get the painting. But you have to buy it at the auction. You only have to wait forty-eight more hours. Think how much more it will mean to Grace when you buy it in a public place in front of the whole world's media."

Vlad nodded. He liked this plan.

"Immediately after the sale we make an announcement. Tell everyone about the museum."

Vlad took Barty's hand and began to shake it vigorously.

"Easy, old chap—I only have two of those," Barty said.

"Proof of love, proof of love. Very good. Good."

. . .

Sitting in his private bank, in a townhouse in St. James's Square, Dmitri Voldakov decided that he would buy *The Improbability of Love*, even if it bankrupted him and incurred the Leader's abiding displeasure. His motivation was simple: to humiliate Vlad. Since arriving in Britain, Vlad had done nothing but cause trouble: investing in Dmitri's patch and driving the art market prices up to unprecedented heights. Furthermore, Dmitri was sure that Vlad had been chasing his fiancée, Lyudmila. It was a matter of pride that Dmitri should win the painting and he had liquidated a significant amount of his fortune in anticipation of triumphing at the auction. He had also put a plan B in place just in case. Voldakov was not a man who valued human life or freedom or moral high grounds. He liked to win—whatever the cost.

From his office on the 87th floor of Brent Towers, on Park Avenue and 73rd Street, Stevie Brent, founder and CEO of SB Capital Partners Inc., looked out over Central Park and considered his options. In ten days' time, the Titan of Wall Street would be hauled up in front of the U.S. prosecutor and accused of insider trading. Nervous investors had already removed $15 billion of capital from his flagship hedge fund, leaving Brent's pool depleted. The trader intended to send a signal to the world's markets that, far from being washed up, he was rich and confident enough to buy the most expensive picture ever sold at auction. *The Improbability of Love* would hang in the lobby of his Manhattan office and its image would feature on the cover of his annual report.

Brent was used to taking punts without security or equity. When the stakes were high, Brent came into his own; he held his nerve when others crumbled. Right now he needed a sucker punch. This would not be the first time Brent had used art to bolster his reputation. Every time his company had come unstuck or the Feds had got close, the King of Wall Street bought a fabulous painting. Just like the Medicis, slave traders, marauding rulers and others before him, Brent understood that art had the power to whitewash his reputation. The Watteau was the perfect way to restore his investors' confidence. The day after the auction, they'd open their newspaper or flick on to the Internet news service to learn that Brent had triumphed again. No guy who was about to be imprisoned or bankrupted would risk such an audacious move.

In her Claridge's hotel suite, Mrs. Appledore signed the last pieces of paper authorising the liquidation of the Melanie and Horace Appledore Charitable Foundation.

At the National Gallery in London, Septimus Ward-Thomas chaired an emergency meeting of the trustees; they unanimously agreed to use all the gallery's reserve funds to try and secure the picture, a total of £2 million.

Darren Lu walked around the auction house looking at the doors and windows. His instructions were clear, but he was still not sure yet how to achieve the goal. It would come. Darren Lu had never been found wanting before.

His Excellency the President of France had diverted his country's reserves in order to secure the painting. In anticipation of his triumphal return, the President imagined his country's media waiting to greet him at the Elysée Palace. Holding the painting above his head, he would shout out, *"Liberté, fraternité, et l'art—Vive la France!"*

In his studio in Hoxton, Mr. M. Power Dub-Box laid the last track on his new album. He had set aside Thursday evening to attend the auction. He would arrive in a convoy of white Range Rovers with his new single, "Witches' Brew," blaring and get a couple of girls to fawn over him. He knew that the picture would sell for more money than he had. He couldn't take this art world seriously. Dumb prices. Dumb people.

Barty's office was covered in possible outfits. He could not decide whether to go as Catherine the Great (and come with a horse tucked under his arm); Peter the Great (and bring a live whippet); a dissolute Earl (dragging empty wine bottles); Louis XIV (with enormous wig); or as Madame de Pompadour, in a ballgown in deepest pink taffeta and lace to be topped with a wig of cascading white curls.

"You wore something like that to my dinner," said Delores.

"With respect, Delores, your dinner was for fifty people in some godforsaken part of London. Over two billion will be watching the proceedings," Barty said crossly. "Bennie, Emeline, where are my people?"

"We are all here," said his PA, Frances, wearily. Barty looked around and saw that all fifteen employees were lined up patiently waiting for instructions.

"If you wear another preposterous wig, no one will know who you are. Why don't you lose the wig?" Delores said. "More Sofia Coppola, less Danny La Rue."

"When he or she buys the picture, I will whip off the wig and everyone will know," Barty said, imagining the coverage on the evening news.

"You'll look like a damp old drag queen—imagine what four hours under hot lights will do to your hair and make-up," said Delores, walking towards the door.

"You can't go yet," Barty wailed. "Why do I have to do everything all by myself?"

Two nights before the sale, the BBC broadcast a feature documentary devoted to the history of *The Improbability of Love*. Settling down to watch it, Larissa thought how unusual it was for the BBC to devote a prime-time slot to a work of art. Once a rather rarefied and contemplative hobby, art was now seen as a popular, populist pursuit. When Larissa had trained as a historian over forty years earlier, she entered a world of dusty archives, mouldy churches and crumbling stately piles. A younger generation could hardly believe such a time existed. Now it was fishnet stockings, digital archives and brand-new museum extensions.

The programme was imaginatively made. Using the latest digital effects, the filmmakers re-created the exact rooms where the picture would have hung. One minute the painting was in an artist's garret, the next it was in the Imperial Tsarist inner bedchamber. Each of the owners had bought the painting as a token of true love. Larissa, along with 12 million other viewers, watched in amazement as this tiny work of art made its way through history, passing from one illustrious couple to another.

Finally, in 1929, it was bought by a young Jewish lawyer, Ezra Winkleman, as a wedding gift for his fiancée, Esther, whom he had loved since they were both children. After their marriage the painting hung in their small Berlin apartment. The couple had four children including Memling and lived simply but happily. Then war broke out and the Jews of Berlin were rounded up. The Winklemans and their children were sent to death camps—most assumed they perished. Their youngest son, Memling, managed to escape from the death train and lived out the war in a remote farmhouse eating nothing but grass and berries. When the Allies discovered him in 1946, all he possessed was his identity card, his mother's photograph and the painting. Larissa felt an unfamiliar lump in the back of her throat.

A few shots later, Memling appeared, handsome, square-faced, with broad cheekbones and those strange blue eyes. Larissa had never really noticed his eyes before. She had never been close enough. Like the rest of the country, she was transfixed by his quiet, authoritative, lisping whisper. His story was appalling, heartbreaking and yet Larissa was not convinced. How strange for an Ashkenazi Jew to have those pale blue eyes, she thought, and noticed that each time he spoke of his parents, he gazed downwards, towards his hands.

Larissa thought back to her last dinner with Trichcombe. The historian had told her he had finally found "evidence." Something about a photograph in Berlin and a birth certificate. Larissa had not really listened to the latest diatribe: Trichcombe had nursed this grudge for over forty years. Yet there was something in the documentary, something about Memling, that profoundly unsettled Larissa. Although it was nearly 11 p.m., she dialled Jesse's telephone number and asked him to come to her apartment immediately.

Chapter 36

THE DAY BEFORE THE SALE

England has never looked more lovely, Jesse thought sadly, as he stared out of the train window at the velvety fields dotted with lambs and at the hedgerows turned white and pink by flowering hawthorns. The deciduous trees had unfurled leaves of vivid greens and their trunks cast lithe black shapes against the soft blue sky. Apart from the occasional gash of electric-yellow oilseed rape, the train passed by fields made up of hundreds of hues of green. On similar train rides, Jesse would have wondered how to capture this majestic, rolling landscape, but since Annie's arrest he'd found it hard to paint. Looking out of the train, he wondered what Annie could see from her window, if she had one. He was worried whether she could stand incarceration for much longer. On each visit, she seemed to shrink deeper into herself. Her bright eyes had become dull and cloudy and the regulation prison clothes hung from her increasingly emaciated body.

That morning, following Larissa's suggestion, Jesse had caught the train to Wrexham, where he changed on to a smaller commuter service. It was four o'clock in the afternoon and every seat was filled with children returning from school. Jesse found a corner seat at the far end of the train and felt like he was caught in a human fireworks display as children shot, jumped and screamed around him. He was the only adult present, yet somehow invisible to his fellow passengers. There were eleven stops between Wrexham and Buckley and for three of these Jesse considered getting off and waiting an hour for the next train. When they crossed the River Cegidog, a group of junior savages gave up one game, leaping the aisles, to start another, throwing smaller children over seats. Sometimes they were caught, other times they fell with a painful thunk on to the floor. At first Jesse worried about broken bones and bloody noses. Later he worried when the children would turn on him. Perhaps he would be trailed by his toenails out of the window or used as a human trampoline. Suddenly at Penyffordd there was a mass exodus and Jesse was left alone with a small girl and her brother who had sought refuge in an overhead luggage rack and now carefully climbed down and sat opposite Jesse.

"Is it like this every day?" Jesse asked.

The little girl shrugged. Her brother looked out of the window.

Jesse tried to imagine a young Trichcombe Abufel in similar circumstances. How had the ascetic asexual survived this kind of childhood? Had he found refuge in inanimate works of art? Had these served as tableaux of stillness and calm?

At Buckley, Jesse took a local bus to Mold, hoping to see

some glorious countryside en route, but the bus had hardly left the suburbs of Buckley before the straggling outbuildings of Mold appeared. Jesse looked at the address again, 21 Ffordd Pentre. He hoped it would be easier to find than pronounce.

After much deliberation with Larissa, they had both decided it would be better to visit rather than telephone or write to Trichcombe's nephew Maurice, particularly as the sale was being held the following evening. Once the brouhaha of the sale had passed, and the press and public had lost interest in the picture, Jesse worried that the police would lose interest in reviewing Annie's case. He did not want her to spend even one extra minute in prison.

"What if they are on holiday?" he asked Larissa, pacing up and down her small apartment.

"They will come back," Larissa answered sensibly.

"What if they threw away his stuff?"

"If so, all hope is lost," Larissa answered. "Jesse, you have to be careful—you have no idea how powerful the Winklemans are."

"So you keep telling me," Jesse said irritably. He had wanted to drive to Mold that night. Only the absence of a car and driving licence stopped him. If he'd had the money, he would have hailed a black cab to take him the whole way there.

"Look at the picture's catalogue," Larissa said, holding up the mighty tome dedicated solely to the picture. Across the front in gold was its title, *The Improbability of Love*, and between the thick hardback covers were eleven essays extolling the picture's importance and cultural significance. There were pieces by Septimus Ward-Thomas on the value of this picture in the litany of art; by Simon Schama on its art-historical pre-eminence; as well as commentaries by Jasper Johns, Peter Doig, Dexter Dalwood, Catherine Goodman, Gerhard Richter and Tarka Kings, and poems by Carol Ann Duffy and Alice Oswald that had been inspired by it.

"No one, apart from us, wants this sale to fail," Larissa said.

"Annie is innocent!" Jesse said emphatically. He had stopped pacing and was now standing in front of Larissa, his eyes blazing.

"I am not saying she is guilty, but the evidence is stacked up against her," said Larissa. "There is no footage of her in the shop on the day of the alleged purchase, but a policewoman recalls her giving a statement the day after the place was burned out and taking particular interest in the death of the shopkeeper. There is even CCTV footage of her taking the painting out of Winklemans' as well as evidence pointing to her amassing information about the picture's history, including visits to the National Gallery and the British Museum. The Winklemans even have records of books taken out of libraries on the subject of Watteau and details of her trying to authenticate the painting in every establishment apart from the obvious one—her employer's. Why didn't she show her picture to Rebecca?"

"She did not want to be seen wasting office time," Jesse countered. "Besides, you know how frightening and unapproachable both Rebecca and Memling are."

"You have to admit, Jesse, it doesn't look good. No jury is going to have much trouble convicting her," said Larissa.

"She's been framed."

"You are a man in love," Larissa said gently. "You have to play this very carefully and coolly if you want to help Annie."

Jesse walked through the centre of Mold. Thirsty and hungry, he looked through the window of the Dolphin Inn wondering if he had time for a late lunch and a pint of Dutch courage. His thoughts immediately turned to Annie and he felt a stab of shame—her future rested in his hands and he was thinking about food. He found Ffordd Pentre easily—it was a housing estate built in the 1980s near the main Chester Road. Each house was a slight variation on a red-brick box: some had bay windows, some had white boarding, all had oversized garages and cobbled forecourts. Number 21 was surrounded by a small wall and a privet hedge. Unlike its neighbours, it had a neatly clipped mini lawn and hanging baskets. A tortoiseshell-coloured cat sat preening in the window and there was a small car parked out front.

Jesse had dressed carefully. He wore a pale blue shirt, a tie and his best corduroy suit, hoping to look respectable but not official. Smoothing down his hair with his right hand, he walked up to the door and knocked firmly.

Inside Delia Abufel had just made herself a cup of tea, got three custard creams out of the biscuit tin, made a note to buy more at Tesco's the following day, and settled down to watch a daily show, *Pointless*. It started at 5 p.m., and at 4:50 exactly, with everything "just so," Delia turned the television on to see Alexander Armstrong's beaming face announcing the first guest. Today, Delia thought, I am going to win. The day before she had been beaten again, another defeat in a long row of disappointments. The doorbell rang. One short but insistent bleat. Delia looked at the cat but he was unperturbed and kept on licking his paw. She turned up the television. It was probably kids from up the road—best ignored.

Outside Jesse moved his weight from foot to foot. He knew someone was inside. He could see ghostly reflections from the television screen flicker behind the net curtains. How long should he leave it before ringing again? He didn't want to annoy the Abufels.

Inside Delia considered the different contestants and which pair would be her main rival. Most were normal middle-aged, Middle England types, but there was one duo that Delia hated on sight, Milly and Daisy from Blackpool. For a start they were pretty—far too pretty to have brains as well as good figures and nice clothes. Delia could have been Daisy or Milly. Delia should have been that kind of girl. But something went wrong. She had not had a lucky hand. She should have married Tod Florence and gone to New Zealand or accepted Ronnie Carbutt, who was now manager of all of Tesco's Wales, but Delia had decided on the nice local boy instead. Maurice was, frankly, a waste of space—a plumber with no hope of promotion. A man to set your watch by, not a man to live your life with.

With each child she had gained a stone; now all four had left home, leaving their mum with a hole in her life and a stomach that hung over her trousers. Glancing at the shelf beside the television, Delia looked at the two neat rows of books: the upper shelves were devoted to cooking, books by Nigella, Delia and co.; the lower were her collection of failed diets, every fad from the South Beach to Atkins, three yards of dashed dreams.

The doorbell again. This time longer and more insistent.

"Which film has Sigourney Weaver starred in?" Alexander Armstrong asked. "If you can guess the least likely and score the least points, you have a chance of going through to the head to head."

Delia frantically tried to think of one Sigourney Weaver film. Was it *Alien*? *The Ice Storm*? *Ghostbusters*?

The doorbell rang again. Delia thought about getting a jug of boiling hot water and throwing it in the face of the offending child.

She had a thought. Maybe it was the military police come to tell her that her eldest boy, Mark, had been hurt in Afghanistan. They came to the door. They didn't telephone. Where was Maurice when she needed him? Delia felt the urge to cry. Heaving herself up out of the chair she almost ran to the front door and pulled it open.

"Tell me the worst," she said, fighting back the tears.

The man before her did not look like a soldier or a policeman or anyone official. He was dressed in a suit that had seen better days. His tie was straight, but his thick dark brown hair shot out in irregular tufts. Looking down, Delia noticed that his shoes were covered in paint.

"Who the bloody hell are you?" she asked.

Jesse looked back at the small, round woman standing in her housecoat and pink fluffy slippers. If he had to match the narrow-limbed Trichcombe Abufel, with his perfectly tied cravats and polished shoes, with the most unlikely person in the world, he would never have dared imagine Delia. Trichcombe had rarely shown any emotion, but the woman before him had opened the door stricken with sorrow and was now sodden with rage.

"Who the hell are you?" she asked again.

"I am a friend of Trichcombe Abufel," Jesse began.

"Are you his bone smuggler?" Delia asked hesitantly.

"Sorry?"

"His cock jockey?"

"I am just a friend," Jesse said firmly.

"What do you think Sigourney Weaver's least-known film is?" Delia asked, looking back towards the television.

"*Gorillas in the Mist?*" Jesse guessed.

"Good fucking idea," Delia said, before closing the door in his face and rushing back to the screen.

Jesse was left standing on the doorstep looking at a shut door. Back inside, Milly and Daisy won that round with an obscure film named *Galaxy Quest.*

"Here are the names of eight footballers—match their British club to the national squad they represent." Alexander Armstrong beamed out of the television screen.

Delia slumped back in her chair—she knew nothing about football. It turned out that Milly and Daisy did—they romped into the lead with a very low score indeed.

The doorbell rang again.

Delia heaved herself out of the chair and went to answer it. "Now what?"

"I am sorry to bother you. It's really urgent."

"I can't ask you in—you'll have to wait till Maurice gets home."

"When will that be?" Jesse asked as politely.

"Six p.m. exactly. Never a minute earlier or a minute later. Now who does Robin van Persie play for and where's the fucker from?"

"Manchester United and he's Dutch."

Again the door shut in his face.

Jesse sat on the wall outside the house. A brisk wind whipped up Fford Pentre. Jesse noticed other people returning from the school run or work, parking their brightly coloured boxy cars in front of their red-brick porches and hurrying inside. Even though it was July, an early dusk seemed to settle on the town. He watched as the lights popped on and spilled on to cobbles. Each house, so nondescript and unprepossessing in daytime, became genial after dark, windows glowing like gentle eyes on a bland face. At exactly 6 p.m. Maurice Abufel's car, a Honda Civic, pulled up outside his house.

"Hi, you must be Maurice Abufel," Jesse said, stepping away from the wall.

If Maurice was surprised to see a stranger lurking in his forecourt he didn't show it. Maurice looked a little like his uncle—tall and thin with exaggerated features and a rather lugubrious expression. Unlike the exquisitely turned out Trichcombe, this Abufel wore a blue boiler suit and rubber-soled shoes.

"Who are you?" he asked.

"I am a friend of your Uncle Trichcombe. I was a friend. I am sorry for your loss," he added quickly.

"What are you doing here?" Maurice asked, taking a front-door key out of his pocket. "Why didn't you ring the bell? Come on in."

Maurice opened the front door and motioned for Jesse to follow. Inside Maurice took off his hat and put it on the table, put the key on a hook that said "Key" and his car key on another hook that said "M's Car." He opened a cupboard in the hall and hung his coat carefully on a blue plastic hanger.

"We have a visitor. Turn the TV off," Maurice said.

"Who?"

"A friend of Uncle T's—he was waiting outside." Maurice and Jesse still stood side by side in the small hall. Through the open door they could see Delia heave herself out of the chair and come towards them.

"I made him wait outside," Delia said, not looking at Jesse.

"Why? It's chilly out there."

"He might have been a rapist," Delia said.

Maurice looked his wife up and down. "In your dreams, woman, in your dreams."

"Shut your face, Maurice, and have some tea," Delia said.

"What is it?"

"Fish fingers and beans."

"Oh yes, it's Wednesday."

"There isn't enough for three," Delia said, looking at Jesse.

"You cook enough for ten—eat enough for nine—tonight you can cut back. Won't kill you." Maurice turned to Jesse. "Come on in and tell us why you're here." Maurice led the way into the kitchen.

Jesse hadn't eaten since that morning, but while he had their attention he talked, telling them about Annie, how she'd bought the picture in a junk shop and how he had encouraged her to get it authenticated. Next he explained how Trichcombe had stumbled on some dark secret hidden in the Winklemans' past and had been literally expelled and discredited from the London art scene back in the 1970s. There was something about this picture, Jesse told them, that verified Trichcombe's hunch. He had waited for over forty years to unmask the Winklemans and when he met Annie and saw the picture, he finally had proof. The art historian had written up his thesis and planned to publish it in a magazine called *Apollo*. On the day before Trichcombe was due to pitch the story to the editor, he suddenly died.

"The coroner said it was a heart attack," Maurice interjected.

"What kind of person deletes all their records on their phone, their computer and all their filing cabinets and then has a heart attack?" Jesse asked.

"Maybe the strain was too much?"

"The caretaker of the building saw him leave that morning. He was carrying a package and told him he was going to the post office. I asked if he looked pale or ill. He said that he was in top spirits—even said 'Good morning,' which was surprising for an old curmudgeon. With all due respect," Jesse added quickly.

"He was a grumpy old sod," Delia agreed.

"Two nights earlier he had dinner with a mutual friend and told her that he'd unearthed a crime that would blow everyone's minds. Said it proved he was right and had been much maligned," said Jesse, leaning towards them. "I don't believe that Trichcombe's death was an accident."

Maurice and Delia looked at each other.

"I was putting out the washing today thinking that nothing ever happened in Mold," Delia said.

"Nothing does happen in Mold. This took place in London," Maurice said.

"My friend said that Trichcombe might have sent you something—a copy of his report." Jesse held his breath. It was Annie's last hope.

Maurice shook his head. "Nothing, I'm afraid."

Delia was quiet and she suddenly said, "The package—I thought it was from ASOS—I walked the whole way into town, had to wait in line for forty-five minutes and it was just one of his manuscripts. He'd rung to warn me a few days earlier."

"What did you do with it?" Jesse leaned over the table.

"I'm just trying to think." Delia leaned back in her chair.

"Don't take your time, will you? There's just the murder of my uncle at stake," Maurice said.

"After the post office, I went to the butcher and got two lamb cutlets. I ran into Lily and she said come to Ivy's for a coffee. So we went to Ivy's—she had done a nice cake. A sponge with jam and cream and real strawberries from Spain."

Jesse did his best not to cry out in frustration.

"Then I came home."

"That was all that happened that day?" Maurice asked incredulously. "I had probably driven from Chester to Birmingham, fixed four boilers, cleaned out a couple of drains and filled in the same number of call-out sheets; you sat around like Marie Antoinette eating cake?"

Delia pursed her lips but didn't reply.

"Did you bring the package home?" Jesse asked.

"I'm just trying to think which bag I went out with."

"Could you have left it at Ivy's?" Jesse asked, trying to keep the panic out of his voice.

"Did I take the big shopper or the string bag?"

"What's that got to do with it?" Maurice asked.

"One's got a pouch."

"Perhaps you could check the pouch?" Jesse asked, already on his feet.

Delia walked over to the cupboard and opened it. The shopper sat at the back behind the ironing board. Delia patted the big front pocket.

"It's not in there." Looking up at the clock she gasped. "It's the *Mac Show* in ten minutes—they've got Rob Brydon on tonight. Shall we go and watch it?"

"Please, Mrs. Abufel, I know that it's a lot to ask but we need to find that package," said Jesse, trying to keep his wavering voice even.

"Don't you worry—as soon as the programme's finished, I'll keep looking."

This time Maurice got to his feet. Maurice, in his worn tartan slippers, with his comb-over, his patched brown cardigan over his Corgi regulation workwear and his 1960s prescription glasses, turned from a plumber into a roaring colossus.

"Get out of that chair and into the attic," he shouted at his wife. "For once in your life put the TV in second place and someone else in first. We are talking about my uncle Trich. He was family. Family comes first. If it didn't, I would have walked out of that door many years ago. Now you go and get every single scrap of paper that my uncle sent you and bring it down here as fast as your tiny legs can carry you."

Delia looked at her husband in astonishment. She opened and closed her mouth and left the room. Jesse and Maurice sat in silence listening to her heavy tread on the stair and then on the landing and a thump as the attic ladder was lowered. There was a creak as Delia climbed up into the loft.

"Should I go and help her perhaps?" Jesse asked.

"Stay there," Maurice replied, staring ahead.

A few minutes later, Delia returned with three carrier bags. Inside there were unopened brown Jiffy bags with Maurice's name written on the front. On the back, also handwritten, was Trichcombe's name and address. Jesse sorted through them quickly. None had been sent recently.

"Are these all his books?" Maurice asked, turning the envelopes over.

"He wrote at least twelve," Jesse answered. He examined each postmark with great care. "It's not here."

"Go and call Ivy. See if you left it at hers," Maurice instructed his wife.

"She'll be watching *The One Show*," Delia grumbled, going out into the hall to use the telephone.

Ivy, they found out, didn't have the manuscript, nor did Lily.

Jesse felt his and Annie's future slip away. He knew that it was hopeless and she would be found guilty and spend the rest of her life in prison for a crime that she had not committed. Her life would be sacrificed to keep a secret safe. Jesse also knew that he would never love again. No doubt there would be other women, memories would be created, pictures painted, but it would be a shadow of the life that he wanted to spend with Annie. Until the moment they met, Jesse realised his existence had been wrapped in a kind of ambivalence and his idea of success was personal freedom—freedom from commitment, worries, poverty, wealth, anxiety and possessions. He had constructed a rather bland, emotionally sealed existence.

He loved painting and his family but little else. Once or twice a woman had been worth crossing town for, but when they drifted off complaining of his lack of engagement or commitment, Jesse had shrugged apologetically.

That all changed when he met Annie. His life, once an orderly, monotonous and pleasant series of tuneful single notes exploded into a cacophony of riotous, unpredictable chords. Sunshine flooded into dark, unknown corners of his being. He had become utterly daft, light-headed and open-hearted. He smiled at strangers, sang in lifts, danced down corridors. He heard melodies as if for the first time; saw colours afresh. Every tiny task became effortless—he ran down streets and bounced up stairs. Some inexplicable film had been lifted from his eyes, allowing Jesse to see the world from a familiar but altogether surprising viewpoint. Everything became heightened, acute and affecting. His painting was utterly transformed: muted tones and careful composition gave way to extravagant bursts of colour and wild flights of fantasy as his brushes flew with brio and élan across canvases. Occasionally the breath escaped from his lungs with such force that he had to hold on to something solid to stop the ground from giving way. He knew with absolute, undeniable certainty that he and Annie were meant to be together.

Along with his new discovery came its opposite, fear of loss. From the moment he saw Annie, he knew real terror for the first time. His insouciant, nonchalant attitude to life evaporated and every move, each tiny event was underscored by a sense of panic and trepidation. Now, sitting in the kitchen of 21 Fford Pentre, Jesse realised he had lost, that Annie and he were never going to be together and that the person he loved most in the world faced a desolate future. Placing his head in his hands, he started to cry.

"There's a stranger crying in my kitchen," Delia said.

Taking his handkerchief out of his pocket, Maurice passed it to Jesse. Turning to Delia he said, "Get the shopper out and the string bag. Go through the recycling pile. It's got to be here."

Delia looked at the clock. She was in a slight muddle about what was on next. What day was it?

Maurice got up and went to the cupboard. He threw out the broom and pans to get to the shopper and other carriers.

"You're making a mess," Delia said plaintively.

"Get the recycling box now," Maurice snapped.

Delia got up and went out the back door to the old coal shed where she kept bundles of papers and plastic. Since the council made its cuts, they only came every fortnight and there was a fair pile.

Maurice turned the shopper upside down. A lone carrot fell out. He turned the bags inside out. Nothing.

In the shed, Delia turned on the light and started to sift through the layers of paper. She was angry now and humiliated. How dare Maurice talk to her like that in front of a stranger? How dare this strange wailing man interrupt her TV schedules? She kicked the pile of papers and they spilled over the floor. Of course there was nothing there. What did Maurice think? That she wouldn't remember putting his dead uncle's stuff in the pile? Delia stopped suddenly. There was a telltale grey padded corner. She pulled it towards her and that now familiar spidery writing appeared. Delia felt a flush of panic. To find it suddenly constituted a further loss of face and made her look even more stupid. It was probably best to hide it and once Maurice had gone to work in the morning she could rip it up or take it down to Tesco's for recycling. The most important thing was to get rid of the weeping man in her kitchen and get back to her TV. Delia could only cope when her world was ordered, otherwise she felt the shakes and panic set in. She had the certain feeling that whatever lay inside that envelope would change her life, and not necessarily for the better.

"What are you doing in there?" Maurice appeared behind her, casting a terrifying shadow over the shed.

"You frightened me," Delia said, stepping backwards and trying to cover up the envelope by moving some papers around with her foot.

Maurice, from the corner of his eye, saw her nervous side-glance.

"What are you hiding?" he asked.

"Nothing—what would I hide out here?" she replied. "Let's go in and comfort that young man. Poor thing. You could drive him to the station." Delia knew that no one must find this envelope.

Maurice pushed her aside and, sinking to his knees, started to go through the pile.

"It's dirty down there, get up," Delia urged.

It took Maurice less than twenty seconds to find Trich-combe's envelope. Grabbing it triumphantly in one hand, he got to his feet and walked out of the coal shed without looking at his wife.

He went back into the kitchen and dropped the envelope in front of Jesse.

"Found it. Who's going to open it? You or me?"

Jesse lifted his head from the table and looked from Maurice to the envelope and wiped his face.

"This is wonderful. This is so wonderful. You do it." He got up and hugged Maurice. He went to hug Delia.

"Don't you dare come near me," Delia hissed, drawing herself up to all of her five feet two inches.

Very carefully Maurice prised open the edge of the envelope and, slipping his hand inside, removed a memory stick, some photographs, a neatly typed manuscript of about forty pages and a letter.

> Dear Maurice,
>
> I hope that you never have occasion to need to read this letter or act on its contents. If that day has come I am probably dead. As you are my closest living relative and an apparently reliable and upstanding member of your community, I have always prevailed on your good nature to keep copies of my work. I suspect that you have neither had the time or inclination to digest my books. I never met one person growing up in Mold who shared my passion for art. I am not at all sure where it came from. Your grandparents' house did not have even one reproduction, let alone an original work. My passion was ignited when the headmistress, Miss Quilter, forgot to book a school trip to the Bournville factory and we had instead to waste time in the Birmingham City Museum and Art Gallery. You may not remember, but I took you there as a small child. I felt everyone deserved a life-changing experience even if they didn't take it up. For me, art was my lifeline; studying it, looking at it, loving it was the only way I could feel a little less lonely and odd. Some love women or men, gambling or the bottle; I love paintings and have devoted my entire life to their study and to trying to explain their beauty and mystique to others.

Maurice readjusted his glasses and, peering at the letter, continued.

*One man helped me establish a career and the
same man destroyed it. His name is Memling
Winkleman.*

Maurice stopped and looked at Jesse. "Is this him?"

Jesse nodded. His tears had dried and his heart thumped in
his chest. "Read on," he urged.

*I hope by the time you read this letter that his name is
internationally recognised and that he has been exposed
for what he is—a duplicitous, dishonest criminal, a
Nazi, who let nothing stand in his way to create the
world's most successful art business.*

"A Nazi. Fancy that," Delia said.

Maurice gave his wife a silencing look and went on reading.

*As you may or may not know, I was his authenticator,
an expert who pronounces if something is right or
wrong. I have a prodigious (if I might claim some
credit) knowledge of paintings and a photographic
memory. Once I have seen a picture, studied it for some
time, I never forget a single detail. Show me a corner
of a Rembrandt and I will tell you everything about
that work. This made me an expert spotter—Memling
and I would roam the salerooms; I would identify and
certify a master painting, Memling would buy it. Oddly
enough, I was never much interested in money. I wanted
the association with great things and the chance to
publish my thoughts and insight. Memling and I had a
great partnership. He got rich, I got approbation.*

"What does approbation mean?" Delia asked.

Maurice and Jesse ignored her.

There was one thing I could never understand. One thing he could never explain. Even when the market constricted, when there were fewer good things around, Memling could unearth great paintings, magic them from nowhere. He would get on a plane and return with one or two canvases. I would ask how and where? He never replied. Once he turned up with a really great Titian, a portrait of a young woman, small but perfect. Something about this painting piqued my curiosity. I knew the composition from an etching I had seen in the Gemäldegalerie in Berlin. I soon established that this painting had belonged to a Jewish family before the war but had disappeared. I started to run checks on other paintings that had been through the gallery—surreptitiously, of course—and found out that during the ten years I had worked for Winkleman, about thirty paintings we had handled had been owned by Jews exterminated during the Holocaust. I think that I knew then what this knowledge might cost me.

One day I walked into Memling's office, forgetting to knock, and there on his desk was a painting by the French master Watteau, called The Improbability of Love—*I knew it from etchings, of course—it is a truly wonderful work of art. It's said that its beauty has the power to inspire love in mere mortals. It certainly inspired some madness in me. Without thinking, I picked it up from the desk and devoured it with my eyes. I should have pretended not to see it. Memling snatched the painting away and shouted at me to leave his office, to leave the building. I was so shocked that I did what was asked. Returning the next morning I found my possessions and books loaded in a box placed outside on the pavement. I was barred from entering the building. The rumours started immediately. The art* world is a tiny place run by a powerful elite. I would walk into private views or galleries to be met with blank stares or outwardly hostile glances. My manuscripts were rejected. I couldn't get published, let alone employed. I tried to blow the whistle on Memling, to tell others of my discoveries, but no one would listen. They knew where the power lay. We are all complicit in a dance with power.

I made ends meet. Just. I had my flat and a small stipend from the Wallace. I have continued to write books—most remain unpublished. You have a copy of all of them. I accepted that this was the way of the world. That the Memlings of this world would prosper and the little men from Mold would moulder away.

One day hope returned. I saw a drawing of the painting—the Watteau, The Improbability of Love— and a young woman told me that she had it. Maybe it was years of latent unexpressed rage or some remnant of Welsh fighting spirit, but I knew that I had the chance to expose the monster. This tiny, beautiful work of art gave me the strength and purpose to do what I should have done many years earlier.

This long essay, which I hope has been published and disseminated in all the world's press, will tell you how I did this and what my evidence is based upon. Though lives have been lost, justice will now be meted out.

If for any reason my life is cut short (and it would not be overdramatic to assume that it might be), I ask you, dear nephew, to make sure that this information sees the light of day. I would urge you to do this anonymously and with great care, but I know that you are the kind of man who wants to see a wrong put right.

Your respectful uncle,
Trichcombe

Delia put her hand on her heart. "I knew we should have left it in the shed, Maurice. This is trouble."

"Put the kettle on," Maurice replied.

For the next two hours, until 10 p.m., he and Jesse read and reread Trichcombe's essay and pored over his detailed footnotes. The art historian had abandoned convention and written his story in the first person, detailing his relationship with Memling and their dealings together. He spoke of suspicions cast aside and of the Titian portrait followed by the other "miraculous" apparitions. Trichcombe spoke openly about subjugating his suspicions in order to further his own career until the day that he saw the Watteau. Each painting that he mentioned came with a detailed provenance showing that they had once belonged to Jews who lost their lives during the war. The most devastating evidence came with the photographs of young "Memling" with the Winkleman family standing before *The Improbability of Love* in their Berlin apartment. Trichcombe had gone straight from Danica Goldberg's apartment at Schwedenstrasse 14 to the public records office. He had a copy of Memling Winkleman's birth certificate and also of that of a lad called Heinrich Fuchs. Trichcombe had not stopped there. The next photographs he unearthed were from the Hitler Youth, showing a young conscript called Heinrich Fuchs, a younger version of the man everyone now called Memling Winkleman. Trichcombe traced the man's career to the Nazi art squad, where Fuchs worked directly under an officer called Karl Haberstock. Perhaps the most astonishing photograph found showed a junior officer standing behind Hitler holding up a painting. Though the photo was smudged and slightly out of focus, the young man with the cap pulled over his face, his back ramrod straight, was, unmistakably, Heinrich Fuchs.

"What the hell do we do now?" Maurice asked, pushing his chair back.

"You pretend you never saw any of this," Delia said. For the last two hours she had been hovering nervously, moving from the television set and back to the kitchen.

"The genie is out of the bottle now. We have to do right by Uncle T," Maurice said firmly. "I can't see the local boyos in blue taking this seriously."

Jesse was taking photographs of each picture and every page of manuscript on his phone and saving that to a remote server.

"Maybe I could email these to someone?" he said.

"We are driving the evidence to London," Maurice said firmly.

"You've never been to London. You won't find it," Delia interjected.

"Some things are too big to miss," he said, looking her up and down.

"You can't leave me here," Delia said.

"I should have left you here a long time ago." Maurice walked out of the room and up the stairs. Jesse and Delia stood in silence at the kitchen table. His face was split by a broad grin. Hers looked like a lump of wax after a night spent on a radiator, with hanging cheeks and drooping eyes.

A few minutes later Maurice appeared with a small suitcase in one hand and his overcoat in the other.

"Come on, Jesse. Let's go."

Chapter 37

FROM THE *Daily Shout*

Art and Arrests: The Improbability of Anything By
Our Chief Arts Correspondent Arthur Christopher

Measuring only 18 inches by 24 inches, made up of oil paint on a canvas backing, the little painting *The Improbability of Love* has an extraordinary history, which has just got even more fantastical. Due to be sold at Monachorum auction house at 8 p.m. last night, the picture by the eighteenth-century master Antoine Watteau had been expected to break all records. Though not as fine or as historically important as a great Titian or Leonardo, nor as fashionable or cutting edge as a Richter or a Warhol, this picture's provenance has captivated imaginations worldwide. Many collectors fancied adding their names to the illustrious roster of history's most notorious kings, queens, great thinkers and lovers who have owned this painting.

Moments before the sale started, a power cut plunged the saleroom into darkness and the auction house into chaos. Automatic security gates descended, locking some 250 important guests into the saleroom. Pandemonium ensued, made worse by the arrival of twenty armed policemen who clashed with the private security teams protecting some of the world's wealthiest individuals, as well as the President of France and the British Minister of Culture. Several shots were fired. Mr. Barthomley Chesterfield Fitzroy St. George was shot in the arm, but the only fatality was the seventy-nine-year-old Mrs. Melanie Appledore, the New York–based philanthropist, who died of a sudden heart attack.

Matters were not helped by the crowds outside who had gathered to watch the live auction feed. When the power loss cut the TV screens, disgruntled spectators tried to force their way inside the auction house.

In the mayhem, no one noticed that the picture had disappeared from under the noses of the world's media, the police and the security teams. Unmitigated confusion followed: had a handler taken the painting to a strongroom? Had one of the grand guests swiped it?

In the early hours of this morning, a journalist from this paper, stationed outside the private home of Mr. Memling Winkleman, reported that uniformed officers had arrived at the house at 8 a.m. and left accompanied by the prominent art dealer. Later, Paddington Green police station confirmed that a ninety-one-year-old man and his fifty-year-old daughter, Rebecca Spinetti-Winkleman, were helping with inquiries. No charges have yet been brought.

At noon today, Ms. Annie McDee was released from HMP Holloway, and all charges have been dropped. Readers will recall that Ms. McDee had been remanded in custody, charged with theft, extortion, conspiracy to defraud and the murder of Mr. Ralph Bernoff, son of the proprietor of Bernoff Antiques, Goldhawk Road, London.

At 10 a.m., the Simon Wiesenthal Center tweeted that one of the last Nazi section leaders, Heinrich Fuchs, had been unmasked. Fuchs, one of the key players in Hitler's notorious "art squad," or the Einsatzstab Reichsleiter Rosenberg (ERR), has been at large since 1945. Unconfirmed rumours suggest that Fuchs had stolen the identity and heritage of a deceased Berlin Jew, Memling Winkleman, who died in 1943 at Auschwitz.

At 11 a.m. the President of France issued the following statement: "Last night I came to Britain to complete the purchase of an important French work of art, Watteau's *The Improbability of Love*, which should be hanging in the Elysée Palace in Paris. It is of utmost importance to my country that the painting be returned as soon as possible."

At midday, Number 10 Downing Street issued the following statement: "We are pleased to announce that one of our operatives was able to rescue the painting by Watteau, *The Improbability of Love*, from the auction rooms last night. The painting is being held at an undisclosed address until further notice."

Chapter 38

As you have probably guessed, it was an entirely put-up job by the young government operative, Mr. Darren Lu, posing as a porter. In the mayhem following the power cut, he cut a hole in my so-called impenetrable glass, put me into a rucksack, walked down the stairs and out of the back entrance.

I felt for poor old Melanie Appledore—a lady who made it through a world war, had navigated the brutal waters of Park Avenue and survived as a lonely widow for nearly quarter of a century, only to snuff out in the saleroom. At least she died *hors de combat*, believing that the deal was as good as done.

I was bitterly disappointed not to set a new world record at auction. The wily Earl was hoping for more than $500 million. Eminently achievable, given that the Cézanne card players, one of five versions, fetched $261 million and my provenance is far greater than the Klimt of Adele Bloch-Bauer, which fetched $150 million.

Don't be shocked by this apparent self-reverence; as you know, my canvas is covered with the brushstrokes of a genius and overlaid with centuries of desire, love and avarice. Each of my owners added an intangible but indelible stratum: the first was my master's outpourings; the second was his friend Julienne's fraternal affection; and these two were followed by the admiration of the great and the downright ugly; even young Annie added a little bit of magic. These layers of appreciation, though invisible to the human eye, are detectable to those with particular powers of intuition and sensitivity.

Does this, I hear you ask, explain the insane prices for works of art and why I and my ilk are more highly prized than gold or diamonds, a more reliable investment than houses or land when we are really nothing more than a patch of cloth stretched over four slender shafts of wood? The answer is simple enough: look around at this crazy, godless, cynical world and ask in what and where can mankind put its trust? I know, you think I, Pontificating Peter, am a frightful old bore for going on like this, and I know I have said this before, but in a declining, degenerate, money-obsessed era, where even Mammon lets most down, art has become a kind of religion and beauty offers a rare form of transcendence.

Like other successful religions, art has evolved and offers glorious temples and learned high priests as well as covenants and creeds. The new churches are known as museums, in which the contemplation of art has become a kind of prayer and communal activity. The very wealthy can create private chapels stuffed with the unimaginable rarities and guarantee a front seat. It was ever thus.

Back to *moi*: there's been a frightful row about who owns me. Annie, true to her word, relinquished all claims, so everyone else is charging around the world trying to find a relation or

distant cousin of the original Winklemans. Ten thousand pre-
tenders have stepped forward; most can be utterly discounted
but there is one woman, in Israel, who looks plausible.

All I want is resolution, not restitution. There has been far
too much movement and I am in desperate need of a period of
peace and consolidation. My blessing is to inspire excesses in
emotion; my curse is being powerless over my fate.

For now, I hang in the Prime Minister's state dining room
for "safe keeping"; his main objective is to annoy the French.
After three hundred years, nothing changes: France and England still quarrelling over very little. That Rock of Gibraltar,
ceded to the British in 1713, is still a bone of contention with
the Spanish, and the British and the Russians are still in and
out of love: it was ever thus. No one talks much about Sweden
these days or the Austro-Hungarian Empire, but there are two
new players, America and China; superpowers come and go,
control ebbs and flows.

Le scandale du jour was that the old Nazi took a cyanide pill
in his prison cell and died frothing and foaming on the floor
of HMP Wandsworth. A letter was produced claiming that the
daughter knew nothing of her father's misdemeanours; pull
the other leg, as the bootjack used to say. The same letter also
revealed the whereabouts of a cache of hidden paintings—
Nazi loot—in a disused salt mine in Bavaria. It happened to
contain eighty-four masterpieces and the Amber Room. Now
there are full-on fisticuffs between Russia, France and Germany about who owns what. Since Helen of Troy, beauty has
inspired warfare.

Annie was released with a full pardon. She came to lunch
with the Prime Minister and brought Jesse, and a man from
Wales. It just so happened that there was a problem with a
blocked water closet of all things! The man from Wales
whipped off his jacket and disappeared with an orderly. Thirty
minutes later he reappeared, problem solved. The Prime Min-

ister was frightfully chuffed and banged on about good citizen-
ship and "big society." I must say the PM is a bit of a bore, but
you probably have to be a little dull to want to go into politics
and even duller to stay there.

The Welshman came up with another idea: what about
making *moi* "The People's Picture." He proposed a campaign
to save me for the nation with every citizen donating £3 to the
great cause. The PM loved that, knowing he would be the first
politician in history to introduce a tax that everyone liked.

Just before she left for America, Annie came to see me.
Looking around to make sure no one could hear, she whispered into my paint.

"Thank you," she said, "for reawakening my belief in this
world and, most of all, for making love possible again. I owe
you a huge debt."

Moments later, Jesse came up behind her, put his arm
around her and kissed her gently on her head. "What are you
thinking about?" he asked.

"*The Improbability of Love*," she replied, still looking at
me. Intertwining her fingers into his, she rested her head on
his shoulder.

One had to admit, one was quite moved.

Tomi Horshaft was confirmed as the grandchild of Ezra and
Esther Winkleman. Born in Auschwitz-Birkenau in 1943,
orphaned soon afterwards, she was adopted by an American
couple who relocated to a kibbutz in northern Israel. Speaking from the shores of the Sea of Galilee, Mrs. Horshaft
said, "While this discovery will never bring back my parents,
grandparents or cousins, I will use the money raised in the
sale of this picture to build a school in their honour."

The people of Great Britain clubbed together to purchase
moi for £240 million (a fraction of my estimated value). It
was a frightful bore; every quarter, I had to move to a dif-

ferent regional museum. There were queues outside each as hundreds of thousands came to admire *moi*. Museums charged hefty fees for couples to marry under my gaze. Every year since the purchase, I have been voted the best British National Treasure, with over six times the number of votes garnered by Stonehenge, Blenheim Palace, the Giant's Causeway or Blackpool Tower, whatever or wherever they might be.

Still, the hoi polloi give good gossip: I overheard that Annie and Jesse moved to a farmhouse in upstate New York, a place which satisfied their love of the countryside but was not too far from the city. Annie's company, called Foodalicious, became the byword in chic, themed, high-end specialised catering. Despite offers to take Foodalicious global, Annie resisted. "For me," she told a scribe, "food is love, food is memory, food is suffering and hope, food is the past and the future, food is who we are and who we want to be; so cooking is all about originality and intimacy and you can't achieve that on a big scale." When the journalist asked if she was the same Annie McDee who had bought the world's most famous picture from a junk shop, gone to prison and refused £1 million in compensation from the Winkleman Foundation, Annie replied, "That was an entirely different person."

Jesse, now her husband, still paints landscapes from memory in his studio, a large converted barn. I am told that these are colourful, abstract and highly sought after.

Charged with falsifying documents and concealing evidence, Rebecca Winkleman was given a five-year custodial sentence but continued to run her business from an open prison. After two and a half years she was released. Most assumed that she only acted illegally to protect her beloved father; she was welcomed back with sympathy into the art world. With her extraordinary eye and steely nerve, the business flourished. In 2025, Rebecca was made a Dame in the King's Honours list in recognition of service to the arts.

Following Memling's unmasking, Carlo Spinetti became an independent filmmaker and won an Oscar for an ultra-low-budget spoof horror movie, *My Father-in-Law*, about a ruthless ex-Nazi who drank blood for breakfast. Carlo died in *flagrante delicto* with two young women at the Chateau Marmont in Los Angeles

Vlad and Grace Spinetti married. He renounced his fortune and they moved back to his hometown of Smlinsk where they had seven children and ran a tattoo parlour. Grace considered returning to England to join her mother in the family business but chose personal freedom over professional rewards.

The Right Honourable Barnaby Damson lost his seat in the 2020 election. He became Albania's media advisor.

Barty's left arm was damaged in the shooting but he received significant compensation from the auction house. He lived till the age of 102, always dressed for every occasion, and fronted his own television show called *Frightfully Common*, an idiosyncratic look at the British class system.

Delores Ryan married a Moroccan taxi driver and moved to Taroudant in the Sous Valley. Following her failure to spot the Watteau, she gave up art history and mass-produced products made from argan oil.

Earl Beachendon left the auction house to run the Emir and Sheikha of Alwabbi's museum. With an annual budget of £1 billion to spend on paintings, the Earl became one of the most powerful people in the art world.

After his ingenious idea to crowdfund The People's Picture, Maurice Abufel was rewarded with the ambassadorship to the Republic of Dagestan. "It's about the same size as Wales but a long way from Mold," he told everyone. His ex-wife Delia Abufel won "Slimmer of the Year," remarried and settled in Pontefract.

Evie successfully completed rehab, gained her A levels and won a scholarship to Oxford University. Two years later she married Bruce Goldenheart (thirty-five years sober) and together they run a counseling service for recovering alcoholics in the Isle of Wight.

After four years of marriage, Desmond's wife left him, citing "unreasonably controlling behavior."

And what about *moi*? Do you still see an old bit of canvas, eighteen by twenty-four inches, encrusted with pigments, oils, a splash of chicken soup and a dead fly? I think not.

My time is nearly up. Frankly, I am exhausted. It is hard work keeping the flame of beauty and excellence burning. Centuries of being ripped out of frames, strapped to the back of mules, loaded into ships, stuffed into plastic bags, hung above roaring fires and subjected to hot breath have all taken their toll. My warp and weft are disintegrating; the moisture has gone from the oil. Soon I will be nothing more than a tiny pile of dust. Luckily, many followers and imitators thrive and survive; some are excellent. All that matters is that artists keep reminding mortals about what really matters: the wonder, the glory, the madness, the importance and the improbability of love.

ACKNOWLEDGMENTS

The characters in this book are inspired by many whom I have met or read about or simply hope might exist. Any likenesses are entirely accidental or intentionally complimentary. Various public personas and institutions appear as themselves, as it would be hard to imagine an art world, real or fictional, without them.

I have been lucky enough to learn from distinguished scholars and also from the directors, conservators, curators and trustees at the National Gallery, the Tate, the Wallace Collection and Waddesdon Manor. These institutions and their luminaries have provided a lifelong source of solace and inspiration.

Thank you also to Catherine Goodman for the writing room and for her insights about painters and painting.

Sarah Chalfant, agent extraordinaire, spotted this book's potential and guided it to the distinguished homes of the peerless Alexandra Pringle and the priceless Shelley Wanger. Thank you to everyone who sails with the Wylie Agency, Bloomsbury and Knopf and to Sonny Mehta, Nigel Newton, Alba Ziegler-Bailey, Charles Buchan, Alexa von Hirschberg and Anna Simpson.

A particular debt of gratitude goes to my family, friends and colleagues for their support, humour and patience; to the careful readers, Jacob and Serena Rothschild, Fiona Golfar, Justine Picardie, Philip Astor, Stephen Frears, Rosie Boycott and the SP. Last and by no means least, thank you to Emmy.